Praise for Robert Llewellyn:

The Man on Platform Five

'Romance, sex, treachery and a frightful accident, which all adds up to a gripping story. Llewellyn's brilliant dialogue brings his characters vividly to life in this acutely observed and genuinely funny book'   *Mail on Sunday*

'A bewitching debut . . . gentle humour and skilful characterisation . . . great subtlety . . . Llewellyn has genuine charm and a tremendous gift for gilding the commonplace'   *The Financial Times*

'Witty, sharp and entertaining'   *Woman's Own*

'Hugely engaging story . . . A fun book, with verve and wit. Think of *Trading Places* written in the clever, forceful style of Ben Elton and you're close'   *The Times*

Punchbag

'A powerful exposition on male violence, women's fears and the need for rapprochement between the sexes'   *Good Housekeeping*

'The most original, though-provoking book I've read in ages . . . A black comedy about rape, violence and men's attitudes to women . . . Handled with great sensitivity by a writer who knows exactly when to tickle the funny bone and when to ask some serious questions . . . The razor-sharp comedy, the acutely observed sexual politics and the underlying serious questions add up to make Llewellyn the rightful heir to Ben Elton'   Paul Davies, *Mirror*

'The characters are sympathetic and convincing and the story is gripping . . . Readers of the future, looking back at our popular fiction, will see that at least some fin-de-siècle blokes had something on their minds other than babes, beer, best mates, kebabs, shagging, football, classic pop and crap TV'   *Independent*

About the author

Robert Llewellyn was a playwright and television writer before he became an actor, and has since juggled both careers. He is the author of several non fiction books, and his best-known acting role is as Kryten in the BBC's long-running series *Red Dwarf*. He lives with his partner, also a writer, and their two children.

Sudden Wealth

Robert Llewellyn

FLAME
Hodder & Stoughton

First published in Great Britain in 2000
by Hodder and Stoughton
First published in paperback in 2001
by Hodder and Stoughton
A division of Hodder Headline

A Flame Paperback

10 9 8 7 6 5 4 3 2 1

A CIP catalogue record for this title
is available from the British Library.

ISBN 0 340 75112 6

Printed and bound in Great Britain by
Mackays of Chatham plc, Chatham, Kent

Hodder and Stoughton
A division of Hodder Headline
338 Euston Road
London NW1 3BH

For Louis and Holly

PREFACE

So many threads feed into a writer's mind that it's normally impossible to trace the source of a story. However, the history of *Sudden Wealth* is slightly different.

It all started on a Wednesday afternoon back in May 1987. I was sitting in a room in Hampstead (where else) with a therapist, not particularly happy about it and hoping the hour wouldn't last too long.

I'd been seeing him for a few weeks and didn't feel I was really going anywhere, personal growthwise. It wasn't his fault. I was a deeply emotionally blocked white English man, classic case, blah blah.

Then, on this particular afternoon, out of the blue, he started to tell me he was involved in a 'flight'. A flight was an absurd system for supposedly 'creating money', also known as a pyramid. If I gave him £50 to join the flight, then asked seven people I knew to give me £50 so they could join the flight, I'd have £300 left over at the end of it. Free money. So the initial £50 wouldn't cost me anything really. The people I had asked would then ask seven people each and so on.

Initially I tried to argue that at some point in the future, when the world's mugs had all been fleeced, surely some people would end up being ripped off. This was obviously a very negative attitude and symptomatic of my depression.

I never went to see him again, but the story started to grow.

I always need to thank Judy Pascoe for all her support

because she always gives it if I ask often enough. My two kids for trying to understand what Dad does in his shed all day. Jamie Rix and Nigel Planer in particular because they've listened and read a lot of ideas related to this book, for years. Also Vadim Jean, Loretta Sacco, Maureen Vincent, Birgit Nakielski for help with German, Sarah Leigh and Robert Kirby, and dozens of other people who have encouraged me to develop this idea over the nearly thirteen years of its gestation.

Chapter One

$\Longrightarrow\!\!\gg\!\circ\!\ll\!\Longleftarrow$

Mario Lupo stepped out of the Lear Jet into what felt like a solid wall of heat. The dazzling white light made anything at a distance shimmer. He rubbed his eyes and put on his Ray Bans; he could already feel a headache coming on.

Mario was standing on a private airstrip just outside Key Biscayne in Florida. It wasn't his jet. Although successful, Mario Lupo was not in the market for a seven-million-dollar private plane. It belonged to a conglomerate of professional golfers, one of whom he was en route to visit. Bruce Yakich was a new client. Over the years he had treated a few pro golfers and Yakich was not one of Mario's favourites, though his discreet professionalism meant he would never admit that to anyone.

'Your car is just over here, sir,' said the well-built black man who stood waiting for him in the searing heat. As Mario had expected, the man was dressed in a smart suit and wearing the obligatory mirrored sunglasses.

'What is your name, young man?' he asked.

'Daniel, sir,' replied the driver.

'So, Daniel, tell me, is Mr Yakich in the car?'

'That is correct, sir.'

'Okay. As you probably know, I am his therapist. I warn you, I may have to use some unorthodox techniques here, but I want you to remain calm and keep your eyes on the road at all times. Is that understood?'

'Very good, sir, I'll keep the privacy button on. Anything Mr Yakich says to you will remain entirely confidential.'

'Very understanding of you, Daniel. Here's a little something for your trouble.'

Mario handed him a carefully folded hundred-dollar bill. The chauffeur smiled and pocketed the money discreetly.

He led the way to a long black limousine with mirrored windows, held the door open and Mario stepped inside. During the entire trip from San Jose in California he had walked barely fifty metres. The whole journey had been meticulously arranged so that he'd done little more than lift the phone to accept the job. Mario always travelled light. His small leather flight bag contained a change of clothes, a healthy selection of credit cards and a shuttle-dial satellite phone with earpiece because he didn't want to fry his brain. The bag was chosen from necessity as much as for easy travel. Mario Lupo had a congenitally disabled left arm. It was next to useless; he couldn't carry or grip anything on that side. The arm just hung limply.

'Hi, Mario. This is real good of you, man,' said Bruce Yakich, the patient he had come to see. He was sitting well back in his seat, cool inside the air-conditioned interior.

'Bruce, you look strained, what's going on?' asked Mario as they drew away.

'I'm totally stressed, man. Something feels like it's snapped. I'm – well, I don't even want to say this out loud, but I'm just so damn' tired of the whole thing. I'm bored, Mario, that's what it is. I'm fucking bored of golf!'

'This is quite normal,' soothed Mario. 'You do a high-stress job, you're used to the challenge, have reached the very top of your profession. All your life your maison d'être has been to win, am I right?'

'Totally.'

'And now that you've done all that, what else is there?'

'But how can I be depressed? Me – Bruce fucking Yakich! I'm the man, know what I'm saying?'

'You've worked very hard.'

'Sure, doing something I love and getting paid top dollar for doing it. But what's the point? I've run empty, you know, in some kind of weird way I don't understand. I need help, man.'

Mario scratched his head and moved his left hand to his lap. He felt so happy, sitting in an air-conditioned limousine, the Florida heat shimmering beyond the tinted glass as they hissed along the busy freeway, with Bruce Yakich, five times PGA champion, in the seat next to him. And if Mario did his job well, very possibly Mr Yakich would make it six. It was a classic scenario and Mario knew all the signs. After the initial burn of desire where all problems could comfortably be put on hold, sometimes for years, the goal was achieved, the energy spent – and then the chasm promptly opened. He had seen it so many times. No matter how often he lectured on the falsity of goals and the inherent danger of task-oriented living, no matter how often he demonstrated that roles, not goals, were the healthy way to live, Mario had more Bruce Yakiches to treat than ever before.

'You have to compartmentalise to survive, Bruce. That's the price you have to pay for the level of success you've achieved.'

'What the hell does compartmentalise mean?'

'When you play golf, do you think about anything else?'

'No. Well, I never used to. That was when I was "the man". You know, I was so focused, nothing got in the way of my game. But now, I kind of keep having thoughts. Like, worries about money, or else I think about sex. It's crazy.'

'Why is that crazy?'

'Well, it ain't like I don't have plenty of both. I've got about a hundred mill in the bank, and Marielle is not above acting like a high-class hooker in the bedroom, if you know what I mean. She even takes it up the ass, which I respect.'

'Of course,' said Mario. 'Who wouldn't?'

'So what the hell is happening to me? My game is shot to fuck, I can't sink a putt, my mind is always wandering off . . . It's the fucking PGA this weekend. I've got to be in the loop, man, or I am yesterday's news.'

'I hear you. Which is why I say, you have to compartmentalise. What do you think of just before you go to sleep?'

'The game.'

'The game?'

'Always the game. I see the lay of the course. I see the rough, can like, actually feel the tee as I push it into the earth. You know, I can smell the fucking grass. It's comforting.'

'Comforting?'

'Sure. Like, I'm lying in bed – usually I've just fucked the hell out of Marielle so I'm kind of spent – and I can actually *see* the course in my mind, like really good quality pictures in my fucking brain. I see different courses at different times. It makes me relax. I know where I am when I do that.'

'And you think this every night?'

'Yeah, but . . .'

'What?'

'Now there's people on the course, in the way, like they've just started to crowd in. There's no room, I can't see the fairway. It gives me a headache just talking about it.'

'So you think about the game a lot?'

'All the time.'

'And you think that's good?'

'I don't know. It's not good? This is what you're telling me?'

'I'm not going to tell you what I think. That would be wrong. We have to reach the answer together. I can only be beside you, that's all.'

'Man, you cost me an asshole to get here and this is all you're giving me? I'm finished – is that what you're telling me?'

'Maybe I can't help you. Maybe no one can. Maybe you are finished.'

'I don't need to hear this!' said Bruce Yakich, shooting a fierce glance in Mario's direction.

'Bruce, do you carry a gun?'

'A what?'

'Do you carry a gun with you?'

'Of course I do. What d'you take me for, a putz?'

'May I see it?' asked Mario carefully.

'What d'you wanna see my fucking gun for? I need help, man, I'm not here to talk about fucking firearms.'

4

'Bruce, please, let me see your gun.'

'Jesus.' He leant forward and opened a leather attaché case at his feet, taking out a black automatic pistol. 'There, happy now?'

Mario gently took the gun from his hand.

'What d'you think I'm gonna do, blow myself away?'

'No, I don't think you're going to do that,' said Mario. Calmly he clenched the gun between his knees and pulled back the arming mechanism. It clicked loudly.

'What the fuck . . .' But before Bruce Yakich could properly react Mario was pointing the gun at his temple, moving with a speed that defied his disability.

'I cannot see the point of continuing to treat you when you are a hopeless case: selfish, stupid, mean and arrogant. You have been praised too many times and it has made you flabby and lazy. You are worthless, Bruce Yakich. I am going to do the world a favour and kill you. Then I will kill your driver and disappear. I have done this many times before. I see it as a necessary part of my job, not particularly enjoyable but essential. Are you ready?'

'What the fuck?' said Bruce Yakich, his face taut with fear. 'You're not serious?'

'Never more so. I am, however, fascinated by what might be going through your mind now. I would be grateful if you would tell me. It's always interesting to know what people think just before they die.'

'I'm not thinking anything.'

Mario pressed the gun into Bruce's temple. 'You must be thinking something, Bruce. Are you thinking about the game now, or Marielle's asshole, or the fact that you will never stand in the sun again? You must be wondering what it's going to be like to be dead. Tell me, you don't have long.'

'Who the fuck are you?' whined Bruce. 'I thought you were a therapist.'

'Oh, I am, a very radical one. I have already killed many of my hopeless cases. Think of me as a therapist stroke hit man. Of course, my withered arm is a big advantage. People aren't scared of me.'

'You're fucking crazy.'

'No, far from it, I am very sane. You're crazy at the moment, and I want to hear your crazy thoughts, Bruce. Tell me what you're thinking.'

'I don't want to die,' said Yakich, his bottom lip starting to quiver.

'Of course you don't. Who does? Life is good. But then we get bored and it all seems like shit. That's called depression and it's very natural. A person who is mature can live through it, they have the foresight to see that it will pass. But very stupid people like you, Bruce, have no foresight, only self-pity. It was always everyone else's fault, wasn't it, Bruce? Until recently when you discovered it was all yours. You have everything yet still you're miserable. What a waste. The best thing to do is die.'

Mario closed one eye and turned away as if preparing himself for the blast and the impact of the bullet on Yakich's head.

'No, please!' said Bruce, dribbling with fear. 'Please, Mario, don't fucking do it, man. I'll tell you what I'm thinking, okay? I'll fucking tell you.' He spoke rapidly, spittle running down his chin, eyes awash with tears. 'Don't pull the fucking trigger, it's a really light action. Okay . . . I see my mom and my dog when I was a kid. It's all so intense! And I can see Marielle's butt, yes, arched up and ready to be plugged . . . Oh, man. I love her, man. Please don't shoot. I wanna see her again. Shit, oh, shit! Yeah, and I can see the first set of clubs I ever owned, leaning against the wall of my mom's house in Denver. And my Maserati . . . I can see that. I can fucking see that like it's in front of me. Shit! And I can see me in it, and I look like an asshole. I am such a fucking asshole! Oh, God, and I can see myself fucking Marielle, and she's so young and beautiful and I'm such a putz, so fat and blubbery and white and . . . oh, man.'

Mario opened his eyes and smiled. He cast a glance at Bruce's groin. A damp patch had appeared on his blue trousers. Again Mario turned away.

'No, no!' screamed Bruce. 'Please, Mario, I'll give you anything. How much do you want?'

He did nothing, just held his position. 'You are going to die, Bruce. What more could I want than that?'

Then Bruce Yakich broke down. He started sobbing. His mouth hung open and he howled like a dog. His fists were balled up tight on his soaking wet lap. There were no two ways about it, Bruce Yakich was a total mess.

Mario smiled kindly and lowered the pistol. Again securing it between his legs, he disarmed it and released the bullet clip. It dropped to the floor. Mario bent down, picked it up, pressed the window button. A blast of hot air entered the now slightly pungent limousine and the clip was ejected with one swift flick of Mario's wrist

Bruce opened his eyes and looked about him, sobbing open-mouthed. He saw that the gun was no longer at his head. Mario noticed he was still shaking violently.

'You must rest for a couple of hours now. You've been through a very taxing experience, Bruce.'

'Ain't you going to kill me?' he asked finally.

'Not now, no.'

'What d'you mean, not now?'

'Well, the exercise wouldn't have worked unless I really had been utterly prepared to kill you. Your life was hanging by a thread there, Bruce, you were very close to death.'

'Oh, man, look what I done. I pissed my pants!'

'Very cathartic,' said Mario. 'Encouraging. How do you feel?'

'I'm blown away, man. What the fuck were you doing?'

'Do you feel your mood lightening?'

'Fuck, man, my feelings are fried. I thought you were gonna kill me. What the fuck were you trying to do to me?'

'The questions are flooding in. That's good. Now take a moment to ponder. Don't worry about your pants, we can sort that out later. Just sit back and relax. I have disarmed the gun, I'm not going to harm you.'

Slowly and slightly uncomfortably, Bruce Yakich sat back. He let his head rest against the seat and breathed a huge sigh.

'Tell me, how do you feel?'

'Shit, man, I feel good.'

Chapter Two

Although Miles Morris had around thirty million dollars to his name, it wasn't as if he was a Lottery winner. He'd worked very hard for it, after a fashion. With several million dollars in a bank in America, a couple of million pounds in a bank in London and some sort of investment in Switzerland he didn't fully understand, there was no arguing with the fact that he was a very rich man. He hadn't been born rich, far from it. The product of an unremarkable comprehensive education, he'd just happened to be the right age, working in the right part of America in the late-twentieth.

Miles was one of the few, a man who understood computer code, a man who had a simple idea that turned into a 'killer app', net jargon for an extremely popular computer application everyone would want. It was buy out time.

Miles Morris, the quintessentially quiet Englishman, was suddenly confronted with a money mountain.

Did he buy an island, a ship, a Boeing 747 with built-in non-spill Jacuzzi? No, he bought a new bicycle.

Did he buy a stately home with a helicopter pad and a Rolls-Royce?

No, he bought a two-bedroomed apartment in North London.

True, his bike was a made-to-measure mountain bike fitted with the very latest equipment: lugless crank, one-touch gear shift for eighteen gears, front and rear shocks, and weighing just under ten kilos. Fairly expensive for an ordinary mortal, but for a man who could buy his own army hardly a major extravagance.

To be fair, the apartment was in an exclusive block on Abbey Road and cost three-quarters of a million pounds, but no one would call it flash.

Miles would have thought it utterly normal if he'd ever thought about such things, which he didn't. He liked riding bikes and his wife was obsessed with the Beatles. To him it all made perfect sense.

A month after his return to England he was riding his bike along a disused railway cutting, the state-of-the-art suspension cushioning any bumps his Kevlar-reinforced tyres encountered.

He had joined Sustrans, a voluntary organisation devoted to sustainable transport – hence the abbreviated name. Sustrans rehabilitated miles of disused railway tracks and turned them into cycle paths. Miles had been looking forward to this event for weeks. That is, he'd been seeing it in his computer diary for weeks, marked out in orange, his favourite colour, denoting cycling, his favourite non-computer-based pastime. To describe him as being excited about the day out would be a gross exaggeration; Miles Morris didn't get excited about anything.

He was not alone. Upwards of one hundred and sixty people were on the trip with him. It was the inaugural ride along a stretch of disused branchline which at one time had run between Guildford, Farnham and Winchester. It wound its way through open country, past golf links and glider clubs; through cuttings partly overgrown with sycamore trees. It was Miles' idea of a good day out; his casual check of breathing rate and pulse indicated he was relaxed.

'Where are you from?' asked a woman cycling beside him. Miles had noticed her earlier, mainly because of the machine she was on: an antique, bone-shaking, sit-up-and-beg model that must have been manufactured before the war. Bar pull breaks and no gears, huge wheels and heavy black mudguards. He assumed it must weigh a ton, wondered why she rode such an outdated contraption.

'London, I suppose.'

'You suppose?'

'Well, I've only been back a month.'

'From where?'

'Pacific Northwest.'

'Where's that?' She seemed genuinely not to know but he wasn't surprised. No one in England understood where he'd been living until he explained it was where the sit com *Frasier* was set.

'America, top left-hand bit. Seattle.'

'Oh, right. Computer programmer?'

'Yes.'

She rode on for a while. Then: 'Aren't you surprised I knew?'

'No,' said Miles flatly. He'd been here before. 'People are always guessing things about me.'

'Are they? Okay, I'll try a few more guesses. Do you mind?'

'No.'

'You're thirty . . .' she paused for a moment, looking at him. He knew she'd guess right. '. . . three.'

'Yes.'

'You're Sagittarius.'

'Yes.'

'You're married.'

'Yes.'

'No children.'

'Yes. I mean, no.'

'Your wife earns more than you.'

'Yes. Well . . .'

'Except you've just received a lot of money.'

'Closer. I don't really earn money any more. It's complicated.'

'You think you might be depressed but you're not sure what that feels like.' She had clearly decided to ignore the fact that she'd been wrong about his wife earning more.

'Yes.'

'D'you still not wonder how I guess all this?'

'Not really. I must be some sort of psychic open book. This is always happening to me.'

'Weird,' said the woman. They rode on in silence for a while. Miles tried to conjure up some interest in the accuracy of her guesswork. He couldn't manage it.

'You're not poor though, are you?'

'No, I'm quite rich.'

'You should see someone.'

'I'm sorry?'

'That's very American, to say "I'm sorry?" like that. Americans always say "I'm sorry" when they're feeling defensive.'

'Is that what I'm feeling?'

'I knew you couldn't feel things. You really do need to see someone.'

'I don't understand. Who should I see?'

'Someone who can help you. You're rich and depressed, blocked and numb. Look at me – I'm rich and happy. I used to be depressed but now I'm not. I'm so happy, so free.' She sang the last word, threw her head back and laughed.

'You mean, therapy?'

'If you want to call it that.'

'Oh, God. I've tried it but it doesn't work for me. I'm English.'

'So am I. That's no excuse any more.'

'Well, everyone I know who does therapy, which was basically everyone I ever knew in America including my wife, seemed to get madder and madder. And they all say I should do therapy, especially my wife. I don't need to talk about my childhood.'

'Everyone needs to talk about their childhood.'

'Well, I don't. All things considered, it was very happy. Well, happy enough.'

'See Mario Lupo.'

'Who's he?' asked Miles out of politeness.

'Doesn't matter, just remember that name. Mario Lupo.'

'Okay, I'll remember it,' said Miles. He smiled at her. She wasn't unattractive, and certainly incredibly confident. She even made riding a rickety, out-of-date bike look cool.

'See if you can guess things about me.'

Miles now noticed that she could possibly be flirting. He didn't really want to try and guess things about her but couldn't be bothered to disagree.

'You are twenty-eight.'

'Well done!'

'You like old things. Distrust modern technology, but find using cell-phones and e-mail rather useful.'

'Very good.'

'You are single, you do not have children. You have had a series of unsuccessful relationships with men who reveal their immaturity at an early stage.'

'Spot on.'

'You have recently had an experience that has changed your life and you feel very positive about yourself and very confident about what you can achieve.'

'Mario Lupo. Remember that name,' said the woman again. She smiled at him. Miles checked again. He didn't feel anything. He had something more to say and pondered for a moment. He wasn't sure if it was motivated by a feeling he just couldn't feel.

'There's more,' he said eventually.

'Really.'

'Yes, it's not going to last. Sorry, I don't mean to be cruel but it's absurd to believe that the state of elation you find yourself in at the moment is sustainable. You've had some sort of pseudo-religious experience which has left your life seemingly sorted out, and you think this is going to last? I have no wish to be cynical but it's been going on for centuries, the salvation myth, hasn't it? Religion, politics, great leaders, great thinkers, gurus. People claiming to have an answer to normal human misery. There isn't one.'

'Oh, I know that,' said the woman, still smiling. 'I'm under no illusions. But I cope with normal human misery, live with it and have a much better time. Mario Lupo.'

'Mario Lupo,' repeated Miles in as tired and resigned a tone as he could muster.

'Remember that name.'

'How could I forget it? He's obviously the second coming.'

13

Miles sat back on his saddle and felt his pulse. He had noticed a very slight muscular spasm when she had told him to remember the name. Only slightly above normal and probably due to the fact that he was pedalling up an incline. A hint of a feeling? Must have been, but not a very nice one.

He seemed to be able to read this woman fairly easily, but then she was clearly self-aware and highly therapied, if there was such a term. It was in the way she sat on the bike, it was in what she was wearing. Very carefully chosen clothes, someone with plenty of time to think about herself.

Nothing she had said about him had surprised him either. Miles was nothing if not self-aware. It was just too easy to guess stuff about him. He had a ring on his wedding finger, he wore American clothes but had an English accent, and his wife Donna told him he had the most depressed expression in Christendom.

He'd grown used to hearing people suggest specialists he should go and see. Mario Lupo was just another in a long list of names.

He started pedalling faster, leaving the woman on the sit-up-and-beg bicycle lagging behind.

'It's not a race!' she called out, laughter in her voice.

Miles pretended not to hear. He didn't want any further contact with her. Maybe that was a feeling? A desire not to talk to someone must be based on a feeling.

He had chosen this particular trip because it fitted in with work. He'd had an all-day meeting with a software company in Bristol the previous day. He no longer needed to work for money, only relaxation. If he did nothing he started to tighten up into a knot.

The end of the ride was near the old family home in Datchet where his father still lived. Miles didn't think of it as home any more. After twelve years in the Pacific Northwest, Seattle was more like home now.

When the ride ended he caught the train back to Windsor and then rode five miles through the Sunday evening traffic to Datchet.

The mock-Tudor building dating from the 1930s that

housed his father's antique shop stood on what might once have been a peaceful village green. It was now home to a set of mini-roundabouts and almost twenty-four-hour congestion.

Datchet was marooned in the middle of a tangle of roads which fed into or out of the M4. Situated just outside London, cordoned off from the capital by the stranglehold of the M25, somehow Datchet had managed to remain suspended in time. Meanwhile the whole surrounding area was pulsating with people who had money and cars, and at some time of the day or night all seemed to need to drive through Datchet.

His father's shop suffered from this constant high-speed procession. Unlike Eton or Windsor, which had a huge tourist trade passing every establishment on foot, very few people walked past Morris Antiques in Datchet. Those who did would notice that the items inside were virtually invisible behind a screen of anti-Europe posters.

'We will never accept Euros here!' they screamed in fluorescent pink and black. 'Save the pound, reject the Eurocrats!' In between the posters hung a selection of Union Jacks in various stages of decay.

Miles and his sister Katherine had lived above the shop until they were old enough to run away, in Miles' case as soon as he'd finished his 'A' levels.

Nothing had changed in the house within living memory. His father held on to everything old with all his diminishing might, fighting the tide of development and newness which threatened to engulf the area. As Miles dismounted by the battered green front door, Concorde roared overhead on its way to New York.

On the days the wind direction dictated, the Heathrow flight path passed directly over the house. Every minute a jet would scream across the sky as it fought its way above the clouds. Datchet was not a peaceful little town.

When he had come into London on Concorde a month earlier, Miles had peered from his window to try and see his birthplace. He'd missed it.

'Hi, Dad. How's it going?'

'Bloody awful to be frank. Are you coming in?' said his father, standing in the door. Miles looked at his watch.

'I haven't got much time.'

'I've got a bit of old pie I could warm up.'

'Okay,' said Miles. He pushed his bike into the narrow hallway and leant it against the wall. His eyes were level with a photograph, badly mounted in a large ornate Victorian frame. It was a picture of a small child, himself, sitting on his mother's knee. She in turn was sitting on the bonnet of their old Ford Escort, parked in a windblown beachside car park on the Kent coast. Miles was six years old in the picture and could remember the moment with startling clarity. He checked himself to see if he felt anything when he saw it. Nothing.

As he walked along the hall he passed three lovingly framed black and white portraits of his mother as a young woman – dark hair, such thick dark hair. Very full lips. Was she beautiful? Miles couldn't tell. He was supposed to look like her, according to all the relatives he hadn't seen since he went to America.

Miles heard the door to the old gas oven close, a sound he knew well. When he entered the cramped kitchen, Mr Morris Senior sat down and sighed. He sighed like an old smoker coughed. Big sighs coming from nowhere. He'd done it for as long as Miles could remember.

'How's business?' asked Miles, sitting on the wobbly stool opposite him. His father was already scanning the pages of an antiques catalogue.

'Bloody awful. Nobody appreciates fine furniture any more. Bloody Ikea, I ask you. Awful European rubbish. Bloody ghastly foreign muck everywhere.'

'Oh. But you're okay?'

'Course I'm not okay. Country's gone down the pan, though'.

'It seems quite prosperous to me. It's changed a lot since I've been away.'

'Yes, for the worse,' said his father. 'Hoard your pounds, Sonny Jim, that's all I can say. There'll be a revolution. The silent majority aren't going to stand for this Euro nonsense. It'll all end it tears, believe you me.'

Miles had spoken to his father regularly on the phone from Seattle, every six months or so. He knew there was no point in arguing, pointing out that America had used a single currency for hundreds of years and it hadn't held them back economically. Miles couldn't really see the problem. Global in outlook, local in activity – that was how he saw himself.

Half a chicken and leek pie came out of the oven. It was a sorry affair, the deep-frozen variety containing the minimum amount of meat legally possible for a product describing itself as pie.

'I get these in six packs from Iceland, they're damn' good value,' said his father as he handed Miles an exquisite old plate with a quarter of the thin pie resting on it. 'Probably get banned next week by some bloody ignorant Belgian chump who's accepting back handers from some bloody awful French cheese manufacturer.'

'Looks lovely, Dad. Got any beer?'

'Hell's bells! Think I'm made of money?' snapped his father grumpily. 'There's perfectly good water in the tap. Don't waste it, though, I'm on a bloody meter now. That's probably a damned Euro directive, too, knowing our luck.'

'D'you need any money, Dad?'

'Don't want charity, thank you very much.'

'It's not charity. I've got more than I need.'

'Lucky old you.'

His father started reading the *Daily Mail*. Miles didn't press the offer.

When the pie was finished, which didn't take long, his dad offered Miles a 'Say no to the Euro!' poster. He folded it carefully, putting it in his pannier bag. He'd noticed posters like it all over the country, but they seemed a little futile.

He got back on his bike and cycled the very short distance to Datchet train station. The level crossing gates were down, he had just enough time to shoulder his bike and run over the footbridge to catch the last train into London.

For a week or so after they had landed in England, Miles

started to have some feelings. Or he'd thought that's what they were, and the nice part about it was they seemed to be good feelings. He'd wanted to get up in the morning and do something other than work or cycle. Make the apartment their own, cook nice meals, have people around to dinner.

Donna Buick, his wife for just three years, bought him a complete set of DeWalt power tools and he willingly put up shelves, turned the spare bedroom into a huge walk-in closet for her, had an ADSL line installed so they could work from home. He built a corner desk so the computer wouldn't look so ugly.

Donna did not suffer from the same ailments as her husband. She was constructed of almost pure feeling. She literally ran everywhere, was always on the phone to her therapist and old friends in Seattle or her new friends in London. She would occasionally dash up to Miles as he measured a piece of MDF for her walk-in wardrobe and embrace him, telling him how happy she was and cursing the fact they hadn't moved to London earlier. She had a thing about the 1960s, hence the importance to her of the Abbey Road address. For some reason everything about London made her think of the Beatles, her favourite band. Not forgetting Jimi Hendrix, and the Who, and the Rolling Stones, and Marianne Faithfull whom she also had a big thing about. Donna seemed to take pleasure in everything.

Miles didn't know what pleasure felt like. Newly found wealth gave him none. It was only after he'd received the money that he realised it clearly wasn't the reason he'd worked so hard for so long. Code-writing for the corporation round the clock, then eight months at his new company working ever harder. Towards the end of his eight years at the corporation he met Kulvinder Bhasker also from England. They jumped ship at the same time when a favourite project they had originated was dismissed by the board. Using their savings and a respectable loan from Donna, they started up a small programming company.

Miles and Kulvinder spent weeks hopping endlessly between Silicon Valley and Seattle, developing a program which emulated the human voice and face, quite crudely as they themselves would readily admit.

However, this system could be transmitted in byte-sized packets over the net. The company was called viaFace, and the industry was soon abuzz with articles in *Wired* magazine, interviews on net TV shows. Soon the big guns started knocking on their door. They realised they had finally struck micro-gold.

Their eight-month-old start-up company was sold for a little over seventy million dollars. Not that much in industry terms, but clearly of immense impact to the two men directly involved.

Celebrations, a change of world view, everything golden. Then came the paperwork and the meetings with bankers, financial advisers, investment brokers. The windfall had resulted in a mountain of paperwork, something Miles had never been faced with before. His partner Kulvinder dealt with the bulk of it, but Miles couldn't avoid it altogether. He suddenly had an enormous amount of money and, it seemed, a lot of responsibility.

It was around this time that he became aware of the numbness. He felt lethargic and fuzzy-headed. Everything seemed pointless.

More meetings followed: Miles and Kulvinder with bankers and venture capitalists on Sand Hill Road in Silicon Valley, Donna with her therapist and publishers, although mainly with her therapist.

A decision was made. They would return to London and start a new company, FullFacial. They would continue their research into the technology they had created. This time they would go the whole hog with little thought for profit.

Once the initial excitement of the move to London was over, Miles found the numbness returned. He didn't want to tell anyone. He was pretty certain he wasn't physically ill, assumed it was stress from the hours he sat in front of a screen. His shoulders didn't go numb, they felt like bags of sharp rubble.

Although he ate good quality food, took plenty of exercise and was engrossed in his work, anyone who tried to give him a massage said it was like kneading rock. Legitimate, qualified masseurs had almost broken their thumbs trying to get him to relax. Of course this much bodily tension caused Miles much suffering. Shoulder pains like blades in the flesh, a neck that could hold up a tree. Constipation? Don't ask.

By contrast, Donna was a flowing stream of creativity. Or Miles assumed that's what it was. The chaos she engendered spread like rampant lichen over every available surface.

A huge black bin bag of rubbish rested beside the front door when he arrived back home. He carried the bloated sack all of two metres to the garbage chute in the hallway outside, began to force it in and naturally it exploded, releasing its foetid contents all over the squeaky clean floor.

'Ah, there we go, as predicted,' he said in a sing-song voice. He swept up all the bits of sweetcorn, cigarette butts and rotten potato salad and deposited them down the chute. Then he returned to the flat, only to realise that none of the lights was on and the blinds were drawn. Donna liked to live in perpetual dusk. Although it was still daylight outside, inside it was a cavern. Miles really didn't much like the dark.

Donna was always happy to shuffle around in the gloom, claiming the daylight hurt her eyes. She was very health-conscious in a chaotic way, using an impressive selection of vitamin pills and seaweed supplements to combat a seemingly perpetual hangover.

Miles pressed the dimmer switches and spun the knob to max. The hall was flooded with light from the recessed spots he'd had expensively installed. Low-voltage, high-output. He had in fact programmed a desktop to run the entire household lighting system, bringing the lights up at the appropriate hour each day according to the time of year. Unfortunately Donna used the same machine for her e-mail and writing and soon it just wouldn't switch on. She didn't know what she'd done and, although apologetic at first, soon blamed him for buying such a stupid computer. He simply hadn't had time to re-do the whole thing.

Once he closed the door all seemed quiet. He kicked an empty fizzy drink can, picked it up and looked at it.

It had all become so familiar. He was used to Donna, and although he wasn't sure what love actually felt like, was more or less certain he did love her.

He'd never heard of her when they'd first met in a coffee bar near the fish market in Seattle, an admission which seemed to annoy her and make her interested in him in equal measure. He'd heard of her books since they seemed to be everywhere, and anyone with children would often refer to 'Milky'.

Donna Buick and Milky were synonymous. Milky the . . . well, Miles was never quite sure what Milky was though he never said anything about it. Some sort of stain on the page with a very moral outlook on life had made Donna Buick a comfortably wealthy woman.

They didn't have children, not for any reason that Miles was aware of, just didn't have them. Their friends in Seattle, particularly Donna's friends, were very happy she was getting married to the patient English guy. That's how they referred to him. 'You'll need to be patient,' Donna's mother had whispered to him at the ceremony. 'But it'll be worth it in the long run.'

Miles was patient, right from their first meeting. Donna was, by anyone's standards, striking. Around five foot eleven of model good looks, if in a slightly crazed way, with enormous, slightly red-rimmed eyes. Jet black hair with a streak of white sweeping from her hairline. He initially took this to be Seattle cyber chic, but it was natural.

'It's Milky,' she once said to him seriously.

He couldn't believe it when she actually asked him out on a date. He found he liked being with her, cooking for her, cleaning up her blitzed apartment while she went through what appeared to be some form of physical agony when in his presence. Writhing on the floor, telling him she had never lusted after anyone so much.

He smiled at the memory as he unwound the cord from the brass hook he had screwed to the wall and lowered the recently fitted Victorian clothes drying rack he had adapted as a bike hanger. Two shining bicycles appeared, a hand-built road tourer and a carbon-fibre track bike. He attached the two spare hooks on to his mountain bike and pulled all three up into the high roof space.

He looked up at them, tidy and sensible, out of the way.

Well-built and beautiful bikes, all three hanging there like ripe fruit.

Donna walked past dressed only in a large bath towel. She was talking on a cordless phone but threw a smile at Miles as she entered the large front room and flopped down on the sofa. It was only just recognisable as an item of furniture due to the mountain of Sunday newspapers, and Saturday newspapers, and piles of glossy women's magazines, dirty plates, half-empty boxes of chocolates, clothes, coats, shoes, socks and underwear distributed over it. Miles followed her in and without hesitation started cleaning up.

He wanted to be relaxed and happy, fall into her arms and lie down in the mess that surrounded them. He wanted not to need to tidy up. He pondered as he picked up the first ashtray if the urge to tidy was a feeling or was it just a need? He needed to go to the toilet or to eat, those weren't feelings. He needed to tidy up. No, it was a need, not a feeling.

The smell from the ashtray was disgusting and the sheer number of butts was staggering. Surely she hadn't smoked all those herself? Then he saw the line of empty wine bottles along one wall and the corner filled with broken glass from what had once been tall-stemmed wine glasses they'd bought in Heal's on a sticky Saturday afternoon.

Miles breathed in deeply and went into the kitchen. He pulled out the dustpan and brush from under the sink. As he stood up again his knee caught the door which slammed back on its hinges, making an ominous cracking sound. He started to inspect it. The kitchen was badly designed. Clearly the doors were going to break under normal use. It was an over-complicated hinge design, and self-tapping screws in laminated MDF wouldn't hold for long. Bad workmanship with bad materials. He wished they'd bought the stainless steel catering kitchen he'd seen in the hotel equipment showroom but Donna had wanted natural wood so they'd bought wood. Or rather wood effect, badly made wood effect, even though it had cost a bomb.

He pulled out a roll of bin liners and carefully closed the cabinet door. The tiny vibration shook the dirty plates that had been piled up on the sink unit. One started to slide. He leant against the kitchen unit to stop its descent, put the dustpan and brush on the floor and opened the dishwasher. It was full of dirty plates and his Opinel wood-handled French vegetable knife which wasn't supposed to be washed in a dishwasher. He pulled the knife out. Its steel blade was rusty, its once-varnished handle scoured clean, the wood cracking where it joined the blade. He placed the knife on the draining board, making a mental note to clean it later, maybe even re-varnish the handle.

Donna walked in, still holding the phone. She glanced at him. He stared at her.

'Miles is back,' she said into the phone. 'I'd better go, I haven't finished clearing up yet and you know what he's like – Mr Anal.' She smiled at him as she said this. 'Are you a bit anal, honey?'

He smiled back. 'I don't know.'

'Yeah, he's a bit anal,' she said into the phone. 'Anyway, I'll see you Tuesday.'

He waited for her to finish, but as usual she started talking again, saying, 'Nooo! Surely not!' and 'Did he!' and 'How could she!' and 'How big is it!' and 'No way, I wouldn't do that for anyone!'

On and on she blathered, walking back into the main room. It seemed hours later when she finally put down the phone.

'Hi, sorry about this, I'll clear it up in a jiffy,' she said as she put the phone on a chair which was already covered in unopened post, newspapers and clothes.

'I tried, I really tried, not to clean up. I'm trying not to be anal. I really am.'

'I know you are, honey. I'll clean it up,' said Donna, making no obvious moves to carry out this threat.

'I can't leave things alone. I just can't,' he said, picking the phone up and putting it in its recharging cradle which was on a shelf directly behind the chair.

'I had some people round Saturday night. They stayed kind of late.'

Miles walked past her into the front room.

Whenever he had been away from her for more than a few hours he always went through a moment's discomfort at being reminded that Donna was slightly taller than him. She only had an inch and a half on him, but it still seemed wrong. You never saw pictures of men shorter than women in adverts. He knew this was just his problem. Donna claimed short men were more motivated and she liked that. However, Miles noticed that this discomfort was without doubt a feeling. Not a good one but a feeling nonetheless. He couldn't be dead.

He started to clean up in earnest while Donna sat on the only chair not festooned with cast-offs.

'Did you have a good time?' she asked as she inspected her feet. 'Cycling,' she added accusingly as though he had been away doing something else.

Miles emptied another ashtray and picked up some more dirty plates.

'I can't remember. I can't leave this, I have to tidy up.'

'Well, talk while you do it.'

'But . . . but surely this isn't right? Is this right?'

'Is what right?'

'Well, that I come home and the place is terminal.'

'I don't know. Does it feel right?'

'Oh, please, Donna, don't do therapy talk. I don't know. I mean, does this not look like a mess to you?'

The phone rang. Donna got up and answered it. She didn't even say hello, just started talking as though she was already in the middle of a conversation. All the people who rang Donna were women, mostly in America, so the phone bills ran to healthy four-figure sums a month. They rang each other constantly.

Miles placed more and more rubbish into the bin liners. He filled three of them and went out on to the communal landing, sending them crashing to oblivion down the chute. When he returned he heard a noise in the main bedroom and glanced in as he made his way to the cupboard where they kept the Dyson. Donna was talking on the phone and making vague attempts at tidying up the bedroom. She was also smoking which he had repeatedly begged her not to do. He had to put up with it in the rest of the apartment, but not in the bedroom. It didn't seem that much to ask. No one smoked in America as far as he could tell, except Donna. It was one of the reasons she loved Europe. More people smoked.

Miles Morris picked up the Dyson and threw it right across the room. He threw the state-of-the-art bagless vacuum cleaner so hard it smashed into the dining table and the handle came clean away. It lay on the floor like a disembowelled goat. Many pieces of broken, brightly coloured plastic lay scattered around the floor.

He started at it, sat down and tried to work out what had happened. He had received no warning he would do something so destructive. It was like he'd just had an electric shock, from somewhere else. From outside.

He checked his pulse to see if there was any sign of emotional turmoil. It felt normal. He looked at the broken vacuum cleaner again. Had he really done that?

Donna appeared at the bedroom door looking anxious. 'What happened?'

'Oh, no. Oh, no,' said Miles as he looked at the shattered domestic appliance. 'I can't believe I did that.'

'Miles, that is really fucked up! Why don't you just tell me you're mad at me? I'm telling him to express his feelings. You know what men are like.'

Miles looked at her. This was an experience he was familiar with. She was having two conversations at once, one with him and one with any number of women on the other line. Donna was the only woman he'd ever met who had conference calls with her friends.

'I'm sorry, I don't know what happened.'

'He doesn't know what happened,' repeated Donna to her phone. 'Have you heard that one before? Yeah, me too. "I don't know how that happened, honey."' Donna started laughing, taking luxurious puffs on her cigarette and smiling at Miles.

'I'm really sorry,' he said. 'I liked that machine.' He stood by the broken vacuum cleaner, moving the pieces around with his toe.

'I'll call you back in an hour,' said Donna. She switched off the phone and let the towel drop, standing in front of Miles completely naked.

'Come on then,' she said. 'Let's have like, sex, yeah.'

He couldn't believe she was interested. Things were really starting to make less and less sense.

As he stripped off, surprised at how the idea appealed to him, Donna dialled a number on her hands-free set and lay on the bed.

'What are you doing?' he asked as he knelt beside her.

'Hi, yeah, we're going to try it,' said Donna to the person on the other end. 'Are you free for ten minutes?'

'What's going on?' asked Miles.

Donna looked at him. 'God, I want to fuck with you so bad.'

'But who are you talking to?'

'My therapist. Don't worry, she can't see anything. It's an exercise we've talked about and now seemed like a good time. Just ignore what I say and fuck me like it's the end of the world.'

'Thank you, darling,' she said as she flopped on to the bed beside him. She was on top, she came, he didn't. Miles had once read a book about tantric sex that Donna had given him. It explained how a man was drained by orgasms and a woman energised. He'd tried it and found it to be true. If he didn't come he could get back to work immediately after they fucked. He hadn't come in six months and felt much better for it.

'That was worth every penny,' she said, lighting up a cigarette.

'I'm so sorry. I don't know what happened!' he said, covering his eyes with his arm.

'The best fuck we've had in years. Ever, maybe. And all we have to do is buy a new Dyson.'

'Are you okay?'

'Never better, baby. Any time you want to smash the place up, I'll be here. Page me.'

She kissed him on the forehead tenderly.

'I hate myself.'

'You shouldn't. You're a wonderful, gentle man with a very tight ass,' she said with a kind smile. 'Try and relax.'

'I can't. I don't know how to.'

'Then get help,' she said flatly.

'I've tried getting help, you know what happened. It made me worse.'

'You're a grown man, sort it out.'

'That's rather cruel, isn't it? You're a grown woman and you . . .' He stopped himself.

'What?' she asked, holding the phone ready to make the next call.

'Well, you can't even look after yourself.'

She laughed, not cruelly but with great confidence.

'I don't need to, baby. You do it for me. And I don't smash things up. That's how I judge a grown up – kids smash things when they don't get their own way, adults don't.'

Chapter Three

———◦◦◦———

When the black Cherokee Jeep rumbled into the spacious redbrick drive of number 314 The Avenue, the owner of the property, one Gaston Bell, was not well pleased. True, his wife was in Florida, his son at Eton. However Mrs Slavic, their cleaner, an illegal Balkan immigrant Bell managed to hire at very reasonable rates, was in the kitchen. He didn't trust her one inch, knew she had been removing certain articles from the house and definitely didn't want her to witness this visitor.

He pulled on his blazer and went out of the front door.

'What the blazes are you doing here?' he said to the heavily built, bearded occupant of the car.

'Came for a little chin wag, Brigadier,' was the rumbling reply. Donald Cooper had an absurdly deep voice issuing from the depths of an unusually large body. 'Got your message, thought I'd drop by.'

'For heaven's sake, you know this area is out of bounds!'

'Get in the car and stop poncing about,' said Cooper. Gaston Bell checked the house. No sign of Mrs Slavic. Hopefully she would be none the wiser. He went to the passenger door and climbed in.

'Don't mess about, I'm feeling rather annoyed,' said Donald Cooper as he pulled slowly out of the drive. 'I didn't drive all the way out here for you to give me the run around. What's the caper?'

Donald Cooper had been in the Green Jackets, as had Gaston

Bell although not for nearly 20 years. This did not stop him on occasion from referring to himself as Brigadier Bell. He had recently hired a man by the name of Redford as his driver. Also ex-Green Jackets, he came highly recommended, and Redford had kept him in touch with certain rogue elements within the ranks of ex-servicemen. They were very useful to know, but not when they came to your house.

Gaston Bell had been through a lot since he left the Army. He was a changed man. He'd reached a crisis point in his early forties – so bad, in fact that he had to seek professional help. This was not a thing it would have been wise to divulge to a born soldier like Cooper. A sign of weakness, frailty, a sign which would immediately encourage Cooper to take advantage. He had to be firm.

'This is completely out of order,' said Gaston Bell. 'You know me, Cooper. The reason I'm useful to you lot is that I'm outside. No contact. Rule one.'

'Oh, bollocks, Brigadier,' said Donald as he took the turn for Maidenhead. 'This is exceptional. This is the biggest job in history and we need to start recruiting the squad.'

'I know that. We also need to keep it quiet.'

'I'm not talking to anyone. You wouldn't actually accuse me of singing, would you, Gasty?'

Donald glowered at Gaston, his huge face exuding menace from every pore. Gaston Bell had always managed to disguise his fear of this dangerous man but on the receiving end of a look like that anyone would know they were in danger. Donald Cooper had been decorated for his efforts in the Falklands, but some of his more violent exploits had been kept from the authorities by his immediate superiors. An effective soldier, Cooper, but a man who relished extreme violence even more than the Army was comfortable with.

'No, of course not,' said Gaston. 'But this is just the sort of job where the whole thing can be messed up by one peripheral idiot blabbing in some seedy public house.'

Donald nodded as he drove. He seemed deep in thought.

'True enough,' he said. 'Mind you, word is one peripheral idiot has had his jaw permanently welded shut.'

'Little Mickey Pilcher?' asked Gaston, referring to a colleague who had known too much and not been afraid to share his knowledge. Gaston had received a coded self-deleting text file saying that Mickey Pilcher was no longer a threat.

'I'm saying nothing.'

'Good news all round, then,' said Gaston, trying not to imagine the sequence of events that must have taken place. He glanced at Donald's enormous hands gripping the wheel as if to stop it escaping.

'So, we need a meet,' said Donald. 'What about next Tuesday at the George?' He burped loudly, a habit of his Gaston could never quite accustom himself to. 'Harris and Pickering can make it. I want to keep the team very tight.'

'Yes, all right. Tuesday. We've got one hell of a lot to organise if we're going to do this one. It's a logistical nightmare.'

'You know me, Gasty. I love logistics – particularly nightmare ones.'

Chapter Four

It could not go on, Miles knew that. He surveyed the wreckage. The Dyson had gouged a large hole in the wooden floor he had laid himself. It had also damaged the leg mounting on the excessively expensive dining table.

Donna was right, he had behaved like a child – or rather not like he was when he was a child, he'd never broken anything then. Now, as an adult, he had thrown a favourite toy across the room and smashed it.

He walked into the kitchen and turned on the wind-up radio. It was sitting on the windowsill where the sun was strong through to power the solar panels.

He sat at the table with a glass of filtered water and half-listened to the radio as he flipped through one of Donna's women's magazines.

A big picture of a healthy-looking blonde woman was on the cover, printed next to it the words ORAL SEX in huge letters followed by the strap line, 'Give less, get more, we show you how'.

Miles flipped through the pages, then a voice on the radio caught his attention. It was American. Still only half-listening, his mind went back to Seattle, to the tall stand of fir trees on the opposite side of the road from their old house. So much space, such a fresh smell in the morning.

The voice on the radio belonged to Bruce Yakich who, the dry-voiced presenter explained, had recently won the PGA Golf tournament in Florida, his sixth victory.

Yakich explained that prior to the tournament he had reached an all-time low.

'I was finished, completely finished.'

'And what made you think that?' asked the interviewer.

'I couldn't hit the ball. I lost my game,' said Yakich. 'I couldn't get through the block. I was real angry all the time because of the frustration, but I was lucky enough to hear about this guy called Mario Lupo.'

Miles turned slowly and looked at the radio.

'Is he a coach?' asked the interviewer who Miles now realised was a well-known newsreader.

'No way. He'd make a good one, I guess, but no. He's kind of a therapist but he's really out there, you know? There's a kind of process you go through with Mario . . . I can't tell you exactly what it was in my case but it was very quick, very profound, and it got me back on line.'

'So one session with this, um, Mario Lupo and you started playing well again?'

'Not only well but better than I ever have before. I was nine under par at the championships. And, I tell you, I sailed it. The guy is a genius. Although he would resent me saying that, I guess.'

'He sounds extraordinary. Who is he exactly?'

'Well, he's kind of mysterious. Doesn't seem to, like, live anywhere, although there's a place called the Lupo Institute in Geneva . . . or I think that's where it is. Some people say it's in Milan. It's kind of hard to see him. You have to be introduced, I guess. He works with some very influential people, senators and CEOs, that kind of thing.'

The conversation changed tack as the presenter introduced a psychologist who was rather dubious about the particular methods of this therapist, even though they were never fully explained. The psychologist was concerned that instant cures always seemed to wear off, even sometimes land the individual in more trouble.

Miles recognised the slow, tedious voice that was the trademark of this sort of man. He imagined sitting in his office being asked questions about his mother's death and how that had affected him. All the dull old theories about nine year old boys and their mothers. This Lupo man sounded a lot more interesting. Miles moved to the sink and listened to the rest of the programme. As the presenter wound it up, he again referred to the Lupo Institute. Miles wrote down the name on a notepad he kept by the phone. The one Donna never actually wrote anything on, choosing instead old envelopes which she always lost.

He turned the radio off, picked up the cordless phone and called International Directory Enquiries.

'I want the Lupo Institute in Geneva,' he stated clearly.

'Geneva, Switzerland?' asked the female operator.

'Yes, I think so.'

'Do you have an address?'

'No.'

The line went quiet, then suddenly a computer voice came on line.

'The number you require is . . .'

Miles wrote it down. It was long, starting with a triple zero. It could only be a satellite digital.

The phone system worked through the long string of digits and almost immediately a voice-mail system answered.

'Hello, *bonjour*, *guten tag*, *buongiorno*. This is the Lupo Institute. Please leave your name and number and we will get back to you.' The message was then repeated in four languages.

A small beep followed. Miles held the phone tight to his head, trying to work out what to say. He wanted to talk to someone and instead got this recorded message. He didn't need this, especially on a day like he was having.

'I need to talk to someone . . . I'm sorry, my name is Miles Morris and I want to talk to someone. I'm very rich and I think I'm going mental. I can't tell because I haven't got any feelings. I'm mentally numb. If it's possible to ring me back, I'd be very grateful. Sorry this message hasn't made much sense. I don't know what's going on in my life. It's end of tether time here. I'd be very grateful for a reply.' He gave them his number and switched off the phone.

Half an hour later Miles arrived at the small but prestigious Covent Garden offices of FullFacial, the new company he had set up with Kulvinder Bhasker.

They were both tired from the start-up treadmill, but Full-Facial had been the obvious step. They knew what the technology could achieve, they had to try it.

Finding a client had only taken two weeks. Their reputation was high after the sale of viaFace.

The Nishin Banking Corporation had signed a two-year development deal with them. The product was a talking, fully interactive, user-configured autoteller. The Nishin Bank didn't have any branches in Europe and had no plans to open them. They had opted instead to lease out sites in shopping malls, supermarkets and petrol filling stations where state-of-the-art autotellers would be the friendly face of the corporation.

It was originating this face, the voice-recognition software and graphic animation related to it, that was the huge task Miles and Kulvinder had undertaken. Miles was code writer, code checker, office manager, communications expert and company accountant. He also made the tea and kept the kitchen very tidy. Jean Chowdry, their secretary, was some sort of distant relative of Kulvinder's and seemed to do very little. She sat in the entrance lobby, usually reading *Hello!* or *OK!* magazine. With only one client as yet, calls didn't come in that often.

One whole wall of their office was covered in layer after layer of high-end print outs of various faces they had tried. They needed to narrow the choice down to just twenty. Ten men, ten women, each different face representing a different racial group. Their primary task was to complete the European characteristic face in time for the visit of the Chief Executive Officer of the Nishin Corporation, Mr Nakasomi.

Kulvinder was on the phone when Miles entered.

'Hey, no problem, we can do that for you. Like I say, no problem.'

Like Miles' wife, Kulvinder was always on the phone. He

seemed to do less and less code-writing, which was after all what
they were supposed to be doing. Miles stripped off his cycling
gear and placed it in the red plastic box beside the door which he
had purchased specifically for this role. He sat down at the huge
desk which ran the length of one wall and clicked his desktop,
the smallest machine in the office. He checked his e-mail.
Nothing.

He sat down at the main console and clicked run. The face
came up on the screen, smiling and friendly.

'Good morning, Miles Morris, welcome to the Nishin Bank.
How can I help you?' The voice was full-bodied with plenty of
bass notes. It was delivered through huge Bose speakers
mounted on the wall. It was very loud.

'Hey, steady, Miles, d'you mind?' said Kulvinder, covering
the mouthpiece of the phone. 'Go deaf over the weekend or
what?'

'Sorry, sorry.'

It was all arrangements with Kulvinder: being on this train at
six, being at that bar at eight, doing the meeting in the morning
at nine. All he did was meet people, for no apparent reason.
They never seemed to get any other commissions.

Meanwhile they had been paid big time to do the Nishin
autoteller and still had a mountain of work to do on it.

Miles put on a pair of headphones so as not to disturb
Kulvinder. He ran the face through its basic routine, watching
the mouth closely. There was a delay on some of the consonants.

'Oh, no. That's all we need,' said Miles. 'Lip synch's gone.'
His main responsibility was to check the code that the two of
them had written. Acres of it. It was the most boring, time-
consuming job the company had to undertake, and Miles was a
master at it. The fact that the mouth's movements were out of
synchronisation with the sound was a code error, therefore his
responsibility.

Kulvinder lifted one of Miles's earphones.

'Morning. Good weekend?'

'Really brilliant. Did about seventy kilometres, the new
stretch down there is awesome,' he said happily. 'Mind you,

as predicted, everyone drove home in their bloody cars afterwards.'

'Very useful things, cars. Digital transportation.' Kulvinder was smiling as he spoke, he enjoyed teasing.

'Oh, please,' said Miles.

'Actually, I meant the meeting you went to in Bristol.'

'Oh, yeah, that was good. I mean, it's an animation company so they're not looking for high-end abilities,' said Miles. 'I don't think it's our area, but they were really nice people. And they all cycled to work which was good. They even had a bike storage area in their office.'

'Revolutionary,' said Kulvinder with little interest. The visit to Bristol had been his idea. An animation company there had expressed interest in using their software. But when Kulvinder heard the sort of money this small company had to spend, he lost interest in going himself and talked Miles into it instead. Kulvinder had been right, as usual. The Bristol company couldn't afford the services of FullFacial.

Miles took off the headphones. He found he wanted to talk. 'I went to Datchet to see my dad on the way back.'

'Oh, yeah. He's still going then, is he?'

'Bit miserable. Lonely. Living in some fifties time warp. Then, well, I got home and found the place had been wasted.'

'Yeah, it was a great party, though,' said Kulvinder, smiling broadly. 'Shame you weren't there, kiddo. We had a ball, I'm tellin' you.'

'Oh, so you went then?' asked Miles. He pondered for a moment on the fact that his wife waited for him to be absent before she threw a party. Then he remembered all the parties they'd had in Seattle, the ones where he'd spent the majority of the evening clearing up and emptying ashtrays. Making everyone feel uncomfortable, according to Donna.

'Everyone did,' said Kulvinder. 'There were loads of ex-Corp people there . . . Johnny Reece, Dave Spath, Spud, Hitch, Gonzo, Mickey Walker – who, I may add, against all expectations has hooked up some tech chic of serious, well, dare I say, beauty?'

'Oh, really?' Miles then recalled he hadn't even asked Donna about the party. He must have seemed such an uptight prat, coming in and tidying up after she'd been whooping it up with loads of people he knew and would liked to have seen. Except they were a bit disturbing, especially at a party where they became drunken and boastful, openly relishing the damage they did to the world. The new super-modern anti-eco ethic had really taken hold. Drive bigger cars, consume more, waste more – and laugh about it at parties.

Miles didn't want to hear any more. He turned back to the face on the screen. 'The lip synch's gone,' he repeated.

'Yeah, bad code, Miles. What can I say? All my fault probably. But, you know, I am an Indian, it's only to be expected.'

'No, it's my fault,' said Miles, concentrating on the screen.

'I was just running through the core prog on Friday after you left. Showing some people from Barclays International. They're very interested. Seriously now.'

'What people from Barclays?'

'Didn't Jean tell you?' He put his head around the partition and called to her. 'Didn't you tell Miles about the Barclays people who came on Friday?'

There was no reply. Kulvinder pushed his chair back to his side of the desk, shaking his head. 'Don't know what we pay her for, she does fuck all.'

'But which people?' asked Miles again.

'The development team. They're well into this. Reckon we've got them bagged there, mate.'

'I didn't know you were bringing them here . . . the place is such a mess . . . what on earth can they have thought?'

'We're artists, man, we're allowed to be messy. Didn't you know?'

'I wish you'd told me.'

'I did, didn't I? I was sure Jean must have mentioned it. She put it in the diary. Positive. You were so keen to get off and do your cycling, I didn't bother you,' said Kulvinder. 'We've got to spread the net. I'm having a meeting with them on Tuesday.'

'Another meeting?' said Miles. 'You're always having meetings.'

'I know. Great, isn't it? I've got to go to another in one minute fifty seconds, actually. Lunch.'

'Brilliant,' said Miles. 'I'll just stay here and spend hours fixing the code on the lip synch like the sad act I am.'

'Hey, Miles, love you, mate,' said Kulvinder kindly as he pulled on his painfully bright blue blazer. He had developed some sort of British cricketer style when he lived in America and failed to see how embarrassing it was since he'd returned to England. All blazers and white chinos, white shirts worn with stripy old school ties. Miles had initially decided it was better than the home-boy chic his partner had adopted when they first met. Now he wasn't so sure.

Kulvinder patted Miles gently on the back as he passed. He heard Kulvinder's mobile ring as soon as he'd shut the door. He looked at the bank of phones on his partner's side of the desk, crouched down under the worktop and unplugged all of them. He didn't want any interruptions.

Miles immersed himself in code. When he had discovered it as a teenager, tapping away on his Sinclair ZX88 in the top bedroom above the shop in Datchet, he had felt parts of his body relax for the first time.

Code was good stuff, it earned him a living and kept him sane. Computer code had been a very benign influence on Miles' life. He felt he understood his own workings by understanding code. The logic was all there, line by line, if you could be bothered to go through it. And Miles Morris could be bothered for days at a time. It would be impossible for an observer to know this, their mere presence affected him and made him tense. Like quantum theory, Miles was changed merely by the act of observation. When he was truly alone with a bible-length stream of code to wade through, he was calmness personified.

Chapter Five

Twelve people sat around the long and very old oak table in the great hall of Château Hatton in the Verdun region of Northern France. They came from many different backgrounds, many different European countries, but they had one thing in common: they were in a mess. These twelve were all clients of Mario Lupo who sat at one end of the table, barely glancing at any of the people talking quietly among themselves.

'Thank you for attending,' said Mario finally, speaking in English, their common language. 'I am impressed by the bravery of everyone here. I know it wasn't easy to do so. You have had to admit to a certain failure in your lives to make this commitment, and believe me, that's three-quarters of the battle.'

It was true, the twelve people seated around the table were not exactly New Age loafers. Not for them the public housing and cheap clothes of the continent's poor. These people were mostly at or near the very zenith of their field: managing director of an airline, car designer, international bank executive, domestic white goods manufacturer, software engineer. They were all comfortably wealthy as the car park outside the delightful medieval château testified: Mercedes sports, BMW 7 series, Porsches, even a Rolls-Royce. People who, if asked, would not know the cost of a loaf of bread but would be able to give you a good idea of the day's exchange rates or the price of a Concorde ticket from Paris to New York. And yet they looked so glum, sitting around the table, some twisted up with physical tension, some morose. Their unhappiness sprang from many sources but mainly an indefinable sense of depression. An inner sadness that wouldn't lift despite holidays, career success, sexual conquest, drug use or even alcoholic stupor. Alcohol was the one thing missing from this gathering; instead bottles of mineral water and coffee cups littered the table. The atmosphere was dark and sombre. There was electric lighting but this was minimal. The light mainly came from candles and a massive fireplace at one end of the room where several enormous logs glowed comfortingly.

'We are here for the weekend,' Mario continued when he was sure he had their attention. 'It's going to be an intense experience, but we are all here together.' He stared around the group, noticing without surprise or disappointment the expressions of anxiety and regret on the faces of his clients. He smiled. 'We are all here to support each other and be honest about how we feel. Including me. Then we are all going to go back to work on Monday morning feeling much more positive. I know this, I have seen it happen on previous exercises.'

'When you say exercises, what precisely do you mean?' asked Helmut Zwiegler, a Swiss German nuclear physicist with a burgeoning career and a massive depression which was on the verge of tumbling him into oblivion.

'I cannot divulge the nature of the exercise at this point,' said Mario. 'I only want you to know that there is no physical danger. This is not some team-building corporate weekend for lower management, we are not going down in the valley to build bridges with old telegraph poles or anything like that. We will start early in the morning so I want you all to get a good night's rest. As you may have noticed, there are no staff here, we have to look after ourselves.'

'I have paid over seven thousand dollars to be here and I have to cook my own breakfast?' queried Luigi Mastrano, a man so high up in Fiat that no one knew he was in the company at all.

'I'm afraid so,' said Mario. 'To make up for it I have chosen this magnificent old place for us to stay in. Château Hatton has every convenience as it was refurbished in the 1920s by a rich

American woman still greatly revered in the locality. The château has survived the devastation caused by two world wars in the surrounding area. It seemed appropriate to choose a location in the very heart of the new Europe.' He smiled at Yves Franchet, Director General of Eurostat, the statistical data analysis arm of the European government. Franchet didn't smile back. Slumped in his chair, he didn't even look up.

'I'm very tired, I will go to bed now,' said Christina Boeri, a beautiful Dutch millionairess who owned a chain of fashion shops throughout the Benelux countries. She was about to expand into the rest of Europe but the wind had gone out of her sails. She got up and walked out of the room, leaving her bag behind.

One by one, the other men and women around the table got up and wandered out. Mario stayed put, staring at the fire. Only one person stayed with him: Anna Benz, once an innovatory firebrand at the VW car design centre in Wolfsburg, now running on empty.

'I love a real fire,' said Mario to her softly. 'In ancient times, a fire was a source of great peace and contentment.'

'It is not very ecologically aware.'

'Very true,' Mario agreed. 'But if every community had access to a fire like this, and people learned to sit by it occasionally and think – maybe talk quietly with a trusted counsellor, take time from their lives to reflect – then I think we would see a great deal less unhappiness. What do you think of when you see a fire like this, Anna?'

'Burning trees, destruction, death. That's all I see all the time. Waste, misery and death. It's all around.'

'You don't see regeneration, life and hope then?' asked Mario softly. 'You don't see something that is dead, the tree, being transformed almost magically into something beneficial: warmth, comfort, sustenance?'

'No,' said Anna emphatically. 'I don't know what's happened to me. I see nothing like that. I just want to die.'

He nodded and said nothing.

'Why am I so depressed, Mario? Why can't I get out of it? Why is my life such a mess?'

'We will find out, Anna. That is why we are all here. It is a malaise that is sweeping the whole world. We have to work together to find out. Isolation is the curse. We have to live together.'

'I hate people, I hate everyone,' said Anna on the verge of tears. 'But I hate myself more for even thinking such a terrible thing.'

She stood up slowly, almost as if she was hoping Mario would explain to her what she should do. He said nothing. She walked out of the room, leaving him alone.

He stared at the flames. He was tired too, had spent all day studying the histories of the people staying at the château. He had never met any of them before. Not for Mario the hour-long session of talking therapy. For him it was make or break in one fell swoop. He looked around the kitchen and smiled. Everything seemed to be in order. He stretched with his good arm and slowly stood up. Mario Lupo felt good. He really enjoyed his work.

At three-thirty in the morning, the moon bright over the hills and valleys of La Meuse, a black Mercedes G-wagon sped along a narrow road leading to Château Hatton. The ancient building was picked out by the moonlight, hugging the bluff of a hill overlooking the flat plain.

As he entered the town at speed, the driver killed the lights and engine. The only noise from the vehicle came from its wide rugged tyres. It pulled to a gentle halt outside the gates and a tall man got out, clad in black. He was wearing a knitted hat which he pulled down over his face, leaving only his eyes visible. Once inside the unlocked front gates he ran across the formal garden in the courtyard, keeping low. With great agility he climbed an exterior wall, using a down pipe and the ancient crumbling stones for footholds. He eventually came to a latticed window which fitted snugly under the ancient eaves. Extracting a fearsome-looking assault knife, he gently eased open the catch, pulled the window wide and with one swift movement launched himself inside. He was in a room containing a single bed in which slept a young woman. The masked man slipped the knife back into its sheath on his belt and removed an automatic pistol. He moved up to the bed and pointed the gun right into the sleeping woman's mouth. She woke slowly, made a vague effort to push the gun to one side with her hands, then opened her eyes and saw the terrifying spectacle before her.

'Get out of bed! Any sudden moves and I will blow off your head,' said the man. He had a very strong French accent and Anna, whose English was only good when she was awake, momentarily failed to understand.

He gestured for her to get up and hissed, '*Schnell, schnell!*' How did he know she was German? she thought. What was going on? Her heart was pounding so hard she was actually aware of movement within her. The man moved back a little to give her room, but kept the gun a few inches from her face. Anna was breathing heavily, making little involuntary whimpering sounds as she moved. She was wearing only a skimpy vest and pants so glanced around the room for something to cover herself. As she did this the man in the mask grabbed her, spun her round with a force that left her senseless for a moment and locked his arm around her throat. He was twice her size. She felt dwarfed by his bulk. Then she felt the gun press painfully against her temple. Without warning the man almost carried her across the room to the door then pushed her towards it.

'Open it,' he said quietly. She stood frozen with fear, could feel her hand shaking as it held on to his huge forearm.

'Open the door now or I'll kill you without hesitation,' he said, even more forcefully.

She slowly reached out and opened the door. Light from the hallway spilled into the room, blinding her for a moment, and before she knew what was happening she was standing out there. The man slammed himself against the wall, holding her with frightening strength.

'Okay!' he shouted. 'Everybody out of their rooms. You have ten seconds or the German bitch's head will look like a half-eaten cherry pie!'

There was eerie silence for what seemed like a very long time to Anna Benz. Nobody appeared, nothing happened. She felt the man remove the gun from her head but before she could react she started as an astonishingly loud report deafened her. He had fired. Anna stood frozen in terror. She could hear nothing, her vision was cut down to a quarter of its normal field, she was barely conscious. She felt herself being shoved along the corridor. In front of her she could just make out several terrified faces. It all seemed to be happening so slowly.

'Move downstairs!' shouted the man in the mask. 'Now!' he screamed when no one moved. He pointed the gun at Anna's head again. Suddenly everyone moved towards the stairs and started to descend.

The terrified group walked along the dimly lit corridor and into the kitchen which was in blackness.

'Turn on the light,' shouted the man. Someone turned on the lights and Anna could see everyone else cowering in a corner. Suddenly, and without warning, the man pushed her towards the others. She fell over and someone helped her up. The French man from the EC.

'Okay, where is he?' asked the masked man, waving the gun around like a madman. No one said anything. He suddenly levelled the gun at the cowering people before him and screamed, 'Where is he!'

'I'm sorry but we do not know who you mean,' said Helmut Zwiegler.

'The bastard, the destroyer, that's who I want!' screamed the man. 'You have three seconds to tell me where he is or I'll start shooting.'

Pleas for mercy began to ring out against the stone walls. The man started counting.

'Do you mean Mario?' shouted the hoarse, terrified voice of Helmut Zwiegler.

'Yes, if that's what he's calling himself.' The man in the mask suddenly sounded more reasonable, which for some reason Anna found even more chilling. 'The fucking cripple, where is he?'

The group looked at each other, started to shrug.

'He's not with us, that's all we know,' said Helmut Zwiegler. 'I presume he is in the château somewhere.'

'Then we will wait for him.' The man walked to the doorway and shouted out, 'I know you're there, you son of a bitch! I am going to kill these people one by one every thirty seconds until you show yourself. You destroyed my life!'

He seemed to wipe a tear from his eye with one black-clad forearm. The gun stayed pointed at the cowering crowd and they cowered some more.

Then the outside door at the far end of the kitchen opened and cold night air flowed into the room. Everyone except the masked gunman turned. Mario appeared, wearing a dressing gown.

'What's happening?' he asked quietly.

The gunman spun around and crouched, holding the pistol with both hands and aiming it straight at Mario.

'You fucking son of a bitch! I knew you'd crawl out from under your rock some time.'

'Jean-Maire, is that you?' said Mario, still maintaining an aura of calmness.

'Yes, it's me,' said the man. 'I want you to know that I killed you. I want to look into your fucking eyes as the bullet hits you, scum!'

'I see. Well, this is all very sudden. Maybe we can let everyone else go back to bed then you and I will talk this over together,' said Mario. Anna thought he looked a little nervous.

'No more talk,' said the man. 'I'm going to kill you. Get used to it, you little cripple.'

'Jean-Marie . . .' Mario started to say.

'Shut up! Shut up until I tell you to speak. I want these people to know what you did to me. I want them to hear how you destroyed my life. I want them to know that this is a mercy killing. If you're dead, you can no longer harm anyone else.'

'Surely there's some way . . .' said Helmut Zwiegler, but the look Jean-Marie flashed at him cut him off mid-sentence.

'Okay, now I want a coffee. You,' said Jean-Marie, looking at Anna, 'make me some.'

She couldn't move. Someone shoved her gently from behind. Jean-Marie loosened his tense shoulders with a shudder. He pointed the gun at Helmut Zwiegler. 'Make me some coffee or this talkative pig gets one in the head.'

Anna slowly moved forward, staring into Jean-Marie's eyes, his only visible feature. They looked crazed, but also pained.

'Don't just stand there staring, you stupid little bitch. Make me some coffee.'

'I don't know where it is.'

Jean-Marie moved very rapidly. He aimed the gun at a cupboard to one side of the fireplace and fired. Screams and whimpers were the first sounds Anna could hear as her hearing slowly returned. She looked at the cupboard door and saw a small hole in it with brown powder pouring out.

'Put the coffee pot under that and add boiling water. I don't want it filtered,' said Jean-Marie.

Anna did as she was told. Jean-Marie pulled a chair out from under the table and sat down, without letting Mario out of his sights.

'Okay, tell them,' he said.

'What d'you want me to say, Jean-Marie?'

'Tell them what you did to me.'

'I didn't do anything to you, Jean-Marie, other than try to help you.'

'Bullshit!' he screamed. 'You tore me to pieces with your stupid experiments and didn't bother to put me together again.' He threw a glance at the crowd of terrified people huddled together in the corner of the room. 'You trust this asshole, don't you? You think he can help you!' Jean-Marie laughed. 'That is so sad. If this is how far you're prepared to go to get help, then you must really need it. He is evil, that's the only word for it. Evil.'

He glanced at Anna who was pouring boiling water into a coffee pot. 'Hurry up with that, slut!'

Jean-Marie, there's no need to be abusive to Anna, she has done you no harm.'

'All women have done me harm!' screamed the gunman crazily. 'Come here with that coffee.'

Anna approached him hesitantly. She put the cup of steaming coffee on the table before him and stood frozen to the spot.

'Come closer, I want to show you something.'

'Jean-Marie, please,' said Mario. Jean-Marie jabbed the gun in his direction. Anna moved closer, her whole body shaking.

'Very nice *balcon*,' said Jean-Marie, looking her up and down. 'Okay, Anna, I want you to turn and face Mario. Stand right in front of me and face the evil bastard.'

Anna did as she was told. She felt Jean-Marie press up against her, his huge body towering over hers. He grabbed her wrist and pulled it up to his other hand, making her grip the gun.

'Put your finger on the trigger, Anna.' Slowly she obeyed. Jean-Marie moved his own finger away and allowed her to replace it with hers. Then he gripped her right hand, sliding his forefinger over hers. Anna was, against all her expectations, fascinated by the sensation. She had never touched a gun before in her life.

'Okay, Mario − if that's what you're calling yourself now. Tell the people what happened,' ordered Jean-Marie.

'There's nothing very dramatic to tell. Jean-Marie was one of my clients. He took part in a trauma therapy workshop five years ago and decided to use the experience to excuse all his own failings. I know his marriage fell apart. I know he went to prison for molesting his teenage daughter . . .'

'Lies!' Jean-Marie screamed.

'I know he is a very unhappy man with a tendency − all too common, I'm afraid − to blame everyone and everything else in his life for his own failings.'

'Scum!'

'I know if he had done the exercise properly and listened to the people who cared for him, he would not be here now, playing out this absurd ritual. I have treated over five hundred people very successfully. Jean-Marie is the only one with whom I . . . well, failed.'

'You bastard!' hissed Jean-Marie.

The pistol flash illuminated the room; the sound hammered into everyone's ears. The recoil jolted Anna's arm. She felt a pain in her chest from the impact and watched, fascinated, as Mario's body flew backwards into the fridge, his chest seeming to explode violently, blood flying everywhere.

Jean-Marie pushed her forward and screamed insanely, 'What did you do that for? You fucking idiot! I was only going to scare him.'

Anna turned and looked at the distraught man who was waving the gun around wildly. She could hear the others screaming in terror. She heard a ghastly coughing sound and glanced back to see Mario's body sprawled on the stone floor, his head propped against the blood-spattered fridge. He coughed again and a fountain of blood erupted from his mouth. His face was ghastly. Anna felt herself heave but wasn't sick. She looked away.

'Look what you did!' shouted Jean-Marie. 'You fucking killed him! I don't believe it. I was only going to scare him.'

'I didn't . . .' she started to say.

'Don't think I'm going to take the blame for this,' Jean-Marie said. He turned to the crowd. 'You saw it, didn't you? You saw what she did.' He turned back to Anna. 'I've got witnesses.'

'But you made me! I felt you squeeze my finger,' said Anna through the tears which had appeared without warning. 'I know I felt it. I didn't shoot him . . .'

'Oh, that's right, bitch. Blame me. Women always do that. I suppose you're all going to believe her too, aren't you?' he bellowed, then pointed the gun at the ceiling and started firing. The sound of the shots was so painful Anna covered her ears. She dived under the kitchen table and in so doing put her hand into something sticky and wet. She looked down at it. It was blood, must be. She stared in horror and pulled back from the pool of red on the floor. Her head banged painfully on the table above. The air was full of screams and gunshots. She found herself in a better light all of a sudden, one of the lamps on the long sideboard was on, and looked for something to wipe her hand on. All that blood . . . She held out her hand and moaned. The blood, Mario's blood, was so red. It was so red . . . in fact, too red.

Suddenly she wasn't scared but intrigued and mystified. The fear had gone.

Immediately Anna felt the texture of the substance on her fingers she began to wonder. She had never put her hand in someone's blood before but she didn't think it would feel like this. It was cold and very glutinous, almost like treacle. She squeezed her hand a couple of times and watched as the 'blood' formed thick ribbons between her fingers. All around her was chaos – people screaming, chairs flying, crockery smashing – but Anna just focused on her hand. When she rubbed her fingers together the 'blood' instantly dried and formed little pellets. She sniffed her fingers tentatively and detected a delicate perfume. Not blood then, but something else. A polymer of some kind. She rubbed her hands together more violently and managed to roll all the blood into a little ball. It was rubbery in texture and left her fingers completely free from any residue. She might never have put her hand into a pool of blood before but she had cut her finger and as a woman had come into contact with blood on many other occasions. Whatever this was, it wasn't blood.

Anna tried to stand up. Again she smashed her head on the huge heavy table she was crouched under. When she finally emerged from beneath it she saw that the masked man was pinning the Dutchman to the table top with the gun forced into his mouth. Other people were trying to pull him off. Some of the women were screaming hysterically in a corner and two men had managed to escape down the corridor outside. She shook her head calmly and walked over to Mario, still lying in a pool of fake blood.

'Excuse me,' she said, quite loudly, but not loudly enough. No one looked up. She took hold of a large poker that leant against the wall next to the grate and walked over to a beautiful cabinet full of stunning examples of crystal wine flutes, goblets and decanters. She held the poker in both hands and swiped at the cabinet with all her strength. The sound of breaking glass was astonishing. Even Anna was shocked at quite how much damage that one movement caused. The shelves in the cabinet were also glass. The impact caused a chain reaction as glass fell upon glass. When finally the cascade came to a glittering halt at the base of the now ruined wooden cabinet, she looked up to see a totally silent group of people at the far end of the kitchen table.

'The blood is fake – the whole thing is a trick. We should all go back to bed,' said Anna flatly.

'What?' exclaimed Helmut Zwiegler as he slowly released his stranglegrip on the masked man.

'The blood is a slow-drying polymer. It's commonly used in the film industry. It's the wrong colour for real blood. Mario isn't dead.'

Anna walked over to where he still lay motionless on the floor, the wound in his chest looking very gory but, to her eyes, totally unrealistic. She gently put the toes of her left foot under his armpit and wriggled them. Mario shuddered and then laughed aloud.

'Oh my God! It's . . . what is going on?' cried a female onlooker.

Mario slowly stood up next to Anna. He wiped the blood off his chin with his dressing-gown sleeve and smiled at her kindly.

'Welcome to trauma therapy,' he said.

Chapter Six

For the first time in Miles' life, the drug of code failed to work. There was no escape from this torment.

There had finally seemed no point in staying at work. He cleaned up and ran the office Dyson over the floor, which reminded him of the previous night. He wiped the city grime off the windowsill and then pulled on his helmet and filter mask and pushed off along St Martin's Lane.

Cars and their drivers, the fatal combination of the twentieth century. A quarter of a million people every year killed as a result of car impacts. Worse than AIDS, worse than hundreds of diseases which received endless coverage in the pro-car press. Worse even than smoking. And yet no car carried a government health warning. How many gardens buried under tarmac or gravel to give room to park; how many towns and villages scarred beyond repair by roads?

Someone, Miles noticed it was a woman, had parked on a double red line outside a dry cleaner's and opened the driver's door directly in front of him. Although his reactions were rapid, he had no choice. His front wheel hit her leg before slamming into the car door.

Miles pulled down his mask and spoke to her as calmly as he could.

'Please be careful.'

The woman looked at him furiously from the driver's seat.

'You idiot, you could have broken my leg. You deliberately rode into me!'

Miles sighed deeply, sounding very like his father. He stared at her, trying to understand how someone who had so obviously been at fault was able to turn everything around and blame someone else. She stared back furiously. He spoke very quickly, but he wasn't upset. His heart rate remained constant.

'A, stop driving a car. Or failing that, B, use your mirror before you open the door. And C, don't stop on a red route where every sign specifically tells you not to.'

'Pillock.'

'Should we just apologise to each other and leave it at that?' he asked calmly.

'Piss off!' she jeered.

Miles slowly pulled his bike back, noticed that the front wheel was slightly bent. Not enough to stop him but another thing in his life out of true. He pulled his mask on, checked the continuous traffic which was missing the little incident by inches, and carried on his journey.

When he got to the apartment and opened the door, he saw Donna standing in the hallway, dressed very smartly in a grey, close-fitting trouser suit. As far as he could remember she was meant to be at some posh lunch meeting with a British children's book publisher, selling Milky to the Limeys. He had returned to the flat because he thought he could be alone, go back to bed, try to find out if he was just tired or if there was something else wrong.

As he started to pull off his cycling equipment, Kulvinder appeared beside her.

'Ah, Miles, I didn't expect you back,' said Donna chirpily. 'How's the lip synch?'

He could remember little of what took place after that. Donna did try to talk, Kulvinder did try to leave. As Miles rode back down Abbey Road, he knew it had been ugly. He knew the TV set was smashed and the large living-room cabinet was lying on its front. He knew there was a lot of broken glass and he knew Donna was crying. But it was all a haze. He knew

Kulvinder had said 'Calm down' too many times for it to have any effect.

He stopped on the corner of Abercorn Place, got out his mobile and turned it on. He never left it on, no one rang him anyway. They always rang Kulvinder. He dialled the number he had called earlier for the Lupo Foundation. The same answer-machine came on the line. Miles switched the phone off. It was all pointless. Then he saw there was a message for him. Someone had called him. Probably Donna or Kulvinder. He called his message service.

'Hello, Miles, this is Mario Lupo. I am presently on my satellite number. Call me.'

This was followed by a very long number. He had to press the repeat key three times before he could scrawl it on to his Palm Pilot. He immediately called the number.

'Hello,' said the voice with the indeterminate accent.

'It's Miles Morris, I rang you earlier.'

'Miles, yes, very good of you to ring. You said you were rich?'

'Yeah.'

'You said you had no feelings?'

'Yeah.'

'You said you needed to talk?'

'Yeah.'

'Well, that's not really what I do. Maybe you can find a therapist in London who can help you.'

'But I need something else. I don't know what. I don't go to therapists. I don't want to talk about my childhood. I know it will only make me more numb. I used to function okay without help but now I've started breaking things. It seems I've just totalled my apartment.'

'It *seems* you have? I don't understand.'

'Well, things were broken, apparently by me, but I'm not in a bad temper. My pulse rate is normal. I don't feel anything – as usual. I'm so constipated I can barely move, and my shoulders have locked until I look hunchbacked.'

'You are angry?' asked Mario.

'I don't know. How do you tell?'

'Are you in pain?'

'I think I cut my thumb a bit.'

'I mean, are you in emotional pain?'

'I don't know.'

'We all have to live with pain, but maybe you are not living with your pain very well.'

'I don't know. All I know is nothing is working and I earn too much for this to be a problem. I shouldn't have problems like this, but I can't buy anything which helps. I've got everything I've ever wanted and everything just gets worse.'

'Where are you now?'

'London. Where are you, Geneva? I'll fly there.'

'I am in La Meuse.'

'Where's that?'

'La Meuse, in the North of France, near the German and Luxembourg borders. I'm in a place called Château Hatton, about fifteen kilometres south-west of Metz.'

'Metz?' said Miles. 'I've heard of that. Where all the First World War graveyards are.'

'That is almost correct,' said Mario. 'They're not actually in Metz, but that is of no consequence. However, there are some complications here I need to sort out. Normally I would come to see you, I go all over the globe visiting clients, but I'm forced to stay here for a while. The only thing I can do is ask you to come here. If you drive you can take . . .'

'I don't drive. I don't go in cars.'

'I see. Well, you can fly to Luxembourg and get a taxi.'

'I don't go in cars. Taxis are still cars. Why can't people understand? I ride a bike.'

'A motorbike?'

'No, a pedal bike. A bicycle. I don't use cars or motorbikes. Just trains, planes and bikes.'

'I don't know what to suggest then,' said Mario, showing a hint of frustration. 'If you can get here, I'll spend time with you. I charge a little more than most therapists. The decision is yours.'

'I don't care what you charge,' said Miles. He was scrawling on his Palm Pilot again, the phone wedged uncomfortably under his ear. 'Château Hatton. Outside Metz. I'm on my way.'

Chapter Seven

To say that Mario's trauma therapy exercise had been a disaster would be grossly to underestimate the opinion of the majority of his clients. In the early hours the sound of high-powered engines shattered the peace of the sleeping village as they left in droves immediately after the revelation Mario was not in fact dead. A few waited until the following morning. Three of them demanded their money back and one threatened criminal proceedings.

'We came here to find peace and security in a crazy world,' objected Luigi Mastrano. 'I already have to have a bodyguard. Have friends who have actually been killed by masked terrorists. I don't need to experience anything like that to lift my depression. I will return home and go to bed for a week. After that you can expect to hear from my lawyers.'

Mario was disturbed by this reaction, which wasn't what he'd wanted, but he hadn't gone as far as he had in the world of top-drawer trauma therapy to stop now.

'A typical initial reaction, all part of the healing process,' he told his assistant over a bowl of coffee. 'They'll be back, you'll see.'

'This isn't going to help your reputation,' said Philippe who had planed the part of 'Jean-Marie'! 'I told you it could backfire. You might have known some of them would react badly.'

'All I was scared of was that you would take the exercise to its logical conclusion and use live ammunition. For me it worked. I have never been more frightened in my life. I feel like a man reborn.'

'Very nice for you,' said Philippe dryly. 'For myself, I did not derive a great deal of pleasure from being seen as a mad gunman – although it was pleasant to grapple with the German lady.'

'Anna?'

'Yes, she is very attractive, *non*?'

'I cannot see that myself. I see only a person in pain.'

'I see a woman in a very thin vest and pants with a very beautiful body. German woman are, in many ways, the sexiest women on the planet,' his assistant enthused. 'I know the stereotype is they're rather lumpy and square, with hirsute armpits and hands like a docker, but with Anna this is not so. What does she do?'

'She is a car designer.'

Philippe looked surprised. 'Not your usual VIP client, Mario.'

'Yes, she is. Anna runs a large design team for Volkswagen. She's in charge of a great many people and her history is in many ways a classic case. From a humble beginning she worked her way up the corporate ladder. Her successes are legendary within the company. The new Beetle, that's hers, and the new Golf. She was due to head up the entire research and development division soon – practically unheard of for a thirty-three-year-old woman. Then it all went flat for her. She started being late for work, sleeping for longer and longer. She's tried everything: talking therapy, massage, joining a gym, weekend retreats with a Bhuddist organisation. It only gets worse.'

'So she comes to see you and then everything gets really bad?'

'Thank you, Philippe,' said Mario with a wry smile.

His assistant stood up and walked over to the stove, his heavy boots crunching on broken crockery. As he poured himself more coffee from the steaming pot, he noticed the soles of his shoes sticking to a towel on the floor. They still had not cleared up the kitchen after the previous night's activities. The place was in a terrible state and it would cost serious money to repair and replace all the broken and damaged items.

'I'll take her up some coffee,' said Philippe, looking through the cupboards above the sink unit. He opened the door through which he had apparently fired the shot the night before. The plastic container which had held the coffee was still taped to it. The wires leading to the small charge of explosives which had actually blown the hole in the wood were all still there.

Philippe smiled. 'Impressive, *hein*?' He ran his hands over the splintered wood. 'Of course, if anyone had looked closely they would have seen the wood splintered outward, whereas a real bullet would have made a small hole on the outside and caused severe damage inside. But in the heat of the moment, who cares?'

'The way the coffee poured out was very impressive.'

'It was a work of art,' said Philippe, stirring milk into the coffee.

'Now, Philippe, I must warn you – Anna is a very depressed woman who is not to be messed with. She's at a crucial period in her recovery so I don't want you trying anything sexual.'

'*Moi?*' he said. 'How could you think such a thing?'

'I suppose based on past experience. You have slept with sixteen of my clients, haven't you?'

'No, fifteen. You know I never touched *la Duchesse*.'

'I often wondered if that was a fantasy. It was certainly most realistic, what she told me.'

'She was a crazy woman,' said his assistant, raising impressive eyebrows.

'They are *all* crazy, Philippe. Why else d'you think they come to see me? They are all very rich and very crazy.'

Philippe walked out of the kitchen carrying the steaming bowl of coffee on a silver tray. As he made his way along the corridor towards the stairs, Mario could hear him whistling a Spice Girls tune.

Chapter Eight

———◦◦◦———

Miles was sitting in a first-class compartment on Eurostar. Somehow, his seat was in the smoking section. He had specifically requested non-smoking when he'd booked it as he rode towards Waterloo. However, he had used his mobile phone earpiece and was moving fast through traffic, so it may have been hard for the operator to hear him.

It had taken quite some time and many phone calls to ascertain that the quickest and least stressful way of getting himself and his bike to the La Meuse region of France was by train. He wanted to fly. Liked flying. He could, with a lot of hassle and expense, have flown to Brussels, but the bike was going to be a major problem and Miles wasn't going without it. He didn't have the flight bag with him and the airline were being very negative about it, which he could understand, but it made his bowels tighten further.

The man sitting opposite Miles on the train was talking loudly on his mobile as they rattled and rolled through the unreconstructed British section of the journey. They were sitting in a beautifully designed high-speed train which was barely managing to stay on the rails, such was the state of disrepair of the track beneath.

Miles looked out at the grubby trails of rubbish to either side. England was a hole, really, and badly put together. He pondered on the way the place had developed. Centuries of people trying to sort the place out, and it just got worse.

A neat little factory with a neat little fence around stood next to a neat little row of houses, but there was a gap between them that was effectively an overgrown rubbish tip. Miles stared at this minor tragedy as they passed it and shook his head. Someone, some dusty-suited planner, had allowed a decision to be made whereby a strip of land no more than two metres wide was, for some medieval reason, left between the factory and the houses. No one had considered that it might not be a good idea. It presumably fitted in with some daft legal notion of land ownership.

Other people in other countries were better at joining things together than the English. They didn't leave gaps like that, Miles decided. He knew there were parts of America that were despoiled in such a way, but in general, because things had been planned in advance and most development in America was on green-field sites, the gaps were better taken care of or didn't exist. Gaps indicated bad programming to Miles. He couldn't leave a gap in a chain of computer code or the whole thing would crash.

As he mused on the quality of the environment, he started to wonder why he had come back to England at all. The effort he had made to help set up FullFacial suddenly seemed futile. What a waste of time! Miles had always wanted to use time well. Even as a young man, time seemed to stream past him so rapidly. He used to think that this was because he was used to operating on computer time which is split into many hundredths of seconds. Miles always made sure that the code he wrote or corrected was lean, streamlined, and didn't waste time on unnecessary commands. Now he was sitting on a train wasting hours and hours of possible programming time.

He wondered if Kulvinder and Donna had actually been doing what they claimed, nothing but talking, when he had walked into the flat. Donna was attractive; Kulvinder was okay-looking if a bit fat. They had known each other for a long time, Kulvinder being best man at their hurried, unromantic wedding. He was still single, more or less. Always having meetings with women and putting projects together that sometimes involved sex.

The view outside had changed. The train was clearly approaching the tunnel entrance. The rails were smoother. They picked up speed. Miles could see the new development around the tunnel entrance: the vast car parks, loading ramps for car and truck transportation. He looked ahead and could see a grass-covered bluff where, presumably, the tunnel entrance was situated.

Just as suddenly as it had entered the twenty-three-mile long bore, the train emerged into bright sunshine. The relief was immense. Miles put his head back and breathed deeply. Immediately the train seemed to be more elevated, travelling smoothly at a far greater speed. It took his breath away. Like a plane just before take off, it was hurtling along.

He watched the rapidly passing French countryside. It was so neat. The drainage ducts and roadways which ran along the track were all new, their edges tidy, boundaries clearly defined. He felt his mood lighten a little. Maybe this unexpected trip was just what he needed. Maybe these were feelings coming back.

He got off the train in Brussels Central station and pushed his bike up the platform. The station was new, clean and bright. It was easy to find the platform for the connecting train to Metz.

He loaded his bike into the postal van and climbed aboard. The train was empty which suited him. He sat motionless for almost the entire one-hour journey. Only once did he move. As the train passed through some particularly steep cuttings, his mobile rang.

'Miles, it's Kulvinder, man. We've got to talk.'

'What about?' he snapped.

'About us, about the project, about Donna.'

'Don't want to talk about Donna.'

'Well, the project then. Nakasomi San is arriving tomorrow, remember?'

Miles hadn't remembered. The Chief Executive Officer of the Nishin Banking Corporation was due in London while he was sitting on a train somewhere in Belgium.

'Yes, of course I remembered.'

'Where are you, kiddo?'

'Doesn't matter.'

'Well, are you going to be there tomorrow?'

'What time does he land?'

'Ten past five, but I've got a meeting. I've cancelled three and rescheduled one but it's still tight. I need you there just in case.'

'I'll meet you at Heathrow,' said Miles and switched off his phone. He didn't want any more calls.

Chapter Nine

Gaston Bell got out of his Jaguar feeling distinctly uneasy. His driver Redford was completely trustworthy. Should be, he cost enough, but Gaston felt a uniformed chauffeur looked out of place before a public house, albeit a rather smart one in Kensington. Gaston prided himself on his discretion, his virtual invisibility. He led a relatively scandal-free public life and any difficulties in his private life were kept very quiet. He had kept his closet skeletons to a minimum. There was very little to find out about him.

He nodded to Redford to wait and keep an eye out then walked into the George, mildly relieved to find it apparently empty. He approached the bar then noticed at the far end a cloud of blue smoke hanging in the air. Beneath it sat three large men most people would instantly recognise as being of military origin. Must have been the moustaches. They all wore them – neatly cropped hair and thick moustaches. Gaston, who had never sported facial hair, wondered why this fashion amongst soldiers had been popular for so long.

'Gasty, what'll you have?' asked Donald Cooper, standing to his full threatening six foot six.

'G and T,' said Gaston, turning to see a barman already reaching up to the Gordon's optic.

With his drink in hand he joined the three men sitting around a table.

'Fucking Euros!' said Harris, a diminutive but dangerous-

67

looking fellow. 'The country's going down the fucking pan, if you ask me.'

'The PM's a total cunt,' agreed Pickering, wiping froth from his voluminous moustache. 'The Bank of England's run by total cunts. Come to think of it, the whole country's run by cunts. It's a crying shame.'

'Yes, fascinating,' said Donald, obviously not listening to a word that was being said. 'Well, we've got one last chance at saving a bit of sterling, lads. And it's a very big bit.'

'Nice one,' said Harris.

'Gasty, fill us in, you posh bastard,' said Donald, knitting together his huge black eyebrows on his huge red forehead.

'Fifth of next month, between the tunnel and London – we've got to find a location. Easy access to the line and a minimum of three escape routes. Shooters are up to you but you'll need metal cutters, Semtex and heavy transportation. Simple job, no security. Yours on a plate.'

'Sweet!' Harris said. 'How much?'

'Five billion,' said Gaston as lightly as he could.

'How much?' asked Pickering.

'Like the gentleman said, five billion,' Donald repeated with a leer. 'Are you deaf, Pickering? Did you forget to wear your ear protectors on the firing range again?'

Pickering was clearly rattled by the notion of five billion pounds. He didn't seem to have heard Donald. 'Five fucking billion pounds? That's a seriously big wad, sir. I mean, we're talking Interpol and the fucking CIA here. The local rozzers won't get a look in. Five fucking billion! You cannot be serious?'

'It's the last chance, is it not?' said Donald to Gaston.

'Absolutely the last. And add this to your pot: you've got just five hours to get it washed.'

'Come again?' said Harris.

'Five hours?' Donald broke in. Gaston had not been looking forward to informing them of this part of the deal. Donald Cooper worked on a short enough fuse as it was. 'Five hours! What are you talking about?'

'After five hours, you may as well pulp it. That's the whole point. Fifth of the month . . . ring any bells?'

'Stone me, sir,' said Harris. 'It's Euro Day.'

'In one,' said Gaston.

'Five hours . . . How on earth are we going do that? Five billion's a very big strategic manoeuvre, Gasty. We need heavy haulage. Vehicles like that stand out a little.'

'It's thirty tons of money so you need an articulated lorry, a big one. And it's got to be kosher. If you can get the lorry to my clearing house in under five, we're in business. Any later, torch it.'

'Thirty tons?' said Harris. 'Fuck me!'

'Hang on, what's the money going to be in?' asked Donald.

'An unmarked container.'

'Crane,' said Donald with a psychotic grin. 'We need a very large crane. I mean, seriously huge. We'll lift the whole thing.'

'Nice one, sir,' Harris told him.

'Bit obvious,' Gaston put in but stopped when he saw the palm of Donald's oversized hand signalling him to be quiet. Donald was thinking.

'Here's how it looks,' he said after an uncomfortable pause. 'Money's in a container, right?'

'Correct, on a train of forty or so.'

'Right, listen up, chaps. We find a building site, track side. If there isn't one, we start one, right? Use that as our operational base. We nobble the foreman, kill him if we have to. Bury the bastard.'

Harris grinned unattractively. 'Nice one, sir.'

'Then we get the crane in. It will look legit, a crane on a building site, no problem there. Then, right, we have to stop the fucking train. Don't care how.'

'Blow the line, sir,' suggested Pickering. 'Couple of ounces of Semtex – I've still got some at home.'

'Nice one,' agreed Harris.

'Get the crane in, lift the container off, drop it on a flat bed. Drape it, and shift it to Gasty's pronto. Shouldn't take more than an hour, top whack.'

'A draped container's going to attract attention,' said Gaston. He was already very nervous about this plan. Cranes . . . building sites? It was fraught with danger.

'Flat liner,' said Harris. 'We could slide the cunt in, sir.'

'Of course! Good thinking, man,' said Donald with a toothy grin.

'What's a flat liner?' asked Gaston. Donald snickered in an unseemly way for a man of his size.

'Mr Bell don't know what a flat liner is, gentlemen, and we are risking our necks for him. Doesn't exactly fill you with confidence, does it?'

'It's an articulated lorry with a frame, sir,' said Pickering, gesturing with tattooed hands. 'Roof on top, reinforced drapes along the sides. Common as shite, if you'll pardon my French, sir.'

'Dead common,' agreed Donald.

'If we can get one that says Marks and Sparks or Weetabix on the side, it'll blend right in,' Harris told them.

'Excellent!' Donald threw back his Scotch in one and bared his magnificent teeth. 'Five billion pounds. Worth it for the laugh alone, isn't it?' He smiled at the small group around the table. 'Gentlemen, let's get busy.'

Chapter Ten

Miles cycled around the centre of Metz until he found a tourist information booth. He purchased a map and located the little village where Château Hatton stood. Within an hour he was well clear of the town and feeling quite happy about riding his bike on the opposite side of the road. He had ridden so much in America, it now felt normal to him to have cars whizzing past him on his left.

The ground undulated gently. All the towns and villages he saw indicated on signs had an eerie ring of familiarity to them. This land had been fought over for so long, he could almost see the carnage and suffering it had known, mile upon mile, death and destruction on a gigantic scale merely to enforce boundaries. Miles understood boundaries, had plenty of them. Maybe he was at war over his boundaries. He wasn't sure what that would feel like.

He rounded a slight bend in the road where the view was obscured by a copse and saw a hill in the distance. There was something castle-like perched on it, just above a steep drop. He checked his map and pressed on.

The final two kilometres were all uphill. Miles used the many gears he had at his disposal and powered the bike upwards, breathing heavily by the time he reached the top and slowly coasted through the small village which lay on the crest. A sleepy dog watched him pass, a few cars were parked here and there, but otherwise the place seemed deserted.

The village street came to an end at the gates of an almost fairytale castle. Not the enormous château he'd envisaged, just a very ancient house with a wall around it, a very rickety tower to one side capped with a pointed roof. The whole place was surrounded by what had once presumably been a moat, now partly filled in. The front gate was reached across a drawbridge. It reminded Miles of Myth II, the medieval computer game.

He dismounted by the gate and knocked. He heard a sound behind him and turned. An old man had come out of a cottage a few metres away.

'*C'est fermé*,' said the man. Miles had no understanding of French. The old man could have said any number of things. Miles pulled out his CD Walkman and took the tiny earpieces out of his ears. He'd been listening to a Corrs CD as he made his way to the château. He knew it was soppy romantic music which was meant to appeal to men in their mid-thirties with the promise of illicit dalliances with thinly clad twenty somethings. He also knew as he listened to the song 'Never Really Loved You Anyway' that he should feel cheered by the sentiments, that he was finally free from Donna and her hang ups. But it did nothing for him other than help him pedal to a regular rhythm.

He stared at the old man and wondered what to do. He didn't want to start talking loudly in English in the hope that the man would understand. The old man looked at him with no obvious emotion.

'*C'est fermé, monsieur*,' he said again. Miles smiled.

'I've come to see Ma—' He was interrupted by another man who had suddenly appeared from the side of the building.

'Miles,' he said. Miles turned and looked at him. A big fellow, tall and powerful. Miles nodded cautiously.

'This way,' said the man with a slight accent.

He followed the man around the side of the château. A narrow path led along the foot of a high stone wall, the ground falling away steeply on the opposite side. The air was full of the sound of crickets. Out of the wind, the sun was hot. It was a beautiful spot. The man held open an ancient wooden door and Miles passed through.

Inside, the transformation was extraordinary. From walking along beside a moat overlooking featureless farmland, he entered a fragrant garden, protected on all sides by a picturesque building and its high surrounding walls.

The man closed the garden door and walked towards the house without speaking. Miles followed him after leaning his bike against an ivy-clad wall.

Inside the building, as his eyes adjusted to the light, he realised he was in a magnificent old kitchen.

'Hello, I'm Mario,' said the small dark-haired man who sat in a battered armchair next to a log fire in a huge grate. 'You are Miles?'

'Yes,' he said as brightly as he could.

'I know nothing about you, Miles,' said Mario, offering him one of the chairs. Miles noticed there seemed to be something wrong with one of Mario's arms. 'I am neither forewarned nor forearmed.' He smiled, and Miles was not sure if he was making a reference to his own arm. 'You have nothing to fear, I have no agenda.'

If English was not his first language he spoke it well, slick and fast with a West Coast twang. Miles nodded and took off his helmet and gloves, loosened his cycling shoes and removed them, unclipped his reflective strip and took off his Gore-Tex jacket. The pile beside his chair was quite impressive.

'Quite a business getting off your bike,' said Mario with a smile. 'Now, before we go any further, we have to discuss my fees. I charge five thousand Euros for the first assessment, is that okay?'

'That's fine,' said Miles. He fished in his cycling coat for his wallet and pulled out his black Amex card. It had been presented to him with great ceremony at his bank, conferring unlimited global credit.

'Good,' said Mario, who likewise pulled a small brown leather bag from beneath his chair and extracted a hand-held card swipe. He pulled Miles' card through and tapped in some numbers before showing Miles the screen. It read €5000. He nodded and Mario pressed another button, slipped the little machine into his bag and handed the card back to Miles.

The two men sat in silence for a long time. Miles was surprised he didn't feel embarrassed. He just relaxed into the chair and held his hands gently on his lap. He was, after all, still recovering from the ride. He glanced around the room, noticing that the man who had let him in had disappeared, then back to Mario who seemed perfectly unthreatening. There was no air of latent aggression or spite about him. He was nothing like Donna's therapist whom Miles had once seen at a gallery opening of her Milky illustrations. She'd looked positively psychotic.

Miles wondered what he would say first. Maybe he wouldn't speak at all, they'd just sit in silence for an hour and then he would put on his cycling kit again and leave, a serious amount of money worse off.

'Miles, I want to break this silence because it's not a game. I don't play games,' said Mario suddenly. 'I make people work on themselves, otherwise there's no point. Life is too wonderful. You could walk through a meadow and breathe in a heavenly scent and it would do you more good than all this introspection. Are you with me so far because I don't want to waste your time? I don't have to be very clever or psychic to see you are in a lot of pain, here, in your heart. Anyone with a little sensitivity can see that. But we are both modern men and we can take a lot of things as read. I only work with people who are highly committed, highly motivated. I don't do social work, Miles. I work with very successful people who have hit a wall and can't get through it. I open up other resources for them, allowing them either to climb the wall, go around the wall, or knock the fucking wall down!'

Mario jumped up as he spoke the last phrase, then with a big grin on his face went through a relatively convincing Kung Fu-type routine considering he did it all with one arm, the other hanging limply by his side.

'Oh, I feel so much better now. I hate the tension of first meetings. How are you feeling, Miles?'

'I don't know. Much the same.'

'Much the same? Fine.' Mario sat back down on his chair

with a resigned grin. 'I sometimes find myself wishing that talking therapy worked, but I think the past one hundred years have proved what an ineffective and time-wasting method it is.'

'Sorry,' said Miles eventually.

'Never say sorry,' Mario told him. 'Never say sorry, Miles. Sorry is for losers. You are a winner facing a block.'

'I'm not a winner.'

'You are a winner with a seratonin deficiency.'

'I don't have a seratonin deficiency,' said Miles. 'Who told you I had a seratonin deficiency?'

'Nobody had to tell me, it's written all over you. How much did you earn last year?'

'Sorry!' said Miles. The question seemed incongruous. He felt anxious as to where this line might lead. 'Why do you want to know?'

'Was it enough to buy a small hatch-back car?'

'I don't know how much cars cost.'

'Was it enough to buy a house?'

'I suppose so, in theory, before tax and depending on the property location.'

'So you're earning around five to ten times the average European yearly income. Therefore you are a winner in simple, fiscal terms. Which after all is the way we measure ourselves against others. And yet you are depressed and demotivated.'

'I don't know if I am depressed. How do you tell?'

'You don't know what's wrong because there is nothing actually wrong, is there, Miles? You're not starving to death. Your children aren't being slaughtered by an armed militia.'

'I don't have any children.'

'I am talking hypothetically here. You don't have a fatal disease which releases you from the grind of life and allows you to be happy and loving for your last six months on the planet. You live in a prosperous, safe, healthy part of the world. You are rich, young, attractive, fit, fertile and fascinating, and yet you are depressed. Am I right?'

'I'm not attractive.'

'That's for me to judge. You cannot comment on that. Am I right?'

'What, about being attractive or being depressed?'

'Don't play games, Miles, your defensive stance does you no credit.'

He felt his eyebrows raise. He'd been told off. Something peculiar happened in his stomach. He actually felt something. It was making less and less sense to sit in a medieval kitchen in some sort of castle in a part of France he'd never even heard of with a weird foreign man with a withered arm. And, on top of that, listen to abuse and pay €5000 for the privilege.

'Am I right?' Mario repeated, though still without discernible anger or malice.

Miles nodded. 'Yes, you're right, I am depressed. Or I suppose that's what you could call it. Although all the depressed people I've ever met were quiet and withdrawn. I'm not, I'm still working – well, up until today. But I think I've smashed up rather a lot of things at my apartment, although I don't really remember doing it. I didn't mean to, I don't feel any anger. But that's not good, is it? It's not normal. So, yes, by your definition I'm depressed, but for very clearly defined, easily explained reasons. Not a seratonin deficiency.'

'Go on,' said Mario, sitting back and making himself comfortable.

'What?' asked Miles.

'Go ahead. Tell me the reasons.'

'Right. Well, where to start? God. Uh, you mean, the whole story?'

'Whatever.'

'Um, well, I think my wife is sleeping with my best friend and business partner. I'm not sure but I know they've . . . and I feel sort of numb. Not absolutely physically numb, but there's a sort of frosted glass panel between me and the world, I think. Although I'm not sure because it's always been there as long as I can remember so I've nothing to compare it with.'

'That's good. Go on.'

'I don't know if it's due to a painless trapped nerve in my

lower back, something which stops signals from my brain reaching my body, or vice versa. I have wondered about it being caused by a psychogenic disorder, my mother's untimely death causing a non-specific illness which manifests itself as numbness and a feeling of detachment. Whatever it is, it's a rather disturbing phenomenon. As you rightly say, I know I should be happy but I'm not. I know this is the golden age. I read about it in last weekend's *Independent* colour supplement, and it's true. I know I am living during the warmest, safest, happiest, richest, most expansive period in the whole of human history. I know this is the longest single stretch of world peace since records have been kept. There has been no all out war in my lifetime – and it can only get worse, that's the thing. But somehow it never actually does. I've been waiting for it to get worse all my life, and it hasn't. It only gets slightly better. But I know there must be more and more insurmountable problems building up out there somewhere. And London . . . I can't believe London. I lived away from it for nearly twelve years and remembered it as a miserable, rundown, dirty dump. Now it's alive, London is glowing, it's warm and vibrant. It's a fantastic place to be. So I know if I'm depressed at this point in history, at this geographical location, regardless of my own personal situation, if I'm depressed now, at the best, most glowing pinnacle of human history, then it's got to be . . .'

There was another silence. Miles felt his lungs empty, felt the energy slowly drain from his body, felt his hard disks spin down. He knew he couldn't adequately describe the dark wall that seemed to be engulfing him. He was trapped behind a black felt fuzz. He knew stuff was going on outside, could hear and smell it, but he couldn't seem to *be* in it.

'A wonderful evocation of seratonin deficiency. I wish I had written it down. Thank you, Miles,' said Mario. 'You must be hungry after your journey. Can I prepare you something to eat?'

'I'm starving.'

'I can only do sandwiches, I'm afraid, but we have some very nice things to put inside.'

Miles watched in fascination as the man with one working

arm deftly put together a delicious-looking sandwich using a whole baguette, some pungent French cheese, slices of salty German sausage, pickles, fresh salad and tomatoes. As he opened the fridge, Miles noticed it had a badly dented door and a strange pink stain down the front. Mario took out two short bottles of Belgian beer.

'You have caught me at a rather unfortunate time,' he said when he sat down again. 'I have just had a setback in my professional life. An exercise I had been planning for months has gone very badly wrong. I have just lost, I think, eleven clients. Now, this is of no concern to you, Miles, I am only telling you this because I am in a position where the whole – how do you say this? – reason for me to be, has somewhat dismantled itself. Normally I run a series of workshops and exercises for groups and individuals which I have loosely termed trauma therapy.'

'Trauma therapy?' said Miles through a mouthful of delicious sandwich. There was something about this man's voice which was totally captivating. Miles hadn't noticed it before but he realised he had relaxed considerably since entering the room.

'Yes, though it's not a term I would use to the press or to people outside my client circle, and I would ask you not to use it if you feel the need to talk about what you are doing with me.'

Miles shrugged as he chewed. Mario looked at him and smiled kindly. He took his damaged arm in his good hand and rested it on the table top.

'An English writer, J. G. Ballard, once said that if a person survives a traumatic experience – a car crash or war or natural catastrophe – then they will be changed forever by that experience, and often for the better, having faced their own mortality. That's very interesting, don't you think?'

'He was in a war, wasn't he?'

'Indeed I believe he was. As a young boy he was captured by the Japanese in the Second World War.'

Miles nodded and kept on chewing. He took a swig of the icy beer. It was delicious, with a hint of raspberries somewhere.

'Well, we don't have a war to live through in this part of Europe at the moment. Sure, there are plenty of wars we could go to, but the people I work with generally don't have time to go to war zones and get themselves killed. So, by careful planning, I allow my clients to experience a trauma, very realistic at the time, which in the vast majority of cases allows them to blast through their problem in a short time. They don't have to spend hours and hours talking to me, telling me about how their mother didn't love them or their father loved them in the wrong way. They might think that's what's going to happen initially, I never give them any indication they're going to experience a trauma, so they walk into the situation with as open mind.'

Mario jumped up then with a speed Miles didn't anticipate. It made him jump and some of his beer sloshed out of the top of the bottle.

'Then suddenly,' said Mario, his face close to Miles', 'their world goes crazy. They think they are going to die. They go through hell, Miles, that is the only way to describe it. And when they come out at the other end, they are hugely changed. I don't wish to blow my own trumpet too loudly, but they are changed in very positive ways. It seems marriages improve, relationships with children become more healthy, they are capable of higher levels of output, become richer and happier.'

Mario sat back in his chair and took a swig of beer.

'You see, I don't work with poor people, Miles. I can't, there's no way to organise it. There is no way I could, for instance, get government funding for such work. It is very much at the leading edge of what is acceptable psychotherapeutic practice. I only work with the very successful. Powerful people, Miles. Very powerful, although not necessarily in political terms, nor in media glamour terms, but behind the scenes. Innovators, designers, creative people who are right at the forefront of what is going on. It's very exciting for me to be working with people like this. I want to be around people who are on fire with ideas. That's what makes me hot as a therapist. And you are clearly one of those people.'

They sat in silence for a while, Miles chewing the last of his sandwich.

'I'm not sure I understand, though,' he said finally. 'It seems you've told me your modus operandi, therefore any potential trauma you might plan to put me through isn't really going to work, is it? Because I know it's going to happen.'

'This is very encouraging. I can see why you are a success in your field. You can see ahead, – can see how a chain of events might or might not unfold. Exactly, Miles. You are the first client I have ever talked to in this way. We are in uncharted territory here, I am as much in the dark as you.'

Mario let his head rest against the back of his chair. He closed his eyes and sat in silence for a moment.

'You may notice I look a little tired. I haven't slept now for close on thirty hours. I have been walking around the beautiful garden running through experiments, trying to find the way forward. Because, Miles, and very few therapists would admit this to a client, I don't know what to do.'

'What d'you mean, you don't know what to do?'

'Trauma therapy doesn't work.'

'What?'

'It doesn't work, Miles. I proved it last night.'

'Well, why did you drag me all the way out here!'

'I didn't drag you here, Miles, you decided to come. I merely furnished you with information.'

'I can't believe you've told me all that and now you're telling me it doesn't work!'

'Are you angry, Miles?' asked Mario softly.

Miles stood up and started pacing around the room.

'Well, no, but I'm probably not very happy,' he said as he clasped his left wrist and took his own pulse.

'A little above average . . . maybe I am angry, I don't know.'

'Fascinating,' said Mario.

'I'm supposed to be in London, working. I've got one of the most important clients of my career arriving tomorrow and we're not ready for him. What was I thinking of coming here now? I must be mad.' Miles stood there, head hanging, shoulders twisted with tension. Mario stared at him. He smiled.

'It's good that you're angry, Miles, because I know why

trauma therapy didn't work for those people. Allow me to explain.'

'For someone who claims he doesn't do talking therapy, you've talked pretty effectively for the last hour.'

'Believe it or not, I am in crisis,' said Mario a little more sharply than usual. 'Okay?'

He looked angrily at Miles, seemed genuinely upset. Surely that wasn't what analysts were supposed to do?

Mario continued, 'My life's work has collapsed but there is a glimmer of hope at the end of a very long tunnel. That is the image I have and it's very exciting. Sit down again, please.'

Miles slowly moved back to his chair by the fire. 'Look into the flames, it will help you to relax,' Mario told him.

'It's so hot already.'

'Take your clothes off.'

'What?'

'Well, if you're naked, you'll feel more comfortable in front of the fire.'

It sounded like a come on and yet it hadn't crossed Miles' mind that this strange little man could be gay.

'I am not propositioning you, Miles, I am a confirmed heterosexual.'

He wondered if this man could read his thoughts.

'It's just whenever we get the chance to get back to basics, back to something grounded, we should take it. To squat in the ashes with nothing on is very basic. It's up to you.'

Miles looked at him for a moment, not knowing what to do. Mario started to pull his own shirt off awkwardly. 'I'll join you.'

'Oh, all right. I've clearly gone mad anyway, may as well go mad and naked,' said Miles. He pulled off the many layers of clothing he was still wearing and squatted in front of the fire, placing another log on the blaze.

'Is that a good feeling?' asked Mario as he squatted beside him, his thin withered arm dangling in the ashes.

Miles felt the tingling warmth sparkle through his skin. He felt his feet, firm and balanced on the warm smooth stone of the hearth. It did feel good. He nodded. He was actually feeling good.

'Twelve people were ushered into this room at three this morning. Dazed, tired, anxious,' said Mario as Miles continued to stare into the flames. 'They were being forced to do so by a masked gunman – Philippe, the man who showed you in. They didn't know him – had never seen him before. They then witnessed this man apparently shoot me in the chest, killing me outright. We have contacts in the special effects industry so it was well done. Rather reminiscent of *Reservoir Dogs*, I thought, but not convincing enough.' Mario sighed, long and slow.

'One of my clients, in fact the only one who is still here . . .'

'There's still someone here?' asked Miles, wondering if he wanted to share Mario's attention.

'Yes, Anna, she's sleeping. The thing is, most of my clients are wealthy enough to want to have a serious problem. They have everything else, so why shouldn't they be depressed as well? But Anna really is depressed. She just sleeps.'

'God!' said Miles, feeling slightly better about himself.

'However,' continued Mario, 'Anna discovered by fate, chance, or maybe it was meant to be, that the fluid gushing out of me was not real blood. She has a good background knowledge of polymers which are used in the motor manu-facturing industry. So the exercise went wrong, people were upset and they left. This has never happened before. Normally it is the start of an intense weekend of traumas which is finally rounded off with a revelation group where everyone is released in a controlled way from the terror they have experienced. It is this final experience that my recent clients missed and they were therefore thrown into despondency and confusion. I too was utterly thrown by events. We have performed the same exercise many times in the past with one hundred per cent success. Of course, I can take good care to make sure no one else finds out the trauma isn't real, but it's made me stop in my tracks. I have to learn from this. Learn from it and strike a new path.'

There was silence. Miles sat feeling very calm. He had listened carefully to what Mario had said, found his accent and delivery had a slightly hypnotic effect which made him feel very good. He could feel a bowel movement approaching. It was a wonderful feeling.

'I want to be involved,' said Miles. 'I have nothing to lose.'

'But where is my new path, Miles?' asked Mario. He too was staring into the fire. 'I don't know what to do. I only know one thing – it has to be real.'

'It has to be real,' agreed Miles.

'It cannot be an exercise in the accepted, therapeutic sense of the word. It has to be more than that. It has to be genuinely dangerous, without putting you in genuine danger. This is what is impossible. I cannot allow my clients to be in genuine danger, it is against all my ethical codes. Their wellbeing has to be my foremost concern. But, on the other had, if the exercise isn't genuinely dangerous . . .'

'. . . it doesn't work,' Miles finished for him. He rocked back and forth on his feet, feeling so good. So in touch for once. Mario was right, it was good to get his clothes off and squat down by a fire. The fireplace was messy, he would have quite liked to have tidied it up, but for once that didn't spoil anything. He was sure he was having feelings again.

'But I bet it could work,' he said after a pause.

'I know it could. If we could find the right thing.'

'The right thing,' agreed Miles.

'And you have got to do it yourself. Make the decision and just do it.'

Miles looked at Mario who was looking at him. Their naked bodies were only a metre apart. There might have been no one else on the planet.

Miles turned back to the fire and stared at the flames. He was feeling very good. He had struck out at last, just thrown everything up and moved himself into another world. He already felt changed, he already felt he could go back to Donna and not smash anything, just tidy up after her and maybe actually have some feelings, good feelings, about her. Maybe he could go and see his dad and actually talk about his mum. He felt he could sit in front of the screen and check code and still talk to

Kulvinder. Get excited about the opportunities that FullFacial had to offer instead of blanking them out. He started to bounce up and down on his haunches, felt energy tingle through him.

'All the time recently I've had the feeling I should just do something,' he said. 'Whatever comes to mind. That's why I'm here. Couple of years ago I wouldn't have dreamed of doing this. Then I was rigidly held in place by everything around me. My work, my relationships, my ambitions. I never went anywhere without six months warning, my diary was immaculate. Still is, but this visit isn't marked in it. Everything is tidy in my life except my wife, but I think she's going to leave me anyway. Maybe she already has. So then everything in my life will be incredibly tidy, but I still won't have any feelings. That's what I realised. Nothing's getting better no matter what I do. I want to change.'

'Just the drive which will make this exercise work,' said Mario softly. 'We have to come up with something huge, earth-shattering, but ultimately safe. There are so many options, so many possibilities. Choosing an exercise is ninety per cent of the process.'

'What about . . .' began Miles, standing up and turning to face Mario, '. . . destroying something we don't approve of? Like a car factory.'

'I'm sorry?' said Mario. 'Why would we want to do that?'

'Why?' said Miles, confused by his response. 'Why? I would have thought that was obvious.'

'Destroy a car factory? It seems a little uncreative.'

'We could do it with no danger to anyone, make sure no one was hurt. Imagine the impact! We could destroy a dozen. There would be no more cars. People would stop buying them.'

'A car factory,' mused Mario. 'How very synchronous. You see, the only client I have left here is Anna Benz. She works for a car manufacturer.'

'You're kidding? Brilliant! Someone on the inside.'

'So what you're saying is, we commit a crime?'

Miles sat thinking for a moment. A crime? He hadn't thought of it in that way. Of course, technically Mario was right. But it didn't feel like one.

'It's a crime to keep making more and more cars when that technological ability could be used to improve modes of mass transportation,' Miles said eventually.

Mario stared at him. 'Forgive me, but you don't strike me as a typical Greenpeace person. They don't normally travel with a black Amex card.'

'I'm not. I just really disapprove of cars. Always have. People say it's because one killed my mum, which is rubbish. We've all seen what they've done. They're simply a very inefficient way of transporting people. They're outmoded and retrograde. So we could bring about the beginning of the end of cars.'

'But it would be a crime,' repeated Mario. 'I am talking about the attitude of the authorities here. They would view the destruction of a valuable national asset such as a car factory as a serious crime. What about committing a crime no one is going to be too bothered by?'

'What's the point?' asked Miles.

'Well, the point is it would cure you and the other clients involved. That's the only reason to do anything, from my point of view.'

'What sort of crime?'

'Let's say, just as an example, a robbery.'

'I don't need any money.'

'Precisely. That is why we will be able to do it, experience the trauma and then carry on with our lives. We return whatever it is we have stolen.'

'Return it?'

Mario nodded. 'We steal something, remove it, leave it somewhere safe and inform the relevant authorities.'

Miles was still imagining lying in a field at night, watching a car factory explode in one massive blast, sending burning debris flying high into the air. Stealing money – what was the point? He had millions in the bank already. But maybe Mario was right. It was the best reason to do it. He really didn't need it.

'Do you think it would work?'

'I know it would cure you.'

Miles stared at Mario for a moment, suddenly seeing him in a different light. He looked crooked, looked like a criminal now, even naked in front of the fire, looked like some poor person who came from a big housing estate on the edge of Paris, the wrong side of the ring road.

'Have you done this sort of thing before then? Is this just a front for a criminal gang?'

'Amazing how you jump ahead so rapidly, but no, it is not like that. I have never committed a crime with my clients before, though we have encountered the outer reaches of the law. It is the obvious next step, so long as we can be sure of safety. I am a well-known figure in my field, I cannot risk your getting caught any more than you can.'

'But d'you think . . . I mean, if I did this, would I stop going mad?'

'Without question.'

The man who had shown Miles into the castle appeared at the door. He didn't seem the slightest bit surprised to see two naked men squatting in the fireplace.

'Michelle is here to see you. She has Dominique and Angelica with her and she's a little upset, I think.'

'Who are they?' asked Miles. He stood up, feeling suddenly exposed as the Frenchman glanced at his penis.

'It is of no concern to you, Miles. They are my children.'

'Oh, you have children?'

'Many, many children,' said the Frenchman sardonically.

A woman appeared in the doorway behind him. She was wearing only a thin vest and a pair of knickers, her thick dark tangled hair all over her face. She glanced at Mario and Miles through her fringe as she made her way drowsily to the sink, filled a coffee cup with water from the tap, drank it quickly and left the room.

'Is that one of your children?' asked Miles.

'No, that is Anna Benz.'

Chapter Eleven

———⟫⟫◦◦◦⟪⟪———

'Mr Cooper to see you, sir,' said Trish, Gaston Bell's secretary.

'Send him in, Trish, and can you get this to Donaldson, please?' He held up a banker's credit for a seriously large sum without looking up from the NASDAQ index on his monitor. Trish took it and opened the door. Gaston glanced up as the burly figure of Donald Cooper appeared, this time, thankfully, wearing a smart suit instead of battle fatigues. His thick moustache looked newly trimmed.

'Brigadier, nice to see you, old chap,' said Donald, shaking his hand and taking a seat. Gaston noticed with alarm that his own hand was only a quarter the size of the man-bull's before him.

'Keep it brief, Donald, I'm a very busy man,' he said, discreetly moving his mouse cursor to the bottom left-hand corner of the screen and bringing up the screen-saver image of his children.

'We've found a site, slap bang next to the line just outside Maidstone. It's perfect.'

'Can we get access?'

'No problem. D'you remember Minty Shawcross, the little lad who took out that bunker at Goose Green?'

'I thought he bought it?'

'No, no, you're thinking of Pinky Shawcross, his cousin. Got his head blown off the same day. Friendly fire, apparently.'

Gaston quickly nodded, not keen to remember the day in question.

'It's his brother's construction company. We're very lucky, it couldn't be better.'

'Very fortunate,' agreed Gaston.

'We'll have to slip Minty's brother a wad. He's very trustworthy because I know where he lives.' Donald smiled threateninglly, never a pretty sight.

'And what about the crane?'

'Sorted. We're getting a seriously big piece of kit. Lifts fifty tons. Like the old eight-wheeler jobs the Engineer Corps used to use. It'll lift a Centurion – obviously without battle armour. Whatever, it'll have no trouble with a container. Harris has got his hands on a flat liner. You know, we explained it to you? Lift it off, slip it in, shift it out. It's a three-minute job. Easy.'

'You think you can keep it quiet?'

'Who's going to talk?' said Cooper. 'None of my team. Who have you been talking to?'

'Come come,' said Gaston. 'As if I'd tell anyone. You are the only person I've even mentioned this to.'

Chapter Twelve

Miles jumped off the Go airlines flight when the doors finally opened at Heathrow and started running. He hated being late, was very close to being so and the thought of it annoyed him. But this was counteracted by the fact that he had evacuated his bowels on the flight. It was the first time he had gone in two days. Miles took it as a good sign. Running wasn't too difficult, he didn't have any baggage, he'd left his bike at Luxembourg airport.

Once in terminal three he checked the arrivals board. The flight from Tokyo had landed, baggage in hall. Miles got out his mobile. Just enough juice for a call.

'Kulvinder, it's me.'

'Where the hell are you, man?'

'Terminal three, where are you?'

'In the arrivals hall.'

'Is he here?'

'No, not yet. Where the hell have you been?'

The line went dead. No power. Miles looked at it. The battery had run down, that was all. He checked his pulse, nothing wrong there. No feelings, but actually, as he walked along, he realised he felt all right. He wasn't excited, he wasn't particularly looking forward to the arrival of the men who could make FullFacial an international name, but he felt all right and that was a step up. He even smiled to himself as he took the escalator down to the arrivals hall.

His exit from the château at the crack of dawn had been hurried. The whole affair was rather mysterious. The woman arriving with Mario's two young children, then the shouting match in the old hallway which took place in French. The hurriedly made meal. Mario talking on his satellite phone in more languages than Miles could remember. Philippe, as he'd discovered the Frenchman was called, feeding the children, reading them a story and eventually taking them to bed. Then his own little room at the top of a flight of spiral stone stairs and the sudden, anxious wake-up call.

As he rushed downstairs he saw Philippe carrying the sleeping German woman, Anna, her face still obscured by her thick mop of dark hair. Mario was carrying one of the children, also sleeping, under his arm. The other one was crying, holding on to a big teddy bear. Miles picked up the child and followed the rapidly departing group.

They seemed very anxious as they walked across the garden in the slowly appearing light. Birdsong filled the air as the dawn chorus erupted. They left through the main gates and before Miles could say anything, Philippe started to load his bike into the back of a large Mercedes four-wheel drive. Miles explained that his decision not to use cars wasn't arrived at lightly, and meant it. He saw that Anna Benz had been placed leaning against a silver-grey Porsche. Once Mario had loaded the children into the four-wheel drive, he walked over to Anna and slapped her face a few times. Without complaining, she got into the car and started it up. It sounded extremely loud and gas guzzling. Without so much as a wave she roared off down the road leaving a cloud of blue smoke hanging like a stain in the crisp morning air.

Philippe and Mario climbed into the Mercedes and moved off with similar haste. Miles got on his bike and cycled through the quiet village. A farmer passed him driving a tractor. As he free-wheeled down the hill towards the main road, following the route he had used the day before, he heard a police siren. He felt slightly alarmed at this, wondering quite what was happening. Mario hadn't given him any explanation as to why they had to leave, had merely told Miles he would explain later. They had arranged to meet in London to continue the exercise. Miles slowed down as he saw a flashing light moving at speed along the main road at the bottom of the hill. It didn't look right, there was no one else about. What if Mario and the other three were wanted criminals? What if *he* was now classified as a wanted criminal? The authorities could easily have bugged the castle. Maybe everything he and Mario had spoken about had been monitored and now they were coming to raid the place.

He pulled off the road and skidded to a stop beside an oak tree. He laid his bike down in the long grass and squatted beside it, checking his pulse to see if there was any change. He didn't feel anything, knew he should feel anxious but there was nothing. His pulse rate was normal for someone who had been cycling. It appeared to be slowing rather than speeding up.

The siren grew louder and louder until two police cars roared past him, climbing the hill, followed by a large black people carrier and another black saloon car, a posh one, the make of which he didn't recognise.

Then, nothing. He waited a while, shrugged, got back on his bike and started to make his way back to Metz. It was all very odd.

He rang Mario on the satellite phone number when he reached Luxembourg airport, got the answering machine and decided not to leave a message. He started thinking about the ease with which the authorities could trace his mobile number. He pondered on what he had done, checked his pulse to see if he was upset. He didn't appear to be.

Miles saw Kulvinder waiting in the crowd in the international arrivals hall at Heathrow, holding a large printed sign with 'Nakasomi' written on it. The logo of FullFacial was above it. When Kulvinder saw him, his face dropped. Without words he managed forcefully to communicate that Miles could have made an effort with his appearance.

'I've been in France, I can't tell you any more,' said Miles, shrugging off the criticism.

'What the hell have you been in France for?'

'I said, I can't tell you. Where have you been?'

'In the blasted office, all night,' snapped Kulvinder. He was angry, the first time Miles could remember such an event.

'What's wrong?'

'Miles, I've been working *all night* getting the voice synch to work, checking code. Your job. We have our only client arriving. Today. Now.'

'I know, I'm here.'

'Yes, and look at you!'

'What's wrong?'

'You look like . . . like someone who doesn't care.'

'Well, I don't very much.'

'I know you don't need the money, but it should be fun. That's what I've been thinking all night. This was supposed to be fun.'

'I know. It isn't though, is it?'

'Well, it should be.'

They stared at each other for a moment. Kulvinder kept glancing at the steady stream of heavily laden passengers emerging through the arrivals gate.

'What is actually wrong with you, Miles?'

'Nothing is wrong with me that a few of sleep won't de-bug. However you look like a pimp,' said Miles. Kulvinder was wearing a dark suit and he'd had a shave. His face was a mass of minor scars. He looked extremely uncomfortable.

'At least I made an effort!' he snapped. 'For goodness' sake, Nakasomi has flown all the way from Tokyo to see us. He's going to pay us several million dollars and we have a product that is, to say the least, a little clunky around the edges.'

'I've spent thousands of hours working on it. Who checked all the code? There were countless mistakes in it. Who stripped the code down so the reaction time was milliseconds? Who made all the tea?'

'How come you make me feel guilty when *you've* messed up? You're so manipulative. I think I hate you, Miles, you know that? I really hate you.'

'You're shagging my wife!' he said flatly.

'I am not! You stupid little man, I'm not doing anything with your wife except being her friend.'

'If I had any feelings, I'd probably be mad right now.'

'You heartless swine!' said Kulvinder, now red-faced with fury. 'How could you do that to her?'

'What? I haven't done anything to her!' said Miles. He could sense people in the crowd around them pulling back. 'She's a nutter. She's started talking to her therapist in Seattle while we have sex, for God's sake!'

'Oh, as if! You little lying bastard!' shouted Kulvinder. 'I'll fucking kill you!'

'Don't keep calling me little,' said Miles, just holding back a desire to check his own pulse, thinking that if anything would make him upset and start to feel things, being called 'little' would.

Kulvinder grabbed hold of Miles' hair. Since he was a good five inches taller it must have been the obvious target. He pulled at it with surprising force. Miles' reaction was to grab his wrists and try and stop the pain. He was definitely feeling that.

'Good afternoon, gentlemen.'

Miles and Kulvinder turned. They saw a very neatly dressed Japanese man standing in front of them. Kulvinder immediately let go of Miles' hair and managed a smile.

'Mr Nakasomi,' he said, holding out his hand.

'No, I am not Nakasomi San, I am Mr Yamaha, Nakasomi San's interpreter. He speaks very little English. He is just over there.'

The tidy man pointed to a grey-haired and very distinguished-looking man standing with two other besuited businessmen, one Japanese, one European.

Kulvinder pulled his crumpled suit into shape as best he could and approached them.

'Good afternoon, Mr Nakasomi, it is a great privilege to meet you.'

'Good afternoon,' said Mr Nakasomi, and muttered something to Yamaha in Japanese.

'Mr Nakasomi is wondering if you are injured?' said Yamaha, nodding in Miles' direction. Miles had held back a little from this initial meeting. His head was still hurting from

Kulvinder's hair pulling. Miles hadn't shaved, bathed or changed his clothes in over twenty-four hours and realised he might look a little unbalanced.

But he stepped forward and held out his hand to greet the Japanese banking magnate.

'This is my partner at FullFacial, Mr Morris.'

'How do you do?' said Miles when Mr Nakasomi eventually shook his hand. Yamaha had translated what Kulvinder had said and Nakasomi raised his grey eyebrows for a fleeting moment. Other than that it was impossible to tell what he was thinking.

'There is a car waiting outside. We can go and see the first demonstration now, then you will need to rest at your hotel. Yes?' said Kulvinder, speaking slowly and clearly.

'That sounds most appropriate,' said Yamaha. As the group moved off Miles started to push the baggage trolley piled high with five enormous yellow, moulded plastic suitcases.

He pondered just disappearing with the cases. They probably contained vital bank documents. He could run off with them. He could find Mario and give him the cases so they could be returned safely. Or then again, maybe they could blackmail the bank – they were bound to be crooked after all. Miles stopped momentarily. For a fleeting moment there he'd felt something. He checked himself. He sensed a sort of excitement, a joyous bubble, although it soon evaporated in the dark fog of his interior. The others turned and looked at him.

'Everything okay?' asked Yamaha.

'Fine, sorry, got a lot on my mind at the moment,' said Miles, and continued walking.

As they emerged from the busy terminal, Kulvinder was waving at a huge white stretch limo crawling through the traffic towards them. It finally managed to pull to a halt, the boot popped open and Miles helped load the hugely heavy cases into the spacious rear of the daft machine. There was nothing he hated more than stretch limos, the ultimate in automotive stupidity.

Two Japanese and one European climbed into the back, Kulvinder holding the door for them. He looked at Miles.

'What are you going to do?'

'Get the train. Meet you there,' he said.

'For goodness' sake, clean yourself up,' hissed Kulvinder. 'Put a suit on.'

'Yes, all right,' said Miles, waving off the comments like flies. He turned and almost bumped into Yamaha.

'Are you getting in?'

'No, Mr Yamaha, I don't go in cars, I think they're stupid.'

'Miles, please,' said Kulvinder, still holding the door.

'I understand,' said Yamaha. 'Many people in Japan are opposed to cars also. Will we see you later?'

'Yeah, I'll be there,' said Miles. Maybe the Japanese were more advanced than the English. They had the bullet train after all. Very few people failed to question Miles' abhorrence of the motor vehicle. They were always tackling him about it, asking him what he would do if his child was injured and the only way to take it to hospital was in a car. Would he let the child die? He had no answer to that, other than that cars injured a lot of children in the first place.

He waved the car off and went back inside the terminal.

He had never used the high-speed service to Paddington before. It took only eleven minutes to go from the airport to central London. Televisions showing BBC World News played in each compartment. It was a clean, quiet, European type of train, startlingly out of place in England where most public transport was Third World standard.

Once at Paddington he caught the tube to St John's Wood station, walked down Grove End Road to Abbey Road and entered the apartment building.

The place was deserted. There was a huge pile of broken equipment heaped up along the rear wall of the front room. He walked into the kitchen. The washing up was done, the food had been put away. The cordless phone stood neatly on the shelf, hand-set actually resting in the re-charger. Kulvinder must have stayed. There was no way Donna would have done that.

Miles showered and shaved and dressed himself in a linen suit he used to wear to meetings in Seattle. He checked himself in the mirror. He looked a lot better.

He wrapped his ankles in his Day-Glo yellow cycling puttees and lowered his touring bike. Leaving the mountain bike in Luxembourg had worried him. It was in the left luggage department at the airport and unlocked. Custom-built for him in America, it was still the best bike he had ever owned and Miles had owned hundreds.

He arrived in the Monmouth Street studio before anyone else and went into the office to find it spotless. Fresh flowers were arranged in a vase that used to be in their apartment. Donna must have given it to Kulvinder. They *must* be shagging, there was no other explanation. How could she? Kulvinder was such a sack of lard and Donna was always obsessing about hard-bodied men. She actually got off on underpants adverts featuring men with well-defined six packs.

Miles booted up the mainframe, reassured by the high-speed disks' ringing song. He loaded up the autoteller and the face appeared. It blinked its eyes and the eyeballs scanned the room, eventually locking on to Miles. The face smiled.

'Hello, Mr Morris,' it said in a very convincing English accent.

It was still quite a chilling moment even for Miles. He knew the tiny camera which sat on top of the monitor had located his position and sent a message to the software engine that controlled the face. The eyeballs then responded by seeming to scan the room until they stopped at a point roughly where the individual was situated. They had then quickly scanned the ten-thousand faces they held on their data bases until they found Miles. Every action complex and involved and all taking less than a second.

It seemed to be working properly. The lip synch was right on cue. Kulvinder must have worked hard. Miles felt a twinge of guilt for accusing him of having an affair with Donna.

'This way, Mr Nakasomi,' said Kulvinder as he entered the outer office. Their arrival gave Miles another twinge, this time of pleasure. They had been sitting in a car all that time, crawling stupidly through the traffic. This was the first time he had seen other people in their studio, which, although not terribly grand, was quite large. High windows cast a flood of sunlight on to the newly laid wooden floor; a large sofa stood in one corner with an oversized exotic potted plant next to it. Donna had donated it as a present to make their new workplace more friendly.

The three Japanese men entered the room accompanied by the large European man. They seemed to take up all the available space, their suits darkening the atmosphere. For Miles it was akin to having grown ups look in your bedroom when you were a kid. He didn't like them being here.

'Allow me to introduce you to Roger,' said Kulvinder proudly. 'The first fully interactive, multi-character, user-configured autoteller.'

Mr Nakasomi said something in Japanese as he looked at the large screen before him.

'Very impressive,' translated Yamaha.

'Miles, if you would be so good as to vacate the chair and allow Mr Nakasomi to try the software.'

'Certainly.' Miles got up off the chair, offering it as politely as he could to Mr Nakasomi. The Chief Executive sat down and his henchmen gathered around behind him, staring at the face on the screen.

'Would you mind standing back a little? I need to conduct business in private with my client,' said the face on the screen. The Japanese men laughed and pulled back. The eyes on the face seemed to look around the room a little then focused on Mr Nakasomi.

'Good morning, sir, how may I help you?'

Mr Nakasomi looked behind him to Yamaha, who translated what the face had said. Nakasomi nodded politely.

'If Mr Nakasomi would just like to ask a question in Japanese, he will start to see the full versatility of the program,' said Kulvinder.

Miles, who was standing behind Kulvinder, noticed his fingers were crossed behind his back.

Mr Nakasomi did as he was invited, said something in

Japanese and then gasped as the face in front of him morphed into that of an Asian woman. She smiled demurely and nodded, then spoke in Japanese.

'Perfect interpretation of the language,' whispered Mr Yamaha to Kulvinder and Miles. 'Most impressive.'

Somehow Nakasomi managed to talk to the charming face on the screen for a full five minutes. This intrigued Miles and Kulvinder because there wasn't that much to the average bank transaction. They wondered what he had said, how she was responding. It all looked very convincing but the language had been downloaded from a Japanese voice-recognition company and the possible response sub-lists, which in code took up thousands of lines, were completely baffling to the two English-speaking programmers.

Eventually Mr Nakasomi stood up, bowed politely to Miles and Kulvinder, and then, concentrating hard, said in English, 'Wonderful. We are very happy.'

His henchmen laughed, Kulvinder laughed, even Miles smiled a little.

'D'you want to have a go?' he asked the European member of the party.

'Are you telling me there's a Dutchman in that box?' he asked, giving away his origins with his accent as well as his remark.

'Every major European language is catered for,' said Kulvinder. 'Although it is a Dutch woman, or would be in your case. We have made the facial recognition system as gender-sensitive as we can. Normally the facial representation will be of the opposite gender to the person in front of the machine.'

'It's been a major hurdle,' said Miles, now very happy to be talking about his work. 'We've had to use as many sampled images of male and female faces as we can to try and reinforce gender difference, but we've not been one hundred percent on this. It's amazing how many similarities there are and although the software is essentially intelligent – using neural paths it can in fact learn from experience – it's not faultless. We're okay with men with facial hair and women with long hair, but bring on a strong-faced woman with short hair, or a fey-faced adolescent male with long hair, and the machine can bring up an inappropriate character.'

'Fascinating!' said Mr Yamaha. He started furiously translating what Miles had said to Mr Nakasomi. The Dutchman, meanwhile, sat in the chair in front of the machine. He spoke in Dutch and the screen face morphed effortlessly into a blonde Dutch woman with nicely cropped short hair. She smiled at the Dutchman who sat open-mouthed in wonder as he stared at her.

'She is beautiful.'

'Thank you,' said the Dutch face in a Dutch accent. This elicited another laugh from the Japanese.

Praise was heaped upon Miles and Kulvinder by the bucket load as each of the Japanese men took turns in talking to the face. They were clearly fascinated by it.

'Mr Nakasomi says this invention has enormous potential,' said Yamaha. 'He would like to set up a big meeting with you both in Japan to discuss the possibilities of exploiting it to maximum effect.'

'Fantastic!' said Kulvinder.

'The Nishin Bank is prepared to invest many hundreds of millions of dollars in such a project and we all hope we can work together on this.'

'Fantastic,' said Kulvinder again. He turned to Miles who was also smiling broadly. Kulvinder embraced him firmly which Miles did find mildly uncomfortable, being a good four inches shorter than his business partner.

'Miles, you little bastard, looks like we've done it!'

'Yeah, great,' he said. 'Let go now, Kulvinder, you're embarrassing the clients.'

'Sorry, sorry. I'm just so excited! Two months, mate, two long hard months getting this thing to work.'

Mr Nakasomi then explained that jet lag had got the better of him. The entire group made their way downstairs. Miles noticed the Dutchman make a call on his interesting-looking mobile. As they left the office the ubiquitous stretch limo was pulling up at the kerb.

They bade farewell to their only clients. As soon as the car had disappeared into the busy London evening, Kulvinder started to jump up and down on the pavement.

'We did it! We damn' well did it!' he kept shouting. Passers by stared uneasily at the sight of a man pounding his out-of-condition body up and down so violently.

The two of them retired to the bar of the Covent Garden Hotel opposite their studio. Kulvinder ordered a bottle of champagne, the most expensive on offer.

'But you don't drink,' said Miles.

'Officially that is correct,' said Kulvinder as he popped the cork. 'But today is very special, and as long as you don't tell my mother we'll be fine.'

He brought out two huge cigars from his top pocket, put one in his mouth and offered the other to Miles.

'No, thanks. I don't fancy tongue and jaw cancer at the moment.'

'Oh, loosen up.' Kulvinder lit the cigar and puffed luxuriously. 'All those years we talked about interactive human friendly interfaces. This is the future and we made it. I know it's not really a big deal in comparison with everything else we've done. Sure, this only took two months to get right, but it was based on all that code we wrote. I mean, it is pretty incredible, isn't it?'

'We've both been very lucky.'

'Hey, I always thought selling viaFace was a one off, but today we're the masters of the tech universe, matey boy. I know we're stupidly rich already – I mean, even I am embarrassed about it. But it was fantastic, watching the program work with people who've never seen it before. I mean, it really does work, doesn't it?'

Miles smiled. His old friend looked so ridiculous with that cigar. Kulvinder didn't normally drink or smoke, something which had made their partnership possible. Donna did smoke, a thing which made marriage and life and everything else very difficult.

'Yeah, it works,' said Miles. He wished he could feel

something like Kulvinder did. Elated, happy, excited. He felt none of these things. He realised it was boring being who he was.

'What's up? How can you be depressed at a moment like this?'

'I'm not depressed,' said Miles. 'I'm tired, I suppose, and there's sort of a vacuum formed by the fact that we've finished the job.'

'God, we haven't finished!' said Kulvinder, suppressing a cough caused by the huge cloud of blue smoke that hung in front of his face. 'We've only just started. Think of the applications. With the right development money we're looking at actual, recognisable interactive software that requires no typing skills, no computer literacy, no reading ability. You just have to be able to talk and listen and your computer does the rest. It's as revolutionary as the silicon chip . . . as quantum physics.'

'Yeah, I know. It's really good,' said Miles. 'I suppose it's just that the struggle to get this far has been so intense, and I've put everything I have into the project, and at the end, I go on a cycling holiday to have a break then come back and my life falls apart.'

'Your life hasn't fallen apart,' said Kulvinder. Carefully he poured two glasses of champagne. Miles took a sip. The bubbles annoyed his nose. He wiped it aggressively.

'You're just going through a bit of a rough patch with Donna,' continued Kulvinder. 'You're really lucky, she's a fantastic woman.'

'You should know,' said Miles, and immediately regretted it. Although he didn't feel like one, he knew he sounded like a sulky twelve year old.

'Miles, Donna and I are *not* having an affair. I'm your partner. I know you and her far too well. I haven't told you about Kerry, have I?'

'Who's Kerry?'

'There you go, see.' Kulvinder drew extravagantly on his cigar and blew out smoke as he spoke, giving his voice a hoarse, forced quality he clearly rather liked. 'She's a young lady I met through an internet chat group. She's gorgeous and bright as all hell. Works for Dell in Cork, but she's coming over here soon.'

'Sounds great,' said Miles. 'So you're not having a thing with Donna?'

'No,' said Kulvinder. He looked at Miles, his brown eyes calm and non-threatening. 'Whatever problems you and Donna are having, they're nothing to do with me. I felt sorry for her. She rang me after you'd got back from the weekend cycling thing, dead upset, and asked me not to tell you. She's got no friends in England other than you or me. I'm always working and you're always depressed. It's not surprising if she's gone a bit wobbly. I was there as a friend. I was supposed to be at a meeting with Morgan Grenfell at the time, but I had to reschedule.'

'Okay, so now I feel like shit. Thank you,' snapped Miles.

'Miles, if you feel bad – and there's no need to by the way – it's not Donna's fault. You've got to get this problem sorted.'

'What problem?'

'The depression thing. Whatever it is you're feeling.'

'I'm not feeling anything, that's the problem.'

'Well, feelings are a bit of a waste of time, I'll grant you that. But you must have them. Why d'you smash stuff up if you don't feel anything?'

'I don't know. It doesn't feel like I smash stuff up. Stuff just breaks sometimes.'

'Oh, yeah? Sure. Well, let me tell you, from the outside it looks like you've got feelings.'

'I check my pulse all the time.'

'I know you do. Drives me round the bend the way you do that.'

'Have you noticed I do it then?' asked Miles. He had assumed this was a very private habit.

'Of course I have. You've constantly got two fingers on your neck or your wrist. Do you think you're dead or something?'

'I wonder sometimes.'

'God, you're a liability. Just as well you're good at what you do.'

'I know.'

'Can't you get help?' said Kulvinder, staring out of the window.

'I am.'

Kulvinder suddenly looked at him again. 'Is that what you were doing in France?'

'Yeah. Can't talk about it, though.'

'Okay, fair enough.' Kulvinder put his hands up and singed his hair with his cigar. 'But you're actually seeing someone – a counsellor or something?'

'Yeah, but I really don't want to talk about it, okay.'

'Sure. What do you think of India's chances tomorrow?'

'What are they doing?'

'Playing cricket. I'm just changing the subject. More champagne?'

Chapter Thirteen

At about the same time that Miles was sitting in the Covent Garden Hotel, Mario Lupo got off Eurostar at Waterloo. He started walking down the platform, followed by Philippe heavily laden with bags.

Mario was a little anxious. He never liked going through passport controls, seeing them as a gross invasion of his privacy and a threat to his independence. As he didn't actually reside anywhere in particular, he found the notion of nationhood or nationality an alien concept. Mario came, he liked to think, from the world. His race was human. Having a passport which showed his nationality was an unpleasant experience for him. He looked through the small bag he was carrying over his left shoulder. Inside were eight passports, all apparently legitimate and accurately containing his details, all in different names.

He found his British passport and pulled it out. The man at passport control barely gave him a glance as he walked through. Mario turned to watch Philippe also sail through. As soon as they were within the station complex, Mario's mood started to lighten.

This new state of mind was blasted from starboard as Paula Bentley screamed out his name at the top of her voice. She was standing a good thirty metres from him but had spotted him in the crowd and wanted to attract attention to herself, something she always did if it was at all possible.

Mario smiled at her kindly and raised his hand in a wave. Paula rushed across the busy railway concourse towards him.

'D'you want me to take her out?' said Philippe in his ear. Mario noticed the Frenchman was already going for something under his coat.

'No, she's fine. I called her before we left. I think we can help her, but we'll have to spend time with her.'

'*Merde!*' said Philippe glumly. 'Thank you for telling me.'

Paula's embrace knocked Mario so hard that if it hadn't been for Philippe's strong hand on his back, he would have been sent sprawling.

'It's so . . . so *fantastic* to see you, Mario! This is just utterly amazing! I am so excited!' She hugged him again. 'I can't believe you're here. I was just saying to Mary – you remember Mary? Oh, no, you never met her. She's my absolute best friend ever . . . other than Monica, of course. Anyway, I was just saying to her that I couldn't believe you were coming.'

Suddenly she pulled back and stood, head downcast, hands up in front of her.

'Shit, shit, I forgot! I got so excited, I forgot. I'm a bitch, kill me, I'm a bitch!'

'Hello, Paula,' said Mario. 'You are not a bitch.'

'I am. I completely forgot about your crippled arm – I am such a nightmare. And I said crippled! Oh, no! God, I am *so* insensitive. That's what everyone thinks, I know they do. I just hugged you and probably hurt your crippled arm. I've got a friend with a crippled leg and I always forget that and ask her to come out for walks with me. I am *so* insensitive. And I had a blind friend, a lawyer with a huge cock, but he was blind and I was always asking him if he'd seen this movie or that movie. I am so evil!'

Paula looked up. She was crying, floods of tears streaming down a face that only seconds before had been ecstatic. 'I do bad things,' she moaned. 'I'm so utterly insensitive,' she wailed. 'So selfish. I just think about me, me, me. I'm obsessed. Why can't I just think about other people for a change?'

'Good morning, Paula,' said Mario, managing to fit the phrase in just as she drew breath for another onslaught. She looked at him for a second, mouth wide open ready to speak, then it started again.

'Oh, God, I'm so sorry. I'm just so excited to see you, and can't believe you're going to stay at my humble abode.'

'Well, we have made other arrangements . . .' attempted Mario.

'It's terrible, but then I am so lucky. I am so lucky and I don't deserve it! All my friends say I don't deserve it. Alan – you know Alan? does the press for Monica. Who I work for. You know I do PR for Monica Simpson, don't you? Of course you do, everybody knows that, I'm crazy if I think people don't know about that, everybody knows about that. Christ, we're in *Hello!* virtually every issue, or *OK!* if we're not. Or *Harper's*, or *FHM*. Every fucking time I look at a magazine there's me and Monica, usually pissed, usually at a party with our tits out. Fuck! Especially since the thing with Max. That was terrible. She's still in rehab and no one is looking after her kids. Mind you, I'm not looking after mine, so what's new? But I must have told you about Alan . . .'

Mario touched her arm and started moving.

'Let's walk while you tell me about Alan,' he said as gently as he could. Paula barely stopped talking to listen to him and they all started walking towards the exit. Out of all the clients he had ever treated, there were just two abject, chronic failures. One was Anna Benz – one trauma session and no measurable improvement. The other was Paula Bentley. Five separate and extremely expensive trauma therapy exercises and nothing had changed her at all. Mario knew Paula much better than he wished.

'Well, Alan said I didn't deserve my place.'

'We are not stay . . .'

'He said I should swap with him. He only has a tiny place in Kentish Town, poor little mouse. Of course he wanted to swap. But I said, no, I need the spare room because I'm always having people to stay. International people. Like musicians, Hollywood stars, psychoanalysts . . .'

'I'm not a psychoanalyst, Paula.'

'Head shrinker!' she shrieked, then covered her mouth while her whole body heaved dramatically, as if she was going to be sick. 'I shouldn't have said that, I shouldn't have said that! Oh my God, please, Mario, *please* forgive me?'

'It's no problem, you can call me a head shrin . . .'

But Paula had already started again, this time telling a story about the dentist who came to her house and tried to seduce her. Apparently he'd also fixed Mel Gibson's teeth and showed her the dental mould he made of Mel's mouth. And told her he'd show her Clint Eastwood's dental mould if she'd only go down on him.

Mario hailed a cab outside the station and he and Philippe got inside with their bags. Mario shouted the address at the driver because not for one micro-second did Paula remain silent. The only gaps were when she paused to draw breath, and Paula seemed to be able to breathe in with unnatural speed.

Mario patted Philippe's knee reassuringly as the cab wound its way through the heavy London traffic. He smiled and raised his eyebrows. Paula leant forward in her seat to get their attention.

'It was only a month ago that I was in Monaco . . . it seems like ages because so much – so, so *much* – has happened since then. It's been unbelievable but I've had, like, men waiting, literally waiting, outside my house. If I get up in time to take Mustoe to school . . . I've told you about lovely Mustoe, my boy, haven't I? I hope so 'cos sometimes I forget him. That's what's wrong with me, I even forget I'm a mother, although I'm so shit at it I don't deserve the title. But these men . . . they're desperate, Mario, absolutely desperate to have me. It's extraordinary. They will go to any lengths and I just say, "No, go away, Paula will not bless you with her body." '

'That is very good.'

'I have to wait for the right one. Isn't that what you said to me, Mario, when we did that exercise in Sicily?'

'Oh, Sicily, yes, what a wonderful . . .'

'That's what you said to me.' She turned to Philippe. 'D'you know what he said to me? By the way, I don't know your name.'

'This is Philippe, my assistant,' said Mario as quickly as he could.

'Oh, Philippe, Philippe! How do you do? God, you must have an enormous cock . . . look at the size of your hands. Fuck me! Anyway, d'you know what Mario said to me? Lovely Mario with the crippled . . . Sorry, sorry, shouldn't have mentioned it. Well, Mario said that I had to wait for the right man to come along.'

'I'm sure I never said . . .'

'That's what you said to me when we were in that hotel with the camp waiter who said he'd never seen a woman before me he could fancy. D'you remember him, Mario?'

'I'm not sure,' he said, looking out of the window, trying to keep the barrage of noise as far away from the newly focused centre of his universe as possible. It was hard. The dog-eared ends of Paula's stories tended to lodge in the mind. He couldn't help wondering who Alan was and what he'd said and where they'd met and about the dentist with a mould of Mel Gibson's teeth. All this stuff went in somewhere, Mario knew that, he just needed to keep it in check. After all, he was about to embark on a radical new project.

They climbed out of the taxi outside an elegant town house in Bryanston Square. Mario paid for the taxi while Paula carried on with five separate anecdotes, mainly linked to whether one should pay for taxis and restaurant bills when lunching with one's psychoanalyst.

'I am not a psychoanalyst,' said Mario as they climbed the few steps to the front door of the house.

'Why are we here?' asked Paula. 'Whose house is this? Is it your house, Mario? My God, I never knew you had a house in London. This is fantastic!'

He found some keys in his bag, opened the door and stepped inside. As soon as they closed the door behind them, Mario deftly tripped Paula up with his left foot and pushed her over with his right arm. She sprawled face down on the floor, screaming hysterically. Philippe dived on top of her, wrenched her head back by pulling her hair and held a terrifying, carbon-fibre, jagged-edged hunting knife to her throat. Mario knelt down on the floor in front of Paula so she could see his face from the extremely uncomfortable position she was in.

'Paula, listen to me . . .'

'What are you doing?' she croaked.

'Paula, shut the fuck up and listen to me! If you don't shut up now, Philippe is going to slit your throat from ear to ear. He's a hired killer with ten years' experience in the Foreign Legion and eight years of prison behind him. You will die in about five seconds as the blood drains very rapidly from your brain. Do you understand the danger you are in?'

'Yes,' she croaked.

'Good. Now I want a ten-minute period in which you will promise me on pain of death to listen, take in what I say, and only at the end respond to it. Do you understand, Paula?'

She nodded as best she could, tears now streaming down her face. Philippe pulled her roughly to her feet and marched her into the exquisitely decorated front room. Using wide grey carpet tape he tied her to an original Louis XV chair. When she was very securely held, he tore off a strip and held it in front of her mouth.

'Are you going to co-operate?' asked Mario.

Paula slowly nodded and Philippe lowered his hand. He did so very slowly. He could see the muscles in Paula's jaw working, could tell she was talking without making a sound. Slowly a noise started to emerge. Philippe rapidly held the tape up close to her mouth again and looked at her threateningly. The sound died away, just the slightest movement in the neck and jaw remaining. Again he began to straighten up, moving his hands away from her face. This time it just erupted from her.

'. . . was a banker. I must have told you about him? The one who gave me the Mercedes. Anyway he wanted to tie me up last week and force me to . . .'

Philippe slapped the tape over her mouth and pressed it on as hard as he could. Paula whimpered a little. Soon it was clear she was still talking under the tape, but the sound was thankfully muffled.

'Paula, I am going to let you do another exercise. I know this one will work.'

Suddenly both Mario and Philippe could tell she really had stopped talking. She stared at Mario, her eyes wide.

'This is something which has to be kept secret at all costs. You will not be able to divulge what you did on this exercise. It can never be one of your stories. You will learn, through the trauma associated with it, that you can keep things to yourself. That it is healthy to filter what you say. You will learn to be happy in silence. Not oppressed by an outside force like you are at the moment. You will become a more peaceful person from within.'

Mario sat down, nursing his limp arm. The embrace Paula had held him in at the station had been fairly intense, like the resulting pain in his shoulder. He looked at her with a flat smile. Tears were pouring from her eyes. Her very beautiful eyes.

Not much about Paula Bentley made sense. The very rich, very beautiful Englishwoman of twenty-eight was one of the most unpleasant people Mario had had the misfortune to encounter, and his list of rich and mad clients was very long indeed.

Chapter Fourteen

The giant orange Hamag crane lifted another flattened car and dropped it in to the back of an open-topped articulated truck. Phil Pilcher was on the early shift at the Meyer Parry scrapyard, tucked behind PC World in Brentford.

He'd worked at the yard for two years, his longest time in one job since leaving the Army. Having been in the Royal Engineers, he found jobs relatively easy to come by. There wasn't a lot of heavy machinery he couldn't fix. He had drifted from engineering firm to heavy contractor, building site to civil engineering project, never finding anything which made him want to stay. But working at the scrapyard was a job he rather enjoyed.

The Hamag cranes were fantastic to drive for the first couple of weeks, state-of-the-art bits of kit from Japan, not too noisy and powerful as hell. A very long orange arm was fitted either with a powerful electro-magnetic dish, if he was sorting small scrap, or a great big four-fingered claw if he was shifting big, unprocessed lumps.

As he swung the crane around to lift the next pancake-flat car, he noticed something out of the ordinary in the yard to the side of him: a shiny new Cherokee parked amid the debris. Standing beside the Jeep, leaning on the roof talking on a mobile, was a man he immediately recognised.

Phil had never actually served under Major Donald Cooper, a known psychopath. His younger brother Mickey, still seemed to get on with the Major. Phil knew they were up to no good but steered well clear of a certain, select group of old Army buddies. The group that seemed to flout the law and get away with it. Lately, though, Mickey seemed to have dropped off the face of the planet. Phil wouldn't have been surprised to discover that Major Cooper had something to do with it.

One thing Phil really didn't need was a visit from this particular ex-officer. He picked up a flattened Ford Granada and dropped it noisily in the back of the nearby truck.

For a moment he thought about dropping the four-fingered grab on the Major, lifting him into the skip and dumping a load of scrap on him. End of problem. Needless to say, Phil Pilcher did nothing of the sort, he wasn't that sort of man.

The engine in the Hamag slowly died and he climbed out of the cab. Donald Cooper pocketed his mobile and walked towards him. Phil pretended to be checking something on the crane. He couldn't bear to stand and watch the man mountain's approach.

'Hello there, Philip. How's it dangling, you scrawny little bastard?' Monstrous teeth glinted as Cooper spoke.

'All right, sir.'

'Hey, at ease, old chum. Need a little word, got a minute?'

'All right, but I've got a ton and a half of shit to shift this morning.'

'I had a word with the boss man, he's very amenable,' said Donald, motioning behind him to the weighbridge at the entrance to the yard where old man Williams was sitting, chain smoking.

'We've got a bit of crane work we need doing.'

'Oh, really. What's that for then?'

'Best not to know right now, old chum. Touch of the classified if you know where I'm coming from, and I think you do. An hour's work, tops, and a very respectable wad of cash in your hand. Euros, mind you, none of this sterling crap.'

'What sort of crane are we talking about, sir?'

'Big bastard, eight-wheeler. Hydraulic jacks and all the stuff you love. It'll be a laugh, Phil, believe me. And it looks like you could do with one.'

'I don't have a licence for a big rig any more, sir. Haven't used one of those since I left the Army.'

'You don't need a licence. No one is going to be checking up on you, we run the bloody site!'

'What about driving it there?'

'No probs. It's all been carefully planned. The operation's taking place on a building site in Kent.'

'Fair enough.'

'Can we count on you then?'

'I don't know about that . . .'

Phil had been here before, offered strange 'jobs' by the Major for serious money. His kids came to mind. Kirsty and Mandy, both at primary school, loved their dad. If he did something stupid and landed in the nick for five years they'd grow up like most of their friends, with no dad around for years on end.

'Can't help, Donald,' he said. 'Just can't do it. Straight and narrow me, mate. Got a good job here and I don't want to risk losing it.'

Donald Cooper ran his massive hands through his thick black hair. He stretched his spine and looked up at the sky. Phil knew the move, he'd seen it on a parade ground. Cooper always did this before laying the nut on someone, but Phil was wearing a hard hat, bright yellow with a sharp peak.

Donald looked down at him and smiled. 'Knew you'd be a pussy, Pilcher. You always were. Say anything about this to anyone and I'll kill you. You know that, don't you?'

Phil nodded. He knew that. Major Cooper took no prisoners, that much was well known.

No more was said. Donald climbed back into his Cherokee and reversed out of the yard at speed, sending up a cloud of oil and metal shards from the filthy ground. Phil Pilcher climbed back into the cab of the Hamag crane and started it up. It was only as he engaged the hydraulics that he noticed how badly his hands were shaking.

Chapter Fifteen

'Yes, I do want to go back,' said Donna.

On reflection, it was obvious to Miles that she'd say this. He had asked her if she wanted to leave him. He was holding a tea cup when she told him. He stared at it for a while, wondering if it would suddenly be broken. It wasn't. He checked to see if he was feeling anything. He wasn't. It was just data. His wife wanted to leave him and go back to America. Simple.

He thought about Mario and the strange château. The woman with the hair over her face whom Philippe had carried out to the car. The rows of graves in the endless war cemeteries he'd ridden past as the sun came up. The emptiness of the countryside. He had felt a change in himself even in that short meeting with the funny little man with the withered arm.

Miles put the cup down carefully. He leant against the sink and sighed like his father, waiting in his case for something resembling a feeling. For someone who theoretically never had feelings, Miles took a keen interest in them. His mother had classified him as a sensitive little boy, saying nothing was ever easy for him. He could see, looking back, that he'd been just as they'd said, a complicated child. Maybe he was a sensitive man now, just missing a bit of vital code which connected his feelings to . . . he didn't know what. To himself, he supposed.

Donna wanted to leave him and he wondered how much difference it would make.

'If I said I'd stop being morose, stop sometimes smashing things up, would that make any difference?' he asked at last.

Donna looked up at him. She shook her head sadly.

'Is it someone else then?'

She didn't react for a long time. The sound of the fridge, that special people-who-live-on-their-own sound, filled his ears.

His eyes wandered around the kitchen, then he noticed something. Donna was crying. There was someone else then. It must be Kulvinder – who else? He had always fancied her, that much was obvious.

Was he, Miles, really that bad? Must be. He must be hell to live with. She had tried everything, poor Donna, everything she could think of to keep him, except tidying up a bit and stopping smoking and stopping talking to her therapist. And she had failed completely.

She was wearing a beautiful business suit, he could tell she'd just had a shower. Her tangled mop of dark hair was tied in a loose bunch on top of her head. The little white streak clearly visible. He liked her, that was the trouble. He did actually like Donna. Big problem. It always had been. She was the only woman he'd met that he liked. Even though she drove him crazy with the mess she made, Miles did actually like being with her.

'Now it's all over,' he heard himself saying.

She nodded.

'It's Kulvinder, isn't it?' he said. She started sobbing even more violently. She was saying something through the tears but he couldn't make it out. Slowly she composed herself.

'I want to go home. I hate it here,' she managed to say.

'But it was you who wanted to come here.'

'I made a mistake. I got a block in Seattle and thought a move would help. But it hasn't. It's made it worse. I need to see Dianne every day, actually *see* her.' Dianne was her therapist. 'I can't write here.'

'What d'you mean, you've got a block?'

'I feel like I've lost Milky.'

'Lost him?'

'Her.'

'Sorry.'

'That sums it all up, Miles,' she said, using her slightly whining voice. 'You've never liked Milky, never understood her. Everybody in this awful country feels like that. I just can't write here. I'm nobody here, and my US publishers want me back. I thought I could do it from here, send them everything over the net, but it's just not working. My dream of teleworking has gone totally offline.'

Miles picked up a copy of *Milky on Parade* which was lying in a pile of newspapers and magazines on the kitchen table. He flicked through, meaning to say something helpful and supportive. The books had always been a mystery to him, uniformly bland, just a series of near-empty pages with splotches of washed out colour on them.

'But there's only about nine words in the average Milky book,' he protested. 'How can you have writer's block?'

He started laughing then. Couldn't stop himself. He knew it was wrong but the laughter came from somewhere deep inside.

He was fascinated that he was laughing because laughter was a sure sign of feeling, a happy feeling. He checked his pulse. About average.

Donna started crying again, sitting on the kitchen chair, her shoulders heaving. Miles knew he should feel terrible, but he didn't.

He walked into the bedroom, where he gently threw a few clothes into a rucksack, then went to the hall. He lowered his touring bike, recently cleaned, opened the door and left. He closed the door as quietly as he could, no architrave-splintering slam announced this departure. After the years of discomfort, the endless tidying, the constant litany of complaints, Miles Morris left Donna Buick with barely a whisper.

He headed to the studio, riding smoothly and peacefully along. He didn't have an incident with a driver and he didn't ride as dangerously fast as he normally would have.

When he arrived, there was no one around. Jean must have gone home, finally bored with sitting behind her desk in silence, reading *OK!* magazine with nothing else to do.

Kulvinder was at lunch with the Japanese, of course. He had suggested that, as Miles was feeling a little stressed right now, it might be best if he bowed out. Kulvinder knew he didn't go for lunch meetings much anyway and Miles had agreed willingly.

He sat down at his desk, booted up the computers, and after a short pause the face came on the screen. The face, the annoying face that Kulvinder had decided to name Roger. Not for any reason. Roger wasn't a clever acronym. He called him that because, according to Kulvinder, the face looked like a Roger.

'Good morning, Miles Morris, can I help you?' said the face. Its pointless existence annoyed him. The face was smiling helpfully. It had taken them days and days to get the wire frame skeleton to adopt a helpful smile, making changes so subtle that most normal human beings would have lost any sense of reality early on. But Miles persevered, challenged by the maths involved in moving one line, one sequence of moves, a tiny fraction.

'Fuck off!' he said to the face. It continued to smile then said, 'I'm sorry, I didn't understand that. Could you rephrase what you said, please?'

'I said, fuck off, you dumb prick,' said Miles calmly.

'I'm sorry, I didn't understand that. Could you rephrase what you said, please?'

He adjusted the sound so he couldn't hear the annoying voice, then sat in front of the screen and abused the face verbally for a full five minutes.

'You mindless piece of shit! You fuckwit! You plastic, spastic, crap technology corporate twat! I fucking hate you . . . I absolutely fucking hate you!'

He checked his pulse when he'd finished. Normal. He sat still for a moment then had a sudden and unexpected insight into himself. Not common and therefore memorable. He suddenly saw himself, a grown man, sitting in front of a computer monitor hurtling abuse at a face on a screen, and not even a human face but a digitised composite.

He was mad. That was the only explanation. There was a lot of it about. Loads of people went mad, mostly poor people, but some rich ones did and he must be one of them. It had to happen to some people, so why not him?

On the other hand he didn't feel mad, in fact he didn't feel anything except a slight dizziness. A little tension in the shoulders and a slightly painful stomach, but that was normal. His fingers tapped rapidly on the desk. He needed to code, but there was nothing to code. The job was done, the code was written. His fingers kept tapping. He could adjust the code. Code can always be adjusted.

He found his laptop under the bench and opened it. The entire code for the talking autoteller was on the laptop hard disk. Their backup was obsessive, recorded on digital tapes, burnt on to countless CDs, downloaded on to remote servers. They all held encrypted versions of the vital code. They even had a paper print out, seventeen thousand pages of it, in a document security vault off the Tottenham Court Road.

He opened the code-editing software on his laptop, scrolled through, found what he was looking for and started typing at a speed which defied the eye.

Miles was lost to the world. A man and his code, that was all that was happening. The letters and numbers poured forth torrentially, the screen a blur of movement. Miles' buttocks and shoulders relaxed, his eyes locked on the screen. Every now and then he chuckled to himself, stretched his arms above his head, swung his head around to free his neck, and pressed on.

Chapter Sixteen

When Mario awoke it was already late. He could hear noises coming from the kitchen far below and felt the first pangs of hunger. However, there was a drawback. Paula was in the house and that meant he had to listen to her. Every now and then he'd hear a louder noise and lift his head off the pillow to see if he could tell what it was.

It was Philippe, shouting. Mario couldn't be sure exactly what he was shouting, but it sounded like: 'Shut up.'

Mario stumbled out of bed, pulled on his clothes laboriously and checked his satellite phone, charging on the bedside table. He'd set it to auto-answer so it wouldn't wake him up. The liquid crystal display told him he had seventeen messages. It had been a quiet night. There were times when he had over a hundred.

Mario carried the phone downstairs with him, the noise in the kitchen growing ever louder.

The house he was using was huge with nine or ten bedrooms, Mario had never counted. It was decorated immaculately, very tidy and utterly devoid of character. It was as if the place had died. There was something missing from the dwelling, always a chill in the air. Mario hated the house. He had spent too long in it and had too many bad memories associated with it. The owner was a very rich, highly dysfunctional woman with one very well balanced child. Mario had never worked out quite how many houses she owned, but it was more than she could possibly ever need. Many years before, during the early years of the system, and before she had her daughter, the woman had benefited from the one-off Lupo foundation trauma therapy exercise.

Mario had her kidnapped and 'tortured', not physically, of course, it was merely a deeply unpleasant psychological experience. Philippe was, as usual, his willing accomplice.

After the exercise, which had taken place in the house he was in, the woman was so grateful for her 'cure' she gave Mario a set of keys, telling him he could stay there whenever he wanted.

Mario didn't actually want to use the house very much, he wasn't overly fond of London, but he had a lot of clients in the city. One client in particular who had failed to respond to five separate trauma sessions. The client he could hear babbling away in the kitchen. Paula Bentley.

She had inherited a serious fortune at the age of fifteen when her alcoholic building magnate father died. He had collapsed under a Range Rover in a multi-storey car park somewhere in London and the owner drove away without knowing he was there. At least that was the story Paula had told Mario. It was impossible to tell how much truth there was in her constant babble.

Her father's demise and her sudden wealth had sent her quite mad. Miles dealt with a lot of people suffering from sudden wealth syndrome, it was a complaint that was becoming more and more common. Trips to Seattle and Silicon Valley were regular, visiting people like Miles Morris who had suddenly become stupidly rich without planning or even dreaming of it.

Paula was a classic case. She had indulged herself in so many forms of therapeutic self-searching for so many years that she had tipped over the edge quite happily. Ostensibly in PR, she represented a very well-known rock chick, one Monica Simpson, ex-wife of three rock stars, the last of whom had killed himself with a cocktail of drugs that would have felled a stable of horses.

Paula was always to be seen at Monica's side, wearing virtually nothing. Mario had seen the pictures and assumed that

Monica must do something. Maybe appear in second-rate films, or write fashion books, or present television shows. Now it appeared she didn't actually do anything other than have a terrible life and attend the funerals of those of her friends most heavily covered by the press. She would then go into rehabilitation clinics and a few weeks later appear yet again in either *Hello!* or *OK!* magazine. The opening sentence of the feature would always start: 'Monica Simpson, happier now after her recent . . .' and the rest of the piece would remind the reader of the latest disaster to befall her. This constant feeding of the press was managed by Paula who was in fact anything but stupid. A very canny operator, Mario had come to learn. Very canny at operating the press, utterly hopeless at leading her own life.

Paula also claimed to be an actress, had indeed been on the stage a few times. She had landed small parts in British TV cop shows Mario had never heard of, let alone seen. She almost always played murder victims, or mugging victims, or both. She had furnished him with video tapes but he had managed to mislay them very rapidly. What Paula did, which was what kept other people away in droves, was talk. Everybody, that is, except for Monica Simpson and the press who loved her. She'd tell them anything.

As Mario entered the kitchen he was not surprised by the sight that greeted him: Philippe sitting at the large table with a bowl of coffee before him, head bowed and hands over his ears.

Paula was sitting opposite, smiling broadly, and filling the air with her incessant anecdotes.

'So I said to him, "Helicopter or no, I am *not* going out to dinner with you." I'd met him at a party a month before this, you see, and I didn't like him then. I told him . . .'

Mario touched Philippe on the shoulder reassuringly as he walked past. Paula hadn't paused for breath as he'd entered, but she did lock on to him with her laser victim vision. Paula Bentley had the double disadvantage of being rich and beautiful, in a frail, use me and abuse me way. She was constantly approached by men, always responded, and no matter who they were or how attracted to her they became, they would shy off fairly soon after they'd heard three or four hundred stories in rapid succession.

Mario knew how they felt as she moved towards him in search of another set of ears to abuse.

'I said, "I don't care if you are the richest man in Europe, I'm not going down on you." But then I did anyway, in the toilets at the hotel, so it was all crazy. Huge cock, which was nice. Mind you, I was absolutely hammered. I'd been drinking since nine that morning so I didn't really mind what went in my mouth. Not that I drink like that normally, I'm not an alcoholic, thank God!'

'Get the tape, Philippe,' shouted Mario over the din. Philippe stood up, went to the bag on a chair near the door and extracted the roll of heavy-duty tape.

'This glue is the devil to get off. I was in the bath for hours last night, all nude and soapy. I used up all the batteries on my phone, calling everybody to tell them where I was staying, but I couldn't get a signal. I think it was working so I left messages for them all anyway. I'm so excited you're staying, and Philippe has such a big . . .'

Paula offered her face, still talking. Philippe applied the tape and without looking at her again, sat back down at the table and lit up a cigarette.

He had disabled Paula's mobile the night before. Mario had plenty of prior experience of her obsessive phone habits.

He was listening to his messages.

'Anna is on her way,' he said to Philippe, and carried on listening, occasionally touching keys to activate his answering service.

'Gunter Hempel has killed himself, it's his wife. She's thanking me for all the work I did with him.'

'Is that the man who owns the steel works in Hungary?'

'No, that's Gunter Matteson. Gunter Hempel was the banker from Geneva. The man who gave me that lovely office overlooking the lake.'

'That was the best office you ever had.'

'Yes,' said Mario, still listening to his messages. 'Oh, sounds like he's left me some money in his will. Very kind. I'll have to get that attorney in Paris to look into it.

'Ah, Mr Morris has rung, again and again. That's good. Looks like he'll be joining us.' Mario punched a number into his phone. 'I will inform him of our whereabouts.'

'What are we going to do with her?' asked Philippe, nodding in Paula's direction.

'She's going to take part in the operation, of course. She's going to be cured by it.'

'You know best,' said Philippe with a dry laugh. He lit up another Gauloise, opened a copy of *Le Monde* and started reading.

Chapter Seventeen

'I've had your suit dry cleaned,' said Kulvinder Bhasker when he walked into the office the next morning. Miles looked at his partner's immaculately pressed khaki Chinos and tasselled loafers. He hated Kulvinder, wanted to write it on the wall.

Miles had slept on the floor under the silent computers. He hadn't shaved and needed a bath. His shoulders were like a bag of sharp rocks. He hadn't checked the time when he'd finally fallen asleep but it had been light outside and there was the peculiar central London phenomenon of a rowdy dawn chorus. He had written and corrected code for nearly eleven hours solid.

He stumbled out of his sleeping bag, still wearing all his clothes. He had only taken off his cycling shoes.

'You look like death,' said Kulvinder. 'Go and have a shave in the bogs. I've got some shaving equipment here somewhere.'

He opened a cupboard and found a toilet bag in a red plastic bin. Miles had bought the bin to keep Kulvinder's rubbish in one place. There had been times when his possessions were piled in every available corner, on every available surface. Miles had spent days organising storage for him, which neither of them ever bothered to use. The only reason Kulvinder could find his toilet bag was because Miles had put it there.

Miles went down one flight of stairs and into the men's toilets. He looked at his face in the mirror. It was ugly, no point denying it. Something had happened to it. Maybe he looked older.

When he got back to the office he felt a little better. Kulvinder was downloading the core program on to a removable drive. Miles looked at what he was doing, anxious that Kulvinder might think of running the program. But it was late, there was no time for messing around.

Miles climbed into his suit, pulled on a clean pair of socks and tied his black shoes.

'That's a bit of an improvement,' said Kulvinder. 'Let's move out.'

Kulvinder had agreed to walk to Whiteley's shopping centre. He knew there was no point trying to get Miles into a taxi, and didn't want his partner to arrive in his cycling kit. Walking was the only option. It was a bright day with a cool breeze blowing down St Martin's Lane as they set out.

Within moments Kulvinder's mobile rang and he started talking, recording numbers and contact names into a digital memo recorder. Miles didn't listen. He'd heard Kulvinder on the phone so often his voice was just an annoying background buzz.

They walked through Hyde Park. Kulvinder was still on the phone. Eventually, as they neared the gate opposite Queensway and the roar of the traffic grew louder, he switched it off.

'I'm really sorry everything's gone off line between you and Donna. Really bad timing, mate.'

'Yes, it's not terribly good.'

'You know it's nothing to do with me, don't you?'

'What's nothing to do with you?' asked Miles, his seething hatred for the man beside him pricked into new life. He didn't want to give him any reassurance. As they walked on Miles noticed a slight feeling of nausea.

'Donna,' said Kulvinder. 'I know you thought it was me, but it isn't.'

'She told me she's got writer's block.'

'Is that what she said?'

'Yeah. A woman who writes books with five pages and ten words gets writer's block. Good, isn't it?'

'Oh, damn. I don't want to tell you this but you're my friend . . .'

'Tell me what?'

'She hasn't got writer's block. She's got a new feller.'

'She has!'

'I'd have thought it was obvious. Jesus, Miles, what d'you expect? You're so blocked off, so distant. Ladies need contact, Miles.'

'But I can never have contact with her, she's always on the phone. I don't do that do I, ring some analyst in America when we have sex. That's not normal, is it?'

'You're both cracked,' said Kulvinder, and started dialling a number immediately. He used his phone as a smoker used a cigarette. If something was too difficult to deal with, he put in a call

'Hi, Kulvinder here, it's eleven-thirty-three, I'll be at the launch for two hours then back to the office before I go to see the Barclays people this afternoon. Can we fit in a meeting together late afternoon at the Covent Garden Hotel? Page me, e-mail me, leave a message. Cheers.' He switched the phone off and glanced at Miles.

'Fellow from Royal Bank of Scotland.'

'Who is it, then?' said Miles.

'James McClintock, Head of . . .'

'No, who's Donna seeing?'

'Oh, I see. Spud.'

'Spud!' squeaked Miles. 'You mean, Spud Gifford!'

'Yes, I know. Bit odd, isn't it?'

Spud Gifford was a charming Australian programmer they had worked with in Seattle. He'd left to form a start up in Sydney and been astronomically successful, selling the company after three years for over a billion dollars. It had made Kulvinder's and Miles' success pale into insignificance. Everyone had heard about Spud Gifford. Well, everyone who read *Wired* magazine. But money hadn't gone to Spud's head. He still dressed like a student, travelled economy and tinkered with programs all day.

'But isn't he in Sydney?' asked Miles as they crossed the busy road.

'Not at the moment. He was at the party at your place when you were away.'

'I suppose he's a pretty happy sort of bloke, isn't he?' said Miles glumly.

'Very happy-go-lucky type. And, of course, financially bloated.'

'Blimey,' said Miles. 'Spud Gifford.'

'He's been hanging around her for years. Knew her before you met her.'

Miles started to ruminate on what he'd done. It was obvious Donna and Kulvinder were just friends and Miles had got it seriously wrong.

'Oh, Lord,' he said quietly. 'It really isn't you, is it?'

He glanced at the bag Kulvinder was carrying. The bag which contained the program. He had a feeling then, definitely a feeling. And not a nice one. He felt like a little boy who had suddenly been caught shoplifting. He didn't mean to do a very bad thing, but he had. He'd done a very bad thing indeed.

'Look, I may have been talking out of my arse,' said Kulvinder as they reached the entrance to Whiteley's arcade. 'I don't know that any of this is true, I'm just hypothesising, but I think Spud is interested in what we are doing. I don't believe he came over just to get off with Donna. He could inject some serious talent into the business. We could go global, be bigger than Sun Microsystems in three years. So all this business with Donna is a real bind for me, too.'

'I want to die,' said Miles, surprising himself.

'Oh, Miles.' Kulvinder bent forward and held his head in his hands. The bag containing the program hid his face. 'Will you lighten up? Please? I know things are bad at home, but look where we are. After all we've been through, this is a great moment for us. Please, you know, this is what we've been working towards. We've dreamed of this moment for ages. Don't mess it up now.'

Miles shook his head and they walked inside. The place was

teeming, people sitting around the fountain eating ice cream and talking on mobiles. At the far end of the mall they saw a small crowd had gathered, a television crew standing by.

As they drew nearer they could see that the crowd had assembled around an area of the wall outside Marks and Spencer's which had been draped in a blue cloth.

Mr Yamaha, the translator from the Nishin Bank, was waiting for them.

'Good morning, gentlemen, this is a very big day,' he said with a small bow. Kulvinder shook his hand.

'It certainly is, Mr Yamaha. Is everything going to plan?'

'Everything is tick-tock,' said Yamaha. 'This way, please.'

They followed him into Marks and Spencer's, through a door and down a long corridor decorated with employee noticeboards. At the far end was a huge, newly installed steel door. A uniformed security guard was standing beside it. As they approached he opened the door, revealing the guts of an autoteller.

Miles could see that the machine had been beautifully built. Right in the centre at eye level was a slot which would take the large-format tape cartridge Kulvinder was carrying.

'If you would like to do the honours,' said Mr Yamaha.

'Certainly,' said Kulvinder. He removed the tape cartridge from his bag and pushed it gently into the slot.

The security guard closed the door after them and they followed the same route out of the shop. When they arrived at the entrance to the store, they saw the crowd part as three security guards gently moved people back. The camera crew turned on their lights and the cameraman shouldered his Ikiyami camera.

Mr Nakasomi walked through the crowd. He smiled at Miles and Kulvinder and shook hands with a little bow. He said something in Japanese which Mr Yamaha quickly translated.

'Nakasomi San says it is a great honour for the bank today, the start of a whole new era of low-impact automated banking.'

'Please tell Mr Nakasomi that it is an even greater honour for all of us at FullFacial to be acknowledged for our modest involvement in a process which will revolutionise the concept of international banking.'

Mr Yamaha smiled and revealed, to Miles anyway, that he thought Kulvinder was a bit of an idiot. It was the first time Miles had noticed anything so blatant from a Japanese bank employee.

Mr Yamaha translated what Kulvinder had said, they all shook hands again and Miles thought he was going to vomit.

'Ladies and gentlemen,' said Yamaha in a voice that was much louder than Miles would have expected from his diminutive frame. 'The Nishin Banking Corporation is very proud to introduce a revolution in personal banking. Behind this curtain is the first fully automated voice-activated, multi-lingual autoteller machine.' He spoke slowly, his English pronunciation very good. 'Mr Nakasomi, Chief Executive Officer of the Nishin Banking Corporation, will now pull back the curtain.'

With a tight little bow, Mr Nakasomi moved forward and took hold of a cord that was hanging by the side of the curtain. With a little jerk he pulled it to reveal a flat, grey panel surrounded by a grey hood trimmed in Nishin corporate orange. Underneath the screen were a slot for a card and a larger mechanism for accepting and delivering cash.

Flash bulbs popped as Mr Nakasomi withdrew a platinum cash card from his shirt pocket and inserted it into the machine. In gratifying microseconds the face appeared on the screen. It was the standard male face, the one they had worked on for many thousands of hours. The default face, rejected and adapted and finally passed by a hundred committees at a hundred board meetings. Behind it was a virtual bank, people moving back and forth, some carrying pieces of paper. At the very back was a window looking out over a pleasant parkland scene. This had been Kulvinder's idea, the daylight effect tied into the real-time clock. At night, it was starlit, in the daytime sunny, with never a cloud in the sky. Even the seasons were catered for, including falling leaves and snow at Christmas.

The camera crew moved in closer to get a look at what was going on. Mr Nakasomi said something in Japanese. Again, in a gratifying, multi-megahertz-consuming nanosecond, the face morphed into a Japanese woman. There was an audible gasp of surprise from the crowd which was steadily increasing in size. The voice spoke in perfect Japanese.

Mr Nakasomi conversed with the female face for a full thirty seconds, then withdrew his card, waited another five seconds, and the little hatch opened below the card slot to reveal a pile of Euros.

Nakasomi turned around and held the money above his head like a sportsman with a medal. There was a smattering of applause from the Nishin Bank employees. The rest of the crowd just stared at the whole scene blankly, clearly not sure what was going on.

Yamaha beckoned to a grey-haired English-looking man in the crowd. Miles checked his pulse. It was slightly above average. He felt sick and wanted to be somewhere else, any-where else. He wanted to be back in the château, squatting naked in front of the fire.

The man walked forward, more pictures were taken, then he stood in front of the machine.

The Japanese woman's face smiled at him. He seemed nonplussed, but Mr Yamaha was at hand.

'Just put your card in and say hello or good morning, the machine will recognise you,' he said politely. The man nodded and inserted his card.

'Good morning,' he said.

The face instantly transmogrified into the default, the mid-thirties male with neat hair. Roger. Miles glanced at Kulvinder who looked a little concerned. The face should have changed into an attractive mid-twenties female with a neat haircut. Kulvinder threw Miles a look but his attention was soon drawn back to the machine.

'Good morning, sir, how can I help you?' the face said the instant the image had settled. The man smiled and looked behind him to Mr Yamaha for support.

'Just talk to it as you would a normal bank teller,' said the interpreter with a kindly smile.

The man turned back to the screen.

'I'd like to check my balance, please.'

'Certainly, sir,' said the face. It looked down and a small box appeared on the screen. Thanks to the intricacies of flat-screen technology, the sum it displayed was only visible if you were standing right in front of the screen.

'Not much of a wad, is it?' said the face, its smile now slightly more menacing. The tone of its voice had changed a little, too. More street, more aggressive.

'I beg your pardon?' said the man.

'You heard me. I said, not much of a wad.'

'I'm sorry, I don't . . .'

'Oh, yeah, act all innocent, you deaf old git!' said Roger. 'I said, you haven't got much of a wad, just a pin-dicked amount. You're no Gordon Gecko, are you? More of a Gordon Bennett, you sad old bastard. Come hobbling up here, asking how much you've got. Hardly worth the fucking bother, was it?'

The man looked around for support. Already the Nishin employees were panicking. Yamaha was looking at Miles and Kulvinder with an expression of unadulterated fury on his face.

'What is going on?' he hissed.

'What does the Jap want – the bloke behind you?' said the face. 'He's standing too close. Get back in the queue, you slanty-eyed, piano-toothed bastard!'

'I'm sorry, have I done something wrong?' asked the customer to no one in particular.

' 'Course you've done something wrong, you senile twat! You've wasted my time.' The face looked off in one direction then seemed to speak to someone just out of the picture.

'I've got a right one here. Dirty old tosser asked me to check his wad. There's fuck all in it. S'pose he'll want to make a stonking great withdrawal now. Thinks I won't notice.'

Miles hit the floor before he knew what was happening. He turned around to see Kulvinder standing over him, fists clenched. He started crawling away through the crowd and felt a kick in his stomach. It lifted him off the ground and he couldn't breathe. He heard shouting, heard feet scuffling on the smooth marble floor, knew he had to get away.

What he had done was terrible, almost evil. No, it really was evil. He'd never done anything like it before in his entire life.

As he managed to climb to his feet, his head ringing and his stomach burning with pain, he realised there was no one else to blame. It was his fault. It was all his fault and he had feelings. Lots of feelings. He felt small and scared, he wanted his mum. He actually wanted his mum to pick him up and take him away. He had never felt that before. It was terrible, worse than any nightmare he had ever had. He had to leave, he knew that, just had to get out.

He managed to fight his way through the crowd. All around him, people were shouting and jostling. He felt someone's hand on his collar and dropped to the floor again, expecting a blow to the back of the head. The hand lost its grip and he scrabbled through a jungle of feet.

Again he stood up and, clutching his stomach, ran. The crowds parted before him. He could feel tears streaming down his face.

He had been bad, he wanted someone to understand that, and there was no one. He was alone with nowhere to go, nothing to do. Behind him lay chaos of his own making; in front of him the bright street.

He ran along Queensway towards the park, past the Arab shops, the multinational crowds, the happy people with lives and feelings. He hadn't noticed them at all when he'd walked in the other direction with Kulvinder not half an hour earlier.

He cried as he ran, cried out loud, sobbing out his distress. There was no coherent thought in his head. He wasn't crying with one part of his brain and thinking things with another. His whole being was alive with grief.

He wasn't any different, he was the same as everyone else, he was human. It hurt and it wasn't tidy.

The park was big and open and just what Miles needed. Without thinking he turned east, running along the northern flank towards Oxford Street.

After a long time running, his stomach hurt a little less, his vision became clearer and his breathing eased. He didn't stop but took a quick glance behind him to see if anyone was following. There was no one. The path behind him was empty.

This brought a fresh wail of despair. No one cared enough even to chase him, and why should they? Look what he had done: destroyed his life's work, alienated the only man who had ever made an effort to be friends with him. Used his skill to cause chaos, not order.

He soon found himself running along Oxford Street. It was packed with milling shoppers and tourists. They made him feel alone.

He turned off Oxford Street and ran through side streets he didn't really know. It was only as he ran into Bryanston Square that he realised what he was doing. He had run to the house where Mario had said he was staying. There was nowhere else to go.

Chapter Eighteen

'Gasty, me old mate, we've got a problem,' said Donald Cooper as soon as he had settled in his seat. Gaston Bell felt uncomfortable in his company as usual. He was doing some consultancy work at the Institute of Directors, his presence there very public. However unobservant the doormen were, Donald Cooper stood out rather in the corporate coming and going in the lobby. He was so big for a start, you couldn't help but see him, and his face had threat written all over it. He was also wearing his favourite garb, a camouflage battledress jacket and trousers tucked into large black boots.

'What seems to be the problem, Mr Cooper?'

Donald looked around to see if anyone was close enough to hear him. 'Is this place bugged?'

'I don't believe it is.'

'I see, I just wondered why you were being so bloody paranoid. I'm not a wanted criminal or anything.'

'It's not paranoia, Donald, I am just being careful. As you should be.'

'Don't worry about me. Care's my middle name, Brigadier. Now, listen. We've got the site, we've got the crane, what we haven't got is the crane operator. Phil Pilcher was always an outside bet – bit of a wet blanket under fire, if I recall. I'd do it, but then I'd probably land the container on someone's head which would be just a little counter-productive. I've tried all my contacts but I've come up empty-handed. Everyone seems to be scared.'

'Well, I have to admit my circle of acquaintance doesn't include a great many crane operators, Donald.'

'Nah, didn't think it would.'

'I can ask my man Redford. He had a lot more to do with the Royal Engineers than you or me. One moment, please.'

Gaston Bell picked up his mobile and pressed a key.

'Redford,' he said into the handset and looked up at Donald Cooper's nonplussed reaction. 'Voice-activated,' he explained. Cooper nodded and smirked.

'Ah, Redford. Quick question – any old contacts in the crane-operating business? It's a fifty-ton heavy lifting job. Thought you might know someone from the Royal Engineers . . .'

Gaston wrote down a name and number on a sheet of Directors' Institute headed paper and slid it across the desk to Donald.

'Thank you, Redford. I'll need to go to the City at about three-thirty. I'll ring you then.'

He closed the phone and looked up triumphantly. 'Don't say I never help you.'

'How do we know he's kosher?' asked Donald after studying the name.

'We don't. You need to check him out. But if you want someone to operate your crane, I dare say he's about the best you're going to get.'

Chapter Nineteen

As Miles checked the number on the door of the house in Bryanston Square, Anna Benz pulled up in her little black car. He noticed she actually skidded to a halt, travelling far too fast for a narrow residential street. He also noticed she revved the engine when she stopped, sitting in the driver's seat with the door open. She seemed to be listening to it. It was spewing out toxic fumes from the exhaust without even moving, using up fossil fuel for no reason whatsoever. What possible benefit could she get from hearing the engine of a car revving away? It was stupid and wasteful. Maybe he was angry about it, he wasn't sure.

As Miles approached she saw him, but instead of being embarrassed and turning the engine off, as he'd expected, merely smiled a little and carried on.

'Is that entirely necessary?' he asked over the din.

'Are you the man from the château?' she asked flatly.

'Yes, Miles Morris. I was just . . .'

'I am Anna. Are you here to see Mario?'

'Yes, well, I think I am, but listen . . .'

'Do not worry. I am okay. I am just checking the functioning of the turbo injection. There seems to be a sluggish point in the cycle. It may need some attention. I noticed a slight lag between the speeds of one hundred and ten to one hundred and twenty miles per hour. Not a good sign.'

'I beg your pardon,' said Miles with a laugh. 'Have you really been driving at those speeds?'

'Oh, *ja*,' said Anna, without pride or embarrassment. 'Not constantly, of course, the driving in this country is very much slower than I am used to. Many people travel in the fast lane at speeds no greater than eighty miles an hour.'

'For your information,' said Miles, relieved that she had finally turned the engine off, 'the speed limit in this country is seventy.'

'*Ja*, I know this.'

'Didn't you get stopped? Didn't you get a ticket? Didn't one of those cameras flash you?'

'Nobody attempted to stop me, merely to slow me down which was very frustrating,' said Anna, getting out of the car. Much to his relief, she stood a little shorter than he.

'I can't believe it,' said Miles. 'It's so destructive. You presumably want to die, is that why you're one of Mario's clients?'

'I have no wish to die, I merely receive great comfort from driving very fast in my cars.'

'Your cars,' repeated Miles. 'You've got more than one!'

'I have five.'

'What on earth for? Five cars just for you?'

'Is it a crime?' said Anna, opening the rear hatch of the car and pulling a bag from inside.

'It should be. It's a ridiculous waste of resources.'

'You are an eco-warrior?' Anna asked, looking at him with hooded brown eyes. Miles couldn't tell if she was making fun of him or just asking a simple question.

'No, I am not an eco-warrior. Or a Luddite come to that.'

'I do not know what a Luddite is.'

'Ned Ludd, bit of a retrograde anti-technology activist in the eighteenth century, went around busting looms.'

'How very strange.'

'That's what I mean, I'm not like that. I work in a high-tech field but I try to live a sensible, productive life. I thought Germans were supposed to be very eco-friendly?'

'We are. I also love cars.'

'I just do not understand that. How can you?'

'I always have. I design them.'

'I knew you worked for a car manufacturer, Mario told me, but I didn't know you actually designed cars.'

'Yes, that is what I do. I work for Volkswagen in Germany.'

Miles looked at the car she had just got out of. It was black and had four wheels. That was as much as he knew.

'Is this a Volkswagen? You really don't know?' she said with a smile that was more alluring than he'd expected.

'No, I don't know anything about them. I make a point of it.'

'You are a very interesting man. I have never met anyone like you before.'

'I'm not surprised. You just drive past people like me in your little metal boxes and make our lives a misery.'

'You are very angry at the moment.'

'Well, I'm always fairly angry about cars, but most of the time I don't feel anything.'

'I don't understand?'

'I don't have any feelings. Never have done. That's why I'm seeing Mario.'

'Everyone has feelings.'

'I don't.'

'You do, you just don't know you are having them. You are angry about cars, that is a feeling.'

'That's a logical argument.'

'No, it's a feeling. I know about feelings. I try not to have them, which is why I sleep all the time. And drive. When I am sleeping or driving, I don't have feelings so much and I can survive. That is why I am seeing Mario, because I cannot work efficiently any more because I am having too many feelings.'

'This really is crazy then. Us being here. We're both successful people who understand ourselves yet we're going to see this weird one-armed man who says he's going to cure us. It doesn't make sense. I mean, you don't need to do this, do you? It's stupid, isn't it?'

Miles noticed she wasn't listening. It was always the way. Unless he actually paid people to listen, they always seemed to switch off as soon as he opened his mouth.

They walked up to the front door of the house together. It opened before he could ring the bell. A tall blonde woman with a strip of silver tape stuck over her mouth stood on the threshold. She was wearing a very thin night-shirt and Miles found it distracting that he could see her breasts so clearly through the cloth. He looked at her face, she muttered something beneath the tape. Anna pushed past him gently.

'Hello, I am Anna,' she said as she walked inside. Typical German, thought Miles as he followed her.

He entered the spacious entrance hall and followed the woman with the taped up mouth into a big front room. It looked like something in a feature in a home-decorating magazine: a beautiful space, high-ceilinged and with three huge sofas positioned around a massive Victorian fireplace. Philippe was sitting at the table in front of what Miles recognised to be an iMac DV, a computer ready fitted out to be capable of editing video tape. A camera was plugged into the side of the computer. Mario seemed to be asleep on another sofa but his eyes opened and he smiled as he saw them enter.

'Come in, come in,' he said, not stirring from his relaxed position. 'Make yourselves at home.'

'I need sleep,' said Anna. She flopped down on the only empty sofa and immediately curled up into a ball.

'Would you like some tea?' asked Mario. 'We are in England after all, we had better drink tea.'

'Yeah, okay,' said Miles, feeling uncomfortable and wishing he could just be alone with Mario.

'Go and make some tea, Paula,' said Mario. The woman nodded and left the room, clearly talking away under the tape. Miles stared at her as she left. He could see her ass through the thin nightshirt. She had lovely legs. The tape on her mouth aroused him unexpectedly.

'That's Paula,' said Mario when she had left. 'A client of mine.'

'Why's her mouth taped up?'

'Because she is extremely boring to listen to. It may seem a little harsh, but for the time being it's the only way we can work as a group.'

'So, is she going to do the robbery with us?'

'The exercise, yes, she is. I take it you have had second thoughts?'

'I haven't had any first thoughts, really. I do think it's a bit crazy, though.'

'Then why are you here?'

'I don't know,' said Miles, slightly accusingly. 'Sorry, that didn't come out right. I really don't know. I'm running on empty.'

'I see. Well, you're here now and we have quite a team. Not exactly the one I would have liked, but buggers can't be choosers.'

'It's beggars.'

'Yes, precisely,' said Mario, without paying heed. 'This is all so exciting. Obviously I wanted you as originally it was your idea, although it has grown organically since your first suggestion. As soon as we came up with this scheme I knew I could help Paula with it, too. She has been a client for some time but I have made no progress with her whatsoever. A very depressing admission to make. So, Miles, sit down, relax. Philippe is just getting a little presentation sorted out so we can see what the possibilities are. Don't say anything to Paula yet, she doesn't know what we're going to be doing.'

He sat on the arm of the sofa where Anna was lying. She seemed to be fast asleep.

'What's wrong with her?' he whispered.

'You don't need to speak softly, Anna is now deeply asleep. She is chronically depressed. She too is one of my rare failures. You could be my last hope, Miles.' Mario smiled, blinked and then looked away. 'Anna's work is suffering and she'll lose her job if she doesn't improve.'

'So, it's me, Anna and the woman with the taped up mouth?' asked Miles.

'Paula, yes.'

'Is that the entire team? Me and two women who are, well, a bit unbalanced.'

'It needs to be a small group. This isn't an exercise for ten or fifteen people. It's very exciting, though. I'm already formulating a paper on it, I'm due to give a lecture on my work in Zurich at the end of the month. Clearly I won't be able to go into too much detail about this exercise, but the theory is revolutionary.'

Miles stood up. He wanted to leave. He wanted to go home and get into bed and sleep. He wanted anything but this.

'You seem very tense, Miles?'

He sat down again, not noticing at first that Anna's feet were under him.

'Sorry,' he said to her sleeping face.

'Don't worry about her, just push her feet out of the way.'

Miles gently moved her feet and sat back on the sofa. They were very light, her ankles seemed frail and thin. He rested his head on the cushions and said, 'I am very tense. I wanted to be treated by you because I seem to be going off my rocker.'

He went silent for a moment, eyes shut, trying to formulate what was wrong.

'Everything's such a mess in my life, it's all got on top of me, I'm sinking in the mire. I can't keep it tidy any more. And now I'm surrounded by women who just wallow in their own mess, and I'm supposed to do some weird robbery with them which isn't really a robbery, and that's supposed to make me feel better? I don't want to do trauma therapy if it makes me feel like this – what's the point? Although, on the other hand, I did just think about my mum for the first time since I can remember, so I suppose it did bring up some feelings. But you didn't organise that particular trauma so it wasn't really anything to do with you . . .

'You see, what I really want to do is talk about my mum. I want to sit in a room with you and talk about why I'm so unhappy, if that's what I am. I want to talk about why I don't get on with women very well and why they make me angry. Maybe hit a cushion or something.'

Miles lay in silence for a while, feeling more relaxed, almost like he had at the château in France. He opened his eyes and lifted his head to see Mario. He was lying flat on the sofa, apparently asleep.

'He doesn't do talking therapy, Miles. It does not work,' said Philippe.

'But whatever it is we're doing here doesn't work either! It's ridiculous,' said Miles, more loudly than he intended.

'Then leave,' said Mario without hesitation. He spoke very softly, as if he were still sleeping but somehow able to continue a conversation. 'Why stay? Go back to your misery and your numbness. I am not making you stay.'

'Oh, please,' wailed Miles. 'You think if you tell me to leave I'll stay because what else have I got?'

'Yes, I think exactly that, Miles. I have no problem with thinking that. I don't play games, I am a WYSIWYG therapist. There is no subtext, this is it.'

'You say that, and I can see you there, but I don't know who you are.'

'I am Mario Lupo,' said Mario with a little shrug.

'Yeah, but that's an Italian name, and you're not Italian.'

'My mother was, although by the time she was pregnant with me she was living in Uganda. My father was North African, but he was actually a Greek born in America, although his father was Central African, from Tanzania. So he was Greek African, I suppose. My mother's father was German, his father was Turkish. I was born in Norway when my mother fled General Idi Amin's military coup. However, I was brought up in Copenhagen until I was eight, then in America until I was thirteen. I lived in Argentina for two years, then France for five. I have never been to Bhutan, New Zealand's South Island, many of the satellite nations of the ex-Soviet Union, China or North Korea.'

Mario stopped talking and looked at Miles.

'What d'you mean, you've never been to those countries? You mean, you've been everywhere else?'

'Yes.'

'I don't believe you. No one's done that. There are too many places.'

'Oh, I haven't been everywhere on earth, just every country, sometimes only for a few days. I spent my formative years travelling,' said Mario. 'I am thirty-seven years old. I live in Geneva and Alexandria, but also spend a lot of time in America. I visit Russia quite frequently. I don't know what else I can tell you.'

'Why do you go to all these places? It doesn't tell me who you are.'

'I am just someone, Miles. I am not special or particularly gifted. I am, I suppose, in some ways blessed in being able to find ways to help people. I have been very lucky and very successful, and I like the company of lucky and successful people like yourself. I know I can help you, but I have also been doing this for long enough not to worry about it. If you don't want to do it, it won't work. I have so many clients, I can't let it worry me.'

Miles put his head back on the sofa. All the way through their conversation Mario had not once opened his eyes or lifted his head so he could see Miles.

'Does that help you?' he asked finally. 'I have nothing to hide, Miles. I prize honesty above any other virtue and trust you will return that favour when we do the exercise. It is vital there is no subtext between us.'

'I just don't understand what we're supposed to be doing? I know we're going to rob this train thing, but then I think, why? This isn't going to help. This is just a way for you to get me to steal money for you. You're just a crook who can't do your own robberies because of a disabled arm. So you get other people to do it for you.'

'It will help you more than you can possibly know. I am not making outrageous claims here, that is a simple fact.'

Paula walked back into the room carrying a large tray piled high with tea and cakes, pastries and toast.

'Paula is a magnificent hostess,' said Mario. 'She will give you anything you want. She has no boundaries, Miles. Money, trust, sex, more information than you will ever need about her life. I suggest you preserve your rather overly developed boundaries in her presence. Paula overspills in all directions and stains peoples lives.'

Miles cast a glance at her as she poured the tea. She looked around and nodded, raising her eyebrows. Clearly she agreed with Mario and took no offence.

It annoyed Miles that she was going along with this absurd game. She looked almost proud to be humiliated by the tape across her face. Everything seemed to annoy him. Nothing was pleasurable or relaxing, especially being in this room full of slightly odd people. He felt his neck twitch. It was a disturbing feeling, beyond his control. If he didn't have so much energy, he might be numb. But he couldn't sit still any more, everything was increasingly uncomfortable, itchy, awkward, distasteful. It really had to stop.

'I've gone mad, haven't I?' he said.

'Not quite, not yet, but you will soon if you don't help yourself.'

Chapter Twenty

Chief Inspector McKay from the National Criminal Intelligence Service entered the briefing room on the eighth floor of New Scotland Yard. He was carrying a thick dossier of papers under one arm and holding a cup of scalding tea with his free hand. Entering through the door, he spilled tea on his hand. Just what he needed. To enter a room packed with so many competitors while cursing was never a good move.

'You all right, sir?' asked a face he recognised. Couldn't put a name to it immediately but it was someone from Europol he'd met in Brussels the previous year.

'Yeah, fine, thanks. Just spilt a bit of this filthy tea.'

'Best thing to do with it probably, sir,' said the officer kindly.

McKay sat down and faced sixteen officers from the South East Regional Crime Squad. Sitting next to him behind the table were officers from the Special Branch, his own unit, the Met Special Branch and the Special Operations Unit. He wasn't happy about this, considering the case to be his own. His team were working on it and anyone else's involvement was bound to gum up the works as usual. He cleared his throat, the room fell silent.

'Gentlemen, as you are all no doubt aware, as of the fifth of next month the pound is no longer a valid currency.'

'Shame!' said Detective Inspector Willis who was sitting in the front row, red-faced and sweating freely. Willis fitted the remit for a hard slog copper. He had many good arrests under his belt, but as was often the case with this sort of officer, his personal life didn't stand close inspection.

'Yes, well, it's not our job to have opinions, is it, Willis?' said McKay with a patronising grin. 'However, the fact we are introducing a new currency doesn't mean certain criminal elements will lose interest in thieving. And in fact some information of a rather alarming nature has just reached us.'

He turned and glanced at the officer from Special Branch. The man was giving nothing away. Talk about co-operation.

'On the fifth the Bank of England is shipping all the sterling currency that's sloshing about in European banks back to this country. Now, officially, by the time it gets here, it's worthless paper. The bank is just going to pellet it and dump it in an Essex landfill site. However, just to make our lives a little bit more complicated, the currency isn't officially null and void until the end of trading that day, which will be at six in the evening. The train is due to leave France at eleven hundred hours in the morning. It is due to arrive this side of the Eurotunnel at eleven-twenty-eight, when it becomes our responsibility. What could that tell us, gentlemen?'

'Bit of a window for some well-organised types, sir?' said Detective Inspector Barber who was sitting next to Willis, well-groomed and obviously heading for higher things.

'Indeed it does leave what could best be described as a whole Versailles of windows well and truly open,' said McKay, feeling rather proud of his analogy. 'Now the Chief is having a word with the Home Secretary about this because it seems to be asking for trouble.'

'Begging for a blagging you could say, sir,' chipped in Willis.

'But of course there's a lot of political sensitivity around the issue of which we are all well aware. H.M. Government doesn't want undue attention brought to this final shipment which could be seen as highly symbolic.

'So we have to tread very lightly. We know it would have to be a very big job so there'll be lot of people involved. Let's get our ears to the ground and find out what's cooking. Something is, I can feel it in my bones. I mean, who amongst our friends in crime is going to be able to resist the temptation of an unmarked container holding upwards of three billion pounds. This one's just too big to miss.'

Detective Inspector Willis was out of the building and in his unmarked car within minutes. When he first read in the papers about the end of the pound, he knew bad boys somewhere would try and make a few quid out of it. Except there wouldn't be any quids any more.

'Who on earth is going to do this job then?' said Willis, more to himself than to Reynolds. 'I mean, three billion quid, it's not going to be a couple of geezers in a Ford Escort.'

'No sir,' said Constable Reynolds, an officer seconded from the Diplomatic Protection Squad. Reynolds was licensed to carry firearms and had been working with Willis as they followed a rather vicious Yardie. It was dull and nothing was happening. The sterling job was a lot more interesting.

'Well, we've got to start somewhere. Let's go to the pub.'

'Which particular pub is that then, sir?' asked Reynolds as they waited at some traffic lights.

'Let me think. What about the Dragon, out at Brentford? There's some tasty bad boys hang around there of an afternoon, we could start there.'

'Brentford it is, sir,' said Reynolds as they pulled away.

Chapter Twenty-One

'We are going to watch a video which Philippe has put together. Okay, everybody?' Mario had slept for a short while, comforted by the small electronic sounds Philippe had been making with his camera equipment.

No one said anything. Mario looked around. Miles was sitting in an odd hunched position with his fists tightly bunched. He was staring accusingly at Mario. Beside him Anna was slowly coming round, looking groggy and unfocused. Paula was sitting directly in front of the TV screen, her mouth still taped.

Philippe plugged the camera into the side of the large flat-screen TV that stood in the ornate marble fireplace.

Mario had been looking forward to seeing what Philippe had come up with. He had often dreamed of presenting his own television series about the human mind and how it responded to trauma, supporting his belief that the brain was pre-wired to survive and that, if prodded, this preordained program would kick in with highly beneficial side effects.

The picture on the screen showed Philippe standing in a railway siding. The camera work was a bit wobbly but he looked good, the wind blowing through his thick mop of dark hair.

'This is the entrance to the Eurotunnel,' he said to camera. 'Fifty-two kilometres in length, not one tunnel but three. Two rail links and one service tunnel.'

The picture on the screen showed a diagram of the layout of

the tunnel, the two larger bores flanking the smaller one. Above the tunnels was a pictorial representation of layers of rock and earth and then the sea.

'Is that what I came through?' asked Anna.

'Of course it is. How many Eurotunnels d'you think there are?' sniped Miles.

'Please, just watch, we can discuss it afterwards,' said Mario. These two were going to be trouble if he didn't keep them apart. Something had obviously already happened between them. Philippe might have to intervene.

The Frenchman appeared on the screen again.

'The service tunnel is just over four metres wide and is used by specially designed service vehicles which are wire-guided. The driver does not have to steer. Sensors on the underside of the vehicle control the steering. So the floor surface of this tunnel is very smooth, with no rail tracks.'

The picture changed back to the diagram of the tunnel. It didn't look too bad considering they had merely pointed the camera at a diagram they had found in a magazine. Philippe's voice could still be heard although the sound quality was a little odd.

'The service tunnel is linked to the rail tunnel by cross passages ever three hundred and seventy-five metres. There are also piston relief ducts every two hundred metres to allow the air the trains force through the tunnel to escape.'

This time the picture changed to a shot of a large railway wagon.

Philippe walked along the side of the wagon as he spoke.

'In two weeks' time, a train will pass through the tunnel carrying a very special consignment.'

The picture cut to a close up of Philippe.

'An estimated three billion pounds in used sterling bank notes.'

Now he was standing in front of the Bank of England in the City of London, looking like a tourist.

'With the final, long-awaited introduction of the Euro to the British economy, the Bank of England is removing all sterling currency from the European banks.'

The picture changed again, this time to Philippe standing in a field.

'Now this is a good shot,' said Mario. 'I did this myself.'

As Philippe spoke, the camera slowly moved around, revealing that they were standing on a wind-blown hill overlooking the tunnel complex.

'This is where the train we are interested in will appear, the Folkestone end of the Eurotunnel. There is a huge high-security complex here. A massive car loading area, hundreds of square metres of railway sidings. Over there, beside the two main rail tunnels, just behind the white buildings, is the service tunnel entrance. It is situated behind twenty-foot-high security fencing which is then encircled by the security perimeter fencing of the whole complex. So, how on earth do you get in?'

The picture changed to Philippe standing outside the tunnel, only it looked a little different here, more open, set in a large flat area of land.

'This is the French side of the tunnel at Sangatte. It is here we have to get you on to the container transportation service. This uses the same tunnels as all other traffic, only the containers are loaded by a large crane at the yard over there.'

Philippe pointed away to his right. A rather wobbly camera shot followed in which Mario tried to zoom in on the site. All that could be seen was a blur of movement and the vaguest impression of a large yellow container crane.

'You three will have to be concealed within a container. Once inside the tunnel, it's a simple job. You create a serious chemical leak which will be picked up by the tunnel's sensors. The train is then automatically brought to a halt so that the staff are near an escape route should they need one. You then open the container, remove the requisite amount of money and leave by one of the safety doors between the train tunnel and the service tunnel. Then you escape by bicycle.'

The TV screen went black. Everyone sat in silence.

'Wow!' said Miles eventually.

'You like it?' asked Mario.

'Wow!' he repeated. 'I don't know what I think. It's madder than I'd ever have dreamed.'

'Good, that's good. What about you, Paula? Do you like the idea?'

She made garbled noises and nodded her head. Mario smiled and looked at Anna whose hooded eyes hid her reaction.

'Anna?'

'I don't want to steal anything. I just want to go back to sleep.'

'This is the beauty of what we're doing,' said Mario, ignoring her comment. 'The sheer exquisite beauty of the project is that we are not stealing anything of value. We are merely moving thousands, maybe hundreds of thousands, of pieces of paper from one place to another. It is no longer money. The fact that this shipment is happening now is very Jungian. Even though I don't hold with all of his writings, it's hard not to think of him. It is synchronistic.' Mario made great play of this word while looking at them one by one.

'What do we do with it once we've got it?' asked Miles. Mario noticed Anna look at him, her eyes watchful. Yes, this was certainly going to be a problem, thought Mario.

'We bring it back here and then we dispose of it. After all, it's only paper. Worth nothing. Or we could even return it in a safe way. That is a minor issue. The really difficult part is managing to get it. That is going to be close to impossible, and that is the challenge. But a still bigger challenge is this . . . and this is for your particular attention, Paula. No one can ever, ever speak about what they have done. No matter what, no matter to whom. The whole exercise will lose its value instantly if you reveal anything. This applies on every level, from legal to psychological. Do you all understand?'

Anna looked at Miles who nodded silently. She then turned to Mario. What was she going to do? Run? Stay? He couldn't be sure.

She nodded. Excellent.

'Paula?' said Mario. Philippe stood up and ripped the tape off her mouth with what looked like a little more force that was necessary.

She was smiling, she was very pretty. She said nothing, just nodded. Mario breathed a sigh of relief. He would live to fight another day.

Chapter Twenty-Two

A group of bricklayers watched in fascination as a huge eight-wheeled heavy lifting crane crept its way on to the site. The road outside was only just wide enough for the enormous vehicle to make the turn. The man-height tyres bit their way into the soft clay, some sliding a little as it made its cumbersome way forward.

'Steady, Abrahams, steady!' shouted Donald over the roar of the crane's massive diesel engine. 'Don't get the damn' thing stuck.'

He watched the young driver carefully. This was the man Gaston Bell had procured. Seemed a decent enough chap, good record in the Army but been a drifter ever since. He didn't ask too many questions, seemed to see the whole thing merely as a job that needed doing. A very well-paid job. He was getting forty thousand pounds for a couple of days work.

Donald had parked his Cherokee on the only bit of hard standing on the site.

'Don't want to get it dirty, do I?' he had said to Paddy Shawcross, Minty's elder brother. Paddy Shawcross looked anxious. There was absolutely no call for a crane this size on a building site where the tallest thing would be the roof apex of a three-bedroomed semi.

'I'm going to get so much shit from the planning authorities,' he complained as the mountainous frame of Donald Cooper tramped through the sticky mud towards him.

'Don't worry about it, Paddy old chap,' he shouted as the crane's engines roared again. 'We'll have decamped long before you know it. Minty'll sort you out. And if any planning people start hassling us while we're here, well, I'll bury them, basically.'

Cooper smiled down at the little red-haired man beside him. 'I'll ethnically cleanse them, Paddy. You know I'm not joking, don't you?'

That was the last time Paddy Shawcross complained. Cooper's reputation was fearful.

The crane finally halted and its engine died. Abrahams climbed out of the cab and jumped down. As he landed, a shower of wet mud sprayed up from his boots, splattering Donald Cooper's trousers.

'You messy bastard!'

'Sorry, sir. Fucking muddy, isn't it?' said a smiling Abrahams.

'It's a tosser's job, building,' growled Donald, walking towards the rail track. He was joined by Harris and Pickering, both carrying cameras.

A train appeared, its rumble steadily mounting until it roared past them at speed. Donald looked at it, nonplussed.

'What the hell was that?'

He scowled at his colleagues, angry because he didn't understand. 'That wasn't a freight train, that was a train full of Frog tourists if I'm not very much mistaken.'

'Yeah, that was the Eurostar,' said Harris. 'Well fast.'

'What's the point of getting a crane if the money's in one of those? Surely we just stop the blasted train, shoot a load of people and steal the bloody money? Gaston Bell's a fucking idiot.'

'Nah, keep calm, Donald. The freight jobs use this line too,' said Harris. 'Here, Paddy,' he called to the chain-smoking builder. 'You get freight trains past here, don't you?'

'Yeah, all the time,' he said. 'Pity the poor bastards buying these houses. The trains come through at all hours.'

'These are houses for tossers,' said Donald as though it was obvious. He looked back at the site. 'Right, we've got to get some serious hardcore down here, chaps. There's no way we can get a flat liner through without getting it seriously bogged.'

His stubby finger pointed to a hedgerow originally planted in the sixteen hundreds. 'And we'll have to rip that hedge right out.'

Chapter Twenty-Three

Miles was hunched over the large oak dining table in the front room of the house in Bryanston Square. Spread out on the table was a huge pile of maps and plans, train timetables and copies of international shipping orders.

'Where the hell did you get all this?' he asked.

'It's all in the public domain. No crime has been committed to supply you with this information.'

Philippe leant over the table and looked at him. 'The shipment is due to arrive at the French side just after ten. That is, if it isn't hit beforehand.'

'Is that possible?' asked Anna who was studying the plan of the tunnel, clearly fascinated by it.

'There is a lot of interest, that is certain,' said Philippe. 'We cannot be sure we will be the only party taking an interest.'

'Philippe has very good contacts,' said Mario. 'He knows what is going on.'

'There don't appear to be any security cameras,' said Miles. 'That seems very odd.'

'The service tunnel is just that, fifty-two kilometres of narrow tunnel only intermittently lit. It is only there to service the main tunnels and act as an emergency escape route in the event of a disaster. There are communications systems all the way along it and very sophisticated safety systems. But the tunnel was not built with internal security in mind. Animal transfer was, however, seen as a problem and you will pass over a high-voltage electric plate set into the floor as you approach the UK mainland.'

'Sounds a bit dangerous,' said Miles.

'If you tread on it in bare feet you will die instantly, but it is perfectly safe to ride over. Towards the tunnel entrance there are some security cameras but these we know how to deal with.'

'I still don't feel comfortable. I mean, how do you know all this?' asked Miles.

'Inside information,' said Philippe.

'What does that mean?' asked Anna. She smiled at Miles as she spoke.

'It means he used to work there. He knows the place like the back of his hands,' said Mario.

'I would rather you had not told them that,' Philippe objected.

'Clarity and honesty are everything in this exercise.'

'Okay, so I used to work there,' said Philippe glumly. 'I know how it works. Now listen. Towards the tunnel entrance to either side there are many security cameras including infra-red imagers. These are connected by fibre-optic cable running the entire length of the tunnel. This is also the main data transmission link between the control centres on either side.'

'Fibre optics,' said Miles. 'So there are booster boxes along the way?'

'There is a signal-boosting box roughly four hundred metres from the UK sump, which is about a third of the way through the tunnel from the English side.' Philippe was holding a large folder. He turned a few pages and studied its contents. 'Should be close to a connection tunnel which is, I believe, number 1276.'

Miles lifted the sheet they were looking at to reveal a wiring diagram beneath. His finger tapped the paper lightly. 'I see it. And is that an EP380?'

Again Philippe checked the sheet in front of him. 'I am not sure. What is an EP380?'

Miles held out his hands. 'Give me a look.' He took the weighty tome and started flicking through the pages. He soon spied the information he was searching for.

'Yes! An EP380 is a fibre optic input device. It's there so that engineers can upload or download data when they are in the tunnel. It's like a small computer in its own right, it can take multiple signals. Basically that means other inputs can be fed into it. I need to see what type it is, see if I can hack it.'

'What is your plan, Miles?' asked Anna.

'I can hack it using software and send fresh signals to both the French and English sides which will disrupt the security overrides at both ends and throw them into confusion. I'll need a laptop, a small one, a Sony Vaio would do. I can also get into the tunnel's mainframe. The computer's here.' He pointed to the central command and control room at the Folkestone side of the tunnel. 'That way we can control the tunnel completely for a certain time. We can open and close doors, stop trains, make them run, anything.'

'How long would that take?' asked Philippe.

Miles pondered. 'A long time. At least fifty hours to work through the code, if we can get it.'

'We can get it.'

'And once in the tunnel,' said Mario, 'would you need a lot of time to set it up?'

'No, it would only take a few seconds, as long as I can see what I'm doing. What's the lighting like? We might need torches.'

'That is a problem then,' said Philippe.

'Why's it a problem?' asked Miles, without looking up from the wiring manual he was studying.

'Because you won't be able to see your hands in front of your face.'

'Philippe, please,' said Mario wearily. 'Let's not jump ahead too far. They've all missed a few beats in the planning process.'

'Missed a few beats?' said Miles, now clearly concerned.

Mario stood back from the table, one hand held up in front of him. 'Please, let's take it one step at a time. We are not approaching the task in a very co-ordinated way. I don't want to interfere in any of the technical aspects, but you must approach the problems step by step.'

The group stood in silence for a moment.

'Well, what's the problem?' asked Miles. 'There are lights in the tunnel, aren't there?'

Again a silence. Mario slowly sat down in his chair again.

'What!' asked Miles. There was silence. Mario felt the tension engulf the room.

'We have to blow the lights,' said Philippe finally. 'The tunnel will be in utter darkness. It is the only way of making sure you are never seen. There could be service staff, there could be firemen, anyone could be in the service tunnel. This we cannot predict. Total darkness is the only way we can be sure that the element of surprise is on your side and you avoid the risk of capture.'

Mario looked at his little group. This was far and away the hardest exercise he had ever undertaken. It was terrifying and exhilarating at the same time. He was also convinced it would never work.

Chapter Twenty-Four

———— >⊷⊶⊷< ————

Phil Pilcher was sitting in the King's Head in Gateshead Road, Brentford. He did so every day after he knocked off the early shift at the Meyer Parry scrapyard around the corner.

The pub was at the end of a cul-de-sac, a peculiar position because the entire residential area it once served had long since disappeared. Ravaged by small industrial development and cut off by the M4 flyover, it was now only patronised by an odd mixture of local workers and some vaguely threatening criminal types. Heavy-built men who were happy to park their overly expensive sports cars outside amongst the rubbish and old tyres that littered the street.

Phil Pilcher didn't notice the unmarked red Sierra pull up outside, didn't notice the corpulent figure of Detective Inspector Willis climb out awkwardly and head for the door. He didn't notice the uniformed officer who emerged from the driver's seat and started talking into a mobile phone.

He was the only patron in the establishment not to notice this. Everyone else who had dropped in to have a quiet pint was very well aware of the intrusion.

Willis moved through the pub, ignoring the many eyes that were on him. It was in the middle of his patch. He had worked the West London suburbs for many years and knew where the big-time villains hung out. The King's Head was a regular haunt.

Willis put his massive hands on the bar and ordered a pint.

'Not on duty,' he lied to the frail-looking barman. 'Is Piggy Greenfield about?'

'No, sir,' said the barman, giving away his Irish background. 'I think you could find him pretty easily, though. C wing in the Scrubs.'

'Gone down, has he? Well, well. Good for Piggy. So he's not up to any mischief then.'

'No, sir.'

'What about Hank Pilgrim?' said Willis, emphasising the grim part of the name.

'I'm here,' said a voice from his right. Willis glanced along the bar, and sure enough, older, thinner and more ravaged, there was the face of an old adversary.

'How's it going then, Hank?'

'Straight and narrow,' he said.

'Where you working?'

'Meyer Parry, round the back.'

'What's that then?'

'Scrap.'

'Been reduced to nicking motors then, Hank?' said Willis. He took a huge swig of his beer and wiped his full lips on the sleeve of his jacket.

'It's legit business, Willis. I'm just on the weighbridge. It's called a job.'

'A job, is it?' he laughed. 'Well, you know plenty about them, my son.'

Willis moved closer to Hank. He leant forward on the bar, the two men staring at the optics hanging in front of the mirror.

'You see, there's a very big job brewing somewhere. Wondered if you'd heard anything?'

'No, I ain't.'

'Right. Of course, quite understand. Upright citizen like you. But you know how it is, Hank. Officers start checking up on what's going into a scrapyard and all sorts comes to light.'

'I tell you, I'm out of that game now.'

'Yeah, but you know . . .'

'Look, ask him over there,' said Hank. He jerked his thumb towards an individual Willis had never seen before.

'Who's he then?'

'Phil Pilcher. He's a crane operator at the yard.'

'And why should I ask him, Hank?'

'So as you stop hassling me,' said the other man, as though it was obvious.

'Yeah, but there's something else, isn't there, Hank, you old lag?' Willis gently pushed a crumpled ten-pound note towards him. Hank's hand shot out and took it without hesitation.

'Some posh bastard come to see him last week.'

'A posh bastard?'

'Yeah, big geezer with a moustache, all dressed up in Army clobber.'

'Soldier then?'

'Nah. Fancied himself as one more like.'

Willis walked away from Hank without another word. The old lag was well past his sell-by-date, had spent the best part of his life banged up. There was a time when Willis would have been very wary in his company, but there was no bite to him any more.

Willis walked up to the table where Phil Pilcher was sitting.

'Excuse me, sir, my name's Detective Inspector Willis. Can I have a word in your shell-like?'

Phil Pilcher spilt a little of his pint as he put the glass down.

'No need to be nervous, sir. Unless you've got something to hide, of course.' Willis smiled as he pulled out a stool and sat down at the table.

'What d'you want?' asked the tidy-looking man.

'Just a routine enquiry, sir. Nothing to worry about. Been having a chat with your colleague over there, Mr Pilgrim.' Again he made much of the 'grim'. 'He says you might know a thing or two.'

'What about?'

'Well, there's a bit of trouble brewing. Seeing as you work in the yard, thought you might know something.'

'Look, I'm just doing my job. If this is something to do with my brother, I don't know anything about it.'

'Your brother? Bloody hell, of course! You're Mickey Pilcher's brother, aren't you?'

'Worse luck.'

'He's a bad lad. Where is he now?'

'No one knows. I haven't seen him for months.'

'Were you in the services too then, Phil?'

'Yeah. Royal Engineers.'

'S'that right? Leave like your brother, did you?'

'No. I left when my time was up.'

'No dishonourable discharge for you then?'

'No.'

'Don't suppose you liked what your little brother got up to, did you, Phil?'

' 'Course not.'

'So if you knew anything . . .' Willis took a final slug from his near-empty mug, looking at Pilcher all the time '. . . you'd tell me, wouldn't you?'

'Look, I don't know anything, all right? I really don't.'

'No, 'course not. I was just wondering if that was Mickey who visited you last week?'

'Bloody hell! Pilgrim tell you that, did he?'

'Got my sources.'

'No, that was my brother's old commanding officer. Appeared out of the blue. I haven't seen him since I hit civvy street.'

'Who's that then?'

'Major Cooper. Total psychopath. Shot a load of Argy prisoners in the Falklands. It was all covered up.'

'Ugly business. And he invited you to a regimental dinner, did he?'

'He wanted me to drive a crane for him.'

'Did he now? Donald Cooper, you say,' said Willis, filing the name away carefully. 'And what did you say to him then, Phil?'

'I told him to sling his hook, mate. I'm not getting caught up in anything dodgy.'

'No, 'course not. Good man. So what did he want you to do with this crane then?'

'I don't know. Honestly, officer. He wasn't about to tell me if I wasn't going to do it.'

'No, don't suppose he would,' said Willis. He smiled, stood up and offered Pilcher his card.

'If you hear anything else, you give us a ring. All right, Phil? Good lad.'

Pilcher took the card and slipped it in the sleeve pocket of his overalls. Willis smiled and left the pub.

'Any luck, sir?' asked Reynolds as they got back into the Sierra.

'Ever been in a helicopter, Reynolds?'

'Not for a while, sir.'

'Good, 'cos I fucking hate them. You can look, I'll just sit there with my eyes shut.'

Chapter Twenty-Five

'No lights,' said Miles. He was having more and more feelings as the interminable process of planning this ludicrous escapade continued. The feelings were all bad.

'You have a problem with that?' asked Anna. Miles noticed that he had moved his hands to his lap and that they were gripping each other with enough force to stop the circulation. It was almost as if he was looking at someone else's body.

'Um, yeah,' he said. 'You could say I have a problem with that. We can't do it, it's impossible. How about that for a problem?'

'I don't think so,' said Anna. Paula seemed to be waffling about something, Miles couldn't make out what but she sounded enthusiastic. They were all completely insane. He'd turned to Anna for support but could see that she was smiling at him, going along with this stupid, illogical scheme.

'We're supposed to get out of the train halfway along the tunnel then ride twenty kilometres in utter darkness on push-bikes, which you and Paula don't do as a regular thing so you'll be hopeless. Of course we'll also be carrying half a billion pounds in used fifty-pound notes. Along a tunnel with a constant upward incline, at high speed. I thought I'd gone mad, but no, we're further along here, aren't we? In the land of total self-delusion.' Miles felt his stomach tighten, his hands jerking involuntarily. He was having a really big feeling. Anger. He was really angry with these stupid people. Hello, my name's

Miles and I'm stuck in a room with a bunch of mad people and I am fucked!'

His chair was suddenly broken. He didn't notice it happen but it was in pieces on the floor behind him. He noticed Anna dive off her chair away from him just before he was crushed by an enormous weight. When he managed to re-focus he found himself pinned to the floor by Philippe with what appeared to be a black hunting knife pressed dangerously close to his throat.

'Don't break things, Miles,' said Philippe with such quiet firmness that the threat was obviously real. 'I will kill you if you do that again.'

He stood up, using Miles' flattened body to steady himself, slipped the knife into its sheath on his belt and moved back to where he'd been sitting.

'Okay, so we have a problem with the lighting,' said Mario. From his crushed position Miles couldn't see Mario's face, but he seeming to be ignoring the little drama that had just been played out. 'This is not impossible to get around, but Miles has a very good point. You are not used to riding bikes like he is, and speed is of the utmost importance. We need to practise.'

Miles stood up and looked at the broken chair. It seemed he had done it again. He rubbed his back where Philippe had landed on him. Checked his pulse. Still normal.

'I used to ride a bike when I was a girl,' said Anna eventually. 'I liked it very much although they don't go very fast.'

Miles pulled another chair out from under the table and sat down. Philippe was also sitting again, looking at the plans. There didn't seem to be any residue of the extraordinary explosion of violence that had just occurred. Miles checked his pulse again. Still normal. It didn't add up. Maybe it had never happened. He glanced over his shoulder and there was the broken chair.

'I went out with a professional cyclist last year, Vincent Benveniste. He wore the yellow jersey in the Tour de France. I met him in Cannes when I was there with Monica while Willy was promoting the film before he killed himself. It was the film I was in – I gave you a tape didn't I, Mario? I was on the cover of the video in a bikini, and this bloke said he used that picture to masturbate to all the time, so we got talking. And d'you know what they do, professional cyclists? They put lumps of steak down their shorts, between their legs, because all the friction caused by those great big thighs turning the pedals makes them wear out their ball sacs, apparently. The only way they can stop that happening is by using the steak. So I said, "What do you do with the steak after a day's racing?" And he . . .'

Without hesitation, Philippe unrolled a new strip of tape and stuck it over her mouth. The rest of the story went unheard by the group. Miles stood up and started picking up the pieces of chair one by one and put them in the beautiful Adam fireplace.

'I'm sorry about that, I'll replace it. Sorry, Philippe. I won't break anything again. It's all my fault, I'm hopeless, stupid. Although actually I'm quite happy now because I definitely had a feeling then. A bad feeling – anger, I suppose – but I felt it. That's good, isn't it?'

Miles rattled off his speech with little outward emotion, standing in front of the group with his head slightly bowed. Then he realised something else. He somehow felt comfortable with these people, even the hugely dangerous Philippe.

'That is very good, Miles. We're all moving on,' said Mario. 'I can feel the power of this exercise already taking effect.' He glanced at Paula who still seemed to be talking away quite happily. 'And I predict its effects will reach even the most obstinate subject within the week. Okay, now what do we do?'

'We have to practise,' said Philippe. 'I have estimated what the money will weigh. We have to get three pedal bikes and fit them with large bags mounted on the frame.'

'Panniers,' said Miles.

'Strange, that is a French word which I chose not to use, thinking you would not know it,' said Philippe. 'With four panniers on each bike and a large rucksack on each rider, we have enough capacity to carry the requisite amount.'

Miles felt his stomach tighten again. What they were being asked to do was impossible. Completely. He cast a glance at Philippe who sat in his chair as relaxed as a hunting tiger. Miles didn't want to be pinned to the floor again, or have the hunting knife pressed to his throat in such a dramatic manner. Philippe came across as a fairly accomplished killer.

'I'm not breaking anything,' Miles assured him, holding both hands in the air. 'But I just want to say now that in my opinion the plan won't work. Even I will have difficulty doing this and I ride every day. The bikes will be unstable. If we ride in the dark it will be impossible to balance them. The money will slow us down so we'll end up pushing the bikes. Plus, if we ever reach the end of the tunnel, we then have to negotiate three rail tracks before we hit the car compound.' Miles scrabbled through the plans on the table and pulled out a large aerial photograph of the tunnel entrance.

'Look, we come out here. And we have to get to here.' He pointed to the large car park to the north. 'All the time we're making that crossing we will be in full view of the security cameras, the tunnel authorities on the ground and the police!' He shouted the last word then looked at Philippe quickly. 'I haven't broken anything, have I?'

Philippe smiled almost kindly. 'We will have to try it out,' he said. 'I will arrange it.'

Chapter Twenty-Six

Gaston Bell watched the distant horizon gently tilt as the glider turned. His right hand calmly gripping the joystick between his legs, his feet controlling the rudder with sure, smooth movements, Gaston was obviously a very experienced glider pilot. In his youth he had even set an altitude record which stood for three years. There was nothing he liked more than gliding. He'd learned to fly as a young man from his uncle who ran an airframe manufacturing company. It was a perfect day, plenty of big, thick cumuli-nimbus clouds above him. Spinning easily upwards, the only sound he could hear was the wind pushing against his wings and the faint creak of the frame as he was lifted higher.

He checked his watch, he'd been airborne for three-quarters of an hour, he'd have to get back.

But landing was a profoundly unattractive prospect. Here he was free, nothing around him except the air he floated on. He didn't even have his mobile with him and for a man like Gaston Bell, that was a radical move.

He was in radio contact with the Lasham control tower seven thousand feet below him, but didn't need to say anything other than ask for clearance to land.

He spun down. The airfield swung into view. There was the old runway, there was the entrance, and then he saw the long low building running along the western perimeter of the airfield: the glider clubhouse and bar. And there, clearly, next to his

BMW sports was an instantly recognisable form. Even from two thousand feet, Donald Cooper stood out like an ugly blemish on the otherwisc dazzlingly beautiful Hampshire countryside.

Gaston glanced at his watch again. He'd have to go down. Although he wasn't scared of Donald, and he knew he himself was too important for Cooper to target, the man was so unstable he might let his temper get the better of him at any time.

Gaston pushed the stick forward and felt the familiar sensation in his stomach as the glider started to dive.

Ten minutes later his wing tip touched the grass as he finally came to a halt. It had been a perfect landing and for those few minutes he'd been aware only of his immediate surroundings. The difficult acquisition of the metal-plating company in Wakefield, the Hong Kong project which had been dragging on for months, even Donald Cooper, were forgotten. He was just a man in a glider coming in to land.

'Wouldn't get me up in one of those death traps, Gasty my old mucker,' said Donald as Gaston walked towards him across the vast expanse of grass.

'It's a wonderful experience, Donald. You should try it sometime. It's the only thing that makes me relax.'

'I don't have time to relax, I work like a twat from dawn 'til dusk.'

'I know, Donald, and we're all very grateful. Would you like a drink? We could sit outside the clubhouse.'

'Sounds all right,' said Donald, and the two men walked towards the distant building.

'Everything ready?'

'Wouldn't be normal if everything was ready. I was just planning the route. We're cutting it very fine, Gasty. I was thrashing the Cherokee up the M3 and did it in an hour and a half. But I was touching the ton all the way. There's no way a fifty-tonner is going to do it. Plus, if the M25's stuffed, which it usually is, we're well and truly shafted.'

Yes, it's a big problem,' agreed Gaston Bell. 'I think the thing to do is avoid the major routes. Come along the south coast and cut up from Bournemouth.'

'Sounds like a twat's route to me,' argued Cooper. 'I don't see why we have to bring it all the way out here. Doesn't make sense.'

'There is method in my madness, Donald. This is a very safe place. No criminal connections. Plus, see over there?' Gaston Bell pointed in the opposite direction to the clubhouse. Just over the horizon the roof of an aircraft hangar was visible. 'That's mine, the black hangar. That's where we'll do the deal. It's the perfect place. No one to notice and be suspicious. Nothing to attract attention and plenty of room in every direction to see if anyone's coming.'

'Get your drift, old chum. Nice one.'

'What'll you have?' said Gaston as he pulled a garden chair from under a table outside the clubhouse and gestured for Donald to sit down.

'What, don't you want me inside the club then?'

'Members only, Donald, very strict rule. Anyway, it's a lovely evening.'

'Pint of lager top then. Driving.'

Gaston smiled and walked into the clubhouse. Donald sat down and pulled out his mobile. He pressed a few keys and inserted the earpiece.

'It's Cooper. Okay, take heed. Lasham airfield in Hampshire. Clock it and get the team familiar. Ex-military facility, now a glider club, right? Very low security. I want the place covered. Bell's a two-timing bastard and I wouldn't be surprised if he tried to pull a fast one. We need to be very ready. *Capisce?*'

Chapter Twenty-Seven

⟪ ⟫

Miles got off the train at Shoeburyness and pushed his bike along the flower-bedecked platform. It was a Sunday, the train had been very quiet, the station was quieter still. He walked his bike through the ticket office and saw a dark blue car parked outside. There were two new-looking mountain bikes strapped to bike-carrying mounts on the rear.

The driver's door opened and Philippe got out. He spread a map on the bonnet and pointed to an area about a mile outside the small coastal town.

'The works run along here. The access point is here.' His thick finger prodded the map. He folded it and gave it to Miles.

'See you there,' said Miles as he launched himself along the road.

The car sped past him as he cycled, its exhaust forcing out a swirling plume of blue-grey smoke. He noticed Mario in the passenger seat, seemingly asleep, and Anna and Paula in the back. Miles shook his head and carried on riding.

He arrived at a large temporary gate outside an enormous engineering development running parallel to an army ordnance range. The sign by the gate proclaimed that it was a drainage improvement project. The gate appeared to be locked and there was no sign of the car.

'Over here,' said Paula. Miles turned around to see Anna and her riding their bikes along a suburban street that led off the main road. They both looked much better, happier even, to be on a bike rather than stuck in the back of a car.

'I haven't ridden a bike since I was a kid,' said Paula as she circled around him. 'I once rode across a field and into a stream and a fire crew had to rescue me. It was recreated for *999* – you know, the police reenactment show on the telly.'

'That show wasn't on when you were a kid,' said Miles.

'I wasn't a kid. I was twenty and out of my mind. Anyway, they let me play myself, which the director told me I was really good at, so then I . . .'

'Shut up, Paula,' said Mario who'd appeared around the corner of the street carrying a large bag with difficulty. Philippe was following him carrying three even larger bags.

'We have to go through the fence, we don't have official access,' said Philippe as he passed Miles without stopping. He crossed the road and walked up to the fence surrounding the site.

'Um, why are we going in here?' said Miles, a little confused as to what was going on.

'All will be revealed,' said Mario. 'Come on.'

One by one they made their way across the road and through a gap in the fence where the security wire had been cut. Miles felt slightly uncomfortable. He looked around. They were not in some isolated spot but right opposite a row of suburban houses. There were kids playing in the front gardens; he could see a man washing a car not fifty metres away.

As he wheeled his bike through the gap he said, 'Are you sure we're allowed in here?'

'We aren't really allowed anywhere, but that shouldn't stop us,' said Mario. 'Anyway, it is Sunday. There's no one in here today. Follow Philippe, he knows where we're going.'

Miles followed Paula and Anna as they rode unsteadily across the lumpy ground. A row of massive yellow diggers were lined up beside some Portakabins. Philippe disappeared behind them.

It was only when Miles rounded the corner that he realised why they had come to this peculiar spot.

'Oh, I get it,' he said as he looked at a long stretch of enormous steel pipe lying on the ground.

'What do you get?' asked Paula. 'I hate it when people get things and I don't know what they are. I feel really left out. It happened to me once when I was in Algeria staying in this man's house. Well, I say house, it was a palace really and he wasn't just a man he was some sort of prince. Anyway, he said . . .'

'Shut up, Paula,' said Mario.

'It's like a tunnel, isn't it?' said Miles. 'The inside of the pipe.'

'Exactly,' said Mario.

'Why can't I get things like that? What's wrong with me? You're so intuitive, Miles. Have you got a big cock? You don't look like you would but I bet it's nice. I love intuitive men. I'll suck you off if you want? Right now. I'll kneel in the mud and you can fuck my face if you want. A lot of men want to do that, and the thing about me is, I don't mind. I know a lot of women wouldn't do that, but I like it. I like to watch a man's face as he comes. It's really nice. Fascinating. I was blowing this guy in . . .'

No one was listening except Miles who was trying not to.

They moved slowly across the broken ground to the end of the pipe. It stood at least three metres tall, the far end already buried in the ground. Presumably it went out to sea.

When they got to the opening, Philippe began pulling out an enormous sheet of black cloth from one of the bags he'd been carrying.

Miles looked down the inside of the pipe. It soon disappeared into darkness.

'Bit murky in there,' he said.

'That's the point,' said Philippe. 'Complete darkness. Can you give me a leg up?'

He stood looking at Miles, nodding towards the top of the pipe. Miles put his bike down and came forward. It felt cold and damp nearer the pipe.

Philippe gripped his hands together to form a step.

'*Comme ça,*' he said.

Miles did as he was told and Philippe put his huge muddy foot in the cradle Miles made with his hands. He was very heavy, it required all the effort Miles was capable of to raise the powerfully built Frenchman. When Philippe had a grip on the top of the pipe, he pulled himself up.

'Throw me the cloth,' he said once he stood up. Miles threw it up and Philippe extracted a roll of silver tape from the pocket of his combat jacket. He started fixing the black cloth like a giant curtain over the entrance to the pipe.

'You see, the one thing we cannot otherwise discover is how easy it is to ride along a tunnel in complete darkness,' said Mario. It seemed to Miles that he was talking specifically to the two women. The horror of what they were being asked to do had struck even Paula into momentary silence.

'The security systems in the tunnel are very sophisticated, the lighting systems less so. With very little application we can put out the lights for twenty minutes. That way you can get out of the tunnel without any of the security cameras being able to see you. There are infra-red cameras which can sense where you are, but they will not be able to record an image which is recognisable. You will be stealth cyclists – a very exciting concept.'

'*Mein Gott!*' said Anna.

'The thing is,' said Miles, 'there's no way you can ride in total darkness, keep your balance and not crash into the walls. We'll lose all sense of direction.'

'We don't know that.'

'Well, you don't have to be a physicist or a biologist to understand the rudiments of cycling. I don't know if you've ever noticed the sad lack of cycling clubs for the blind?'

'Get in the tunnel and try it,' said Philippe from the top of the pipe. 'You never know, you may enjoy it.'

Miles pulled back the black drape and peered into the murk. He could see nothing, only smell the slightly sharp odour of metal. He pushed his bike into the tunnel. Mario came up behind him, holding the drape back. Bright sunlight pierced the gloom.

'Just go a little way and then come back, okay? Let's try it.'

Without saying anything Miles mounted his bike and started to freewheel along the tunnel. He followed the shaft of sunlight provided by Mario. He could feel the curve of the tube and quite easily kept to the lowest point. Suddenly, the light went. Mario had closed the drape. Immediately he lost all sense of direction. The only way he could tell he was moving was the feeling of the foetid, metallic-smelling air rushing past his face. He could just about sense that the pipe was on an incline. From the pressure he needed to apply to the pedals he could tell he was building up speed, going downhill. He couldn't tell how fast he was going or in which direction. It very quickly became terrifying. His heart rate went up, he was convinced he was going to smash into something at any moment. He applied the brakes hard and the wheels skidded on the smooth metal surface. He couldn't tell if he'd stopped. He pulled his feet out of the pedal straps and tried to reach the ground. He was still moving, his feet skidding. He lost it, couldn't tell which way was up, the bike slid from underneath him and he slid along the bottom of the pipe.

He finally came to a stop and lay on his stomach. He patted the surface around him. Couldn't even find his bike. He was stuck down a steel tube, not knowing which way was out, on a Sunday afternoon in Shoeburyness. He wasn't having a lot of fun.

Chapter Twenty-Eight

Detective Inspector Willis was not a timid man, but he found sitting in a shuddering helicopter when he could see nothing out of the windows except white cloud just a little disconcerting.

'We're coming over the beginning of the target area now, sir,' said the pilot through the headphones he was wearing. 'It's as we feared, visibility at this height is a bit problematic.'

The helicopter shook violently. The thought crossed Willis' mind that the rather heavy lunch he had just eaten may not have been a good idea. He sat back in his seat and looked at the quilted ceiling of the small cockpit.

'You feeling all right, sir?' asked Reynolds, who was sitting next to him and obviously loving every minute of it.

'Yeah, I'm fine. Just be happy when we can see the bloody ground. Clouds give me the willies.'

'There you go, sir,' said Reynolds, pointing out of the window. The light increased dramatically as they flew out of the dense mass of white nothingness. There below them, serene and peaceful, was the rolling Kent countryside.

'I'm going to have to reduce height a little, sir, we're flying into Gatwick airspace,' said the pilot.

All Willis wanted to do was fly as low as they could. He was feeling decidedly green at this height. However it was imperative that they kept as high as possible to ensure no one on the ground could tell what sort of helicopter it was. The words

'Police' were written in large blue letter along the side of the craft. Bit of a give-away in a surveillance operation.

'Do whatever you have to do, mate, just try and be discreet.'

Willis saw the pilot nod and felt a surge in his stomach as the helicopter started to loose altitude rapidly. It had taken quite a bit of string-pulling to get the ride in the first place. Running a helicopter was not cheap, and Chief Inspector McKay ran a tight budget. He didn't jump at the chance of shelling out serious money to pay for any hunch one of his officers had. But Willis had a very good track record. Britain's prisons were bulging with unsavoury elements he had had a hand in putting there.

Willis had been in touch with the Ministry of Defence and found out rather a lot about Major Cooper. Large parts of his file were either blacked out or kept back. He'd been a very busy man in the Army. Stints in Northern Ireland, Cyprus, the Falklands of course, but also trips to Australia, Namibia and the Gulf. There were substantial periods of his service career simply not included in the file. Classified. Willis knew the regs.

However, there was not a lot for him to go on other than the fact that Cooper either inspired deep loyalty or tremendous hatred in the men he commanded.

Willis had spent a good many man hours trying to trace Cooper's present location. No tax records, no passport details, driving licence, credit cards. It was as if Donald Cooper didn't exist. He was either living out of the country or was a very clever man who knew how the system worked well enough to circumvent it.

Careful cross-referencing of a few ex-servicemen with a criminal past, however, showed Cooper in a pivotal role in their misdemeanours. He seemed to have had contact with almost all of them at some time during their stint. Willis did not believe he was out of the country.

'Levelling out at three thousand feet,' said the pilot. 'That's the main line down there.'

He pointed down on Willis' side of the helicopter. Willis peered out of the window and could clearly see the tracks and a long, white-roofed snake of a train speeding on its journey to London.

'Keep your eyes peeled,' he said as the pilot started to steer a course that followed the line.

'Hey, look at that!' said Reynolds suddenly. Willis tried to lean over to the other side of the cabin but his lap strap stopped him.

'What is it?'

'Building site,' said Reynolds. 'Right alongside the line.'

'There's a lot of building work going on in the area,' the pilot confirmed. 'What with the new line and everything. Whole of East Kent's a building site.'

'Let's have a look see,' said Willis.

The pilot banked the helicopter steeply and moved towards the area Reynolds had pointed out.

'We can have a closer look on the camera,' said the co-pilot.

Willis leant forward to where he had a clear view of a video monitor mounted between the two front seats. The co-pilot operated a simple control panel which was resting on his lap. The picture on the screen showed the rail line in surprising detail; eventually some half-finished houses came into view.

'That's it,' said Reynolds, now also leaning forward and peering at the screen.

The co-pilot adjusted the shot until the whole site was visible. It was a development at the edge of a small town.

'Lenham,' said the pilot without being asked.

'See the big green thing – what's that?' asked Willis. With a few deft movements the co-pilot zoomed into the shape at one end of the building site, adjacent to the rail line.

'Just a crane,' said Reynolds.

'Why's it covered up?'

'Search me.'

'Would you use a crane like that to build houses?'

'Dunno, sir.'

'No, nor do I, but it looks well suspect to me, Reynolds. Mark it.'

'Will do, sir.'

The helicopter turned again, Willis felt his lunch knocking at the door marked 'chunder'.

'Any sick bags on board?' he asked.

'Have you use your hat, I'm afraid, sir,' said the pilot happily.

The helicopter turned again. It seemed to Willis as if they'd gone in a complete circle for no reason. They were having a laugh, they must be. He glanced out of the window. The rail lines glinted in the sun as they continued towards the coast.

'Brilliant, isn't it, sir?' said Reynolds with a grin.

'Gimme your hat,' said Willis.

Chapter Twenty-Nine

Suddenly Miles was engulfed by thick cloth. Light flashed around him and the bike came to an abrupt halt. He felt a sudden pain in his back, followed by another more jarring one in his leg. There was screaming and crying and confusion all around. The cloth was pushed tight to his face, he couldn't breathe. He had to escape but seemed to be pinned down by wriggling bodies and metal.

It was the end of Miles' second descent into metal hell, the first time he had crawled out on his hands and knees. This time Anna and Paula had joined him, all of them screaming the entire time they were inside the pipe.

'You won't have this problem coming out of the tunnel,' said Mario cheerfully as they scrambled to their feet. 'When you come out of the tunnel, you'll have a huge, smooth car park to ride across.'

'Eventually,' added Philippe cautiously.

'It is ridiculous,' Anna protested. 'We can't do it. We're not even carrying anything and we were riding very slowly. At least, I think we were riding slowly, it was impossible to tell.'

'It's incredibly difficult and the sound is a nightmare,' said Miles, rubbing the side of his head just underneath his teardrop-shaped helmet. 'You can't tell where anyone is, how far the person in front of you is . . . it's incredibly dangerous and stupid and it's clearly not going to work.'

'This is all good,' said Mario. 'This is just what I wanted to happen.'

Philippe slid down the side of the huge pipe and joined them.

'Pretty tough, *n'est ce pas?*'

'I'd like to see you do it!' retorted Miles.

Without hesitation Philippe took Miles' bike and pushed his way past the drape. The clouds had lifted and they stood in the dazzling sunlight as they heard Philippe's screams and bellows rapidly recede as he rode off down the dark tube.

'He loves a challenge,' said Mario.

'Well, why doesn't he do the robbery?' asked Miles.

'It's not a robbery, it's an exercise. And besides, Philippe doesn't have any problems.' Mario smiled broadly. 'There would be no advantage in his doing it for you.'

Paula started crying. She was still lying on the ground, legs tangled painfully with the frame of her bike.

'Can someone just kill me now?' she wailed. 'I'm never going to get better. I'm so boring anyway, what's the point trying to cure me? I'm incurable and I can't ride a bike in the dark, I just can't. I couldn't even do it for a man I loved, and usually I'd do anything for a man I loved. But I can't do this. I just can't . . .'

'Shut up, Paula, you have no choice, you are doing it,' said Mario sternly.

She threw the bike off her violently and stood up. Her leg was cut and bleeding through her white leggings. Miles thought it probably looked worse than it was, but it was still rather shocking. Paula was actually angry, Miles could see that. He had never seen this frail-looking woman be anything other than ludicrously sexual, needy to the point of desperation and generally annoying.

'I want to die, Mario!' she screamed. 'Is that so bad? I just want all this pain to stop. Nobody loves me, nobody would miss me, not even my own son! Everyone would be relieved if I were dead, even Monica. She could get into the papers again which would make her happy. She'd be happy if I was dead. No one would even bother to come to my funeral, I'm so awful . . .'

Miles noticed the drape suddenly billow out behind Paula. Anna instinctively moved forward and grabbed the sleeve of her pink long-sleeved T shirt. Miles could hear a screaming noise, not unlike a Formula One car approaching at top speed. Suddenly the drape burst forward with such power that both Anna and Paula were thrown to the ground. Miles saw a man on a bike-type shape fly past, covered in heavy black cloth. He soon collapsed to the ground in a billowing heap, accompanied by a wail of pain.

'I think Philippe has got the hang of it,' said Mario. 'Looks like he was travelling quite fast.'

'The idiot could have killed me!' said Paula. 'Look at my leggings, they're ruined. Look at my leg! Oh my God, it's bleeding! I'm going to die from blood poisoning.'

It seemed to be the first time she'd noticed the nasty-looking gash on her thigh. She almost touched the blood but then her hands shied away.

'I haven't cut myself since I was twenty,' said Paula with barely a pause for breath. 'I was in a car with a coke dealer from San Diego and he was being chased by the cops. Anyway, I wasn't shagging him or anything but he . . .'

'Oh, please, shut up, Paula!' Anna told her. Miles stepped between them. This was looking very ugly. Then he stopped himself.

'What am I doing?' he said, and walked around in a small circle. 'This is mad. We must be mad. Riding along a tunnel in the dark . . . We've lost it, we really have.'

Anna looked at him with incredible sadness. Paula didn't seem to mind that he had called her mad, but clearly Anna was offended. Miles felt guilty.

'I mean, it's chaos, it's a total mess. It's hopeless and pathetic and . . .' His head started swimming. He could feel the control he'd always had over his life slip through his fingers. He was descending into the mire, into chaos and disorder.

Without hesitation Paula started talking again. 'That's just what *he* said when he was driving. That's amazing! Because I was telling him how my first ever boyfriend . . . I was only fourteen

. . . drove really fast and *he* told me he'd heard enough of my stories to last him a lifetime, and just then he smashed the car into a huge freeway sign and that's how I . . .'

'We don't want to know anything else you have done!' screamed Anna. 'Do you understand?'

She walked away. Miles looked at Mario who was paying scant attention to them. Behind Mario, Philippe was struggling to free himself from the black drape. Everywhere he looked people were lost in confusion.

'How can you remain so calm when everything is so utterly hopeless? This isn't going to work, Mario. Haven't you realised that yet?'

'Everything is really good, Miles. This is all part of the process. I am very much enjoying it.'

'I think I have broken my leg,' said Philippe from beneath the black cloth. 'And maybe my arm.'

'Okay, let's re-hang the drape and this time we do it fully loaded,' said Mario. He revealed that inside the large sports bag he was carrying was a selection of newly purchased pannier bags. He started to try and fit them to the bikes with one arm but with little success.

Miles and Anna left Philippe to his moaning and went to help Mario. Paula merely paced around, crying and wailing about her leg.

'We estimate that if you go for fifty-pound notes only, you should be able to get around a million in each bag. So that's four million on each bike, another million in a rucksack on your back, five million each rider, which totals fifteen million between the three of you. Not bad, huh?'

'Fifteen million pounds?' asked Anna. 'Why do we need to take so much?'

'Well, why not? If it's there. You may as well take as much as you can. It will be more of a challenge.'

'We *have* all gone mad, haven't we?' said Miles. He looked at Anna, finding something very forlorn in her eyes. She smiled faintly and nodded.

'Completely.'

Chapter Thirty

If there was one part of the job Detective Inspector Willis didn't like, it was giving away hard-won information to his group of highly competitive colleagues in the new-broom, team politics of New Scotland Yard.

He'd done a lot of footwork, not to mention helicopter work to find out what he knew. Why on earth should he tell anyone else and let them steal all the glory?

'Looks like the Serafino family are very busy in Northern France all of a sudden,' said Hopkins, an officer from the Met who had been seconded to Europol and thought that meant he was better than anyone else.

'Just 'cos he speaks a bit of French, thinks the sun shines out of his own rectum,' Willis whispered to Detective Inspector Barber who was sitting next to him. Clean-cut DI Barber didn't respond in any way.

'The family have been gathering at one of their places in Normandy and we've been keeping a weather eye on them.'

'Thank you, Hopkins,' said Chief Inspector McKay. 'Now, one of the things we can be sure of is that the less scrupulous members of the City banking community will be up to their necks in this if a blag does go ahead. Barber, what have you got for us?'

DI Barber stood up and read from his notes. Willis looked away in embarrassment as he did so. Barber was such a brown nose.

'If it gets this far, Chief, it's going to be very tricky to finger a culprit. Vast sums are flowing through the City on an hourly basis, and any number of people are buying and selling sterling at any one minute. There's a kind of frenzy going on around the currency at the moment. I don't know how many of you read the financial pages . . .'

'All the fucking time,' put in Willis sarcastically.

'Yes, well, those of us who do will have noticed that at present sterling is a very popular currency globally. It's incredibly strong and everybody seems to want to buy it, partly because of the huge trading advantage it has over the Euro. Five years ago no one expected the Euro to be so weak, so, to put it simply, the temptation's there. If you have several million pounds on your hands, and convert it to Euros at the last minute, you could easily end up a Euro billionaire.'

'This is all very well, and we're grateful for your lecture on the current state of the money markets, Barber,' said Chief Inspector McKay. 'But that's all pants! What we want to know is, are there any bent bankers we should be pulling in for a grilling?'

'Well, that's the difficulty, sir. Bankers tend to be very well represented in the legal department. Unless we have some firm evidence there's very little we can do at this stage.'

Willis smiled when he saw the look on the Chief's face. McKay was not well pleased.

'Well, that's pants too, Barber, if you'll excuse my saying so. For a start, what about Sir Philip Galton? Bent as a nine-Euro note and just out of Ford open prison.'

'I doubt he has the clout any more, sir,' said Barber, still standing, not a trace of embarrassment on his clean-cut visage. 'There is Mr Gaston Bell, however.'

'Oh, so now you're going to tell us something useful? Thank you very much,' said an increasingly exasperated Chief Inspector. 'Who the hell is Gaston Bell?'

'An investment banker, Chief. Partner in Bell and Duchamp, small private bank, turnover last year of a little over seventeen billion. He handles mostly foreign currency, clean as a whistle in the open trading department. However, we've been running checks on him for years and he knows it. Very canny operator but there are rumours. He's a fantastically rich individual with holdings all over the world and fairly impressive contacts in this country. Some big political donations in the past and some rather unsavoury acquaintances. Some of the investors in his bank are not exactly what you'd call kosher. We think he may well do a fair amount of laundry, but can't get any proof. Impeccable books and not a leak from his office – and believe me, we've tried. But my money's on him. I'd suggest we put a watch on him, sir.'

'You want me to devote more of my already seriously stretched manpower to watching some little pinstriped toe rag around the clock, do you, Barber?'

'I think it could pay dividends, sir.'

'You've been listening in on those phones too long, son. We don't go for dividends in this job, we go for nicking crooks. We go for getting bent bankers seriously banged to rights.'

'Of course, sir,' said Barber, with no obvious discomfiture.

'We'll have a look and see what we can do. Willis!' said the Chief, suddenly looking at him.

'Sir.'

'What have you got for us?'

Willis was a little taken aback. He had just been jotting down the name Gaston Bell. There was a Brigadier Bell mentioned in Donald Cooper's file. He pursed his lips, looked around the room and sighed. It was painful, but he knew he had to do it. He coughed.

'Yeah, we've got a few leads, Chief. I've had a word with a couple of contacts, there's definitely something going down. We've spotted a possible site where a team could try and hit the train, just off the side of the track near Lenham in Kent. Building site, sir. Nothing much to go on yet but I've posted Barker and Reynolds out there and they're doing a twenty-four-hour surveillance on the site.'

'Good man,' said Chief Inspector McKay. 'At least one of

you is on the case. If this goes pants, there's going to be a lot of heads rolling. Seriously rolling. And you know what they say? A rolling head gathers no pension.'

'Twat!' muttered Willis as he sat down again.

Chapter Thirty-One

Miles arrived back at the house on Bryanston Square and walked up the steps. Anna opened the door. The rest of the group had driven back. His train from Shoeburyness was delayed; the ride back through the City had not been pleasant.

'Hello, Miles,' she said as she let him in. 'I am glad you came back.'

'Why's that then?' asked Miles as he stripped off his cycling gear. Anna stood and watched him in silence. When he had finished he turned to face her. She just stared at him with a slight smile.

'I like watching you get undressed,' she said. He felt embarrassed. This was the first nice thing anyone had said to him in ages. 'Remember when I first saw you in the château? You had no clothes on.'

'Oh, yeah, sorry about that.' He had almost forgotten. The château seemed like ages ago and yet it was barely two weeks previously.

'You don't need to be sorry. *Du bist ja ein süßer Engländer.*'

'Thank you,' said Miles. 'I don't know what that means, but it sounds nice.'

They looked at each other for a moment. And Miles was aware of the fact that it *was* a moment, one he wouldn't forget. This attractive German woman, in the hallway of a strange house, telling him he was a *süßer Engländer.*

'I thought you were with Philippe,' he said.

Anna smiled broadly. 'Philippe! *Mein Gott, nein!* He is a very disturbed man, no?'

'He's a bit odd,' said Miles, then thought about everyone he'd met since ringing Mario. 'But then, so is everyone else.'

'Do you think I am odd?'

'No. But . . . well, I mean, you're here, aren't you? You have to be odd to do this.'

'You are right. I don't know why I am doing it, but anything is better than what I did before.'

'But why are you seeing Mario? You don't seem as mad as Paula.'

'Hopefully no one is as mad as Paula,' said Anna with another shy smile. 'I am here because I think I am going to die soon.'

'Why d'you think you are going to die?'

'Because I can't wake up properly unless I am driving very fast, and as you say, driving very fast is dangerous. I have no reason to have a problem. I am very successful at work, I am paid very well, I have everything I could want in my life. I have done everything I can think of to make my life better and yet I am still depressed. Is it the same with you?'

'Exactly the same. Crazy, isn't it?'

'I don't know. Do you think it could be something bigger than just a personal thing?' said Anna. 'Like an evolutionary thing. You know, as people achieve more and more in the world, every experience starts to be worth less and less.'

'Oh, God,' said Miles. 'I wish I'd come to see you instead of Mario. That's exactly what I think. I'm in just the same position.'

'Do you think this is what attracts us to each other?'

Miles couldn't help his eyes opening a bit wider. He wanted to embrace her. Somehow it didn't feel like the right time.

'I don't know.'

'I do,' said Mario. They both turned to see the diminutive figure of their therapist standing in the darkness of the hallway behind them.

'And before you ask, I have been listening to both of you, and I think it is very touching, but I want to emphasise right now that any relationships formed during the exercise are going to destroy everything we are working for. I would ask that you don't speak to each other again outside the group. It is only another couple of days after all. After that, you will both be cured and happy and I can only wish you the best.'

He smiled and disappeared into the main room of the house. Miles felt like a teenager caught by his dad trying to have a snog with a girl outside the shop in Datchet. He had just started to move towards the main room when the doorbell rang. He turned and looked at the door, then back to Anna.

'Who could that be?' she said. She walked towards the door but before she reached it Mario and Philippe came out of the main room in haste.

'Wait a moment,' said Mario. 'We don't know who this is.'

Philippe pushed Miles firmly behind him as he passed. 'You must go into the rear of the house,' he said. He then pulled a fearful-looking revolver from the back of his trousers, cocked it efficiently and waited behind the door. Mario turned to see if Anna and Miles had left. They were moving backwards towards the kitchen but both of them were fascinated to discover who it could be.

Mario leant his ear against the door. 'Who is it?'

Miles didn't catch the muffled reply, but Mario sagged a little when he heard it and opened the door. A woman in her early-thirties stood on the threshold. She was carrying a sleeping toddler. Another child of about seven was holding on to her low-slung shoulder bag. Philippe quickly concealed his gun and walked back to Miles and Anna.

'*Comme d'habitude*,' he muttered as he passed them.

The child spoke first. 'Hello, Daddy,' he said to Mario.

Miles glanced at Anna who was staring at the touching scene before them.

'Dianne, what are you doing here?' Mario asked the woman.

'Your children wanted to see you, though it's a wonder Max remembers who you are.' Dianne was well-spoken, clearly of mixed African descent.

Mario squatted down and embraced the child in a one-armed hug.

'*Bonjour*, little Max, how are you?'

'I've got a Nintendo 64,' said the boy. 'I'm on level three.'

'Goodness, what a clever chap you are,' said Mario. He stood up, ruffling the child's hair. 'This is very awkward, Dianne. As you can see, I have some clients at the moment.'

She looked past Mario at Miles and Anna. 'Don't trust him, don't believe a damn' word he says,' she said to them. When she spoke she was smiling, a pained smile, but it didn't match her words. Miles felt very confused.

'Please, Dianne.'

'I have to go to Jersey. My mother is very sick. I need some help with the children. You are their father although it's hard to believe.' Miles could tell she had been rehearsing these lines. She seemed to be delivering them by rote and they sounded unnatural.

Mario looked crushed. 'I can't, Dianne, not at the moment. Can't you see, I'm right in the middle of something?'

'You have no choice. I have no choice. They have to stay with you for three days.'

Paula joined Miles and Anna in the hallway and stared at the child. 'Oh my God, he's just like my little Mustoe. Who is he?'

'Mario's son,' said Anna.

'Oh, wow! He's got so many kids, he must be really fertile. I wouldn't shag him, though, would you, Anna? God, I hope Mustoe's okay. I can't phone my mum 'cos she wants to kill me. She's looking after Mustoe while I go mad. That's the idea anyway. He's probably at school right now. What day is it? Maybe he's on holiday. I'm such a useless mother, he hates me anyway.'

Anna didn't respond.

Dianne saw Paula and started to move into the house. Mario made a pathetic attempt to stop her, but the look she flashed him seemed to knock all the spirit out of him.

'Are you poor buggers doing one of his exercises? Are you?'

She glared at them. Miles didn't know what to do. He nodded very slightly.

'For Christ's sake, don't! Don't listen to anything he says. He destroyed my life. Look at me.'

She was ignoring Miles, looking only at Anna and Paula. 'Look what happened when I did an exercise. Oh, yes, he cured me all right. I don't have any of the problems I used to have, I just have two new ones to deal with.'

She handed the toddler to Anna who took the child and patted it gently on the back. Miles thought she looked very nice holding it. He couldn't tell if it was a boy or a girl, its little face was scrunched up, fast asleep on her shoulder.

'That's my sister Josie,' said Max, the little boy. 'She's always being sick, it's really yukky.'

Dianne squatted down and held her son's face in long fingers. 'Okay, Mummy's going to see Grandma now. You stay here with Daddy and I'll come and get you on Friday.'

'Okay, Mum, don't worry about me, I'll be fine,' said the boy. He gave his mother a hug. Without saying another word, she walked out of the house and closed the door.

'Have you got a Nintendo 64?' Max asked Miles.

'Um, no, not here.'

'What about a Gameboy? I'm really good at Super Mario. I've got up to level six – that's where you have to jump on bombs and if you're not careful they go "kaboomph!" and blow up and you lose a life.'

Mario walked down the corridor looking ashen-faced. He gently took the sleeping toddler from Anna and started walking up the stairs.

'Come with me, Max, we'll see what we can sort out,' he said as he climbed. He glanced around at Miles, Anna and Paula, smiled weakly and said, 'I'll be back in a moment. Can you tell Philippe to go out and buy a Nintendo 64, and a pile of games?'

'Fantastic, Dad!' said Max, and rushed up the stairs making explosion sounds with every step.

'What do you think?' said Anna. They had all walked into the kitchen without saying anything.

'It's totally heavy. I've met other children of his when I did the exercise in Cyprus with him. This Greek girl . . . really, really beautiful girl, I think she was the daughter of some really, really rich Greek shipping bloke . . . she had a three-year-old who looked just like Mario. She'd been one of his clients so he must shag them.'

'What about those children in the chateaux?' Miles looked at Anna.

'What children?'

'You must have been asleep, the morning we all had to leave early.'

'I don't remember. It's all a blur.'

'Some kids arrived in the night. I bet they were his too.'

'He's never tried to shag me,' said Paula sadly. 'Not that I want to shag him but he could at least have tried. Has he tried to shag you, Anna?'

'No, he has not,' she said flatly.

'Maybe we're not his type. I've never met a straight bloke who doesn't fancy me, though. You fancy me a bit, don't you, Miles? I mean, I know you're not in love with me, but you'd like to shag me, wouldn't you?'

'Look . . .' he said.

'No, just a dirty shag, a quick dirty fuck, that sort of thing. I'd let you, you see, you're nice and clean and I bet you've got a really hard cock. I'm having a period at the moment, but if you don't mind, I don't.'

'Look, please, Paula . . .'

'Yes, shut up, Paula. We need to think,' said Anna.

'Yeah, look, this woman obviously knows Mario better than we do . . .' Miles started.

'I don't think she really meant any of that,' said Anna.

'What?'

'I think it's part of the exercise. I think it was all set up, like the shooting thing in the château. It was like she was doing what she'd been told to do.'

'But the kids must be Mario's, they both look like him.'

'I do not question that. I only think we should suspect everything, including the possibility she could be part of the exercise.'

'It's always so weird doing anything with Mario,' said Paula, who had been standing holding her mouth shut with both hands. 'Always weird but interesting – like me. Don't you think, Miles? You can tie me up if you want to . . .'

'Please, Paula,' he said. 'Now I'm totally confused. Is that part of the process, d'you think?' He looked at Anna. She looked straight at him. He felt nervous but excited. These were definitely feelings and they were getting intense.

'Very much so. This is what it's all about. I say we keep going.'

'I'm not sure. I feel really nervous.'

'So you are feeling something?'

'Yes.'

'We must do it. I feel awake,' said Anna. She turned to Paula. 'It hasn't had any obvious effect on you yet, but it's only a matter of time.'

'Don't worry about me,' said Paula. 'I'm a hopeless case. But it's great to be with you two anyway. I'm loving it, I just feel very horny. You're not a lezzie are you, Anna? I'm up for a bit of that if you're interested. A lot of butch dykes have said they want to take me to bed . . .'

Anna walked out of the kitchen and started climbing the stairs. Miles followed her and although he didn't look around he could hear Paula behind him, going on about being a lesbian and how she was just so sexual, it didn't matter what way.

They found Mario in one of the bathrooms. He was sitting against the wall watching his son and daughter in the bath. Their clothes were strewn across the floor amidst heaps of damp towels. He looked up at them forlornly.

'It's okay, you don't have to explain,' he said. 'You can go. The whole thing is crazy anyway.'

'We don't want to go,' said Anna. 'We have discussed it and we want to continue.'

Mario put a hand to his eyes and his face crumpled. Tears started to stream down his cheeks.

'Don't cry, Daddy, it'll be all right,' said Max from the bath. He was smiling, a mound of foam on his head. 'Look what I can do – tear my hair off!' He swept the foam off his head with one swipe, an action that made his little sister laugh in delight.

'Ouch, that was my hair!' said Max.

'I don't know what to do,' said Mario. 'Every attempt I make just ends in disaster. Something has changed and I can't identify what it is. Trauma therapy doesn't work. It just shifts problems. Dianne was right, I ruined her life.'

'We know what's going on,' said Miles calmly. 'We've talked about it. None of us is under any illusion. Not even Paula.'

'No, I'm under none at all.' Paula clamped her hands over her mouth when Anna and Miles gave her a look.

'Trauma therapy is already working,' said Miles. 'I already have feelings, Anna is already awake, Paula is . . .' he looked at her '. . . really trying to shut up.'

She nodded and grunted something from behind her hand.

'She's funny,' said Max.

'I'll go and get the Nintendo, Anna and Paula can make some food for the kids, and we'll sort out the latest problem when they've gone to bed.'

'There's no way it's bedtime yet. It's still sunny outside,' protested Max.

Mario stood up very slowly. He lifted his arm and the four adults embraced.

'Oooh, sexy!' said Max, and the little girl laughed and splashed her hands in the water in excitement.

An hour later Miles walked into the house. In the front room he saw Max watching television in the corner. Mario was on the sofa feeding the little girl from a bottle. There were wine glasses on the glass-topped coffee table. Anna was looking at the plans on the large dining table while Philippe sat toying with some odd bits of cardboard tubing that littered the other end.

Miles unpacked the Nintendo and plugged it in. Max danced about him in great excitement. Super Mario appeared on the screen and Miles breathed deeply.

'Mission accomplished,' he said as the familiar 'boings' and crashes of the computer game started to emanate from the TV set.

Paula entered carrying a bottle of wine and some clean glasses. Her mouth was taped again.

'I couldn't let her talk in front of the children,' said Mario. 'I have explained it is a game we play.'

Miles nodded and joined Anna at the table.

'So tell me, Mario, how many children do you have?'

'Fourteen.'

Miles felt his eyebrows shoot higher up his forehead with no encouragement.

'And three who are at present being contested. Not by me – the mothers are claiming I am not the father.'

'Fourteen!' said Miles. 'How come you have so many?'

'It is hard to explain, and very easy to judge. It was part of a therapy process I used to practise, which is no longer as productive as it once was.'

'You had sex with women as part of their therapy?' said Anna flatly.

'It was far more involved than that.'

'Sounds like it,' said Miles.

'The mothers of my children are much happier now, and generally better off financially. It was meeting Paula last year that stopped the whole thing. She was a prime candidate for my sexual therapy but I knew it had to finish. The cost to myself is too high. Fourteen children take a lot of looking after and cost a lot of money.'

Miles looked at Mario for a while. He was feeding the toddler with quiet confidence, totally at ease. He looked down at her. She was already sleeping. He removed the bottle and with considerable skill, taking into account he did everything with one arm, lifted her on to his shoulder and patted her back gently. After a moment, they all heard a gentle burp. Mario smiled.

'So, you help support your children?' asked Anna.

'I support them all, yes, even the ones whose mothers are now either married or living with someone. I take my children's welfare very seriously. As Philippe will testify.'

Miles turned to look at him.

'We have a problem,' said the Frenchman as if on cue. He was still toying with the cardboard tube. Mario shifted slightly, the baby grunted.

'But it could work greatly to our advantage. How is your grasp of physics, Miles?' he asked.

'Bit sketchy.' He felt Anna move beside him, standing closer than she had previously.

Philippe had a bicycle pump in one hand. The flexible pipe was attached to a series of cardboard tubes he had stuck together with the same tape he used to silence Paula. One end of the tube had a red plastic lid attached, held in place with yet more tape. It didn't make much sense to Miles.

'There is an air lock on the service tunnel,' said Philippe. 'We haven't taken that into consideration.'

'What d'you mean, an air lock?' asked Miles, rather louder than he had intended. He checked his pulse, it was racing.

'Philippe will explain,' said Mario as another gentle burp emanated from the child on his shoulder.

'As the train passes through the tunnel, the air in front of it is pushed forward very fast . . .'

'Yes, we know about that.' Miles felt exasperated. His spirits had lifted on his trip to the Oxford Street branch of Dixon's. Now this.

'We knew about the piston ducts, as I explained in the video. Most of this air is forced into the opposite tunnel, though some can be allowed into the service tunnel through special valves built in above the connecting safety doors, as we described. However, in the event of an emergency, if the security safety doors were opened, sudden gusts of wind, about one hundred and fifty kilometers an hour, could blast through the service tunnel and endanger the people working there . . .'

'Wait, wait, wait!' said Miles, holding his head in his hands. 'Blasts of air, people working in the service tunnel . . . How come this job only gets more impossible?'

'Please wait, Miles, we haven't got to the end yet,' said Mario.

'But there are people working in the service tunnel? How come we didn't know that?'

'The tunnel is under twenty-four-hour maintenance sche-dules. There is almost always someone in it somewhere: checking systems, replacing filters, cleaning,' said Philippe. 'This isn't a problem, they are not security personnel. They won't attempt to stop you. They won't even see you because there will be no lights then.'

'But there's the fucking air lock!' said Miles, feeling his fists tighten.

'Please,' said Mario, nodding towards Max at the end of the room.

'He said the F word,' said the boy without turning or stopping playing.

'Sorry. But, I mean, it's quite a big point, don't you think? I thought you said you worked there, Philippe?' Miles started pacing around the room.

'Don't break anything,' warned the Frenchman.

'I'm not going to break anything. But how are we going to get past a F—blasted air lock? We are·screwed! How come you didn't know this? You never worked there, did you? This is all based on bull—on rubbish.'

'I never worked there but I know people who did,' said Philippe sulkily like a defensive teenager.

'Oh, great. So as we ride happily along this dark tunnel carrying fifteen million quid on our backs, we'll just occasionally slam into some poor sod checking the pipes aren't leaking?'

'Sod is rude, but it can also be a not rude word, meaning a lump of grass and earth,' said Max helpfully.

'They will be in vehicles on which the lights will be working. You will see them in plenty of time.'

'And they'll see us.'

'Correct,' said Mario. 'Although it is doubtful they will see very much. However, we have been thinking about this and you will be wearing something rather sophisticated over your faces. Something very useful. Can you show them, Philippe?'

He lifted a grey cardboard box on to the table and extracted what to Miles looked like a virtual-reality headset.

'Military issue night-vision goggles. You will be like cats, you will be able to see in the dark, and they will protect your identity.'

'But if there is an airlock, we cannot get out,' said Anna.

'Well, this is the thing,' said Mario. 'Philippe is just experimenting. Show us, Philippe.'

He straightened himself and smiled. He held the bike pump in front of him and started to inflate the cardboard tube.

'This,' said Philippe, 'is an incredible stroke of luck. The gods are smiling upon us. This is what we think is going to happen.'

He carefully picked at the sticky tape that was holding the plastic stopper in place at the end of the cardboard tube. Suddenly there was a loud pop and a ping-pong ball shot out of the end of the tube and bounced around the room.

'I challenge any of you to catch that!' said Philippe proudly.

Miles leant against the wall and slowly sank to a crouched position on the floor.

'Oh, sh—blimey!'

Chapter Thirty-Two

'Smells like a bloody perfume shop in here,' said Donald Cooper, holding a handkerchief over his nose. He used it to mop his expansive brow. 'What's happened to us? Have we gone soft in our old age?'

'Got to keep clean, Major,' said someone from the back of the crowded room.

'We've turned into a team of Euro-poofs,' said Donald, grinning broadly. 'There was a time when you could smell a pack of English squaddies a mile off if the blessed wind was in the right direction.'

He pushed open one of the aluminium-framed windows behind him. The view outside was dismal, a messy building site in the grey drizzle.

The team sitting around the edges of the crowded Porta-kabin were an odd assortment of ages, ethnic backgrounds and builds. All male, mostly ex-servicemen, and every one known to Donald Cooper personally. All except one: Steve Abrahams, the crane operator, the man Gaston Bell had suggested. Abrahams was clearly a hard man but he seemed kosher from what Cooper could find out. He'd been dishonourably discharged from the Royal Engineers for some scam he'd been working in Cyprus.

Donald knew that the rest of the lads would muck in, do any job necessary, but the crane operator was vital. They couldn't afford to mess up. Abrahams had done three jobs previously which had involved engineering skills. They'd all gone off smoothly and he'd never had so much as an interview with the boys in blue.

'Okay, if I can have your attention, please?' said Donald. The room fell silent immediately. Donald Cooper was used to being listened to and launched into his speech without a pause.

'You all know why you're here. At eleven o'clock tomorrow morning we're going to stop a train out the back there, blow the roof, lift off one of the containers and get the hell out of here as quick as.'

'Excellent!' said Sinbad, a moniker that suited the psychopath and Semtex expert to whom it belonged.

'Now, what you don't know is that the container is carrying upwards of five billion pounds sterling.'

'Fuck me!' said Freddie O'Brien quietly.

'The down side of this information is that Her Majesty's police are going to be seriously miffed. Consequently we have to work very fast. I don't want any mucking around. There's time for that later. We get the job done, leave no trace and disappear. Understood?'

There was a murmur of agreement from the men. 'And on that score, at the moment we're severely hampered by the mud.'

'Aye, it's terrible sticky,' said O'Brien, who surprisingly with a name like that was Scottish.

'Basically,' said Donald Cooper, looking around with an expression that was the nearest he could get to sympathetic and pleading, 'we've got to finish the road in the next twenty-four hours. We've all gone a bit soft, lads. So no boozing, no lounging. We've got to finish, tamp it, make it solid, or come the job tomorrow the rozzers are going to turn up and find a bunch of sad ex-soldiers sitting in the shite with five bill in the back of the wagon. And that'll take a bit of explaining.'

There was silence in the sweet-smelling Portakabin. The men all looked at the floor.

'Is that okay with everyone? I'm only asking to be polite because basically it's too late to pull out now.' Donald smiled.

'Either you pitch in and start some spade work, or I bury you under it.'

One or two of the more nervous members of the team looked at him with alarmed expressions. Donald laughed, an ugly sound not often heard.

'Just my little joke!' he said as kindly as he could. 'Come on, let's get our wellies on.'

Harris, who was sitting nearest the door, stood up and opened it. A blast of fresh air entered, reducing the aroma by a few degrees. The team got to their feet and shuffled, muttered and smoked their way out. As each one passed Harris, he handed over a pair of black wellington boots and a large shovel. Donald followed the last man to the door. Harris handed him a pair of boots.

'What's that, Harris?'

'Come on, Donald, muck in, mate. Be good for morale,' said Harris.

'I've got to oversee, Harris. That's why you never made it up the ranks, dear boy. Any trouble, I'll be having a kip in the Cherokee.'

Donald stepped down from the Portakabin on to an up-turned milk crate that doubled as a step. The crate gave way, splintering and showering the mud around it with blue plastic shards.

Donald's military-shod size twelve foot sank five inches into sticky building site clay.

'Bollocks!' he said. He kicked what remained of the crate off his foot and squelched his way towards his Cherokee.

Chapter Thirty-Three

'I don't think I should be doing PR any more, what d'you think? I think I should be an actress again. That's what I trained for. Well, I never finished my training because I started having an affair with the vice-principal of the drama college and his wife left him and he lost his job and threw himself off a cliff, so I lost interest. Anyway, I always got offered the parts of single mums or mad women or rape victims. I've been a rape victim in *Casualty* and *The Bill*. I was a single mum in *Brookside*, *Byker Grove*, *Coronation Street* and *Only Fools and Horses*. I was a single mum with a dead baby in *ER* once because my American accent is so good and I was shagging the director. Well, I wasn't shagging him, he kept hassling me for a blow job at this club I used to virtually live at in New York. So I said if he gave me a job in *ER* I'd go down on him, but I wanted the contract first. I'm not stupid although people think I am. Mario knows I'm not, he respects me, he's the only man who ever forced me to shut up without stuffing his cock into my mouth. I think that's why most men want to put their cocks in my mouth. I'm not stupid, it's just a very good way of shutting me up. But loads of men have complained that even when I'm blowing them, I manage to talk in between each session. Like I have their cock in my mouth, I'm very good at it, I've done it a lot – but don't get me wrong, I'm not cheap. I won't go down on just anyone. I am a connoisseur of erections and I appreciate a nice one. Some cocks are bent, or stubby, or still wrinkly when they're erect and

I don't like that. I like a straight shaft with clean lines. It doesn't have to be that big. I'm not bothered about size, and in fact if they are very big it makes oral sex a bit of a nightmare. Have you got a big one, Miles? I imagine yours is about normal size but straight and very hard. Hardness is more important than size – I don't think many men know that. So I was blowing this guy in the club in New York as he was calling his people to make sure I got the part. I was really happy at that point because I thought, At last, I am going to be an actress in Hollywood. Because although ER is set in Chicago, it's filmed in Hollywood so I was actually there. Only the part was this single mum who'd lost her baby but the story centred on the baby and how they found it and I only had two lines. They cut it out in the end and anyway Monica was freaking so I had to get back and start doing her PR again. That was just before Dave topped himself. Did you know Dave? No, I don't suppose you did, but the press were every-where when I got back. Like maggots on a dead dog – that's what Monica and I said as we looked out of her window. The kids were crying and I had Mustoe . . . my mum was on holiday so I actually had to look after him. That's my little boy. Loads of people can't believe I've got a kid because my nipples are still small even though my tits are quite big. Not massive, I haven't had them done like Monica did, but they drive blokes wild. Are you a tit man, Miles? Don't suppose you are. You look at my face when I talk, not my tits like most men. You're probably an arse man. Most clean men are because really they're poofs and they like to fuck a woman from the rear because then they can pretend she's a pretty boy. Weird, isn't it? So I think I should just give up being an actress and try to do something useful, you know, like aromatherapy. Have you ever had aromatherapy? It's amazing. Mind you, most men I know think it's stupid. I think it would be nice. I could maybe do aromatherapy for men, exclusively. You know, like a massage parlour only I wouldn't do wrist jobs. But I'd look very sexy in a white coat, quite a tight one that rode up a bit when I bent over. I'd like to do aromatherapy for a man and not do anything to his cock, just see it standing up under a towel. Does that sound cruel? I suppose I have a cruel streak in me but I do love to get a man going and then leave him to suffer. Is that bad? It doesn't feel that bad, more of a tease thing . . .'

Miles and Paula sat on the train facing each other. Miles was looking into her eyes, his palms up in front of him as Mario had shown him. It didn't seem to be having any effect.

They were on Eurostar, economy class, heading for Paris. Paula was in fine form. She hadn't stopped talking for a second since they'd met each other at Waterloo.

He had been back to the flat to get a change of clothes and some hardware for his computer. He didn't really want to go, his feelings were coming to the surface so much more. He knew he was having them now, he knew he always had, it had just been a bad connection. For a reason he couldn't fathom, whatever it was Mario was doing to him was slowly mending that connection.

The apartment was empty and cold. A lot of stuff had already been shipped back to the States. A neat pile of boxes stood in one corner and Donna had lined up every edition of Milky against the window facing the street. She wanted the world to know who she was. Even if the books were facing the street from some seventy feet in the air, it was her way of saying she existed. It was such a tragic sight, even Miles felt sad. She was such a tragic person. But he realised as he stood looking at the forlorn row of books that everyone he knew was tragic. That the whole world was tragic and he, himself, was part of that deep tragedy.

He had packed the things he needed into a small back pack and was just doing up the Velcro when Donna put her key in the door. Miles felt his heart leap, a really strong feeling, a surge of adrenaline and an increased heart rate so obvious he didn't need to check his pulse.

Donna stood still when she saw him in the middle of the room.

'Hi, you,' she said softly.

'Hello,' said Miles.

They stood looking at each other for a while.

'You okay?' she asked.

'Actually, yes, I'm pretty good.'

'I don't want to pry, but it's kind of hard not to want to know where you've been,' said Donna. She dropped her bags on the floor and walked into the kitchen. She appeared again, fitting the earpiece from her hands-free digital into her ear.

'Who are you calling?'

'My therapist of course. My God, I haven't seen you in ages, d'you expect me to be able to deal with that on my own!'

'Do you have to call her now?'

'Hi, Miles has shown up,' said Donna, not taking her eyes off him. 'Sure, he seems fine.'

'Donna, it would be good to talk without . . .'

She held up one hand and pressed the earpiece into her ear with the other.

'Sure, sure. But he looks very cute. He hasn't shaved in a while and it kind of suits him.' As she spoke her voice went up at the end of each sentence, which Miles had always admired.

'Donna, I can't stay.'

'Of course he wants to leave again already. Do I deserve this?'

'Are you asking me?' said Miles. He felt so different. He had never questioned her multiple conversations before. Had always sat and waited patiently or taken advantage of the fact she was talking to tidy up the flat. He looked at the pile of bags on the floor, the shoes she had just kicked off, the coat she had dropped by the kitchen door. There was nothing inside him any more that made him want to pick any of them up.

'What is it you want?' asked Donna. Miles glanced at her. She was looking at him. He pointed to himself, she nodded.

'Oh, right, just my bag. Needed a few things.'

'He just needs a few things,' she said.

He checked his watch, quickly worked out it had to be three in the morning in Seattle. He raised his eyebrows and snorted through his nose. He suddenly felt more sympathetic to the poor woman on the other end of the line.

'What about the apartment?' asked Donna.

'What about it?'

'Well, what are we going to do with it?'

'I don't know. I haven't thought.'

'D'you want to sell it?'

'I don't know. Do you?'

'No, I just want to move out and never see it again.'

'Okay, well, I can buy you out, I suppose.'

'But you bought it with your money.'

'Yeah, but we're married, you own half of it.'

'He says I own half of it,' Donna said to her therapist. Miles could just make out a voice on the other end.

'I may not want that responsibility,' said Donna. 'I may not want to deal with the fact that I own half of it. Why don't you keep this, and I'll keep the house in Seattle?'

'Suits me.'

'He's happy about that,' said Donna.

'Are you okay?' asked Miles. He had to wait for a reply.

'Yeah, okay,' Donna said. She switched off the phone and pulled out the earpiece. 'Sorry?'

'I just asked if you were okay.'

'Oh, well, I've been better. I'm flying back tomorrow. I've got to finish a new book by the end of the month, but I feel good about it. I know as soon as I get home Milky will be back. I still love you, Miles.'

She added the last part with no change of tone that he could detect. It came as a shock. She loved him. He felt waves of new and still unrecognised feelings.

'I still love you too. Weird, isn't it?'

She put her hands up in front of her, reminding him of the technique Mario had taught him for dealing with a Paula onslaught. It must be a therapy thing, he thought.

'I can't deal with that information right now.'

'Okay, fair enough,' said Miles. 'I'll change the subject. Have you seen Kulvinder?'

'Yeah, he's okay. Mad at you though.'

'What happened?'

'He laughed it off. You know what he's like, managed to wriggle out of the whole thing. He's still doing the whole

Nakasomi Bank thing, only not in this country. They're launching it in Europe first.'

'That's good,' said Miles. They stared at each other for a moment. 'Well, I'd better be off.'

'Okay. Bye-bye, English boy.'

'Yeah,' said Miles. 'Bye.'

On the train he wasn't listening to what Paula was saying, he just studied her face as she yabbered on and on. She didn't need any response from him. Although her diatribe was peppered with questions, they required no answers.

He was thinking about other things. He had so much to do in the next twenty-four hours and no time to do it. Although he had spent the entire previous night going through code he felt he had barely skimmed the surface of what he had set out to do. He looked at the slimline Sony Vaio laptop that Philippe had furnished him with, and spun through one of the huge files of code.

He lifted a massive spiral-bound document bearing the Eurotunnel logo which explained an incredibly complex list of instructions for a staggering array of machinery. Thumbing through to page 907, piston duct operating systems for the French sump area, he realised it was clearly going to take more time than he had.

'The coke dealer from San Diego that I was in the car crash with had one of those – he did all his deals via e-mail. He used that as he drove along. He was seriously cool until it all got out of hand and then he turned into a scared little boy, just before he died. I didn't tell you he died, did I? I think he was the only man I ever really loved. I mean, seriously loved. I met him while I was filming *ER*, the same night I met the artist formerly known as Prince and told him he was very short . . . that was a crazy night, I was completely hammered. So utterly hammered out of my tiny mind, I can't remember much about it . . .'

Miles was deep in code as the train went into the tunnel. His heart leapt, or stopped, he wasn't quite sure which. He wasn't scared of tunnels but the tunnel now meant something very different. It certainly did something. He felt things. He was feeling anxiety, nausea, constipation and exhilaration. He was actually excited. He was sitting opposite a young PR woman who claimed she excelled in giving oral sex. She was very beautiful in a ravaged sort of way, barely dressed and completely mad. He was going to France to stay for one night in a little hotel before he took part in the biggest robbery in the history of crime.

He smiled to himself. He actually felt something. Although he knew he and Paula were deeply tragic and flawed people, it felt good, it felt life was worth living. He assumed by logical deduction that what he was feeling was happiness.

Chapter Thirty-Four

Mario checked his satellite phone answering service. There were no messages. In all the time he had been running the Lupo Foundation this had never happened before.

He was trying not to worry. He was breathing into the fear that it had finally come to an end: twelve years of incredible success, more money than he knew what to do with and the adoration of a côterie of rich and powerful people. Word of the disaster at the château must have spread through the closely linked community in which he worked.

He was sitting in a little room of a small family-run hotel in Coquelles, just outside Calais in Northern France. He was alone, Philippe having gone out to track down essential supplies. Mario had spent ten minutes on the phone to the very expensive nanny he had hired on previous occasions to look after the various children he had fathered. She assured him both children were fine and there was nothing to worry about.

He tried to reassure himself that everything was going to plan, but it was a very high-risk venture. He had his paper on trauma therapy to present in Zurich in one week and had barely started to formulate what he was going to say. So much to do and so little time to do it.

There was a knock on the door. He opened it. Anna Benz stood on the threshold.

'Anna, good to see you. You okay?' he asked.

'Everything is fine. I have left the car Philippe supplied in the car park in England as you said. I came across in my car. Everything seems to be in order.'

'This is good. And you are pleased with the car?'

'It seems very good, perfect for the job. It is the Jaguar XKR coupé. It has a 4-litre V8 with manual gears which is unusual as the type is usually fitted with a sophisticated auto box, but I am happier with manual.'

Mario smiled. He was amused by the fact that this woman's obsession was so unlike Paula's. A great many of his female clients fell into the Paula Bentley mould. The Anna Benzes of this world were a rarer commodity.

'And you have said nothing to the others about this aspect of the exercise?'

'I have not mentioned it. Just as you asked.'

'Good, this is good. It will all become clear tomorrow. As soon as you are out of the tunnel, you are in control, Anna. You will have to be forceful and determined, no matter what happens.'

'I understand.'

Mario smiled at her. If only, he thought, if only his old method of therapy would still work, or if he at least believed it worked, he would love to engage Anna in one of his old exercises in bed.

It was not to be. He had to turn over a new leaf if he was not to go stale and tire of his work. He loved the controlling aspect of this new method. Keeping each individual member of the team in the dark as to what the others would do. In the tunnel, it was Miles who was in control. He knew everything about the tunnel, the two women knew very little. Outside the tunnel, Anna took over. Paula, on the other hand, merely had to do the exercise and not tell anyone about it after the event. That was enough for her. Each experience individually tailored to suit the person concerned.

'You don't want to sleep, Anna?'

'No, I am not tired. I think this idea is crazy and I'm sure I will end up dead or in prison, but whatever is happening, it seems to be working. I feel wide awake.'

'This is excellent. Excellent. Have you heard from the others?'

'No.'

'I can't help worrying that they will not appear. There is nothing I can do to make them.'

'I think they will appear.'

'You feel you know Miles already. You feel you have some special bond with him.'

'I think so.'

'This is fine. As long as nothing happens before tomorrow, I wish you well.'

Anna looked at Mario for a minute. She had started to turn back into the woman he had first met eighteen months before. Dark and mysterious but very attractive. He had registered a tinge of jealousy when he'd overheard her express her desire for Miles. It was normal, he'd experienced it before. The relationship between therapist and client was always a delicate one. He had learned from first-hand experience that relationships with clients could become very complex. Destructive even. He looked at his bedside table where he'd left the little leather folder where he kept pictures of his fourteen children. It was something he normally kept out of sight of his clients and he hoped Anna wouldn't notice it.

'I just want to thank you, Mario,' she said finally. 'You are the only person who has ever really helped me.'

'Don't thank me now,' he said. 'Thank me tomorrow, after the exercise.'

Chapter Thirty-Five

Miles and Paula arrived at the hotel in the early evening. As they approached the check-in desk Miles saw Philippe pull up outside in yet another car. He extracted several large bags from the rear and entered the hotel as they were checking in.

'Everything okay?' asked Philippe with a broad smile, dumping the heavy bags on the floor beside them.

'Suppose so,' said Miles. 'We've been sitting on trains for the best part of seven hours and I've certainly learned a lot about Paula.'

'He's been so good, he's listened to me solidly ever since we met at Waterloo. I haven't stopped, have I? Not once. And he's been working away on his little computer and smiling at me. He never taped my mouth up. Even when I asked him if he wanted me to go down on him under the table just to give his ears a rest, he was a real gentleman and said it wouldn't be necessary. Isn't that English? Only an Englishman could say a blow job wouldn't be necessary. You've never said that, have you, Philippe?'

He was completely ignoring her, filling in the little form the grey-haired lady behind the desk had given them.

Ten minutes later they were all crowded into Mario's room for the final briefing.

'This is the stage that makes me most tense. There is still time to stop, any of us can still pull out. We do not have to do the exercise. I want to make that very clear indeed.'

Philippe shook his head in disbelief.

'You have a problem, Philippe?'

'I have just spent the last three weeks setting up this crazy thing, and now you are saying we can all pull out?'

'It is essential that people do not feel coerced into doing it. It has to be undertaken of their own free will. If not, it's just a crazy game that no one really wants to play, and that won't help anyone.'

'I'm in,' said Miles.

'Me too,' said Anna.

'I'm trying to nod and not say anything like I have done before but I've started talking again which is really depressing. I really hoped that by now I'd be all calm and peaceful inside and all at one with myself and just be able to sit here and say nothing, be sort of mysterious like Anna is. That's why Miles is attracted to her because she's mysterious, and I'm all open and on display. It's all very genital, isn't it? You know how a woman's genitals are sort of hidden and mysterious, except when she has her legs really wide apart and the lights full on which is what I always thought men wanted. But if I could be like Anna, I wouldn't need to do that. I could have sex in the dark which would probably be really nice and romantic and make you feel close to the person, maybe even in love. I'd love to be in love, I've never done it. What's it like? Will I find out after tomorrow? I hope so . . .'

Philippe gently stuck the tape over her mouth and stroked her hair.

'Thank you, Philippe, that was very kind,' said Mario. 'Now, let us go over the plan one more time. As you say in England, the devil is in the detail.'

Chapter Thirty-Six

The sun was just coming up over the low flat horizon as Miles set out on his bike from the hotel. He rode along the seafront. A cool wind was coming off the grey expanse of water. He knew that in a few hours he would be deep underneath that same sea. It looked very cold although the wind was fairly warm.

France. He decided it felt good being this side of the Channel. He looked towards England. He didn't feel like he belonged there now. France felt right somehow, or maybe it wasn't France, maybe it was Europe. People felt like grown ups in Europe while England was a naughty teenager who didn't want to join in but still wanted the sweets.

He stared at the beach as he made his way along the deserted road. To one side was a large expanse of featureless flat sand, the waves barely breaking on the shore. A few gulls did their lonely swooping stuff.

He remembered the opening sequences of the film *Saving Private Ryan*. It would have been about this time in the morning that the landing craft appeared, sailing towards the slaughter. He knew that geographically they had actually landed to the south, but the look of the beach and the light must have been very similar. He remembered watching the film in Seattle with Donna. He'd had no desire to see it but she was obsessed with the film; watched it nine times as soon as it came out.

He had checked his pulse to see if the brutal, visceral images at the start of the film were having any effect on him. Nothing.

He smiled at the memory. That was then. Now he had feelings and he felt good. He wouldn't be able to watch the film again, it would affect him too deeply. He worried for a moment about what other things would affect him after the exercise. Maybe he would be hampered by feelings, unable to do anything because it was all too intense.

He looked out at the beach again and felt a shiver of fear run through him. How did anyone cope with running into a hail of bullets? He had lived to the age of thirty-five and never been in a war. He was so lucky. He could do more or less anything he liked, anything he felt like doing. He could just turn around and cycle off through France, forget the whole stupid exercise, but he knew he wouldn't. It was impossible to stop now.

He rode towards the empty factory as directed, feeling even happier. What he felt like doing right there and then was stealing a huge amount of money for no reason whatsoever.

Before he left London he had been to an autoteller, the normal variety, and asked for a statement. He had £32,000 in his current account and just short of £3 million in a special savings account. He knew he had another £3 million in bonds in America. Then there was the Swiss thing, about £8 million in that, and a £750,000 flat with no mortgage which his estranged wife didn't seem to want. Then he remembered that he had started an ethical investment portfolio looked after by a brokerage company in the City. This made him smile, he'd actually forgotten about it. His total wealth was close to £15 million. He really didn't need to steal any more, but it made total sense.

He liked the feeling that he didn't need money. He had withdrawn £500 which was still in the Velcro-fastened wallet in his inside pocket.

The empty factory looked deserted, there seemed to be no one around. Miles pedalled slowly towards the gates and was just becoming concerned that he had gone to the wrong location when he heard a 'Pssst'.

Philippe appeared from a rubbish-filled doorway and beckoned him. Miles got off his bike and pushed it along.

'Everything okay?'

'*Oui.*'

They walked past some rusting scrap metal and Miles saw the container lorry parked to one side of the stripped out factory building.

Mario was at the rear where the doors stood open. Miles looked up inside the lorry. On top of a huge pile of brown cardboard boxes, which by the printing on them must contain computer monitors, he saw Anna and Paula. They smiled down at him.

'Nice of you to come,' said Anna.

'Wouldn't miss it for the world.'

'This is a totally legitimate cargo,' said Mario. 'These are computers bound for the UK market, shipped from Holland. All the paperwork is correct.'

'There is, of course, additionally all the necessary equipment we discussed. You will find it in the boxes at the front here,' said Philippe, pointing to a row of cardboard containers resting directly by the doors.

He gave Miles a leg up and he slid in beside the two women on the boxes. There was only enough room between the boxes and the roof of the container for them to lie down.

Philippe passed up the bike and Miles manoeuvred it behind him to where two other bikes were lying.

'You look fantastic,' said Mario. 'I am so proud of you. Whatever happens, we will never forget this moment. I know that when I see you again, you are going to be very different, very happy people. I love all of you very much.'

Miles noticed a tear forming in the corner of Mario's eye. It could just have been the chill morning air, he thought, until Mario wiped it away, a little embarrassed.

'In a few moments I will drive the lorry into the container loading yard at the tunnel entrance. The container will be lifted on to the train by an enormous mobile crane. The train will take it into the tunnel. You will know when the container is locked into position because the levers which fix it are quite noisy. Once the train moves, you wait fourteen minutes exactly before you start the operation. Okay?'

'Okay,' said Anna.

Philippe looked at his watch. 'We must go,' he said flatly, and gave them a little salute.

'*Bonne chance, mes braves.*'

'*Merci,*' replied Anna.

'*Oui, merci* me too,' said Paula.

'Thanks,' said Miles.

'Think safety, always, all the time. That is the most important thing. Think safety.'

'We will.'

Philippe slowly closed the doors and it went very dark.

There was no sound. Paula didn't say anything. Miles could only hear himself breathing. He held his breath for a moment and then noticed he could hear Anna and Paula breathing as well. He could sense Anna near him. He wanted to hold her. He was having some very serious feelings and they were fantastic. He smiled to himself, could almost hear the smile. He was feeling deliriously happy. This was the best thing he had ever done in his life.

'What was that?' whispered Paula. There was a sound, quite far away. Miles felt a slight jolting sensation. It could have been Anna or Paula, but the movement was suddenly joined by an unmistakable sound: a large diesel engine starting up.

'What's that?' asked Paula again.

'Philippe has started the truck,' said Miles. 'Here we go.'

'I'm scared,' said Paula.

'That is good,' said Anna. 'So am I.'

I'm not, thought Miles. Not in the least.

The container started to move. The silence turned into a noisy, creaking, ominous rumbling. They began to slide around on top of the boxes. Miles felt his head bang into something.

'Ouch!' said Anna.

'Sorry.'

'It's not your fault, Miles,' she said. He felt her hand against his face, reached up and took hold of it.

'Who's that?' said Paula. 'Someone's holding my hand.'

He let go at once. 'Sorry.' The container swung violently

and they all slid to one side. Miles felt himself land on top of Anna and Paula but couldn't tell which was which. He was still smiling. Even this was fantastic, sliding around on a load of packing cases containing computer screens, finding himself lying on top of two young women in the total dark. He was in heaven.

The sliding and jolting went on for quite some time, then everything went quiet. The engine died and they heard the cab door shut. Two thumps rang through the container.

'What was that?' asked Paula.

'Philippe saying goodbye,' said Anna.

'Yeah, that must be it,' Miles agreed.

There was a slight pause then a fairly violent shudder, followed by the same feeling Miles got when he travelled in fast lifts. A heavy feeling, followed by a light feeling.

'We're up on the crane.'

This was followed by an equally rapid descent which ended in a metallic clank as the container was lowered on to the train.

They all heard the securing levers clunk noisily into place, the container shuddered and then there was silence.

'Everybody ready?' asked Miles.

'I am,' said Anna.

'I don't know if I am,' Paula faltered. 'I . . .'

'Try not to start,' said Miles quickly. 'Try with all your might not to speak.'

He could hear her struggling, making little constipated, grunting sounds.

'We should have the night-vision goggles on in here,' said Anna. 'Then at least we could have seen what was going on. Seen each other. It's very disorienting.'

'The batteries wouldn't have lasted long enough,' said Miles. 'We'll really need them in the tunnel.'

They lay waiting for what felt like hours. Miles checked the watch Philippe had given him, pressed the little button on the side until the face lit up. 9.22. They had been in the truck for over three hours.

'We've still got a long wait,' he said.

'We could always have some sex. That passes the time,' suggested Paula.

There was a silence. Miles didn't say anything but he would very much have liked to have had some sex. He didn't really care who it was with, he'd probably never know. They would know, of course, which would be strange.

'No. No sex,' said Anna.

'Don't think it's a very good idea,' said Miles quickly.

Silence engulfed them. Miles moved his feet inside his shoes. He couldn't feel them. Numbness descended. He checked his pulse. Very low, almost stopped.

After a long time of complete silence, they felt a slow, subtle movement.

'The train is starting to move,' said Miles quickly as he checked his watch. 10.05. They had exactly fourteen minutes before going into action.

Chapter Thirty-Seven

DI Willis had spent many hours of his life sitting in the rear seats of Ford cars waiting for something to happen. It was nothing new, although this operation was rather different because the other three officers in the car with him were all from the Territorial Support Group, and as their name suggested, were seriously tooled up.

Only a few inches from his right cheek was the snub-nosed barrel of a matt black, very dangerous-looking sub-machine-gun being cradled by a very professional-looking fellow. Willis too was wearing a heavy black bullet-proof vest. It was tight and uncomfortable and he worried about it stretching the sports jacket he had pulled on over it.

Their unmarked car was parked in the private driveway of a bungalow not five hundred yards from the entrance to the building site. The owner of the bungalow, a pensioner, was very happy to help. Not all members of the public hated the police, the old man had informed Willis when they first met. He only hoped there wasn't a big ugly shoot out and the old soldier caught a stray bullet as he leaned over his gate to watch. They always told members of the public to stay indoors, but when serious police action was taking place, who'd want to miss it? He knew he wouldn't.

Barker and Reynolds, the two officers who had been posted in the disused garage opposite the entrance, had made positive sightings of at least four ex-servicemen who had done time.

They hadn't, however, seen Donald Cooper. Willis still had no concrete evidence that a job was going down and was trying to work out why McKay and the Yard were throwing so much manpower and hardware into his hunch. The area was flooded with police marksmen, armed rapid response squads and, ominously, three ambulances, parked in a school playground half a mile away.

'Barker to DI Willis,' crackled the radio.

'What is it?' he snapped. They were meant to be maintaining radio silence.

'Cooper's just arrived, black Cherokee Jeep, nice motor, registration Kimono four three, Charlie Alpha . . .'

'Yeah, all right, leave it out or the whole thing is pants,' growled Willis.

He dropped his radio on the seat.

'What a fucking tosser!' he said, although inside he was hugely relieved. The elusive Major Cooper really *did* exist.

'One in every team,' said the driver of the vehicle.

'Speak for yourself,' said the occupant of the passenger seat, a very large black officer.

They sat in silence for a moment. A tipper truck carrying a mound of earth drove past, thumping its wheels into a broken manhole cover with an alarming noise which resulted in large clumps of earth and rock being dropped on the road in front of them.

'Look at that pillock,' exclaimed the driver. 'We should pull him over. Unsafe load, innit?'

'Excellent idea with only ten major drawbacks,' said Willis sarcastically. 'One, only a twat would blow their cover at this moment. Two, only a total twat would even think of such a thing. Three . . .'

'All right, calm down,' said the black officer. Willis looked at the back of his head. He wasn't sure of the bloke's rank, but was pretty certain he wasn't an Inspector.

'Who are you telling to calm down?'

'Look, we're all a bit tense, okay? Let's just stay calm until we have to move because then the shit's really going to hit the old ventilation. These are all ex-forces blokes, they love nothing better than a good ruckus. Okay?'

The officer turned around and smiled at Willis who smiled back sarcastically then stared out of the window at the privet hedge all of a foot away.

'I'll tell you a story,' said the black officer.

'Oh, we're fucked now,' said the officer sitting cradling the sub-machine-gun beside Willis.

'When I was a rookie . . .'

'Oh, not this one!' groaned the driver.

'No, you haven't heard this one. Right, okay, there was this little fellow, Patrick. He was only about eighteen and was trying so hard, know what I mean? He was extra nice to me 'cos I was a darkie, thought he needed to prove there isn't any racism in the police and all that bull. Well, he went to see this family what had been burgled and wrote his report out, stuck by the book all the way. Two days later he was hauled up in front of the Chief Inspector who, for your information, was a fucking fascist bastard. The Chief was shouting so loud we all heard him.

'"How many times have we got to tell you not to use racist language?" he says. "Look at this report!" And he started reading it out. "The burglary happened while the Paki family were out shopping and the Paki family state that they lost a video recorder and a hi-fi system." He went on and on, bawling his head off at this poor mug, Paki this, Paki that, until finally this little guy Patrick managed to explain that the family's name was Paki. Get it? It was Mr and Mrs Paki. Poor little sod! We fucking pissed ourselves.'

There was silence in the car.

'Maybe you had to be there,' said the black officer. Willis sighed and checked his watch. Still another hour at least.

Chapter Thirty-Eight

'We move now,' said Miles. He had been staring at his watch for the previous three minutes, watching the digital display of the numbers as they headed for zero. The journey had been highly disorienting as the movement of the train, once it had started, was minimal. The tracks in the tunnel were so smooth and level it was hard to tell if they were actually still moving.

He reached for his belt and felt for the night-vision goggles strapped there. He pulled them over his head and switched them on as Philippe had shown him. The first thing he saw was the ghostly green outlines of Anna and Paula. Also clearly wearing their goggles they looked like bad aliens in a science fiction TV series. They were staring at him.

'Have you had yours switched on a long time?' asked Miles.

'We had to,' said Paula. 'I was going to go, like, totally insane if I couldn't see anything. I can't take the dark because it confronts me with who I actually am, and that's not nice. You should know that.'

'Yeah, but if the batteries run out when we're in the tunnel, we're really in trouble,' said Miles.

'Oh, God! Oh, God!'

'Don't worry, we're going to move so fast they won't have a chance to run out,' snapped Anna.

Miles slid himself off the top of the boxes and clambered towards the doors of the container. He looked into the bag slung over his shoulder. Inside was a battery-operated steel cutter. He had only used it a couple of times before, cutting the front off a car in a scrap yard while being given constant tuition by Philippe. Miles pushed a foam plug in each ear and turned to look at the women.

'Ears!' he shouted then switched on the machine. The noise it made and the kick it gave in his hands were surprising for such a compact little tool. He forced the rapidly moving blade between the two doors at about shoulder height. Philippe had drawn a chalk mark to help him. He moved the blade down slowly. It ripped through the rubber seal on the door with ease, sending shreds of rubber flying in every direction.

The whole point of the exercise was to not leave a trace that they had been there If Miles cut the lock in the right way, there would be no external evidence.

As soon as it hit something solid the noise was painful, even with the ear plugs inserted. It was the hasp of the door lock, a hardened steel bar fifteen millimetres thick. Miles' hands started shaking violently as the blade got to work. Before long sparks started to shower the inside of the container, appearing dazzlingly bright in their night-vision goggles.

Before long the blade moved swiftly downwards. The job was done. Miles switched off the cutter, his ears ringing from the noise. He put the blade guard back on it and slipped it inside his bag.

With one powerful shoulder barge the doors opened and the noise of the train suddenly increased.

'Move!' shouted Miles. Or thought he shouted though he couldn't be sure. It didn't sound like a shout, but then everything seemed a bit muffled.

They clambered down the now half-crushed mountain of boxes and pushed the doors wide open. They pulled up the night-vision goggles and stepped out on to the well-lit freight train.

The noise was much greater outside the cocoon of the metal box. Miles looked at Paula and Anna. They both seemed terrified.

'We must start,' he said as loud as he could. He was surprised when, without hesitation, Anna and Paula moved off in different directions between the surrounding containers. Miles went back into theirs and started ripping open cardboard boxes. He opened three, all packed with various items of equipment, before he found the one he was looking for. It was a plastic drum with a screwtop lid. He heaved it out of the box and manhandled it out of the container.

He tipped it on its side and unscrewed the lid. Immediately a gush of diesel fluid glugged out of the spout, pouring and splashing through the grid floor and on to the concrete track bed speeding past below.

Soon, hopefully, it would do its job.

Miles left the plastic drum to empty and moved along the length of the container, the sides of the tunnel shooting past only feet away. As he passed each container he checked its serial number against a small slip of paper he was carrying. He passed three before he saw Anna out of the corner of his eye. She was looking up at the container in front of them. She glanced over at him and nodded. He checked the numbers. P38/9/F03. She was right. He gave her the thumbs up sign, she returned the signal and started back in the direction they had come.

Miles moved to the container doors and checked out the door-locking mechanism. This was going to be much harder than cutting his way out from inside the container. This lock and hasp were secured within a toughened steel hood.

He had practised the operation with Philippe, but that was on a stationary container in a factory yard. Here he was hanging on as a high wind buffeted him.

He pulled out the metal cutter and pulled down his night-vision goggles to protect his eyes. He flicked the switch and got to work. Sparks immediately flew about in a frenzy as the blade bit deep into the steel body of the large padlock. There was no way of reaching the steel hoop of the lock; that was buried deep within the mechanism. A bolt cutter would be useless. The cutting blade glowed red, then white, before it finally cut through. The padlock fell on the floor at his feet. Miles looked up and saw Anna and

Paula watching him. They were standing with the three bikes leaning against the side of the next container.

'You are so sexy,' said Paula. 'The way you operate tools is a total, and I mean total, turn on.'

He smiled at them.

'Did you pour the diesel fluid?' asked Anna.

'Done.' As he spoke they felt the train start to slow down. The sound changed around them as the brakes squealed on, the noise echoing around the tunnel.

Miles held on to the locking mechanism with his left hand and used his right foot to kick at the door. Slowly it opened as the train braked. This container had its opening facing in the direction they were travelling. Not something they'd considered at the planning stages.

As the forces from the train's braking continued to increase, the contents of the newly opened container started to shift like badly packed shopping in the rear of a hatchback. A plastic-wrapped block of notes slipped off the top and crashed to the ground. Miles stepped back rapidly as it was followed by three more, then it seemed a whole wall of money came thundering out of the container.

'*Verdammte Scheiße!*' shouted Anna. '*Ich werd' verrückt!*'

'I don't believe my eyes,' said Paula. 'Look at all that money!'

'*So viel Geld!*'

The train juddered and finally stopped. The noise around them rapidly died and Miles was suddenly aware of his own breathing. It was rapid, almost panicked. He quickly checked his pulse. It was very, very high. He smiled.

The sight before him was, to say the least, overwhelming. Tipped on the floor and piled up to the roof of the container in very neat, plastic-wrapped bundles were billions of pounds sterling in used notes.

'Bloody hell.'

'*Gott in Himmel.*'

'Fuck my old boots.'

Anna tugged at Miles' sleeve. 'I'll start looking for fifties, you and Paula get the bikes ready,' she said calmly.

Miles couldn't take his eyes off the money. He had never seen anything like it. He picked up one bundle that lay at his feet. It was heavier than he'd expected, the plastic wrapping slightly torn from its fall. The identification docket attached had all the information he needed.

£3,000,000 *Sterling. Denomination 20.*

It had been sent from a bank in Austria.

'Now!' said Anna. Miles looked at her. He wanted to kiss her. He dropped the bundle and felt his pulse again. It was racing like a wild horse.

'Fantastic!' he said with a broad smile.

He turned and started fitting pannier bags to his bike. Then he extracted a rucksack from inside one of the panniers and handed it to Paula.

'No one is ever going to believe this,' she said as she wriggled and struggled into the straps.

'No one is ever going to hear about it.'

'Oh, my God! Oh, my God! I've never done anything I haven't told everyone I know everything about,' she said. Then turned and smiled at him.

'This is fantastic! I love Mario so much. I will never tell anyone, I can feel it.' She thumped herself in the stomach. 'Here. In my womb. I can feel it there. It's going to stay with me forever.'

She threw herself at Miles, wrapping her legs around his waist and kissing him on the lips. He pulled away, not wanting Anna to see this display.

'Shag me here. Hold me down and fuck me on the metal floor. Make me dirty,' Paula said between kisses. 'Defile me – make me filthy. I haven't had a good, hard, dirty fuck in weeks.'

Miles lifted her off and put her down in front of him. He was surprised by the reaction he'd experienced. He was sexually aroused, uncomfortably so.

'Sorry, baby, no can do,' he said, then started laughing. Paula was laughing too and shaking her head. He stroked her cheek gently.

'You're gorgeous,' she said.

'You're not so bad yourself.'

Their moment of rapture was shattered.

'How long have we got?' Anna shouted from inside the container.

Miles checked his watch.

'We have two minutes thirty before the driver will receive clearance to re-start the train. We have to be off by then.'

He glanced inside the container and saw that Anna had tidied the fallen plastic-wrapped bundles to one side.

'We've got to get everything back in here when we've finished,' she said, pointing to the bundles that had escaped. 'That's going to take time. We have to work extra fast.'

Without a word Paula started to stuff a bundle into her pannier bag.

Miles checked his watch as another three bundles came flying out of the back of the container.

'Two minutes!' he shouted. He stuffed the bundles into the panniers of the bike he was supporting. It was a tight fit and the bike immediately became very heavy.

'I can't find any more fifties. It's all in twenties,' Anna screamed from deep inside the container.

'Make it twenties then, we have to go!' shouted Miles. He was dreading the feeling of the train moving again. They would have to jump for it and leave the money and the bikes. It didn't bear thinking about.

It was only then that he noticed a sudden movement of air. Something was happening in the tunnel around them. There was a distant rumbling sound which Miles rapidly realised was a forerunner of what was to come. A ferocious wind suddenly blasted past them, rattling the panelling on the side of the containers. The smell of diesel fumes was very strong.

'Quick, we really have to move!' he screamed.

'What is it?' Anna shouted back.

'They've started the ventilators. Huge fans are sucking air through the tunnel to remove the fumes. This is only going to get worse.'

Two more bundles dropped at his feet. He pulled the empty

rucksack from his back and opened it, slipped one of the bundles inside, pulled the toggles tight and slid it back on. It was very heavy. He worried about Paula. How was she going to cope?

He glanced at her. She seemed completely happy. She had her rucksack on and by the look of the bulge and the way the straps were digging into her slight shoulders, it was already loaded with money.

Anna appeared by the opening of the container. She kicked three more bundles down and jumped after them.

'We have no more time, we have to go.' She stuffed a pack of money into her rucksack and the remaining bundles into the panniers on her bike.

Miles leant his bike against the side of the container and started throwing the fallen bundles back into the chaos inside. One kept falling back out.

'Grab the doors, pull them half closed, I'll chuck it in and then slam them!' he ordered. Anna and Paula ran to either side of the container and did as they were told. Miles threw the heavy bundle as far up as he could. It wedged itself between the piles of other bundles and the door. He could see Anna pushing the door as hard as she could. Nothing was happening.

He joined her and they started to make some headway, but then – disaster. Paula let go of her door and walked towards them. As she did, a huge pile of bundles toppled out, knocking her on to the floor grating. She screamed in pain. Miles and Anna let go of their door and even more bundles started to fall. Miles grabbed Anna and pulled her back. By the time the avalanche had settled, it seemed like half the contents of the container were on the floor in front of them.

Miles checked his watch. 'Thirty-two seconds over. Houston, we have a problem.'

Anna climbed over the fallen bundles to try to free Paula. She clambered to her feet with difficulty but clearly wasn't totally out of action.

'I'll get up there, you pass them up,' said Miles as he clambered into the back of the container.

The three of them worked frantically for a further two

minutes, throwing and stacking million-pound bundles of twenty-pound notes. The last two were very difficult, they had to be stuffed right up on top of the pile. Anna and Paula held the doors while Miles jumped down and they closed easily.

Without hesitation he fished in his shoulder bag and found an identical padlock to the one he had cut open. Philippe had done his research well. He slipped the lock through the hasp, turned the key and stepped back.

'Good as new. No one will ever know we've been here.'

'They will when they open the container we were travelling in,' said Anna

'But that won't be for a long time. Now, let's go.'

'I love you!' said Anna.

'I know,' said Miles with a broad smile.

Paula looked at them and said nothing.

There was a half-metre gap between the train floor and the safety walkway that ran alongside the track. Miles jumped over and pulled the first bike across as Anna pushed it towards him.

Paula pushed her bike forward and again Miles strained to heave its unbalanced weight over the gap. By the time Anna pushed the last bike, it was all he could do to hold the weight. He was sweating profusely, eyes stinging from the rivulets of perspiration that ran down his forehead.

The train started to move just as Paula jumped to the raised walkway. She lost her balance a little. He grabbed her arm and steadied her.

'Close,' he said.

'Thanks,' squeaked Paula.

They started pushing the heavily laden bikes along the raised walkway. Unfortunately, this was against the direction of the powerful wind now blasting right into their faces. The noise was painful as the train built up speed, containers passing them faster and faster and only half a metre away.

'The nearest connecting tunnel should only be about fifty metres along here,' shouted Anna. Miles looked back over his shoulder. For as far as he could see there was the endless rattling train and the string of lights along the tunnel's roof.

'Here!' shouted Anna. They gathered around and saw the door, just as Philippe had described it. 'Emergency Use Only' it said in English and French, large black letters on a bright yellow background. Just below this legend ran the dire warning: 'Opening doors creates danger of very strong wind'.

There was a loud noise coming from just above the door, an ear-piercing scream of wind, and behind it a ground-rumbling thunder of machinery.

Anna pressed the large mushroom-shaped plunger to one side of the door and instantly all hell broke loose. Lights around the door started to flash; there was the repetitive blast of an alarm klaxon coming from somewhere nearby. Miles and Paula looked up and down the track but saw no one. At any moment he had been expecting to see black-clad security police rushing towards him carrying machine-guns and stun grenades.

With a steady increase in the wind noise, the doors started to open. Miles felt his trousers pull on his legs. The force was immense as the crack in the doors widened. Like three pieces of litter on a train platform, they were literally blown through the door and down a shallow flight of concrete stairs. All around was confusion and chaos. The panniers dropped off the bikes and continued their journey downwards. One bike jammed against the wall and stopped Miles' descent. He couldn't hear anything, all he could feel was choking dust and the incredible force of the wind. He realised he was holding Anna's leg, and Paula was holding Anna's head. He glanced at her face and could see at once that Anna was not particularly comfortable or relaxed.

When the wind suddenly died the effect was most disturbing. The dust just seemed to drop from the air. Everything stopped moving. Miles' ears rang, reminding him of the after-effects of standing in the front row at a very loud rock concert when he was a teenager. He glanced back in the direction they had come. The lights of the end of the train flashed past the emergency escape. The door was still open, so the wind should still be blowing. His mind raced through the details of the control systems he had studied in such detail.

'The safety systems must have reversed the ventilation,' he said. 'But the suction from the train could pull us back up there – we've got to close the doors!'

As he spoke they started to feel wind blowing in the other direction.

Anna scrambled to her feet and pushed the large yellow button mounted on a control box on the wall. The machinery spun into life and the doors closed smoothly. As the wind and the noise from the receding train died, all they could hear was a low mechanical rumble somewhere in the distance.

Within a few seconds they had managed to reload their bikes. They bumped them down the flight of stairs, the noise of machinery growing ever louder as they descended.

When Miles reached the bottom of the stairs he looked around frantically. The walls were covered in pipes and wires of various diameters. The whole scene was far more complex than he had imagined or Philippe had explained.

He ran his hand down the wall, over the various pipes, until he noticed a yellow plastic conduit. It was pure guesswork that this contained the fibre-optic cable that ran the length of the tunnel, but as he followed it he could see it did go into a box which looked like it had a power supply feeding it, and the box was big enough to house an EP380 booster, the type he was hoping for.

He motioned for the others to stop. Anna checked her watch.

'Three minutes,' she said.

'I need two.' Miles unzipped the pocket of the small bag he had strapped to his front and pulled out the Sony Vaio notebook computer. He placed this on the floor and opened it. Pressed the on key and stood up.

'What's this for?' asked Paula, looking at him in utter adoration.

'This is our ticket to the other side,' said Miles. 'Prepare for the ride of your life.'

He pulled out a Braun electric screwdriver and undid the maintenance plate on the box. He let the plate drop to the floor. Inside, sure enough, an EP380, exactly the unit he and Kulvinder had had to master in their designs for the autoteller.

The fibre-optic cable fed in at one side. He unscrewed the front housing of the unit and blinked. More complicated than he remembered. Seventy-five sets of wires, three control chips and a neat stack of circuit boards. He checked the colour coding on the wires leading to the mother board.

He knew it was the green and yellow striped wires, not the green and yellow banded or the blue and green co-ordinated. With a tool on his Leatherman he bared enough wire to do the job.

He cast a glance at Anna and Paula who were both watching him with fascination.

'I like watching men's hands when they work,' said Anna.

Miles smiled, winked at them, and found a small black connection box in his shoulder bag. Two fine red wires ran from the box, ending in minute brass crocodile clips. He attached these to the wires he had just bared.

He squatted down, pressed two keys on the keyboard of the Sony and a little window appeared.

Miles typed **r u** and **n** at the end of the code and clicked the return key. Text started to scroll across the screen at invisible speed. He moved the cursor using the touch pad and opened another window. This one had a series of sliding bars which moved rapidly up and down.

'Who's that?' asked Anna.

'An encryption cracker. It's actually illegal.'

'What does it do?' asked Paula. She squatted down beside him. 'Do you really, like, actually understand what's going on on the screen?'

'Well, yes, I designed the program.'

'God, you are *so* clever! I love you.'

'Oh, right,' said Miles. 'Well, this program is checking the central computers that control the tunnel. One in England, one in France. It's sending little messages to both computers asking for password confirmation from either. Once one of them sends it to the other, this little computer will pick it up en route, and bingo, we're in.'

The computer made a plaintive little beep noise and a new window appeared on the screen. On it was written **long dark tubeXIF**.

'That's the password. Bit naff, isn't it?'

Miles typed rapidly and opened another window.

'This is the program which will help us. Get your helmets and goggles on. As soon as I press this,' he pointed to the return key, 'the program will start to run. The batteries in the laptop will be under a lot of pressure. They should protect us for about twenty, maybe twenty-five minutes. If all goes well, we should reach the air-lock doors at the tunnel's entrance just as the program opens them. There can be no stopping en route or we're dead meat. Okay?'

The women nodded.

'Okay. Now, I don't know quite how quickly it's going to kick in so . . .'

They all pulled on their helmets and night-vision goggles.

'Ready?'

'Ready,' said the women in unison. He pressed the return key and nothing happened. He pulled up his goggles to get a better look at the screen. A little box flickered, the egg timer symbol hovering in front of it. Miles bit his lip and stared at the screen, not knowing what to do. He looked at the wires. All the connections seemed good. Maybe they had security systems he didn't know about. Maybe there was something happening he wasn't aware of. He had assumed that as soon as he pressed return, the system would shut down and he would take over.

Suddenly the egg timer turned into a cursor arrow and all around them the lights went out. He knew then they were okay. A little slower than planned, but clearly the program was doing its job.

Chapter Thirty-Nine

Jean-Paul Marionne purchased his favourite coffee from the Pret-à-Manger concession in the passenger waiting building of the Folkestone terminal. He walked back through security and made his way across the windy car park to the main terminal control building in the heart of the Eurotunnel complex. He climbed the concrete steps thinking about his son, Christophe, who had just started school in Paris. Although Jean-Paul now lived and worked in England, his family still lived in France. It wasn't that far away, he visited constantly, but he felt uneasy. He didn't know if his marriage was over or if this was just a phase he and his wife Katya were going through.

He slipped his card through the security swipe and pushed his way through the heavy revolving gates. As he entered the building he saw Maisie, the cleaner, whom he usually found having a cigarette outside the entrance when he arrived.

'They're screaming for you downstairs, Mr Marionne,' said Maisie. 'Something's gone wrong. Search me what it is.'

Jean-Paul looked down at his bleeper. The screen was blank. Was it turned off or was the battery dead?

'*Merde!*' he shouted as he started running for the stairs.

'Ooh, I don't speak much French but I know what that means!' cackled Maisie behind him.

Jean-Paul slid his card through the security swipe outside the door to the central rail control room in the sub-basement of the building. He slid it too fast and the door held firm.

'*Putain de merde!*' he shouted, and with a shaking hand slid the card through again, this time slowly. The little light went green and he entered through the door.

Once inside it was instantly clear there was a major incident in progress. John Fletcher, the night controller from whom Jean-Paul was taking over, was speaking on two phones and simultaneously shouting at the head of line security who was sitting in front of him. Jean-Paul ran up the few steps to the controller's position and looked at the huge map of the tunnel which was displayed across fifteen metres of the wall in front of him. He got the picture immediately. A freight train, FR 9110, was stationary just by the UK sump, twenty-two kilometres from the Folkestone terminal.

The controller was running the resulting backed up trains across the interlink and down the other tunnel, but this meant the tunnels were operating at half capacity. It was summer, the traffic build up outside was already heavy. Jean-Paul knew it would be a busy day but that was normal. A train passed through the tunnel every two minutes. They could move a great many vehicles, as long as there was nothing in the way.

'Fuel spillage,' said John Fletcher. 'Every alarm went off. We had to stop that freight, forty containers, plus the you know what.'

'The sterling delivery?' said Jean-Paul. '*C'est pas possible!*'

'*C'est* very *possible*, I'm afraid, Jean. Look at the security monitors.'

Jean-Paul glanced down to where a technician was working away at a computer console with controlled fury. On the screen was a crude computer representation of a human face, grimacing and morphing into another face with every second that passed.

'Who's that?'

'Search me. Someone's pissing about with the security cameras.'

'How can they?' asked Jean-Paul. 'What in hell's name is going on!'

'The fire service trucks are going in, so are the police.

Apparently the spillage has already been cleared so we should be moving out soon.'

'But this is a freight train,' said Jean-Paul. 'Just containers, no vehicles. How can there be a fuel spillage? There *is* no fuel!'

'I was thinking the same thing,' said John Fletcher.

Chapter Forty

According to Miles the first law of cycling is that if a rider is making a journey from A to B and back again on the same day, the wind will adjust so that it is blowing directly into the ongoing direction at all times, no matter which way the rider turns.

He had experienced this law on many occasions. Wind was a bike rider's worst enemy – worse than rain, worse than bad drivers. There was nothing you could do about wind. Until now. He smiled at the thought. It was so utterly wonderful. This was the best wind he had ever known. A perfect, helpful, warm, powerful, almost loving wind.

He had managed to break the perpetual negative wind law with this one and only golden opportunity. As Paula, Anna and Miles pedalled their hugely overladen mountain bikes up a slow incline through the endless service tunnel, an eighty-mile-an-hour wind blasted into their backs.

Through his program on the notebook computer, Miles had managed to hack into the Eurotunnel's air-flow control system. This was a part of the tunnel's operating system not under the highest security. He had arranged to open several release valves ahead of them in the tunnel, allowing the passing trains to suck out the air before them. These valves would then close with the passing of the train, and valves behind them would open as the train pushed a steadily increasing volume of air before it. This air was then rammed in behind them, initially blasting though the service tunnel at over one hundred miles an hour.

This wasn't the way the system was supposed to work and the strange environment around them was making disturbing noises as they rolled along the smooth narrow road. The service tunnel was a good deal bigger than Miles had imagined; large enough for a truck to drive down as long as it didn't meet anything coming the other way. It wasn't straight either but curved and went up and down. He found the descents slightly alarming, worrying all the time that they might be going in the wrong direction. He subdued the feeling of panic by the logical process of checking the steadily decreasing numbers on the emergency doors they were passing. The plan had been that they did the exercise at a point about twenty-two kilometres from the Folkestone terminal, near the UK sump. This was a massive pump set into a deep pit which cleared any dangerous spillage from the tunnels in seconds.

Miles saw Anna slow down in front of him. They had been taking turns at being in the lead, Paula especially enjoying being first. He couldn't hear anything above the screaming roar of the wind buffeting him in the back and blowing him along faster than he would be able to pedal himself downhill on a light-weight tourer.

'People up ahead!' Anna screamed in his ear when he pulled to a stop beside her. He looked into the fuzzy green murk. Sure enough, he could see what looked like flashing lights and vehicle headlights.

'What d'you think, police road block?' he shouted back. Anna shrugged as much as she could with the huge weight of money on her back.

They both jolted forward a little as Paula slid into their stationary bikes.

'Sorry. What's up?'

Miles found it hard to turn his head in the wind, the pressure on the bulky goggles was fierce.

'There's people up ahead,' he yelled. 'We can't make out who it is.'

'Let me go in front,' screamed Paula. 'I'll sort them out.'

They reformed their angled line so that all benefited from the ferocious gusts at their rear. They didn't need to push off. As soon as they released the brakes they started moving with alarming speed, uphill. As they drew closer to the vehicle they could see figures darting in and out of the lights. Through his goggles Miles couldn't be sure what colour the flashing lights were but the two headlights seemed very close together. Maybe it was a police motorbike. Paula didn't slow down as she got closer to the vehicle. He started pedalling to increase his speed. Maybe she was going to try and ram her way through.

As they got within metres of the vehicle with the flashing light on the roof, it became clear it wasn't a police car. In fact, it wasn't like any vehicle Miles had seen before. It was more of a delivery van that had been squashed to half its normal width. It was very long and fitted with numerous roller doors, some of which stood open, revealing an assortment of tools and control systems.

Immediately after the vehicle they passed an access tunnel. The figures he'd noticed earlier were down this with their backs to the rapidly passing cyclists, using torches to check the conduit which ran along the roof of the access tunnels. Miles only just noticed them, and felt sure they wouldn't have seen him.

The wind was now partially impeded by the stationary vehicle and they found they had to start pedalling to keep up their speed.

'We did it!' said Paula.

'Not out yet,' warned Anna.

'But we're so nearly there,' said Miles. 'We'll get a fresh blast of wind very soon.'

They were still travelling very fast. Miles took a quick look at his watch. They had been going for nearly ten minutes. They were on time, but he was worried.

If the maintenance men found the laptop he'd left on the floor at the UK sump access tunnel, they were in big trouble. Being a responsible programmer, he hadn't infected the mainframe with any form of computer virus. As soon as the crocodile clips were removed, the system would return to normal. The pressure valves would close, the lights would come on and they would be sitting ducks.

Chapter Forty-One

Gaston Bell had dropped his son off at Eton at eight-thirty in the morning. The boy had spent the weekend at the chilly family home, and although Gaston watched TV with his son on Sunday evening, he did not carry a picture of the child in his wallet.

As he made his way towards the M3, grinding his way through the bottleneck of Datchet, his mobile rang, as expected. He glanced at the screen of his on-board satellite phone. It was who he thought it would be. He moved his thumb slightly and touched a button on his steering binnacle.

'Donald, how's it going?'

'Delivery is running late.'

'How late?'

'Don't have that data this end. We're all ready to rock, wound up like serious springs, but there is no bastard delivery. Another ten minutes and we pull the plug. What's the traffic like?'

'Normal, not overly heavy.'

'Later.'

The line went dead. Gaston sighed. He was doing his best not to get anxious about the whole thing. He assured himself it didn't matter if this didn't come off. He certainly didn't need the money, but there would be huge satisfaction in carrying out the plan.

He pulled on to the M3 and started to pick up speed. Then

he slowed down. Wouldn't do to be pulled over for speeding, although he wasn't going anywhere unusual. Only a few moments later a police car sped past him at very high speed, lights flashing. He hadn't seen it in his rear view mirror. The sight shook his normally even temperament. He needed to keep his wits about him today.

He looked in the mirror. There was a white van behind him. The driver could be an undercover police officer. It was possible they were on to him. They could be following him from the air, in a helicopter. They could be tapping his mobile.

He glanced in the mirror again. The driver was talking on a mobile phone and laughing. Gaston smiled to himself. As if.

The phone beeped again. Without checking, he pressed the button.

'Gaston, hello.'

His glanced at the little screen. It wasn't Donald Cooper. It was a satellite phone number he didn't recognise, no name in the memory.

'Who is this?'

'It's Mario, Gaston. We need to talk.'

Chapter Forty-Two

The scene in the emergency siding was one of utter panic by the time Jean-Paul Marionne arrived. The train was surrounded by what looked like the entire contingent of armed police usually housed in the security block.

The emergency siding had been built for just such an event. Any problem train was taken out of the tunnel as soon as possible and put in the siding which stood hard by the entrance. Here it could be dealt with safely and not interfere with the normal running of the traffic.

The first thing Jean-Paul noticed was that there was nothing to notice. The train looked normal enough, a long line of containers pulled by a traction unit. The driver was climbing down as he arrived, being helped by an armed officer.

'Nothing,' he was saying as he reached the ground. 'There was nothing at all. The alarm went off, signals went to red, so I stopped. The alarm stopped, signals went to green, I carried on.'

'You know what you are carrying on this train?' asked Jean-Paul. The driver looked at him blankly.

'Containers?'

'That is all you know?'

The man shrugged.

'Who are you?' asked a uniformed officer.

'Jean-Paul Marionne, chief tunnel systems controller.'

'Ah,' said the officer. 'We've spoken on the phone, Detective Sergeant Thomas.'

The two men shook hands and walked along the side of the train together.

'I don't understand. The sensors detected a fuel leak, but there is no fuel on this train to leak. Have you checked all the containers?'

'All in order, all locked, no sign of anything.'

'Very strange,' said Jean-Paul. 'And then our computers went crazy, we lost control of certain of the tunnel's systems – not signalling or safety, just air locks and lighting.'

'Yeah, there's a snarl up with the service tunnel air lock this end. We can't open it. The fire boys are checking it now, that's why I've got my lot here. Thought we might have an incident on the train.'

'I cannot believe this happened by accident. Nothing like this has ever happened before,' said Jean-Paul.

'Well, there's no sign of tampering. If it's all right with you, we want to send the train on. Bit of an important cargo.'

'Of course.'

'I'm putting five of my officers on the train for the rest of the journey, and we are covering the rest of the journey with a police helicopter, just to be on the safe side.'

'As you wish,' said Jean-Paul, feeling a huge sense of relief that the train was no longer his responsibility.

Chapter Forty-Three

'That's the airlock,' said Miles between laboured breaths. In front of them stood two enormous yellow doors, firmly closed.

The wind had almost ceased in this part of the tunnel as there was nowhere for it to go. Miles knew, however, that the three of them were experiencing almost double normal surface atmospheric pressure. There was a thundering noise all around them as a train passed and he felt an uncomfortable sensation in his ears.

Paula had pulled off her goggles and was resting her head on the handlebars. Anna pulled up her goggles and wiped her brow with her sleeve. They had pedalled the last kilometre with virtually no help from the wind.

'What do we do now?' asked Anna eventually.

Miles checked his watch. 'We wait about another thirty-five seconds, then we go like hell.'

'I just don't have anything left,' said Paula. She looked up at them, her face plaintive but not dramatically so. Not like the Paula they had both come to dread. She looked older and calmer.

'It's not far,' said Miles. 'The road slopes downhill and we'll get another blast of wind – I mean, seriously strong. Use everything you've got to steer, don't worry about pedalling. It's going to be a pretty intense drop in pressure. Your ears are going to pop, like when you land in a plane.'

'I hate that,' said Anna. 'I usually get ear ache.'

'It won't last long.' Miles checked his watch again. 'Dump your goggles, glasses on, the sunlight is going to dazzle us for a bit. Here we go!'

The two women did as they were told, Miles kicked his night-vision goggles off to one side of the tunnel, pulled his helmet down over his forehead and pushed on his dark glasses.

A yellow light started flashing to one side of the door and Miles gripped the handlebars. He had re-written the code which controlled this switch, done it himself with no help. He was a grown man who could understand highly complex systems and change them at will. He looked at himself. It was almost as if he stood outside his own body, seeing himself sitting astride a heavily laden bike, the wind whipping against his clothing.

He was just a little boy, he was lost and alone, no one knew he was here and, what's more, wouldn't care if they did.

His pulse was racing, his eyes filling with tears. He felt his throat tighten. Nobody knew he was here, in a tunnel, in the dark, with a yellow light flashing before him. Suddenly and without warning he saw an image of his mother as clearly as if someone had held up a picture of her before his eyes.

'Oh, God,' he said as a klaxon started blaring. 'I'm having feelings!'

He turned and looked at Anna. Her hair was blowing in front of her face as the wind steadily increased. He was on his own. He looked at Paula, cowering down, almost hidden behind her handlebars. They were all on their own, each in their own private hell.

The blast was sudden and terrifying. From resting on their bikes in almost still air, there was a sudden and devastating rush of wind from behind them, pushing them forward with the force of a truck. As the massive hydraulic rams pushed the enormous yellow-painted steel doors apart, the inner section of the air lock became visible. Miles saw a man in ear phones crouching next to the wall. He started to tumble as the outer doors opened. They followed fast, staring in horror at the sight of a fully grown man being blown along like a dried leaf in a storm. Dust swirled in front of him as the air blasted out. They were pushed forward at terrifying speed, past the inner air lock, deafened by the roar of the wind and the screaming alarms. They ripped past the still opening outer doors and along a half-covered concrete entrance way.

The light outside was brilliant, dazzling, beautiful. Miles let out a scream. He didn't know where it came from, but somewhere very deep inside. The scream was a word.

The word was, 'Mum!'

He screamed again as he rocketed forward. 'Mum, where the fucking bastard hell are you?'

Reality closed in on him like icy water. As the road levelled before him Miles saw fire officers running. Oddly they were running away from him. It was as if he was chasing them. As he saw a very large officer fall to the ground and then tip head over heels he could see why they were running. The wind. The explosive force of a two-hundred-mile-an-hour tornado wasn't something you wanted to stand and watch. No matter how fast the officers ran they couldn't get out of the way. There wasn't room to pass. Although they were now outside, the brightness of the sun and the narrowness of the passage made manoeuvring an impossibility. Miles saw Anna's bike hit one fireman in the back of the legs and send him sprawling across the concrete roadway. He tumbled and slid along as the wind pushed them both.

Miles couldn't help but clip another man who was sent spinning into a parked fire department vehicle which was beginning to pull out of a building to their left. He closed his eyes, didn't want to see what happened to the fast-moving, flailing body.

Everywhere was chaos and noise and the odd glimpse of a face frozen in disbelief. Dust and debris were flying past, windows smashing by the dozen from the shock wave, vehicle doors ripped off their hinges hurtling through the air.

Ahead of them, just visible through the blitz, a double set of massive steel gates were standing wide open. Philippe had assured them that the gates would be open, but Miles had been very anxious about this aspect. He had no way of controlling the gates with the program he'd run in the tunnel. They were controlled by an isolated unit in the guardhouse. A police officer appeared from a building. He seemed to be trying to talk on his radio. The officer was running along trying not to fall over but Miles and his two co-riders shot past him with ease. The gates ahead were slowly closing but it was obvious they had time to get through.

A small white car suddenly appeared in the gateway. Miles saw it all in slow motion. He was still screaming for his mother, still feeling more than he had ever felt before. He was astonished at the speed with which he was travelling. The whole complex, a fire and ambulance station, police headquarters and security checkpoint, had been passed in the blink of an eye. He saw Anna shoot through the gates in front of him. The road sloped down and she moved very fast, legs pumping the pedals for all she was worth. Paula passed through next, knocking another policeman flying with the panniers mounted on her front forks.

As Miles approached the slowly closing gates, the car stopped, the driver's eyes wide in amazement.

The jolt from the impact between pannier bag and car bumper lifted Miles from the saddle, but his heavily laden pannier bag only just glanced the front wing of the car and somehow didn't tear off. He knew if the bike had been unladen, he would have gone flying. He had run into enough cars in his cycling career to realise they don't normally shunt out of the way when run into, but that's what seemed to have happened here. He kept his momentum, kept moving. He kept shouting for his mum.

The sudden contact with the car did, however, send him off on a new trajectory. He was heading straight for the glass and steel entrance of the police station. The steps in front of the door were his only hope and without thinking he applied the rear brake with all his might. The rear wheel locked and he felt the bike start to slide. He leant over, putting his right foot on the ground to steady himself. The rear wheel made contact with the side of the step first and the jolt pushed him off in a new direction, the one he wanted to go in. He was pointing downhill and although for a split second he thought he felt a hand on his back, he was moving fast and gathering speed. He was catching up with Anna and Paula and heading for the huge expanse of car park.

A thought flashed through his mind. Up until that point he had known exactly what was going on, why he was doing what he did and why he had to do it.

From the car park onward, Anna was taking over. He had to do as she said, that was the deal. Suddenly, chaos and terror closed in again. There was no plan; no clear, logical step forward. He was riding headlong into oblivion.

Chapter Forty-Four

Jean-Paul Marionne held his head in his hands as he watched the symbol for the freight train leave the UK side complex. It was through, it was clear, there was no fire, no emergency and everything was getting back to normal.

The only people in the control room who knew what was in that container were himself and John Fletcher. As far as the rest of the control staff were concerned, this was just a fuel spillage on a freight train, end of story.

Jean-Paul's radio beeped. He pressed a key to receive the call. 'Is that you, Terry?'

'Ah, Jean-Paul,' said Terry, a technician who had been in the service tunnel when everything went wrong. There had been no response from him for a while.

'Been trying to get through for ages. It's all been very strange down here.'

'Did you see anything?'

'You're not going to believe this – someone has been having a laugh.'

'What is it?'

'A notebook computer, very nice one, wired into the control conduit.'

'*Non!* Whereabouts is it?' asked Jean-Paul, looking around the control room to make sure no one was too close.

'Tunnel 315, next to the UK sump. Very expert job, someone certainly knew what they were doing.'

'Is it still on?'

'Seems to be. I'm a bit worried about disconnecting it. Who knows what it could do?'

'You are right,' said Jean-Paul. He sat for a moment and thought. Something was obviously going on, or had already gone on, or had maybe gone wrong. Whatever, they needed to find out. 'Leave it for a moment, Terry. The security teams are on their way, and the police, and the customs. The whole place is very busy today.'

'Aha!' said Terry.

'What is it?'

'The lights have come back on.'

Jean-Paul checked the monitors in front of him. They all flickered and went blank, then they started to re-boot. Technicians began trying to tap into the vast mainframes at either end of the tunnel. The screens changed again, back to normal.

'What the hell is going on?' asked Jean-Paul.

'I think the batteries on the notebook have run out. The screen's dead here,' said Terry.

'Did you see anything unusual?'

'Nothing. Mind you, couldn't see much with the lights out. Whoever did this had a pretty good grasp of how things work. They'd opened pressure release valves all along the service tunnel, the wind was incredible.'

'I'm sure we are going to find out soon enough what's been going on,' said Jean-Paul. 'Please wait there, Terry, and don't touch anything.'

Chapter Forty-Five

——————&ox&——————

'It's a car!' said Miles. He was still crying, and then laughing, then crying. He wasn't sure which was which. He was exhausted by it all. The sun was bright, everything seemed new and fresh and exciting. Even a car park full of glittering metal looked wonderful.

They had only travelled a matter of one hundred metres but at such glorious speed. They skidded past a closed automatic barrier and into the car park.

Miles felt everything. He was mourning the loss of his mother for the first time; feeling incredibly happy that he was definitely alive, his heart pounding. Uncontrollable noise was coming from somewhere really deep down, the real him, the person. He was without doubt there, a being, at the centre of events. He, Miles Morris, was having feelings!

Now he was standing in front of a long, dark blue sporty-looking car which only appeared to have two seats.

'Get in,' said Anna.

'But you know . . . you know about this!' he screamed.

'Don't be so dramatic,' said Paula quietly. Even in his heightened state, Miles noticed a change in her. She was loading the heavy pannier bags into the boot of the car as fast as she could. 'Get in the car.'

Miles threw his bike down and started kicking the panniers around the car park. They were very heavy and it hurt his foot to kick them so hard, but he needed to do something crazy.

'Damn!' he screamed. 'Mario set this up, didn't he? I can see it all now. Get him to go in a car to get over all his problems. Well, I haven't got any problems any more, so fuck it. It's not going to work!'

Anna started revving the engine and the noise was incredible. An animal, a furious and monstrous animal, was held under its metal carapace. Miles saw a huge cloud of blue smoke billow out from the exhaust.

'Look at that! Look what you're doing, for fuck's sake, Anna. How could you?' he screamed.

She leant out of the window. 'Look over there,' she said, pointing behind Miles. He turned. In the distance, with a blue light distinctly flashing on its roof, was a police car. 'And there!' said Anna, pointing in the other direction. Behind the car, still the other side of the car-park fence but much nearer, was a police van, also with a flashing light on its roof and this time with a siren howling away too. 'Get in the fucking car!' screamed Anna. 'Now!'

Miles watched Paula open the passenger door, pull the front seat back and climb in. She tugged two pannier bags after her, sat back and looked at him through the rear window, smiling calmly.

'I will give you three seconds and then I leave,' said Anna firmly.

Miles started moving. He wasn't sure what was making him move, then he realised. It was pure, screaming, stomach-churning fear. The police were closing in. The fact that he was now a major league criminal on the run with absolutely no choice but to escape by car made him feel sick.

'Okay, okay!' he shouted. He picked up the pannier bag by his feet and rushed to get another one. He turned to see the car starting to move. He could see Paula's face in the back. She was laughing.

The fucking bitches were going to leave him! How could they? How could they do that? Mario must have set the whole thing up!

'You fuckers!' he screamed as he ran towards the car. Anna

spun the wheel and the engine screamed. The rear tyres started to spin and disappear in a cloud of white smoke. He had never seen anything like it before in his life.

'Fucking hell!' said Miles, rooted to the spot by the sight. The car slewed around somehow. He could not grasp the physics. Anna had managed to make the rear wheels spin at such enormous speed they lost all traction. The car was behaving as though being driven on ice.

She turned in a complete circle before him so that when she brought the car to a violent halt, the passenger door was directly in front of him. The electric window wound down and she leaned across the passenger seat.

'Throw in the bags. We go, now!' Miles threw in the two bags he was holding and ran back to get the others. He hadn't managed to kick them very far but had to pick his way through the abandoned bikes and equipment they had dropped.

As he returned Anna was already moving the car, not so fast, he could catch her, but he had to run. He ran as fast as he could, caught up with the car and threw one bag in the window, and in doing so nearly tripped over. As he regained balance and speed he saw through the rear window Paula pulling the bag into the back seat. He pushed the other bag through, his heart pounding wildly and his teeth grinding, spittle and sweat flying off his face in every direction. It was clear Anna wasn't going to stop the car. He would literally have to jump in through the open window.

He grabbed hold of the rear of the window frame and pulled himself forward. His head was in the car, legs sticking out as he felt an enormous surge of acceleration pinning him in position.

'Oh, give me a fucking break!' he managed to say as his face rubbed into the carpet on the foot well. He could smell the interior of the car. It was new with a distinct and special smell, one he hadn't experienced for many years. He couldn't remember how many because so many memories were crowding in at once. Going to college, meeting Kulvinder, losing his virginity with Francesca, smoking dope in that room in Brighton when he was seventeen. Meeting the black girl at the cinema in Notting Hill, going back to her wonderful bedsit. He could remember going to America, meeting Donna, moving into their house. Could remember checking his bank account and seeing that he had $700,000 in a current account. And that was only the memory spikes. He could remember everything, all at once.

He could feel Paula's hand on the back of his jacket. She was pulling, but it wasn't helping. He could hear the engine of the car roaring like . . . like something that made a lion sound weak and powerless. This roar came from another planet. It was the roar of atomic nature, planet-shattering ferocity.

'Get your legs in the car, we're about to go through a gate!' screamed Anna. Miles twisted himself as much as possible. He was now three-quarters inside the car, upside down, with his abdomen resting on the pannier bag full of money which had somehow taken up residence in the front seat. He pulled his legs in as best he could; they just wouldn't seem to move of their own accord. He tucked his left foot to the far side of the passenger seat headrest which gave his right foot room to enter the car. He saw something big flash past the window at dizzying speed.

'What was that?' he shouted, craning his neck to look up at Anna. Her face was set, hands moving in a blur between the steering wheel and the gear lever.

'Gate,' she said rapidly.

'Look out!' screamed Paula from the back seat. Miles couldn't see her from his position. The car lurched violently, the engine screamed right next to his ear, the tyres screamed even louder and Miles noticed another cloud of white smoke outside the window.

He started to struggle and wriggle and try to get into a more normal travelling position. He started to make some headway, moved his left foot and inadvertently kicked Anna in the head.

'Sorry, sorry!'

The car veered again as Anna reeled sideways, seemingly dizzled by the blow.

'*Dumkopf!*' she hissed as she rubbed her head. 'We are doing one hundred and twenty-seven miles an hour and you kick me in the head?'

'What!' said Miles. 'How fast?' He had finally managed to manoeuvre his way round to a position where he could see out of the windscreen.

His eyes could not adjust to what he was seeing. Everything looked familiar and yet blurred. Lurching, deadly, insane.

'Fucking hell!'

It was like a badly speeded up film of a car chase. They were passing buses, trucks and cars at such a speed it was as if they were stationary. Then Miles realised they weren't on a motorway, they were on a two-lane A road. There were other vehicles coming directly at them.

'Shit!' he whimpered as a massive truck, lights flashing, horns blaring, smoke coming of its locked wheels, came right at them. With a reaction speed Miles couldn't imagine possessing, Anna seemed to throw the car to one side at the last possible moment, only to swing it back into the lane as soon as the truck had screamed past.

'Nice one,' said Paula from the rear seat. She was looking out of the rear window.

'Can't see any cops behind us, but don't slow down.'

'Don't worry,' said Anna. She was smiling.

'Keep your eyes peeled, we don't want to miss the turning,' said Anna as Miles felt a further surge of acceleration.

'What turning? What fucking turning? How can we turn?' he said. 'How can we fucking turn when we are going so fast!'

'This car has very good brakes,' said Anna. 'Put on your safety harness.'

Miles looked around. He saw Paula's arm appear in front of him, holding an expanding belt with a metal and plastic attachment on it.

'Oh, wow. You know, it's been so long since I went in a car, I don't think I've ever used one of these.'

'Check the sign,' ordered Anna.

'What sign?'

'The road sign. Please help, Miles,' said Anna.

Miles looked ahead. There was a large sign approaching. It said London, it said Canterbury, it had numbers and a little square in blue which had M20 written in it. They flashed past so fast he wasn't sure. Anna overtook a car pulling a caravan.

'It must be the first turning off the roundabout,' said Miles.

'Good, that is good. That is what I shall do. Hold on!'

Miles' face smashed into the windscreen, Anna had applied the brakes with such force he had no time to react. The car lurched and swerved violently as he pushed himself back into his crushed position, sitting half on the passenger seat with the pannier bag taking up most of the room.

'I thought you had your belt on!' said Anna.

'I haven't had fucking time!' he screamed.

Anna swerved past several vehicles and took the turning for the motorway. As soon as she was on the downward-facing slip road she started to gain speed. Such speed. Miles heard the tyres squeal again. He glanced out of the window. A plume of smoke was coming off the rear tyres. Even though they were already moving, Anna had managed to accelerate with such power the tyres couldn't get a grip.

'Now we will see,' she said.

'What will we see?' asked Miles queasily.

'Just how fast these English motor cars can go.'

They carried on to the motorway. Anna pulled past several slow-moving trucks, although as they passed Miles assumed they were probably all doing over the official speed limit. It was insane. He looked over at the clocks and dials by the steering wheel. He couldn't make any sense of them.

'How fast are we going now?'

'One hundred and forty-seven . . . one hundred and fifty. She's still steady. One hundred and fifty-five . . .'

Miles smiled. He felt a bubble of joy in his throat. He hadn't been in a car since he was a twelve-year-old and had made his pact. Now, at thirty-five, he was sitting in the passenger seat of some sort of racing car doing well over twice the speed limit.

'One hundred and sixty miles an hour,' said Anna calmly.

'Fan-fucking-tastic,' he screamed.

Chapter Forty-Six

'Got you,' said Donald Cooper as he pressed the little button one of the engineering lads has set up for him. It was connected to the signalling system half a kilometre down the track and a squeal of brakes indicated that it was working. The train pulled to a halt. A long freight wagon stopped right next to the building site where his team was waiting.

Donald looked up the track and saw two lads Pickering knew, a couple of ex-special forces boys who didn't want to mingle with the rest of the team. They climbed up the side of the train and entered the driver's cab. A few cracks of gun fire followed, then the low thud of a concussion grenade and silence.

'Must have been some security,' said Pickering anxiously.

'Well, there isn't anymore,' said Cooper. 'Okay,' he shouted to his troops. 'Let's find the wagon.'

The only information he and his team had was that the money was in a container on this train. The train was nearly two kilometres long and carrying forty containers. They'd had someone watching the loading terminal outside Calais, but due to the lie of the land, getting a clear view from ground level was very difficult. Their source indicated that the container they were after was around the centre of the train, not at either end.

A crowd of men ran up to the fence and lurched over it, split up and ran in opposite directions along the track. In teams of two, they had to blow open each container in turn to discover which one held the money. Donald had given them one minute to place their charges. He knew this was pushing them, but they had to work fast.

He stood up and surveyed the site. Everything was looking good. The large articulated lorry's engine was running, the driver peering anxiously out of his cab. The crane was ticking over, its operator rolling himself a cigarette.

Donald checked his watch. 'Time to blow,' he said to Pickering.

Pickering took a deep breath then bellowed, 'Fire in the hold!' A warning to the men who had set the charges.

Donald flipped the safety cover off the remote firing box, pulled the aerial to its full height and pressed the red button. There were muted cracks of explosives charges up and down the train. After a few moments puffs of white smoke billowed from the end of each container.

Donald turned quickly when he heard a whistle. About fifty metres down the track one of the lads was waving frantically.

'Got it,' said Pickering.

'Tell the lads to reverse the train,' said Donald. 'We need it to come back, what, thirty metres, then we can get the crane in.'

One of the lads got on a radio. The train started to move backwards.

Chapter Forty-Seven

Slowing from one hundred and sixty-seven miles an hour to fifty in very little distance, Anna cut across three lanes of traffic and pulled up the exit ramp leading to the Little Chef motorway services just outside Deal.

As they roared up the exit ramp, she pressed a button on the indicator lever.

'We have travelled twenty-nine miles at an average speed of one hundred and fourteen miles an hour. It's not my record but it is very good.'

'How d'you know that?' asked Miles as she swung into the car park.

'On board computer. I could also tell you our average miles per gallon, but you would be depressed by that fact, I think.'

She drove across the car park to the far side where a row of waste disposal skips were lined up next to a gate.

Parked just the other side of the gate was a large white van. 'Everything is in order,' she said. 'Philippe is very reliable.'

As soon as the car stopped they hauled themselves out. Anna opened the doors to the van and Miles passed her the first package.

Three minutes later they were driving sedately along a country lane in an unmarked white van which held anything up to fifteen million pounds in the back. They hadn't had time to count it.

'Did we do it?' asked Miles.

'So far, so good. We have a long way to go yet, and don't want to spend too much time with this in the back of the van. We do not know how the authorities will react when they discover what we have done.'

'Take a left here,' instructed Paula.

Anna did as she was told and they drove through a village. They passed a row of small shops, all bearing the same poster: 'Save the pound, no to the Euro!'

'That is very appropriate for us to see at this time,' said Anna.

'Did we do it?' asked Miles again. He was feeling his pulse and it was racing so fast he'd started to worry about his heart.

Paula put a hand gently on his shoulder. 'We did it, Miles.'

'D'you feel any different then?' he asked. 'When I say, "Did we do it?" I mean, "Did it work?" Are we all better?'

'I am,' said Anna. 'I have no desire to sleep. I can even drive this vehicle at a sensible speed and keep within the restrictions.'

'I'll never tell anyone about this,' Paula declared. 'Don't need to.'

Miles sighed deeply. His whole body felt alive. He could feel his feet in his shoes; his fingers delighted in rubbing along the material of the seat.

'I'm better too,' he said. 'I've got so many feelings, I don't know what to do with them all. And memories . . . I'm just flooded out with them. And I need to talk about them. I've never done that before. I want to see my dad and actually talk about my mum, which I've never done before either.'

'That is good, isn't it?'

'Is it?' asked Miles. He rubbed his face with his hands, felt the stubble around his mouth. He hadn't shaved in days. But he could feel so much, the numbness had completely gone.

'I'm beginning to wonder,' he said. 'I mean, sure, it's good to have feelings, and I can tell now I was only operating at half speed, but this is too much. How am I ever going to work again after this? All I want to do is consume experiences, be somewhere, with people, in love, alive, in the sun, happy. I never wanted to be anything before. I even want to have children – to look after children and be a father and spend time with my kids –

and I've never even thought about that before. And I want to bury my mum . . . I mean, say goodbye to her properly so I can grow up and be a man. I can't believe I'm even saying these things, they don't sound like me, but they are me. This is who I am. Can you see who I am?'

He looked at Anna, who looked back and smiled at him. 'Yes, Miles, I can see who you are. You are a very beautiful man. Will you come to Germany with me and be my husband?'

He looked into her eyes. He couldn't believe she had said that but it made total sense. What else was he going to do? He had nothing in England except a few scrappy memories of his childhood and a period of intense misery since he had come back from America.

'Do it, Miles,' said Paula.

'This is very interesting, isn't it?' said Anna, pulling slowly back on to the motorway they had just turned off. 'Have you noticed how we are already saying before and after? We all seem somehow to know that this day is a turning point in our lives and we will never be the same again.'

'Yes,' agreed Paula. 'It's true.'

'Oh, God,' said Miles. He felt the fear again, like he had in the car park. 'I don't know if I want to change this much. I was used to how I was. I know it wasn't good, but I'd learned to live with it. Who am I now?'

Anna laughed. Miles looked at her. Suddenly he didn't want to go to Germany with this strange dark woman whose hair had always been over her face. How come it was pulled back behind her ears now, making her look all open and strong, like the girl on the bike he had met on the Sustrans ride? How come everything was so weird? How come he felt so sick and strange and upset and happy and horny and frightened, all at the same time?

He had to breathe, had to get out. What was he doing here, riding along in a van, an internal combustion engine-powered metal box? He didn't hate that side of himself, the side that said, 'No, I will not condone or use such a stupid piece of technology.'

But he *was* in a van. He'd been in a car and he'd loved it, then he got out of the car and into a van as if he'd been doing it every day all his life, like every other stupid prick he had despised all those years.

He wound down the window and started shouting: 'Who am I? Who the fuck am I? Mum, tell me, who am I? Why me, eh? Why the fuck is it me?'

Then the tears came in floods, the tearing sobs. Miles totally lost it.

Chapter Forty-Eight

Donald Cooper pulled himself up on to the train and peered inside the container.

'Well, well, well,' he said. 'So that's what five billion pounds looks like. Very nice, eh, chaps?'

The oddball collection of ex-servicemen surrounding him cheered, and at that moment, as if on cue, the crane's massive jib swept the sky above them. A man was riding the hook, guiding the crane operator over a walkie-talkie. Donald felt a tingle of excitement. He loved working with a good team, a bunch of lads who took a bit of initiative and got a job of work done without being prodded. The whole plan was going like clockwork.

'Okay, let's get this little beauty out of here,' he said. He gave a few of the lads a leg up on to the roof of the container. They started to secure the lifting shackles dangling from the crane's main hook.

Within a few seconds the container started its journey skywards. A gaggle of men had decided to 'ride' the container, cheering and hanging on to the chains as they went.

'Incoming!' shouted one of them suddenly. Without hesitation Donald Cooper's hand went to his service revolver which was tucked inside his battle fatigues. He ducked down and scanned the building site. There were flashing blue lights everywhere, dozens of armed police swarming all over the place. He looked behind him. Coming across the field in the other direction were three police Land-Rovers, men already spilling from the open doors before the vehicles had stopped.

'Bollocks!' said Donald. He jumped off the wagon and crawled under it, working his way along the sleepers as fast as he could. He could move very fast like this. After all, he was the man who had crawled right up to an enemy position at Goose Green under covering fire from his men, and popped a grenade practically into the mouth of an Argy sub-machine-gunner.

He could hear shouts all around, could see the legs and feet of people running past him along the side of the train. He crawled even faster and before long reached the coupling device between the locomotive at the front of the train and the container wagons. He quickly turned over, and pulling a small pack of Semtex from his side pocket, wrapped it around the coupling pin. He inserted a two-pronged electric detonator and moved back under the locomotive. As soon as he was clear he opened the firing safety switch on the remote he was carrying and pressed the button. At this distance the blast was fiercer. He heard someone scream in pain moments later. Too bad.

The charge made a lot of smoke and Donald took advantage of that to climb out from under the locomotive and run full pelt towards the driver. He hauled himself up the ladder to be confronted with the snub nose of an UZI 9mm.

'It's me, for fuck's sake. Let's move.'

The locomotive's engine burst into life as Donald stood next to two very neat young men, both armed to the teeth, standing at the controls. He glanced behind him and saw the bodies of four police officers neatly piled against the bulkhead.

He quickly peered out of the window and saw a few police officers running after them, but without its load, the locomotive soon picked up speed.

'Good thinking, sir,' said one of the soldiers beside him.

'Always got to have a contingency built in for when shit happens,' he said. 'Any of you boys got a smoke?'

Chapter Forty-Nine

The pilot of the Kent constabulary helicopter had been under pressure all morning, so when he snapped at his controller it was hardly surprising.

'I can't be in two fucking places at once!' he screamed into his headset.

He was under orders to keep a watch on the building site next to the Eurotunnel main line outside Lenham, and it was clear a great deal of non-building activity was taking place there. As well as that four times he had been asked to go towards the M20 to follow a high-speed chase that had been taking place. Something about illegal immigrants who'd cycled through the tunnel and then stolen a car in Folkestone.

He loved following high-speed pursuits, but he also had to contend with this bloke Willis on the ground who had been given carte blanche over the helicopter as far as the pilot could tell. He was getting a headache from the constant yabbering in his ear.

'We're moving!' shouted Willis. 'Keep an eye out for any runners.'

The pilot brought the helicopter lower. He'd been keeping well away, over ten thousand feet and a mile away, out of earshot of people on the ground. The co-pilot trained the powerful camera on the scene as the building site started to erupt into chaos. What looked like hundreds of officers entered through the main entrance.

What looked like chaos from the air felt like total pandemonium on the ground.

'Come on, you little toe rag, get in the paddy wagon before I break your fucking arm,' said DI Willis. Cold, wet and miserable, he wasn't in the mood to mince words. He'd been sitting on his arse for five hours before the order came to move in. No one had told him that an officer from the Met Special Branch had been infiltrated into the hi-jack team as a crane operator, and that had pissed him off a treat. So everybody who counted already knew about this bust, which made Willis a fucking foot soldier yet again.

As the car he'd been sitting in for so long finally drove into the yard, he saw immediately what was going on. There were villains running every which way, he'd never seen so many, but high in the air was a container load of them hanging from chains under the jib of an enormous crane. And the crane driver, an officer he had seen before, was climbing out of the cab being congratulated by some MSB officer who looked like cock of the fucking walk.

Then there was an explosion. Everyone on the building site ducked for a moment and a shout went up.

'What the fuck was that?'

'The train's started moving!' shouted an officer in the distance. Willis started running across the muddy site, together with what looked like half the Met. He saw in the distance as he ran not the whole train, but the engine, shrouded by a cloud of white smoke, starting to pull away.

'Who the fuck left them up there? What the fuck is going on?' shouted Willis between phlegmy intakes of breath.

'We've got a man down,' cried an officer next to him.

Willis turned on his heel and started walking back towards the police vehicles. Handcuffed miscreants were being led towards them from all over the site.

'Did we get Cooper?' he asked the officer from the Met Special Branch he had eyed with bitterness at the last briefing.

'Who?'

'Cooper! Donald fucking Cooper,' said Willis testily. 'The geezer who set up this whole heist, you twat.'

'All right, Willis, keep your shirt on. I'm sure he's here somewhere.'

'Bollocks! You've let him slip, haven't you?' said Willis as he strode away through the mud. 'He was on that fucking loco-motive which is now bound for London!'

He spat heartily and pulled out his walkie-talkie.

'Can you see the locomotive?' he asked the helicopter pilot.

'Yes, it's still gathering speed.'

'Come down in the field opposite the site and pick me up, we're going after it!' screamed Willis. He needed to scream as the helicopter was only a hundred feet above the site now.

Two minutes later he was scanning the track beneath him as the helicopter soared above the line.

'They won't get far, sir,' the pilot promised.

'There they are!' shouted the co-pilot. Willis peered be-tween the two men. The locomotive had already pulled to a halt and they could just see two figures jump from it and run into some woods that ran alongside the track.

'Oh, these boys are good,' said Willis. 'Let's get a bit more height so we can see where they go.'

As soon as he'd spoken he wished he hadn't. Up until that moment he'd been utterly unaware he was flying, intent only on chasing down his prey. His fear of helicopters hadn't even entered his head. But the sensation of climbing so suddenly brought it all back with chilling speed.

'Fucking hell!' he half-burped, half-grunted.

The helicopter lurched sideways. Willis glanced to his left. There was the top of a tree, spinning round in an unnerving way. The helicopter was banking hard, the feeling in Willis' stomach close to terminal.

'Jesus wept!' he moaned, screwing his eyes tightly shut.

'There's one of them,' said the co-pilot. Willis managed to hold on to the edge of his seat and peer out of the opposite window. At first he could see only sky, then suddenly the horizon swung into view and below, not far away, the figure of a large man, clearly carrying a firearm, was running at great speed across a field.

'Stay well clear,' Willis managed to say. 'Let him get away, make it look like we haven't seen him, keep going around the copse.'

He got his radio out. 'This is DI Willis in the Kent chopper, we're above a wood . . .'

'. . . Harlots Copse, outside Tenterden,' said the co-pilot helpfully.

'Yeah, Harlots Copse, Tenterden. We've got two suspects pinned down here, both armed and believed to be highly dangerous. We need an armed rapid response team here right now. They'll need off road vehicles, this place is in the middle of nowhere.'

Willis switched off the radio and craned around, looking for the figure in the field. He held his head in his hands for a moment.

'What do we do, sir?' asked the pilot. Willis knew this was his call. Whichever way he turned he was probably letting a seriously dangerous criminal get away. He shrugged.

'Let's get that big bastard running across the field.'

Chapter Fifty

———⟫◈◈◈⟪———

Anna pulled the white transit into a parking space right opposite the house in Bryanston Square.

'Parking meter,' she said as she moved the gear stick around.

Miles jumped out and searched through his pockets for some change.

'I've never done this before, I don't know how they work,' he said as he stood next to the meter.

Paula joined him.

'It's not that complicated. You put a pound coin in the slot there.'

'A pound!' said Miles. 'It's that much, is it?'

'For ten minutes.'

'Ten minutes! Is that really how much people pay to park their cars?' he said with a laugh. 'I don't believe it!'

He inspected the contraption, bright yellow and very new looking. It didn't take him long to realise it didn't accept pounds. Paula noticed and looked at the machine too.

'Shit, it's a new one. It only takes E's. I haven't got any E's.'

Miles looked through his pockets. He had a small collection of change, still some American coins in amongst the pile.

'I don't even know what a Euro looks like,' said Miles. He found a coin that had the word Euro milled on its face and pushed it into the slot. The little liquid crystal screen changed to show ten minutes.

'How long do we need?'

'How much have you got?' asked Paula.

'We have about fifteen million, so I think we could afford to insert another coin,' said Anna.

Miles put in another coin and glanced at her. She looked radiant, her hair pulled back from her face, her dark eyes staring into his. She didn't seen mad, she wasn't asleep. She was wonderful.

Anna double checked she'd locked the van and the three amateur criminals walked up the steps to the front door. It was opened by Philippe before they could ring the bell. He looked up and down the road as they slipped past him.

'Were you followed?' he asked in a stage whisper.

'No,' said Anna calmly. 'We have travelled a very long, slow route and I was checking in the mirror all the time.'

'They know you will do that, they are trained to expect it,' said Philippe flatly. Anna smiled at him, not a defensive smile, she seemed genuinely happy.

'I took turnings I didn't need to take and checked to see if any vehicles followed us. They didn't. We waited at the side of roads to see if anyone stopped behind us or passed and looked at us. They didn't.'

'How did you get back here so fast?' asked Miles.

'We flew from Le Touquet,' said Philippe as he took one last look out of the door before closing it. 'Mario is in the kitchen.' They followed him down the corridor. Mario was sitting at the table, looking rather worn.

They stood in a row before him. Miles was smiling. He looked at Paula and Anna who also had broad grins on their faces.

'I take it this is a good sign?' said Mario.

'Very good,' agreed Anna.

'Brilliant!' said Miles. Paula just nodded.

Miles felt a sudden surge of compassion as he watched Mario's face crumple. Tears were streaming down his cheeks, his shoulders juddering silently. He was wearing a washed out grey T-shirt which revealed his arm for the first time since Miles had sat naked with him in the fireplace at Hatton. He looked at them as a child would look at a long-lost parent. The intensity of his emotion reminded Miles of footage he'd seen of refugees whose lives had been shattered by war. He felt a lump in his own throat and started crying too.

Mario stood up, his limp arm swinging slightly as the sobs tore through him. Somehow they all came together, all except Philippe who leant against a kitchen unit smoking a cigarette. Miles held Mario tightly, Anna and Paula also joined in the group hug. Miles patted Mario's back. He was still sobbing. No one had spoken and yet Miles knew that everyone understood what was happening here.

Eventually Mario pulled himself away and looked at them.

'I had lost all faith. I just sat here, feeling utterly lost. I didn't think I would ever see you again,' he said between sobs. 'I know you're not late, but it didn't matter – I was just convinced you would be caught or worse. It was horrible.'

'We're okay,' Anna soothed him.

'Have you really done it?' asked Philippe.

'There's a white transit van parked outside containing over fifteen million pounds,' said Miles. 'And I've been in it.'

'It wasn't easy, but we made it,' said Anna. Mario turned to Paula. She smiled at him and gave him a kiss on the cheek.

'Thanks,' she said quietly. He stared at her for a moment, then smiled through the tears.

'Aren't you going to say anything else?'

Paula smiled and shook her head. Mario, wiping tears from his eyes, turned his dark gaze to Miles.

'You say you've been in a van? A fossil-fuel-propelled vehicle!'

'Not only that, I've been in a car, a really fast gas-guzzling monster that Anna drove incredibly well. We were doing . . . how fast did we go, Anna?'

'We went one hundred and sixty-seven miles an hour at the very fastest point.'

'She is incredible, Mario. I couldn't believe it. Although I hated you when I realised what you'd set up.'

'I understand,' he said. 'I totally understand. And did the computer override actually work?'

'Like a dream! All the way through the tunnel we barely had to pedal.'

'It was fantastic,' agreed Anna. 'The night-vision goggles were extremely useful, but I think we could have done it without them.'

Mario sniffed, moved back to his chair and sat down.

'I don't know what to do now, you're all so different. I feel you should be helping me. I'm so hopeless, I can't even look after my own children.'

'Where are Max and Josie?' asked Miles, half-hoping to see them again.

'They're back with their mother, they're fine,' said Mario. 'I took them back to her before we went to France. Max can talk of nothing else but the man who bought him the computer game.' He sat in silence again. Miles smiled and smiled.

'I don't understand how you did it,' said Mario finally. 'It was a near-impossible task. This is an incredible experiment, and also extremely frustrating. How can I ever tell anyone about it? My biggest success ever and there's no way I can go public.'

Philippe coughed and tapped his watch. Mario turned and looked at him angrily.

'I know, I know!'

'What?' asked Anna rather sharply.

Mario put a hand up in front of his face as if to protect himself. 'Now this is so unfair. I want to have many cups of tea and sit and listen to your stories. I want to know what happened, in detail. We've been listening to the radio but there's been no mention of anything. I want to hear all about it but if we are all to remain safe, I must accompany Philippe to return the money immediately.'

'We understand,' said Miles. 'It's fine, that's what we agreed.'

'I would like to go too,' said Anna.

There was an uncomfortable silence. She stared at Mario with no obvious threat, but very clear intent. Miles sensed at once that she didn't trust him and marvelled at the way he'd picked that up. His nerve endings had changed from blunt instruments of rudimentary sense to tingling receptors of the tiniest vibrations.

Mario looked at Philippe who shrugged and took a puff of his cigarette. There was another silence. Mario sighed. He seemed to be studying his useless hand which was resting on the table. Finally he looked up at Anna.

'I don't think that would be appropriate.'

Miles felt uncomfortable. The atmosphere in the kitchen had changed markedly. He couldn't tell exactly what was going on here but knew he didn't like it. He felt awkward and confused. He remembered he hadn't eaten in a while and thought maybe his blood sugar level was a bit out of whack.

'Why wouldn't it be appropriate?' asked Anna.

Mario smiled. 'It is like this,' he said kindly. 'You have just committed a very serious crime. You are now safe. It seems no one knew you did it – there are no criminal records in existence that can trace finger prints or DNA traces back to you. The risks Philippe and I are now going to take in returning the money are serious. However, that is our job, our side of the bargain.'

'But where are you taking all the money?' Anna asked flatly.

Mario put his hand up again as if defending himself against a blow. He spoke fast and clearly.

'Anna, this makes me concerned. It is as if you feel some sort of proprietorial connection to this money which is very worrying. That was not the idea.'

'I just don't know what you are going to do with it.'

'I am not going to do anything with it except leave it in a safe place where the authorities can recover it and dispose of it as they see fit.'

Miles looked at Anna and startled himself by seeing that she was troubled. He had never previously felt he understood what someone else was actually feeling. Other people's motives and mood swings, particularly women's, had always been cloaked in mystery. Now he could look at Anna and see that she was concerned, maybe slightly angry and very suspicious. It was in the tension in her forehead, the tightness around the eyes and the odd way she was holding her mouth. She thought Mario and Philippe were going to steal the money they had taken. Miles wanted to help. He actually wanted to get involved and help, join in the mess, not stay clear of it and watch it from a distance. He was totally involved in what was going on around him, part of it, not apart any longer.

'Anna,' he said. She snapped him a look. Her expression hadn't changed.

'What?'

'There's nothing to worry about. For a start the money isn't worth anything. It's just a vanload of oddly printed paper, not even any good for writing notes on or using to make *papier mâché* puppets. Mario is doing us a huge favour.'

She stared at him with unconcealed suspicion.

'I don't trust him.'

'I do,' said Paula.

'Well, I don't even care if I trust him or not,' said Miles. 'I've done what I set out to do and I feel much better for it.'

'That's good,' said Anna, and seemed to soften for a moment.

Mario breathed in. They all looked at him but he said nothing. He nodded at them, signifying they should carry on.

'What?' asked Anna.

'I just think you should sort this out for yourselves. At the moment everything is yours, I have no power.'

'You have Philippe,' said Anna.

'He does as I tell him,' said Mario flatly.

They all looked at Philippe who stubbed out his cigarette on a saucer and smiled briefly.

'I'm not going to say anything.'

'Okay,' said Anna. She sat down at the kitchen table opposite Mario. 'Take the money. But if I ever hear you have stolen it for yourselves, I will track you down and kill you.'

Mario laughed, slightly nervously.

Philippe coughed and stood up.

'Sorry. Yes, must leave,' said Mario, also standing. 'I feel rather uncomfortable about this. It is as if your mistrust has soured the air. We'll all meet this evening – not here but in a hotel. My treat. How about the Covent Garden Hotel in St Martin's Lane? Do you know it, Miles?'

'Yes, I know it very well, it's right opposite my office.'

'Of course. We shall meet there at eight o'clock. Everything will be explained and shared then. Is this okay with everyone?'

Paula and Miles nodded. Anna sat in silence.

'Anna?' asked Mario.

'*Ja*,' she said, and dropped the van keys into Philippe's open palm

'Good, we'll see you later then.'

Philippe opened the door and he and Mario left the kitchen. Miles and Paula followed them down the corridor. Philippe opened the front door and looked around cautiously. He made a little hand movement to Mario and they left the house together.

Miles and Paula stood at the front door and watched them cross the road and get into the transit van, Philippe driving, Mario looking like a little boy in the passenger seat.

'I'm going home,' said Paula.

Miles smiled at the relaxed face of the woman he knew more about than any other. She was so serene, a perfect image of inner calm. They stood on the front step together and held each other tightly.

'Thank you, Paula,' said Miles, looking over her shoulder at the disappearing transit van.

'What have I done?'

'Just been an amazing person. One I'm really glad I met.'

Paula nodded. Miles smiled at her. They broke their embrace but held hands. Not like lovers, Miles knew, he could easily sense the difference. Paula wasn't coming on to him at all. She wanted to be an intimate friend. The line was clear and he felt happy about that. Everything that happened he had a feeling about. Very odd.

'I'll see you at eight,' she said, and gave him a light kiss on the cheek.

'Are you going now?'

'I need to sleep. I'm the opposite of Anna. She needed to

wake up, I needed to sleep. I am so deliciously tired, I can't wait to get into my bed. Alone. Besides, you and Anna don't need me around at the moment.'

She smiled at him and descended the wide steps of the grand town house.

'Bye,' said Miles. 'Sleep well.'

He closed the door. The house felt cool and fresh, wonderfully silent. The darkness of the hall wasn't depressing, it was exciting. He felt a rush of joy and wanted to see Anna. He walked back along the corridor, treading lightly on the highly polished wooden floor. He opened the kitchen door and Anna turned to look at him.

'Have they all gone?'

'Yes.'

She stood up and sighed. 'I am very glad.'

'Why?' asked Miles with a smile.

'I want you.'

'I want you too,' he said.

Chapter Fifty-One

—————◦◦◦———————

Donald Cooper found the fact that he was a hunted criminal an exciting challenge. He trained every day, he hadn't let himself go soft like so many of the chaps. Crouched down in the driver's compartment of the locomotive, he felt quite at home facing the danger he was in. The floor was sticky with blood, but for a man like Cooper spilt stood was not a new experience.

As the rattle of the helicopter diminished he slid open the door and dropped onto the hardcore at the side of the track. The sky was clear, but it was obvious the chopper was still about. One last check and then he dived headlong into the drainage ditch. As he made his way through the mud he felt pretty confident he was home free.

He glanced up over the bank and saw the helicopter still circling above the stationary locomotive. He needed to get well away, and fast. He didn't fancy being held responsible for the deaths of four police officers and a train driver. Other than that, things weren't too bad.

True, they'd been thwarted in their main task of getting the money, but he wasn't going to worry about that. However, because so many of the team had been arrested, someone was bound to spill their guts. He'd seen it happen; he'd helped it happen when he'd been in charge of prisoners. His immediate escape from the country was of paramount importance, and to do that, he needed to get to Gaston Bell as soon as possible.

He ran along the length of the ditch, keeping his head down.

He heard the helicopter move away and he crept under a thick blackthorn bush that grew in the corner of the field. As the rotor blade sound died down, he scanned the skies. They had given the position to support groups and moved off. Any minute now the whole area would be swarming with police officers. No time to lose. He climbed up the bank to get his bearings, saw a housing estate in the distance and made his way towards it over the field. Compared to yomping across a windswept moor down on the Falklands, carrying a full pack and heavy weapon, this was easy.

The houses were neat and tidy, the fence that ran between the gardens and the field he was in a low wire affair. He trotted along the fence looking for a suitable dwelling. He saw one or two people inside the houses. A small child playing in the back garden of one looked rather startled as he ran past.

The house at the end of the row appeared deserted. With a quick check for obvious witnesses, he vaulted the fence, knocked on the kitchen door and counted to five. Nothing.

One accurate kick to the door and it smashed open. Cooper was in. No sign of occupants. He was glad. He would have had no hesitation in killing them but he didn't relish the prospect. He had no desire to kill unarmed civilians.

He scanned the room he was in, a neat kitchen. His eyes locked on a set of car keys hanging on a hook near the fridge.

Thirty seconds later Cooper was sitting in the driving seat of a Volvo estate car, reversing out of the driveway of a neat suburban house. Donald Cooper didn't like to hang about.

Chapter Fifty-Two

They fell about the kitchen, crashing into furniture, tearing at each other's clothes and holding each other as if their lives depended on it.

Miles had watched scenes like this in films but he had never taken part in one. It was enormous fun.

These two people, a woman who couldn't wake up and a man who couldn't feel, were goading each other into a frenzy of passion. Miles' heart rate was sky high, he was covered in sweat as finally, with Anna lying supine on the kitchen table, he entered her, very, very slowly. She breathed out with an animal lust that sent his already overloaded mind spinning out of control. His hands grabbed her small breasts and she reacted, heaving and arching, writhing and grinding, against him. Real, fully fleshed, grade one intercourse took place. And a conversation of sorts.

'You dirty pig. You are fucking me.'

'I am going to fuck you forever.'

'Your cock is very big.'

'Your cunt is very tight.'

'Don't come yet.'

'I won't. I don't come very often.'

'You can come today. I want you to. Fuck me 'til I cry.'

'I will.'

'Oh my God!' said a voice that wasn't either of theirs. Miles looked up. Standing in front of him was a very well-dressed woman holding the hand of a terrifically intrigued-looking young girl in a smart school uniform.

'Who the fuck are you?' said Miles eventually, still inside Anna and unable to stop a certain amount of discreet thrusting.

'This is my house. Who the hell are you?'

'I'm . . . Well, we're . . . This is *your* house?'

'Yes. This is my kitchen too. How did you get in here?'

'We . . . well . . . Mario had the key,' said Miles. By now Anna had covered her naked breasts and Miles pulled out of her as slowly as he could. His erection bounced up rather firmly and the girl's eyes locked on to it.

'Go to your room,' said the woman sharply. The girl ducked out of the room and the woman stared at Anna who was attempting to get dressed.

'Who are you?' she said, still holding the kitchen door and glancing at each of them in turn.

'I'm Anna Benz. May I ask, do you know Mario Lupo?'

'Of course I do. You're clients of his, I suppose. Is this one of his exercises?'

'Well, this bit isn't, exactly.'

Miles raced through a thousand possible explanations for what was going on. He felt scared and confused. He was partly naked in a kitchen with a very angry-looking woman staring at him. A woman who knew Mario, knew about his exercises. He had learned that whenever he found out more about Mario, it was generally not encouraging information.

'So how do you know him? Have you ever done one of his exercises?'

'You could say that,' said the woman. 'Mario is my daughter's father.'

'What?' said Anna and Miles in unison. They looked at each other. Anna turned back to the woman.

'Do you trust him?'

'Do I look like I trust him?' she said, a bitterness in her voice that Miles detected with startling clarity. He was noticing so much, even the texture of the wooden table against his naked thighs.

'Do you suppose coming into your home and finding two

people having sex on your table inspires trust? I don't think so. Mario Lupo is a lunatic. A dangerous lunatic. This time he has gone too far!'

'We have to go,' said Anna.

'You're not kidding! You'd better go right now or I'm calling the police,' said the woman. 'How long have you been here anyway?'

'Only a few weeks,' said Anna.

'Weeks!'

'We have been very careful not to damage anything.'

Anna looked at Miles. 'He has stolen the money, you know. He is a thief who has conned us. I tried so hard not to think it, but this is the situation.'

Miles loved the way she said 'situation'. It had a 'D' in the middle. 'Sidduation'. It was so sexy.

'Miles, we have to catch him. He's only been gone a matter of minutes, we still have a chance.'

Like hell, he thought. Then a rush of anger swept through him. Mario Lupo, the little git!

'Have you got any pushbikes?' he asked suddenly. Anna looked at him as though he was mad, and he could understand why. He looked at the owner of the house.

'Are you asking me?'

'Yes, do you have any pushbikes?'

'Why, what are you going to do?' she asked.

'Buy them from you. For as much as you want, money no object.'

'There are two mountain bikes in the basement. A thousand pounds each,' said the woman with the hint of a smile leaking through the permafrost.

'Two thousand pounds for the pair,' said Miles. 'Done!'

Anna looked at him again. He was smiling, enjoying the moment immensely.

'Have you got two thousand pounds?'

'I think so,' said Miles. He pushed his hand into his still half-mast trousers and pulled out a wad of notes which wouldn't have embarrassed a second-hand Jaguar dealer.

He counted out two thousand pounds and put it on the kitchen table. The wad was still a fair size when he stuffed it back into his trousers.

'Did you . . .' began Anna.

'Didn't come from an autoteller,' said Miles.

'Which way would they go?' asked Anna as they mounted their very expensive bikes on the street outside. The woman and her daughter were standing at the front window of the house, watching them. Anna and Miles gave them a friendly wave as they set off.

'I don't know, I don't really care, just thought we ought to get out of there. And you don't have your car.'

'We have to get him!' said Anna. Her face looked different. Hard and angry.

'Oh, forget it. It doesn't matter. Let's go for a ride through the park, it's only just down the road.'

'It matters,' said Anna coldly. 'He's spoilt the exercise for us. He has walked all over us, used us. He will pay for this. Paula would agree, I know it.'

'Well, how the hell are we going to find him?'

'I don't know.'

Anna started cycling off through Bryanston Square. Miles didn't have anything else to do so he followed her. They reached George Street and Anna turned right. She started riding on the wrong side of the road until Miles reminded her that she was in England.

'You had better go in front.'

'Why? I don't know where we're going.'

'*Feel* where we are going.'

'How the fuck do I do that?'

'You said in the car that you had lots of feelings now. Use them.'

'I want to use them on you.'

'Be angry, Miles. We have been duped. Be angry and use that feeling to find Mario.'

God, that's a sexy thing to say. Can't we go to a hotel and carry on? I've still got wood.'

'Keep your wood, Miles. I will not waste it, do not worry. Now which way?'

'Okay, I'll try and feel which way.'

He laughed at the absurdity of the situation but could feel something, something very odd. He looked up and down George Street. They were in the middle of the West End of London, there must have been at least eleven thousand possible routes Mario and Philippe could have chosen. Miles kept looking towards the west. He could feel a pull there, his head kept facing that way. He remembered how birds found their way across oceans, something to do with the magnetic field of the earth. Subtle systems developed over millions of years of evolution. Now, here he was, a computer code-writer in the middle of a heavily developed urban conurbation. There were trillions of signals from TV broadcast antennae, mobile phones, police radios, taxi radios, common or garden radios, and he was somehow feeling a signal from a crippled North African therapist and a French thug in a white transit van. It didn't make sense.

'This way,' he said and set off down George Street towards the Edgware Road. As soon as they reached the junction Miles felt this operation might not be as hopeless as he'd thought. As far as he could see in either direction the road was blocked solid. Buses and taxis vied for space, cars and vans were stranded in yellow boxes. Miles smiled. This was the London he loved, its great heaving mass of machinery ground to a smelly, noisy halt.

'There!' shouted Anna. She was pointing towards Marble Arch. Sure enough, a white transit van was stuck behind a tourist coach. They moved through the traffic towards the vehicle. Miles passed by it on the driver's side; it was being driven by an Indian man wearing dark glasses. He met Anna at the front.

'I suppose white vans are a fairly popular vehicle.'

'It is also a Volkswagen,' said Anna. 'I was so excited I didn't notice.' She looked genuinely ashamed. 'I designed the rear-door latch moulding in my first year at VW.'

'Let's keep looking anyway,' said Miles as they rode through yet more dense traffic. 'I've got this funny feeling . . . well, I've got about a million funny feelings and some sad ones, but there's a feeling dragging me this way.'

'They cannot have got far in this mess.'

'Which you helped create,' said Miles, a giggle building in his throat.

'Traffic needs to be managed like data,' said Anna. 'This is like a badly designed program that is always going to crash – you should understand that. We have to cope with what we have.'

They rode around Marble Arch. All around them vehicles had ground to a complete standstill. They eventually headed west along the Bayswater Road. The traffic was moving slowly here. They passed hundreds of cars and trucks moving at a geriatric walking pace.

'Aha!' said Miles as they approached Notting Hill. Up ahead was a white van that looked very familiar. 'Let's have a look at this one.'

They rode along the pavement, which was the only way they could move, until they were level with the front of the van. Inside, clear as day, was Mario Lupo. Philippe was driving. Mario saw them first and said something to Philippe who immediately drew a large and threatening-looking revolver.

'I'm not sure they're exactly happy to see us,' said Miles with a broad smile. Somehow the gun didn't scare him. He could tell that Anna wasn't bothered either.

They kept level with the van. Miles stood on his pedals and zig-zagged along the pavement to keep his balance. Anna had got off her bike and was walking along the pavement pushing it.

'What are we going to do?' he asked.

'Well, we'll have to wait and see. They're not going any-where fast.'

Miles bumped down off the kerb. He had barely noticed they had come to a turning. The traffic edged forward slightly and without warning the van lurched forward, in doing so making a very nasty dent in the rear of the large black car directly in front of it. The engine of the van was screaming as it pushed its way past the car. All around horns started blaring, people started shouting. The screaming engine sound was joined by the painful screech of tearing metal and shattering glass. The van was heading straight for them. Miles could see Mario looking terrified, Philippe looked murderous.

Miles jumped the bike on to the pavement. He had seconds to live, the van bearing down on him. He shot past a lamp post and seconds later heard a loud crunch.

He skidded to a halt to see that Philippe had driven straight into the post, which seemed a very stupid thing to do.

Before he could collect himself, Anna had appeared by the driver's door and started pulling a half-dazed Philippe out by the hair. The gun dropped to the ground. Miles saw Philippe twist expertly and throw Anna across the road. A taxi screeched to a halt, missing her by inches. Miles picked up his bike, lifted it over his head and ran towards Philippe. He brought the frame down on his head with maximum force. Philippe sagged limply.

Anna joined him, deftly picking up the gun and tucking it under her coat.

'Quick, we are in great danger! Get Philippe in the back of the van. I'll drive.'

Miles saw Philippe's blood-stained head. He glanced inside the van and saw Mario, his good arm covering his face, body rocking slowly. Mario looked at him from behind the raised arm. He looked scared.

'It's okay, Mario, we're not going to hurt you,' Miles said as kindly as he could.

'I will hurt you very badly,' said Anna, wielding the bike lock above her head.

'Anna, get a grip! It's only Mario. Look at him, he's not going to do anything.'

'This is very bad,' he said.

'You are right, this is very bad,' Anna agreed.

'We are in big trouble now. This has attracted a lot of unnecessary attention.'

'Well, we didn't do it. It was Philippe who flipped out.'

'He is like a rat. If you trap him, he will do anything to escape.'

'I do not trust you. Where were you going?' Anna asked as she sat in the driver's seat. Miles leant down and lifted a very heavy Philippe by grabbing him under the arms. He dragged him backwards into the rear of the van then, breathing heavily now, ran back and picked up his bike. He threw that on top of Philippe, then Anna's bike. He climbed in afterwards, closed the doors from inside and slammed his fist on the roof. Anna started driving immediately, reversing the van off the pavement and pulling back into the traffic which was now, miraculously, moving.

'Pretty amazing that we found you, wasn't it?' said Miles as he leant across the seats and looked out of the cracked windscreen. 'I mean, you could have been going anywhere but Anna said, "Just follow your feelings." So I did. And look what happened – I found you. I've got you to thank for that, Mario.'

'This is very bad,' Mario repeated. 'This is very dangerous.'

'We want to come with you, to see what you do with all the money,' Anna told him.

'This woman came into the house while we were still there . . .' Miles began.

'We were fucking on the kitchen table.'

'Yeah,' said Miles, full of delight. 'Just fucking like animals. And this woman came in with your daughter, and she said you were mad, and we thought, maybe he is, and maybe this whole thing has been a giant con and maybe we should come and find out. Well, I didn't really want to, but Anna was very keen.'

'I am very keen.'

'There's nothing I can do to stop you,' said Mario. He leant over the seat and looked into the crowded rear of the van. Miles turned with him and saw that Philippe was not looking too good, crushed as he was underneath two mountain bikes.

'I fear for Philippe. He is bleeding rather heavily,' said Mario.

'I'll sort him out,' said Miles. 'I'll tear my shirt up and make a bandage for him. It's like being in a war, isn't it?'

'I hope not,' said Mario. 'Let us move quickly. The police will surely be here soon.'

Miles climbed over the huge pile of money and started to lift the bikes off Philippe.

'Here, take this,' said Anna, passing the gun over her shoulder, keeping one hand on the steering wheel.

Miles took the gun. It was heavy, he had never held one before.

'Wow, cool!'

'If he makes any trouble, you have to kill him.'

'Yeah!' said Miles.

'I'm sure that will not be necessary,' said Mario.

Miles stuffed the gun down his cycling trousers and removed the second bike from Philippe's still unconscious form. Then he started to move the money to try and make the ride more comfortable.

Chapter Fifty-Three

'It was a fucking set up, wasn't it, Gasty?' said Donald Cooper. 'And what's more, you knew, didn't you?'

He was speaking to Gaston very loudly, helping him to listen by pushing the muzzle of an automatic pistol into his mouth.

The two men were in the cavernous interior of the black hangar on Lasham airfield. Two gliders, seven very expensive cars, a small mountain of large wooden packing crates and a twin-engined Piper Ceneca V all sat inside the echoing building.

Gaston had been sitting at an ornate desk when Donald arrived unexpectedly. He had heard about the police raid but decided to wait a little longer before starting the plane and opening the big doors.

Gaston gently pushed the gun out of his mouth and swallowed.

'It was not a set up, Donald. We are all in deep trouble now.'

'Oh, I know that.'

'The police are on to me. I have been investigated by the Serious Crime Squad more times than I'd like to admit, but they've never found anything. However, I've heard through contacts that I have been linked with this job. They are closing in, Donald, and there's nothing I can do about it.'

'Don't try and same boat me, Gasty. I was out there, in the

fucking mud, loosing my team big time. I just want to know who's paying you to get rid of me? Is it the company?'

'No, it's nothing to do with the company,' said Gaston, referring to MI6. 'Please think carefully, Donald. Think through what you are saying. What possible reason, what possible profit motive, could I have for setting you up?'

'To get yourself off the hook, you little cunt!' snapped Donald. 'You've done some deal with the authorities, haven't you? Deliver me and you get off, is that it?'

'No, that is not the case,' said Gaston firmly. 'I've had no contact with the police. I'm intending to fly out of here very soon, and it would seem that your best option is to join me.'

Donald looked around the hangar. His bug-like eyes landed on the light aircraft.

'What, in that?'

'Yes. We can get to France in about thirty minutes.'

'Fuck me! I've heard of operations going down the pan, but this is a total fucking nightmare. I don't believe it, we haven't even got the money!'

'That's not strictly accurate,' said Gaston Bell, looking at his watch. 'There's still a chance we'll be able to do a deal.'

Donald was about to ask something, but Gaston put up his hand. Outside the hangar a car was rapidly approaching.

Donald moved swiftly to one side of the entrance and peered out of a dusty window.

'Someone in a Range-Rover. Foreign plates.'

'Ah, that is my man,' said Gaston. He leaned forward. 'I would beg you to be on your best behaviour, Cooper, this man is seriously well connected, very nervous and we desperately need his help.'

Gaston walked calmly to the heavy sliding doors and opened one a little way. An immaculately dressed individual entered, carrying a large stainless steel case.

'This is Monsieur Flanchard from the Belge Banque in Brussels. He is here to complete our transaction.'

'What transaction?'

'A little insurance policy I didn't even know I had,' said

Gaston with a broad smile. 'Tell me, Donald, is that gun of yours actually loaded?'

'Don't be wet, man.'

'Very good. Might come in handy if things get a bit tense. Now, let's see if I can't rustle us up a nice cup of tea.'

Chapter Fifty-Four

The rain was just starting to fall over the vast expanse of Lasham airfield when, at the furthest point from the black hangar, a police helicopter suddenly appeared over some trees at a point where the land fell away into a valley.

Detective Inspector Willis, green-faced and half-dead, virtually fell from the machine when it finally touched down. The rotors spun to a stop and his ears rang in the silence that followed.

The pilot would have liked to have landed a little nearer the control tower of the airfield but an alarming shortage of fuel meant he had little choice. Another minute and they would have reached the earth even more rapidly.

The last ten minutes of their flight, following the dark green Volvo estate along the M3, had been accompanied by an incessant buzzing at the helicopter's controls. This noise had informed the occupants that they were about to leave the sky in a falling rock-like manner.

'He's bound to have seen us,' said Willis as he staggered to his feet.

'I've informed control of our whereabouts,' said the pilot, now standing next to him.

'Very good. Well, you stay with your jalopy, I'll go and have a look see.'

Willis started to trudge up the slight incline, hugely relieved still to be alive but one hundred per cent focused on hunting down his man. They had watched the Volvo make a wide circuit of the airfield and drive up to an isolated hangar. That was just before Willis felt his stomach hit the roof of his mouth as the pilot made an emergency descent.

Over the large expanse of windswept grass, the roof of the hangar came into view. Willis had the advantage of having seen the entire layout of the airfield from ten thousand feet. He knew there was only one road to the building; a few hundred yards to the rear was a long strip of woodland. The only explanation for Cooper having driven all this way was that he was flying out.

Willis lay on his stomach on the grass and watched the building like a hawk. All he had to do now was wait for back up.

Chapter Fifty-Five

'We have to turn off here,' said Mario. He was studying a map, sitting in the passenger seat of the transit as they drove along the M3 motorway. Anna at the wheel maintained a steady seventy miles an hour. Mario had noticed that not once in the whole journey had she gone above the speed limit. She looked wonderful, alive, awake. Everything had gone so well until he had seen Miles and her on their bikes, chasing him through the dreadful London traffic.

Mario didn't like London. He didn't like England much, but it was better to be outside the great ugly city which, for reasons he failed to understand, received so much attention around the world.

He turned to look at how things were progressing in the rear of the van. Two men sat facing each other on plastic-wrapped bundles of money. Miles was smiling, his face dirty but radiant. He looked wonderful, a picture of mental health. It warmed Mario's heart to see such joy. Sitting opposite him was an image he found far less rewarding.

Philippe was in a bad way, but it was his own fault. There were times when his gung-ho spirit got the better of him and landed them both in trouble.

The reasons Philippe looked unhappy were twofold. He had a very nasty gash on the side of his head that had bled heavily during the journey, despite the application of a kindly donated strip of Miles' shirt. The other reason he looked glum was that Miles was pointing a gun at him. His own.

Philippe looked straight at Mario. He shrugged.

'I could very easily disarm him.'

'I know that,' said Mario.

'I could kill him before any of you could possibly stop me.'

'I understand that, Philippe. It is a worthy skill, and one you use very rarely.'

'He does not know how to use a gun.'

'He doesn't. We are relying on you to control yourself,' said Mario calmly. He breathed deeply, remembering incidents in the past when Philippe's rage had boiled over and caused serious problems.

'I'm very glad to live in such ignorance,' said Miles with a smile. 'However, they are not overly complex machines, are they? The bit my finger is resting on is called the trigger, if I'm not mistaken, and all I have to do is twitch that and a high-speed projectile comes out of the end of the tube I am pointing at your head and you die rather quickly.'

'But you're not going to do that, are you, Miles?' said Mario, turning back to look at the road. He smiled to himself. He loved dramatic situations like this, even if they weren't part of a planned exercise.

There was silence in the back, but Mario knew Philippe's multiplicity of problems. He would not be able to let it lie.

'I am only saying I *could* disarm you, not that I am going to. I am saying if I wanted to, I could.'

'Okay, well, I'm not asking for a demonstration of your martial arts skills,' said Miles. Mario smiled to himself. He was half-tempted to raise the stakes, see if Philippe would make one of his incredible high-speed lunges. He knew it wasn't a good idea, though. They were in enough trouble as it was, and who knew what powers the exercise had unleashed in his two patients? It was uncanny how Miles and Anna had found them, stuck in traffic in London along with two million other cars. There was still so much to learn from what had happened. Trauma therapy was back on the map and would turn the world of psychotherapy on its head. He couldn't afford to lose his two success stories.

'You can put the gun down,' said Mario. 'Philippe is on your side.'

'Oh, really?' said Anna suddenly. She had been quiet for a long time. Mario glanced at her. 'It did not look like that when we saw him driving towards us.'

'Yes, that was unforgivable,' said Mario. 'But desperate situations sometimes require desperate measures. It was a vital part of the whole exercise that you were kept out of the dangerous process of returning the money. By its very nature, we are having to deal with certain types of people who live on the edges of the law. I had no wish to involve you in any of this. Now it is too late. We just have to hope everything will turn out all right.'

Anna pulled off the motorway at a slip road and slowed as she approached a roundabout. 'Which way now?'

Mario consulted his map again. 'Turn to the left and follow the A339 towards Alton.'

Anna turned on to the road and picked up speed. 'So, what happens now?'

'I am sorry, what happens when?'

'When we give the money back. And to whom are we giving it?'

'A client of mine who works for a large merchant bank in the city. You do not need to know his name. It would be so much better if you never saw him and he never saw you. I don't like the risks this represents for all parties, it is very compromising.'

'But you have lost our trust,' said Anna flatly.

'Yes, it would appear so.'

'So, you just give the money to him and that's it?' asked Miles from the back of the van.

'More or less,' said Mario.

'Oh, *merde*!' shouted Philippe. 'Can we please stop playing these silly games? Tell them, Mario, it's not a bad thing we are doing.'

He glanced around at his difficult assistant. He had to acknowledge to himself that every now and then Philippe would burst a bubble of tension and allow the truth to be told, very often with beneficial results. However, it was complicated.

Gaston Bell had been a client of Mario's some three years previously. He had reached a position of such huge wealth, but spent all his spare time chasing young women. It was putting his family and his health in jeopardy. When he reached a crisis, which took place in a night club largely frequented by people under thirty, Gaston Bell got in touch with Mario. The treatment was short and sweet and seemed to have been entirely beneficial. Mr Bell was not one of the clients who called back for more. One session and he was, to all intents and purposes, cured. However, Mario had discovered a lot about Mr Bell's business dealings during their brief period working together. He was, it seemed, the one person in England who would be able to deal with a very large sum of money in plastic-wrapped bundles and not ask any questions.

'It is so easy to misinterpret,' said Mario after a little thought. 'It is so easy to see the negative side of what we are doing.'

'Try us with the positive side,' said Miles with a smile. 'I love all this, I'm so happy.'

'I am glad you are happy, Miles. That's the positive side. The system works. That is what it is all about, making people feel better. No matter what you may think, what the world may think, this is my primary concern. The positive side is that I feel a huge obligation to spread my work among more people, less motivated people, poorer people. But that costs money.'

'So you were always planning on keeping the money?' said Anna. 'Just as I suspected.'

'I am not *keeping* the money,' said Mario. 'I don't need or want the money. I am merely using it to further the work of the foundation.'

'In other words, keeping the money.'

'Do you need the money, Miles?' asked Mario.

'No.'

'Anna, do you need it?'

'No.'

'Does Paula need the money? No. So what's the problem?'

'The problem is,' said Anna angrily, 'we feel used.'

'But you used me too. You used me to help you get to where you are now. Two very happy people who are in love with each other. Why destroy that?'

'He's got a point,' said Miles.

'It is wrong,' objected Anna. 'We have committed a crime, all of us, the first time we have ever done such a thing. We have risked our lives, and Mario walks away with the profits of that crime. It is just wrong.'

'In those terms it is wrong, but that is not why you did it. You didn't rob the train to get the money, you robbed it to make yourself better. To wake up. Are you feeling sleepy, Anna?'

'I know it has worked. That is not the point.'

'Turn off here,' said Mario. 'It should be on the right somewhere.'

Mario watched Anna drive for a while. He could see her battling with her reaction to his words. She was very angry, a natural occurrence after deep trauma.

He turned again to see how things were going in the back. Philippe was still leaning against the side of the van, the blood now dried dark on his cheek. He was a very strong man and a minor flesh wound like that wouldn't hold him up for long.

'What?' said Philippe suddenly. He was staring at Miles.

'I am just trying to, sort of, well, feel my way through this situation,' he said. 'You know, rather than think my way through like I always have before.'

Mario smiled. The change in Miles was so profound. He had become human, profoundly troubled, torn asunder by feelings, incoherent and magnificent. Mario felt a surge of pride.

'Merde!' said Philippe.

'Look, I'm trying to feel if you are really not going to shoot me if I give the gun back.'

Philippe smiled. The dried blood on his cheek cracked a little as he did so. 'You will not be able to feel if I am going to shoot you or not. I am too well trained to allow information like that to be read from my facial expression or body language.'

'Who trained you?'

'The Foreign Legion, *naturellement*.'

'I thought so,' said Miles. He leant towards Anna. 'I can't decide, I'm confused about so many things. Shall I give him the gun, Anna?'

'*Ja*, why not? He will not shoot us. It is too much trouble to get rid of our bodies.'

'Oh, yeah, I wish I could think that logically. With me it's all feelings now. Feelings, feelings, feelings, that's me.'

Miles sat back and Mario watched as he handed Philippe the gun. The Frenchman very slowly took it, pulled back the firing bolt and ejected a bullet.

'It was loaded and the safety was off. You only needed to brush the trigger with the slightest pressure and it would have fired,' he said as he tucked the gun under his jacket. 'I am very lucky.'

'I know. Mind you, we all are,' agreed Miles.

Mario turned and faced the road. He saw at once that they were approaching the entrance. 'Here we are.'

Miles leant over the front seat next to him. Mario felt a hand on his shoulder. Miles would never have done that previously.

'Are we flying somewhere?' he asked as directly in front of them a red-winged glider was drawn into the sky on the end of a long wire.

'No, we are merely using a safe location to transfer the money.'

They drove along a wide road Mario assumed was an old runway. He had never been to the location before and was feeling uneasy. Grass sloped off in every direction. Nothing else could be seen.

'What a weird place,' said Miles. 'Makes me feel very fuzzy inside. My back is tingling, you know, like there's someone watching us. I feel very exposed.'

Mario heard Philippe struggling in the back. He turned to see him looking out of the rear windows of the van. 'It is possible we have been followed.'

'I don't think so,' said Anna. 'If they were going to stop us, they would have done so in London. I have been very observant for the whole journey, no one followed us.'

'There it is!' said Mario, pointing towards the roof of a large building that was suddenly visible above the horizon.

Anna slowed down as they approached the building. It was a ramshackle hangar, stuck out in the middle of the airfield. An observation tower and a collection of small buildings were just visible across the vast expanse of grass. The wind was blowing strongly, carrying with it a light drizzle.

The enormous sliding doors of the hangar opened. Mario waved to his former client through the car window.

A very smartly dressed man appeared. He walked up to Mario and they shook hands.

'Just in time,' said Gaston Bell. 'We have to work fast. Bring the van inside.'

Chapter Fifty-Six

Miles and Anna climbed out of the transit and stood in the echoing gloom of the hangar. They both blinked a little, allowing their eyes to grow accustomed to the low light. Miles felt the side of his body nearest Anna tingle with delight. He wondered if these sort of feelings would last. Would he still be feeling these things when he was an old man, sitting in a sunny garden with an old lady called Anna Benz?

He looked around, breathed in deeply, a wonderful damp smell. Sexy somehow, new and interesting.

He could make out a small twin-engined aeroplane in the centre of the hangar, surrounded by a lot of boxes.

Mario appeared from behind the plane and walked towards them with the man who'd opened the door. A third man joined them from the darkness. He was equally well dressed and looked European.

Miles turned to Anna. 'What d'you think?' he asked softly.

'I don't trust any of these people. We had no idea any of this was set up while they clearly did. A lot more people knew about what we were doing today than we thought. This is very bad, no?'

'I'm really sorry, Anna, I just can't get worked up about it. I know it's a bit of a con and all that, but I feel so much . . . well, I was going to say better, which I do. But I just feel so much . . . more. Everything Mario said would happen to me has happened, and I'm crazily in love with you.'

'Are you?'

'God, yes,' he blurted. Then he knew. A flash of doubt and pain entered his stomach. Like a Zulu spear, it was twisted and wrenched out. This was really difficult to deal with. He could hear everything, he could sense everything now. The way Anna had responded could only mean one thing: she didn't feel the same about him. He could see now that the explosion of sex in the house on Bryanston Square was just that. An explosion of tension, a release. No more. For Anna, at least. And yet in the van she had said she wanted him, wanted to go to Germany with him, to marry him even. Maybe, despite his feelings being on full alert, it was still possible to be confused by women.

'This is Mr Gaston Bell,' said Mario. 'He is here to help us.'

'How do you do?' said Gaston. 'You've pulled off a remarkable feat.'

'Thanks,' said Miles. It was like being congratulated by a headmaster.

'And this is Monsieur Flanchard from the Belge Banque in Brussels.' said Gaston. Monsieur Flanchard bowed discreetly. 'He is carrying a substantial number of Swiss bank bonds which he is prepared to exchange for the sterling currency you have brought.'

'There you go,' said Mario, Miles thought slightly nervously. 'It's as simple as that.'

'What is the present exchange rate?' asked Anna.

'Well, clearly due to the nature of this transaction, normal rates of exchange don't apply. I think you can understand why?'

'I can understand why there may be some extra expense, but you still have not answered my question.'

Anna stood her ground, looking up at the well-groomed man before her. Miles stood and stared in open admiration. He loved her so much, even though this love was tinged with bitter hopelessness.

'We're about to start counting the money. When we have finished we will carry out the final transaction,' said Monsieur Flanchard. His English was as impeccable as his suit. 'Come with me, we can watch the process.'

Miles and Anna followed the men towards the transit van. Another man joined them then. Miles thought he looked a bit scared and felt sorry for him. Everyone he was meeting looked so different, he could see so much on their faces he had never noticed in his life before. This man obviously felt uncomfortable in a business suit, Miles could just tell. His haircut was un-necessarily short and severe. He saw himself as a man of action, but he was dressed in a silly suit. Miles could also see that underneath the suit's clean lines lay a powerfully built body.

Mario opened the back doors to reveal Philippe standing inside, gun in hand. The man in the uncomfortable suit also levelled a gun in a move so fast Miles was really impressed.

'Bloody hell, that was quick! How d'you do that?'

'Please, Miles,' said Mario quietly.

Gaston Bell looked mildly concerned. 'What's all this, Mario? This isn't necessary.'

'I am very sorry,' he said. 'This is Philippe, my assistant. He is perfectly safe. Please put the gun away, Philippe.'

'Who is this?' asked Philippe, without moving his eyes from the other man with a gun.

'This is my driver, Redford,' said Gaston Bell. 'I think we can continue, gentlemen. On my count of three, let us holster our weapons. One, two, three.'

Philippe and Redford both moved at once. They pointed their guns to the floor and slowly slid them back into their shoulder holsters.

'I want to check out the building before we go any further. We shouldn't have brought the van in so quickly, we don't know what's going on here,' Philippe growled.

Mario sighed and smiled. 'Philippe, Mr Bell is a legitimate businessman. He is not a criminal surrounded by armed thugs. I believe Mr Redford is also an ex-soldier. Am I right, Mr Bell?'

'Perfectly correct,' said Gaston Bell. 'There really is no call for firearms.'

'Philippe was in the Foreign Legion,' said Miles. 'You can't tell anything about his emotions from his facial expression or body language.'

'Is that right?' said Redford.

'*Oui*,' said Philippe proudly.

He jumped down from the van and the two men moved off, talking to each other in French. Miles raised his eyebrows. This was all so cool.

Gaston Bell clapped his hands together with delight as he looked at the stacks of money inside the van.

'Right,' he said. 'Let's count it.'

Chapter Fifty-Seven

Detective Inspector Willis was chewing a nail already horribly bitten and disfigured, trying to decide what to do next. Lying in damp grass was beginning to feel very uncomfortable.

Due to the fact that his walkie-talkie was about a hundred miles out of range of the rest of his team, and his mobile one to nobody service was showing a healthy 'no signal' sign, he had already been back to the helicopter to see if anything was happening. It was a risk, anyone could have seen him, but he had to know.

As he approached the helicopter, the co-pilot was smoking a cigarette sitting in the open doorway of the machine. The pilot was still on the radio, explaining where they were, that they were out of fuel and that they needed backup very swiftly.

He pulled off the headphones and turned to Willis.

'Full alert by the sounds of things, sir. A bunch of boys from Met SO are on their way in a helicopter.'

'Another fucking helicopter? Very discreet.'

'They're also sending a local Special Operations unit from Basingstoke. Should be here in about twenty minutes.'

'Brilliant. What do we do meanwhile?'

'We have to wait, sir. Team work and communication, that's what it's all about these days.'

'Yeah, I read about it in the *Guardian*,' said Willis moodily. He turned to the co-pilot. 'Go up that clubhouse we saw and get us something to eat, will you?'

'Bit of a trek, sir.'

'Bollocks! Can't have been more than a mile. I'm fucking starving.'

The officer sighed heavily. 'Okay, sir, what d'you want?'

'I don't fucking know! Something to eat, and a can of beer.'

'I'm a bit short of readies, sir,' said the co-pilot with a sly grin. 'Not much call for petty cash when you're up there. I leave my wallet in the locker at HQ.'

'Bloody hell!' said Willis, fishing out his wallet from his back pocket. He handed the officer a fiver. 'Get yourself a bag of crisps, too.'

'Very kind, sir,' he said flatly.

As he watched the officer walk towards the clubhouse Willis looked up at the thick grey clouds. 'This is going to be pants, I fucking know it is.'

As he started back up the grassy slope to his former position, he saw the roof of a vehicle going along the perimeter road.

'Pants!' he shouted to himself as he started running. 'I knew something would happen.'

He threw himself down on the patch of flattened grass where he'd been lying before, just in time to see a white transit van enter the hangar. The large doors slowly closed, he could just about make out some figures inside, but had no chance of identifying anyone.

He checked his watch. It was 3.40 in the afternoon. If the back up didn't arrive in fifteen, he would have to go in himself, unarmed, and at least try and stall them.

Chapter Fifty-Eight

Miles sat on the edge of a crate and watched the proceedings dispassionately. The two smartly dressed men counted and recounted the plastic-wrapped parcels of bank notes, taking careful records of their contents and operating little calculators. Anna also watched everything very carefully, while Mario stood slightly away from the makeshift table where the counting was taking place.

Miles started to study Mario who was shifting about uncomfortably. It was possible he found the whole process disagreeable, or it was possible he was nervous because he knew how dangerous it was. But Miles could sense no danger, he felt very relaxed.

'It's okay, Mario. Chill,' he said gently. Mario looked at him and smiled, then he saw that Anna was looking at him with a slightly different expression, one women generally reserve for mildly annoying husbands who've made yet another fart joke at a family gathering.

He heard a faint noise behind him and looked around. He was surprised to see Philippe crouching behind another packing crate, gun in hand. Miles was about to shout a greeting when he saw Philippe's hand come up rapidly, telling him to be quiet. Miles shrugged and smiled.

Philippe was all right really, just a bit crazed from his training. Miles could see in his eyes that he was essentially a well-controlled and gentle person. The violent front was just that, all a front. His job meant he had to appear hard.

'Thirteen million three hundred and fifty thousand,' said Gaston Bell. 'Do you agree?'

'That is correct,' said the Belgian banker. He pulled a credit-card-sized calculator from inside his jacket and carefully pressed a few numbers.

'I can give you three million Euros.'

'Is that all?' said Gaston Bell flatly.

'I promise you, that is very generous. I have to get this back to my people in the next two hours.'

Gaston turned to Mario. 'What do you think?'

He bit his lip, glanced at Anna, then at Miles. 'I don't think we have a lot of choice.'

'Well, let's not waste time,' said Gaston. 'I would suggest you accept the offer.'

'Okay,' said Mario, and that was that. Monsieur Flanchard opened his smart case and extracted a large sheaf of papers. He counted through them, peeled a fair-sized wad off and handed them to Gaston Bell.

Miles flew off the packing case and landed heavily on the floor. He didn't feel pushed exactly, simply transported from one point to another with such speed, he didn't notice how or why.

Once his senses had returned and he'd got his breath back, he looked up and saw a very large pair of shoes next to his hand.

'I think you'll find, gentlemen, it'll be best if you let me have that,' said a very deep, but clearly well-educated voice. The man was holding out his left hand, his right was gripping a very efficient-looking automatic pistol.

'Wow, that gun's even more amazing!' said Miles.

'Don't move, Miles, just for a moment,' warned Mario.

'Please, Major Cooper,' said Gaston Bell. 'Everyone will get their share.'

'No, they won't, I'll just get mine. Drop the carbine, Redford.'

So this man was in the Army too. It was all very intriguing, and now he had recovered from the physical assault Miles still didn't really feel scared. He felt invulnerable, presumably because he was so happy.

He looked towards Mario, Anna, the man called Mr Bell and the Belgian banker, all staring at the neatly dressed Redford who gingerly removed his gun from under his jacket and placed it on the table.

'Good thinking. Now, place all the bonds back in the case and if Monsieur Flanchard would kindly hand me the keys to his Range-Rover, I will discreetly take my leave of you.'

The next sudden movement did send a shock wave through Miles. The thigh of the large man standing above him popped open. That was the sound it seemed to make to Miles – a pop. He was close enough to be splattered with warm blood as the man's leg erupted in front of him. The man shouted and, as he did so, Miles' ears closed down. The noise of the gunfire was so loud it was as if his ears said, 'Oh, enough's enough, we're going offline.'

He had no idea how many shots were fired, but more than a handful. When he slowly raised his head, the very large man was lying on the ground, his left foot occasionally twitching. Redford was standing above him, gripping his gun with both hands, pointing it at the now very dead Major's head. Miles took a moment to work out what had happened. The last time he looked, Redford had put his gun down on the table. He decided it must be some kind of soldierly trick to be able to pick up a gun again very fast and kill people with it.

Miles stood up and saw Anna and Mario kneeling by someone else a few metres away. Philippe.

'What happened?' asked Miles as he reached Anna's side. She looked up at him, eyes full of tears.

'Philippe laid down his life for us,' she said.

'Bloody hell. Is he actually dead?'

Anna nodded slowly. Mario was holding Philippe's head in his good arm, sobbing loudly.

'Aahh, *mon brave*,' he kept saying. '*Mon brave, mon brave*.'

Miles felt a sob well in his throat. His eyes filled with tears. Philippe looked like a child, very serene and innocent, and also very dead.

'Okay everyone, the game is up, you are all under arrest,' said Redford.

As Miles turned another loud crack was heard. Redford dropped to the floor with the suddenness that can only spell instant death. Miles saw Mr Bell holding a small, still smoking pistol.

'This is all getting very fucking weird,' said Miles.

'*Mein Gott. Laß uns gehen,*' said Anna.

The hangar suddenly filled with light. The large doors had started to open and the view outside was transformed. The low grey clouds had blown away to reveal a dazzling, sunny afternoon.

A noise attracted Miles' attention. He turned in time to see Monsieur Flanchard, the Belgian banker, drive his Range-Rover away from the hangar at high speed. But that wasn't the noise that made him turn.

Then he saw what it was. The propellers of the twin-engined plane started to rotate slowly as the starter device whined into action.

'Talk about emotions, is this an exercise or what!' screamed Miles. He stared down at Mario who continued to shudder as sobs ripped through him. The engines kicked into life and they were suddenly buffeted by a very strong wind and billowing smoke.

'Oh, fuck this for a game of marbles, let's go!'

Miles walked towards the transit van and pulled the bikes from inside. The plane started to taxi past him slowly. He saw Gaston Bell at the controls, staring resolutely ahead.

Miles wheeled the bikes towards Anna and Mario, only turning when he heard the plane's engines wind up to full throttle. He saw the figure of an overweight man running across the concrete apron towards the plane. If didn't stop or swerve and the man threw himself to the ground at the last moment. Miles couldn't be sure but it looked like one of the plane's wheels went over his leg, or at least his foot. It definitely wobbled a bit as it taxied forward. The man lay on the ground writhing. It was all too theatrical.

Miles continued to hurry towards Anna and Mario.

'Come on, let's get out of here!'

Anna stood up and looked at him.

'What about Mario?'

'I'll give him a saddle ride.'

Anna squatted down next to Mario. Putting her arm gently around him, she encouraged him to stand. Miles saw his face, smeared with blood and streaked with tears. If this was an exercise, it was the best yet

The sound of the plane was dying away, but a new and far more alarming sound was steadily growing louder. Police sirens.

'We have to go, and we have to go now!' said Miles. Anna got on her bike.

'Go to the back of the hangar, there must be a door there somewhere,' said Miles.

Mario stood motionless as Miles leant his bike to one side and positioned the rear wheel between Mario's legs. He shoved the bike backwards until the saddle was under Mario's crutch then heaved it upright. Mario did nothing to resist, just allowed himself to be raised like a rag doll. Miles stood on the pedals and started to ride. He rode towards Anna who had located a door at the rear of the hangar.

'Locked!' she shouted as he approached at speed.

'Too late!' said Miles as the front wheel smashed into the door. It gave easily and smashed back on its hinges before falling on to the stony ground outside.

'Hold tight!' said Miles as he steered the bike the only way he wanted to go, downhill. The ground sloped steeply away at the back of the hangar. A row of long, low trailers was parked to his left as he bumped over the roughly mown grass. Glider transporters, he presumed. He was travelling at a good speed and the bike felt stable. He was uncomfortable though because he had to stand on his pedals, Mario clinging on with his good arm as they bounced along.

It wasn't until they reached a chain-link fence that Miles slowed enough to see who was behind them. It was a great and uplifting relief not to see ten police cars, only the woman he'd decided he loved, on a bike, in the sun. Anna was rushing towards him, smiling, her face radiant.

'I fucking love you!' shouted Miles.

'I will love you too if we ever get away from here,' Anna told him. She skidded to a halt beside them, looked up and down the fence and then moved off to the right.

Miles followed her as best he could. Now the going got tough. He was riding along an unmown grass surface with another man perched precariously on the saddle. It was very hard work.

He saw Anna dismount up ahead and start to push her bike through a hole in the fence leading to a small copse behind.

She followed the bike and Miles followed her example. Mario got off the bike without being told and stood next to the hole in the fence.

'You should leave me here,' he said flatly.

'What are you talking about? Come on,' said Miles.

'My life is over while yours is just beginning. I am finished. Everything I have ever worked for has been destroyed. I destroyed it. I was so stupid to think this sort of thing could work.'

'It did work. Now come on,' said Miles. He grabbed Mario by the shirt collar and thrust him through the hole. Mario fell badly and cried out in pain.

'Sorry about that,' said Miles. 'I had no choice. Fucking hell, I feel good!'

Once they were all through the fence they slipped and clambered down a steep slope. The light was weak due to the thickness of the trees overhead. The place was no nature reserve, the ground littered with rusty metal, old bottles, pages from pornographic magazines, bits of old rope and gutted domestic machinery.

A helicopter suddenly thundered low overhead, going in the direction of the hangar.

'That was a police helicopter,' said Anna.

'How d'you know?' asked Miles.

'I saw it through the trees. But do not worry, it did not see us.'

As the helicopter noise died down, Miles heard another noise overhead.

He looked up and saw a flash of white just above the tree tops accompanied by the confident whine of two turbo engines at full throttle.

'And that was Mr. Bell,' said Miles. 'It's all go today.'

They slid and tumbled down the steep slope a little further before the police helicopter rushed overhead again, this time clearly following Gaston Bell's plane.

'Well, whatever they're doing, they're clearly not very interested in us,' said Miles.

'It is the end,' said Mario. He was barely making any effort. It was only the pitch of the hill that kept him moving. His face was bedraggled and tear-stained, clothes muddy and blood-soaked.

Miles looked down through the trees and saw something he recognised. It was, he mused, the very last thing he'd expected to see. He could just make out through the dense tree cover the roof of a newly built wooden structure. A resting house or rain shelter built on the side of a disused railway track.

'Bloody hell,' he said.

'What is it?' asked Anna. She looked worried, she had seen the building too.

'This is too perfect for words. It's a fucking Sustrans track!'

As the three escapees stumbled into the sunlight, Miles looked up and down the track. It was smooth and level, and curved very slightly away to the right.

'It is an old railway line, am I right?' said Anna, staring at Miles, trying to get an answer. He was just grinning and chuckling.

'I know where we are,' he said proudly. 'We don't need a car to escape now. We've got it sorted.'

'Which way is Europe?' asked Anna. Miles pointed.

'This way,' he said. 'We can even stop for tea on the way.'

Chapter Fifty-Nine

'Willis, you are a prick!' said McKay as he crouched clear of the helicopter's still-turning blades. 'What the hell did you think you were doing, high tailing off like that without so much as a blasted message?'

The helicopter rattled skywards again in hot pursuit of the plane that had run over Detective Inspector Willis' foot.

'Doing my job, sir,' he said with an agonised smile. He was sitting on the ground, his suit torn, his face grazed and his foot hurting like hell and swollen like a melon.

'Doing your job? Wonderful, Willis. Absolutely fantastic.'

'Thank you, sir.'

'You see, I've just been talking to the Prime Minister on the way here, as you do,' said McKay. Willis raised his eyebrows, feeling very proud.

'Not,' added McKay. The Chief was such a tosser, thought Willis.

'I don't like talking to the Prime Minister, Willis, and d'you know why? Of course you don't. Why would you? That requires a level of sensitivity and intelligence you will never possess. I'll tell you why. He is not a happy man, and I can't say I blame him. Instead of a discreet undercover operation we now have a major fucking incident on our hands. The whole thing has been blown up out of all proportion because you wanted to have your fucking day of glory. Well, Willis, you've had it.'

'Thank you, sir.'

'Consider yourself suspended. I want a full report on my desk by tomorrow morning at 9. How about that?'

'I've got to go to hospital, sir.'

'Is your hand injured, man?'

'No, sir.'

'Fine, I'll accept a hand–written report.'

Willis sighed. He knew it would all blow over. Whatever they said, he'd been the one to lead them to the crooks. His only regret was that he had failed his firearms training on so many occasions he wasn't allowed to carry a weapon. He could have holed the tanks in the plane and caught the bloody pilot then.

What if they really did suspend him, though? What was he going to do with himself? Gardening? He didn't have a garden, he barely had anywhere to live.

He scratched his head and looked at the hangar, now swarming with officers and forensics teams. There was still something bugging him. It just seemed too easy. There was something missing. Why had Cooper come all the way out here? Why did they start shooting each other? And why did they try and escape in a plane, before they even knew the police were there? Or maybe they did know . . . but how? This case had a lot of holes. Willis rubbed his face sorrowfully as he finally realised it might never now be his job to plug them.

Chapter Sixty

'This is brilliant,' said Miles, who was more comfortable now as he was able to rest occasionally on the crossbar of the bike. He had stopped for a moment and padded it with Mario's leather jacket. Mario hadn't said anything, just did as he was told, eyes oddly blank.

There was blood on one sleeve of the jacket which Miles found rather disturbing, but the sun had come out and nothing could stop him feeling incredibly happy.

He could easily cast his mind back to the first time he had ridden along this track and met the girl on the sit-up-and-beg bike who had told him Mario's name. It seemed like years before and almost film-like in his memory. He had become such a different person; he could still recall the tension his body had exuded then, the feelings that were so completely cut off from him, the world, everything. Now he was stripped of all that, he knew some of it had been self-protection, but he felt he didn't need to be protected any more. What was he protecting himself from anyway? The world? Billions of people lived in the world, lived, got injured, got ill, suffered and eventually died. That was all, it wasn't so bad.

'Mario, did you have a client, a woman, about twenty-eight-ish? Bit of an old hippie. She was English, had a knackered bike.'

Mario said nothing.

'I met her when I was riding along here before and she told me your name.'

'Helen,' said Mario after a while.

'I wonder if that was her. She was very keen on you, kept telling me to remember your name.'

'That would be Helen. She's the only other female client I have had from England, other than Paula.'

'Wow, how amazing! And what exercise did you do with her?'

'Philippe killed her mother.'

The smile slid off Miles' face for a moment. He rode on in silence but for the sound of the chunky tyres crunching grit.

'You mean, actually killed her?'

'I don't know. I didn't ask.'

Another silence. Miles was used to Mario explaining everything in a clear monologue.

'What d'you mean, you didn't ask? What happened?'

'Philippe arranged it,' said Mario. Miles heard a sob. 'Philippe could arrange anything.'

'Well, not quite. He didn't arrange for himself to survive the Major and his gun,' said Miles. Then he heard what he'd said and felt terribly guilty. 'God, sorry, Mario, that didn't come out right.'

He took one hand off the handlebars and touched Mario's arm behind him. His crippled arm. 'Sorry,' said Miles.

'It was very realistic,' said Mario.

'What was?'

'It seemed to help Helen. She had a lot of problems with her mother. Her mother was very critical of her, and although Helen did everything she could to boost her confidence as an adult, her internal parent was very dominant. Just like her external parent. It was a trauma exercise so I assume no real harm was done, but I do not know exactly how Philippe managed to make it look like he'd killed Helen's mother without actually killing her. It was, as I said, very realistic.'

'Bloody hell! But it seemed to work. She was very happy when I met her.'

'Oh, yes. It worked. It nearly always works. She really blossomed after that.'

There was another silence. Then, 'I haven't heard from her in a while.'

It was the first time Mario had spoken freely since they'd left the hangar. They'd been riding for an hour, the sun now hot on their backs as they headed east. Miles watched a combine harvester work its way through a field of wheat to one side of the track.

Anna seemed to be enjoying herself. She rode slightly ahead of Miles and Mario, weaving to left and right happily. She wasn't trying to ride fast, wasn't complaining about needing a car and wasn't looking nearly so fierce.

'This is a very beautiful track,' she said as Miles rode up beside her.

'Nice, isn't it? I still can't believe it. We got clean away.'

'Did you get any money?' asked Anna.

'No,' said Miles. 'What about you, Mario?'

Mario said nothing, just held on to Miles with one arm as they bumped along the track.

'I have been thinking,' said Anna. 'We could all go to Germany. All three of us.'

'Oh, right,' said Miles. More silence followed as he experienced a variety of feelings about what Anna had just said. They all concluded in delight. It seemed he was still to be included in her plan. He wasn't sure how he felt about Mario's involvement. He decided these were what would be called mixed emotions, then realised he was quite happy about someone else making all the decisions. He was just going along with whatever happened, not forging his own way against all the odds.

'You and Mario are unknown in Germany. Well, you are, Miles.'

He saw Anna look at Mario. She smiled to herself, then added, 'It might be good to be somewhere you are not known. We don't know if the authorities have pictures of us. We need to wait and see. I have a large house in Hanover. We could stay there and work out what to do next. I could go back to work, we could see what happens.'

'Let's go to my father's house first,' said Miles. 'It's not far away, we can catch a train to London from there. We can wash and eat and rest and work out how to get to Germany.'

'That's a good idea,' Anna agreed.

Miles followed exactly the same route he had done on his original Sustrans bike ride. Within an hour the three of them got off the train in Datchet, walked across the green and approached the shop. It was closed. Miles went to the green front door to the side of the shop and knocked. After a few moments he could hear someone moving inside. A man opened the door. Miles did not immediately recognise him until the man smiled.

'Miles! Well, I never!' he said. The face loomed out of Miles' past and caught up with him.

'Hello, Uncle Patrick. How are you?'

'Very good, thank you. Very good. I haven't seen you in, well, it must be . . .'

'Sixteen years, give or take a month. It's really good to see you, Uncle Patrick.' And without thinking of the implications, he embraced his uncle warmly. The embrace was responded to, gently. Miles was yet again amazed that he could sense his uncle's embarrassment.

'Well, come in, everyone's here,' said Uncle Patrick. 'We've just been talking about you.'

Miles entered the house, introducing Mario and Anna as he did so. He felt strangely elated as he saw his two friends in the dump where he used to live as a boy. It tied together two very disparate parts of his life. Donna had never visited the house. They had always met his father in some swanky restaurant in town, which was always a disaster.

Mario and Anna's presence felt like it actually meant something. Although Miles knew it didn't, the feeling was good.

His father was sitting in his old armchair in the cramped front room.

'Look what the cat dragged in!' said Uncle Patrick. There was a small cheer of delight from the uncomfortable-looking gathering.

'Miles, how lovely!' said his Aunt Sally.

'Hello, Invisible Man,' said Katherine, his sister.

Miles embraced everyone from his family, feeling incredible warmth towards all of them. Even his sister, someone he had secretly hated for most of his life, suddenly seemed like a wonderful and caring person. He felt pangs of guilt for all the dreadful things he'd said about her over the years. He had avoided his family as much as possible since the day he'd left home, didn't want them dragging him back down, and when he made his serious money had wanted to keep away from them even more. Now he was surrounded by them and felt very happy. They accepted him, they wanted to see him. He was an important part of all their lives.

'Hello, Dad,' he said when he'd finally finished hugging everyone.

His father stood up and offered his hand to shake. 'Hope you're not going to cuddle me.'

Miles smiled, grabbed his father by the shoulders and held him tightly.

'Good God, what's got into you?' said his father when Miles finally let go.

'Just pleased to see you.'

Anna was already talking to Katherine, Mario was being looked after by an aunt. Miles could tell he was doing his best to appear normal, but he was, now Miles saw him in the familiar surroundings of his childhood home, a pretty odd-looking man. He was wearing a leather jacket which had one sleeve stained with blood, his trousers were crumpled and looked stained. His withered arm hung limply by his side as he took a drink from a vaguely recognised cousin.

'Miles, what have you been doing then?' said his father, sitting in his old armchair again.

'Been a bit busy, Dad.'

'I've rung you a dozen times or more. Just the infernal answer-machine.'

'Oh, sorry, I haven't been at home.'

'I can see that. Who's the filly?'

Miles looked over to see Anna sitting on the arm of the old sofa, talking politely to Aunt Sally.

'Anna, she's German.'

'Heil Hitler!' said his father, without flinching. 'So where's mad Donna?'

'In Seattle, I would imagine.'

'I see. Well, it's none of my business.'

'I'll tell you if you want?'

'No, no. It's your life, Sonny Jim.'

Miles smiled at his father. This sort of distancing behaviour was so typical of him, but now Miles could see exactly what was going on. On previous occasions he'd always left his father's house feeling slightly confused, not understanding what he was saying. Now he could see it all so clearly. It was a revelation of enormous proportions. His father had buried all his pain and was consequently terrified of anything emotional. It was fair enough, he was old, didn't need trauma therapy. Miles was happy to leave him in that state and love him for who he was. A scared old man.

'I might move to Germany for a bit.'

'Oh, well, you'll have to polish your jack boots. They'll think you're a right scruff otherwise.'

'I think the Third Reich ended about fifty years ago, Dad.'

'Don't you believe it, Sonny Jim. They're already here, aren't they? Everywhere you look, BMWs, Volkswagens, Bosch, everywhere.'

'Anna designs Volkswagens.'

'There you go then.'

Miles laughed. He wanted to hug his dad again and tell him everything was all right. He didn't, he knew it would disturb him, sitting in his comfortable old chair, being looked after by his brothers and sisters.

'Why is everyone here, though? It's not a Sunday.'

'We've just been to a memorial service.'

'Who for?'

'Your bloody mother, who d'you think?'

'Oh, God. Sorry. Was that why you were ringing me?'

'Thought you might like to come.'

'Sorry, Dad. I feel awful now.'

His father said nothing, sipped some more beer from his old pewter tankard.

'Lovely drop of stuff. Got a drink?'

He cast Miles a glance, only a brief look, but Miles saw into his soul in that instant. The man he'd known longer than anyone else, the man who'd showed him how to be. It was all so clear now. He didn't blame his father, it wasn't his fault, but he was the reason. Keeping everything inside, keeping the terror and pain of the world away. If only he'd realised earlier.

'I'll go and get one,' said Miles. He stood up and made his way across the small room, smiling at all his relatives. He reached Mario.

'You okay?'

'I need to rest.'

'Sure. Come with me.'

Miles led him through the crowd and into the hallway. They walked slowly up the stairs. Miles opened the door at the top, his childhood room.

'You can lie down in here. I'm really sorry about my family.'

'They are good people,' said Mario as he took off his leather jacket. Miles knelt down and undid Mario's shoes and took them off for him. It was a special moment, Miles knew it was touching even as he did it. Touching because Mario let him. It was special, real. To be kneeling at someone's feet and taking off their shoes was so symbolic.

'They are good people, aren't they?' said Miles. 'I never saw it before. I can now.'

'You can see everything now, can't you, Miles?'

'I can. Thank you.'

'That is my job. That was always my job.'

'Look, rest now. We're all exhausted. I'm just so high I'm not going to be able to sleep for a while, but we can stay here tonight. Tomorrow is another day.'

Mario flopped back on the bed and Miles pulled the thin quilt over him, the one he had slept under as a child.

He folded Mario's clothes and put them on the chair in the corner of the room. He looked at Mario. His regular breathing indicated he was already sleeping so Miles left the room quietly, closed the door and returned to the family gathering.

'Your mother was a good woman,' said Uncle Patrick. He was her younger brother and bore a strong family resemblance. Although he was in his early seventies, his hair was still thick, grey but lush.

'I know,' said Miles. 'I wish I knew more about her, she's always been a bit of a mystery.'

'She was a complicated soul,' said his uncle. He leant on the kitchen dresser, a can of beer in one hand, already a little drunk. 'It must have been a terrible time for her, to make her leave her two babies like that.'

Miles didn't quite understand what he had said. It didn't fit in with the picture he had. Being in a road accident while she was on her horse, how would she have had time to worry? She'd been killed instantly. Miles looked at his uncle. The back of his head tingled. He could sense he was about to discover something, something that would change his life yet again. The noise from the rest of the family subsided, it was just he and his uncle.

Patrick spoke without looking away from his beer. 'It's a terrible thing for a family to have to live with. No one wants to talk about suicide. I realise you never knew. Your father couldn't speak of it for years, didn't want to tell you, and no one else dared. It's been on my mind for a long time. I always wanted to tell you but I never saw you. You were living in America and became so rich I didn't like to get in touch. You know, poverty-stricken relative crawling out of the woodwork. You didn't need that. But now you're here, and you look so well, I just think you should know.'

Miles stood frozen. The sound around him returned. He was in the kitchen, the very room where his mother had fed him as a baby. The ceiling was so low he could touch it if he reached up. He had travelled so far and come back to this spot. He had so many memories connected with the kitchen: as a little boy coming back from school with a drawing and showing it to his mother. Her lovely hands holding his picture. The way she'd hugged him to her. Then the day he'd come back and she wasn't there. Instead his father was in his chair crying, and all the relatives were coming and going and giving Miles sweets and he didn't know why. And his sister crying and screaming in her room upstairs. And then they told him, 'Your mummy has gone to heaven, Miles. She won't be coming back. She's with Jesus and the angels now.'

'This is a fairly momentous bit of news,' he said finally. His uncle nodded without saying anything. 'I mean, it did affect my life pretty dramatically.'

'I know. Believe me, it's affected all our lives. I took comfort from the fact that it didn't hold you or your sister back. You've both done well in the world, especially you.'

Miles felt a wave of anger wash through him.

'But I haven't been happy, Uncle. In fact I've been very unhappy until this morning.'

'What happened this morning?'

'Oh, nothing, but . . .' He couldn't speak, felt his face tighten. He wanted to scream. He knew he shouldn't, but he was going to burst if not. 'Why didn't someone tell me!'

It was only when he realised that everyone else had fallen silent that he knew he had shouted. His uncle glanced at the family gathered in the small back room. Miles looked around. They were all staring at him, an odd group of badly dressed people with a ravishing dark beauty sitting amongst them, also looking at him. He turned back to his uncle.

'We did what we thought was best at the time. We were all upset. We made mistakes. I'm sorry.'

'Well, I've got some questions now. So many questions.'

'What d'you want to know?' said his uncle, still fingering his beer can.

Miles heaved a huge sigh, just like his father. He didn't know where to start. Was she on the horse or was that just a story? He glanced back into the other room. People were talking again, although in hushed tones.

'Just tell me what really happened. Do we know why she killed herself?' he said as quietly as he could. He didn't want his father to hear. 'Does Kathy know?'

'Kathy has known for about five years,' said his uncle.

'She never told me.'

'She hasn't seen or spoken to you in ten years, Miles.'

He covered his face with his hands. This was too enormous. The day was too big for one person. How could this be happening?

'I know.'

'Your mother had a history of clinical depression. She was very bad after your sister was born, but when you were born she seemed happy. It didn't last. She got worse and worse. Wouldn't see anyone. Her doctor put her on anti-depressants but they just made her sleep. Then, somehow, we don't know how, she got hold of a lot of sleeping tablets and took them all. There was nothing anyone could do.'

'So she wasn't on her horse?'

'No, she wasn't. She was upstairs, in her bedroom.'

'But wasn't Dad here?'

'In the shop.'

'Oh, God. This is terrible.'

'Miles,' said his uncle after another bout of sighs from both men.

'What?'

'I can only ask you this. Please don't say anything to your father. We worry about him. He's going downhill fast at the moment.'

'But I want to know what happened.'

'Ask me. If you need to know anything, ask me.'

Miles felt tired. Very, very tired.

He spent the rest of the evening barely conscious. He tried to cover the shock of what he'd learned, but it was impossible. He decided not to speak. One by one the relatives drifted out. Anna sat on the sofa, looking uncomfortable, looking for guidance, but Miles had no idea what to do.

'You're tired, is there anywhere we can sleep?' she asked when only his Uncle Patrick and Aunt Sally were left. And his father, still sitting in the old armchair, now watching television.

They went upstairs together. His sister Katherine's old room had a three-quarter-sized bed. Miles pulled off his clothes, so did Anna. He couldn't even be bothered to look at her naked body. They slid under the slightly damp covers together, her warmth comforting him as he fell into a deep sleep.

Chapter Sixty-One

'And this is the main pressing shed,' said Anna as they drove along in the little white car with no doors or roof. Miles looked in wonder at the huge machine quietly working. He'd seen films of car-making plants. They had always looked noisy, but this pounding monster was almost silent behind its double-glazed housing.

'If you look down there, you will see that this is a very big building.'

Miles looked in the direction Anna was pointing. He couldn't see the far end of the building. It was too big to be real. It looked as if the view had been digitally retouched.

'It is nearly three kilometres in length,' said Anna proudly. 'It is the largest car plant on earth. The roof covers a greater area than the country of Monaco.'

'Terrifying!' said Miles.

'It is very impressive,' said Mario, who was sitting in the back of the strange little car.

Miles turned round to talk to him.

'But it's terrifying, isn't it, Mario? When you think of what they're making.'

Miles laughed again. The bubble of joy in his heart seemed never to end. Of all people to be driving around a car factory, sitting in a little petrol-engined car with no doors or roof. Sitting next to a car designer who owned six cars. The whole thing was absurd still, even after the exercise.

It was something Miles had discussed with Mario on the train to Hanover. Although he felt totally different about himself, his family, the way he moved in the world, his opinions hadn't changed. He didn't suddenly want to learn to drive and buy a fleet of fast cars, which he could easily have afforded to do. He didn't want to stop cycling, none of that had changed. He didn't suddenly grow his hair, or shave it off, or start wearing different clothes. He was still the same person, only better. Or was he? It concerned him that he still wasn't actually a good person, although what he was doing was essentially beneficial.

'These are the main assembly lines for the Golf,' said Anna as they turned a corner into yet another enormous building. Miles had wanted to walk around the factory, but Anna said it would take many days to do so. It was so big, the journey she was taking them on was at least twenty kilometres and they would never go outside.

'As you can see, the working environment is very benign.'

Miles raised his eyebrows. It wasn't exactly what he would call benign, but it was very clean and relatively quiet. He'd expected more noise and sparks flying, but all the dirty and dangerous processes had been fully automated. Rows of complex robots welded body parts together almost silently, huge sheets of double glazing and sound proofing protecting the workers outside the units.

Anna turned another corner and drove down a ramp. Everywhere Miles looked, cars, or parts of cars, were slowly moving along mechanical racks attached to the ceilings. Thousands of metres of cars, slowly moving along, as they would again once they got on to the world's crowded roads.

'In many ways, this is my favourite section of the construction process,' said Anna as she stopped by another giant, unmanned machine.

'We call this the marriage. This is where the bodywork is joined to the engine, drive system, wheels and brakes. We saw them being constructed on the lower levels. This machine brings them up through the floor and completes the whole process here. Watch.'

Miles and Mario did as they were told. A car body, complete with windows, wing mirrors, seats, wipers, lights, everything in fact except engine and wheels, was pushed into position by a giant hydraulic system, too complex for even Miles fully to comprehend.

As soon as it came to rest an engine and four wheels were pushed up underneath it, and as soon as they were in position dozens of little screwdrivers and spanners whizzed into action. In the blink of an eye, a car was born.

'That is amazing,' said Miles. 'It's so fast.'

'We make a car every twenty seconds,' said Anna proudly.

'Bloody hell!' said Miles.

'You are impressed?'

'I don't know. It's all a bit much. One every twenty seconds? I mean, what's going to happen when the world is full?'

Anna smiled at him. 'You are a little naive about all this, aren't you, Miles? Cars do not last forever. Even Volkswagens. We recycle an enormous number of old cars. Only ones we produce, of course, because we know what went into making them. The world will never be full of cars.'

'Still crazy,' said Miles.

Anna carried on her tour. At the end of it he couldn't help feeling slightly depressed.

They ate lunch in a very brightly lit and clean staff canteen. It overlooked a wide canal, and in the distance the low flat town of Wolfsburg could be seen through the grey drizzle.

'Thank you very much, Anna, that was very informative. I shall never look at a car in the same way again,' said Mario.

'I am very happy you came,' she said. Miles looked out of the window. He wasn't sure what to think, felt very uncomfortable. Being in love with Anna was never going to be easy.

He had lived in Hanover for a month, a very busy time for all of them. Anna's house was delightful, a large old place in a leafy suburb. Trams running along the end of the road, lots of people on bicycles everywhere. In some ways it seemed there was less traffic in Hanover than in London. Anna put this down to better traffic management and good public transport. She'd told Miles she had started using trams more often since he had moved in.

For the first couple of weeks he did very little other than sleep, wash, eat and read. He read avidly, anything he could get his hands on. First English newspapers, full of stories of the failed robbery on the train from Europe. The arrest of a prominent Belgian banker had started a massive enquiry into the banking system in the whole of Europe. There was doom and gloom about the weakness of the Euro and the sudden and huge price hikes in the UK since the currency was introduced.

He even read *Hello!* magazine which had a big feature on Paula Bentley and Monica Simpson, who was, according to the article, apparently 'happier now' since she had decided to sell her palatial London home and start an orphanage in Kent. Paula was pictured with her son Mustoe who looked very happy and well balanced. Like his mother.

Most nights Miles slept in his own room, a nice space on the top floor of the house, the window being in a little turreted tower in the corner.

Anna said she needed time to get used to his being there and her family needed to get to know him too. Mario had his own little flat in the basement, and since they had settled into the sweet-smelling old house, he had started to work again.

He'd spent the first week of their stay in bed, Miles supplying him with soup and vitamin supplements. They'd talked a great deal, and then Miles had met Mila who worked for Mario. She travelled up from Geneva and eventually agreed to move to Hanover.

Miles eventually agreed to do occasional work for Mario, though he worried at first about what this would entail. He didn't want to step into Philippe's shoes. Mario assured him this wouldn't be necessary.

Word had got out that he was once again in business. Mila had been contacted by some new clients.

Not only that, but Anna's return to work, and her complete change in personality, had so impressed her bosses that within a week she had been promoted to head of department. She had been questioned by her chief one day, and in conversation discovered that he was feeling very depressed for no obvious reason.

Their visit to the Wolfsburg factory had two purposes: the tour they had been on, and the first meeting between Mario Lupo and Heinz Stevesant, chief executive of world marketing at VW cars.

As Herr Stevesant approached their table, Miles sat back and folded his arms. Whatever happened, this was going to be interesting.